Joan Eadith lives in the Lake District but grew up in Manchester, where she was educated and became a nurse. She also worked in the University Dental School and Royal Eye Hospital, and as a nursing visitor. She has served her time as a wife and mother, and now considers writing her career.

The Blue Cornflower

Joan Eadith

WARNER BOOKS

A *Warner* Book

First published in Great Britain in 1994 by Warner Books
Reprinted 1995, 1997

A CIP catalogue record for this book
is available from the British Library.

ISBN 0 7515 1013 0

Typeset by Solidus (Bristol) Limited
Printed in England by Clays Ltd, St Ives plc

Warner Books
A Division of
Little, Brown and Company (UK)
Brettenham House
Lancaster Place
London WC2E 7EN

Contents

Foreword   vii

Chapter 1
Beads   1

Chapter 2
The Photograph   24

Chapter 3
A Sunny Day at All Saints   39

Chapter 4
Lodgings   60

Chapter 5
The Insult   78

Chapter 6
The Alder Tree   105

Chapter 7
The Studio   129

Chapter 8
The Paper   144

Chapter 9
The Baby   164

Chapter 10
Naples Lodge   192

Chapter 11
Chrystallised Syrup   211

Chapter 12
The Mother   234

Chapter 13
A State of Fate   255

Chapter 14
Just a Statue   271

Chapter 15
Confrontation   290

Chapter 16
Lone Souls   304

Chapter 17
Summer   312

Foreword

I enjoyed writing this book because it evoked so many memories of All Saints as it used to be, over fifty years ago. When trying to remember some special part of the past, I find that one needs to have one's own memories verified.

With this in mind, I should like to thank the staff of the Grosvenor Building of Art and Design in the Manchester Metropolitan University, who generously furnished me with two very interesting books: *School of Art – A Hundred Years and More* by D. Jeremiah, and *A Walk Round All Saints* by Derek Brumhead and Terry Wyke, which revived many personal childhood memories for me.

I spent some happy evenings attending life classes at the old School of Art and was delighted to find that it is still standing amongst the modern buildings next to the now closed Righton's drapery store, which was once a feast of wonderful textiles. This store was also the place one of my grandfathers served his time as a draper and ended up as a managing director. The shell of the store has been saved as part of the university building, and is a relatively unaltered example of an Edwardian shop. What a delight to see it again.

Joan Eadith

CHAPTER ONE

Beads

'You'll fall off that wall . . . Just you see . . .'

Ten-year-old Milly Dawnay was perched on the broken, mottled red bricks with their crumbling mortar, smiling with calm defiance and idly sucking a sweet. She was swinging her legs beneath her calf-length dark skirt and starched pinny, kicking the wall with the backs of her heels and leaving scuff marks across the fine black leather of her shoes. They were good shoes, passed on by a rich cousin who lived in Timperley. By the time they reached Milly they were a third-hand cast-off from her eldest sister Effie, who was much older but was of a small neat build. Milly herself was regarded as fast becoming a bit of an elephant by her family, even though her Grandmother Smith said secretly that she was charming and beautiful and would grow into a wonderful specimen of womanhood, after her barefoot days.

The elephant at this moment, if it didn't watch out, was about to topple to the small dry mud path running through coarse, sun-bleached grass and yellow dandelions. The piece of old wall belonged to the back of some half-collapsed buildings behind the old steam laundry in Crabapple Lane, not far from Stretford Road, and was banned to all children.

'You just think you're *it*, Milly Dawnay,' said Arthur Fallowfield, 'but just you wait. My mother says you'll come to a bad end.' He smiled with dimpled smugness. He was wearing a perfectly tailored tweed knicker-bocker suit, and his stiff white collar shone as he tried to stare her out from beneath the shade of his flat tweed cap.

She sat there like a duchess holding court with her three slaves: 'I shall *never* fall off it. I expect that's what you'd like, wouldn't you, Arthur Fallowfield – just to see what colour my petticoat is so you can blab it to everyone.'

Arthur blushed slightly and turned away and the two others began to dance about and make whooping noises and turn somersaults in the grass, thanking their lucky stars they hadn't got posh suits to stifle them.

'So I'll tell you right now – it's *not* red flannel with *I love you* embroidered all round the edges. It's emerald satin with diamonds and pearls!' She gave such a kick of triumph at the wall as she said it that a loose brick freed itself from beneath her bottom and in seconds she was lying on the ground with half the wall around her as she howled with terror and pain.

'Me legs ... me legs ... Get the bricks away! Fetch our Effie quick!' She gave a huge groan, and then there was silence as she lapsed into semi-consciousness, unaware of the bleeding gash on her face from a sharp bit of slate. Dull scarlet streaks trickled down from the frail, huddled, helpless form.

Arthur Fallowfield turned and fled for his life, but the other two – Hewy Edmundson and Mackie Bright – ran for help, and within minutes they were back with a man from the laundry buildings.

'Little tikes ...' muttered the man as he carefully removed some broken bricks and freed poor Milly with his large, gentle, calloused hands. 'You all want your bloody heads seeing to. This place is private. Trespassing isn't allowed. There's a flaming big notice in red only two seconds away.'

'Please, sir, we can't read, sir ...'

'Can't read, you bloody little liars? Don't give me all that! You with the red hair and scabs on your nose – get along to the porter's office at the laundry and tell 'em to bring a stretcher!'

Mackie Bright did as he was bid, running like a startled hare to the cobbled street near the laundry works.

'And you standin' there with them big fluttery eyes – 'elp me to get shot of all this rubble. An' let this be a lesson to ya.'

Hewy Edmundson stared at him like a hypnotised stoat.

'*Get a move on, boy*! It isn't a picnic!'

Milly opened her eyes. She was as white as raw pastry, but the bleeding had stopped.

'Where do you live then, lass?'

'She lives in Hatching Street ... Just rount' corner.'

'I didn't ask *you*, laddie. I'm asking 'er to see if she's compus mentus ...'

The stretcher arrived quickly and a first-aid man pronounced no bones broken: 'But she'll know about it termorrer. The poor little devil'll be black and blue, and she'll need summat more for that wound on 'er face.' Then he gave an exasperated sigh. 'Kids ...'

News of a stretcher being carried by two men from the laundry into Hatching Street spread like a bush fire as gossip travelled in all directions, and a huge crowd gathered. Many of them worked at the laundry and everyone was wondering if it was one of theirs. 'What the 'ell's 'appened? For Christ's sake, don't say there's been a burst boiler . . . Mary Mother of God, don't let it be one of our folks . . .'

But as the front door of number six Hatching Street opened and the stretcher was placed on the uneven flagstones beside it, the crowd dwindled away – still wondering if there were yet other casualties to follow.

By the time Dr Daley had visited and tended to Milly, verifying that it was a case of severe shock and no bones had been broken, she had been awarded a week of complete rest. 'Keep her in bed for a couple of days and let her just relax. I'll call again tomorrow. And keep away from those death traps in future.' He smiled slightly with wry compassion. He knew that unless he gave official notice about Milly needing a bit of recuperation she would probably spend more time on household chores – working longer and harder than she would in any normal school day. It was always the same with big families.

When he'd gone, Clarry Dawnay stared mournfully at her daughter. 'You look a right little sight, child. You've been warned and warned not to play on them loose walls . . .'

'*And* she's ruined her face, Ma,' remarked seventeen-year-old Effie bluntly. 'I bet she'll have that scar for life. Sometimes they split open again and bulge with the flesh from underneath. No man'll ever look at her –'

Before she could let out another breath her mother slapped her across the head. 'And no man'll ever take you on either, our Effie, if you don't learn to keep your mouth shut. Get to the wash house and sort out those shirts!'

Two days later, Milly was almost her old chirruping

4

self, but she played it down a bit because if she recovered too well she would be roped in for things like washing the yard and donkey stoning the front.

The doctor had been each day to change the dressing on her face, and although there was a terrible looking wound it didn't worry her at all, for at least it no longer hurt much, except when she chewed, and Dr Daley had promised her that all the bruising and swelling would gradually disappear. In fact it was nice to be the centre of sympathy and attention for once in a family of seven other children.

But the main advantage of being an invalid for a bit was that she could do what she really wanted to do, and that was to draw. Yet the word 'drawing' was banned in the Dawnay household. Whenever she said she liked drawing they all said: 'Drawing what? Water from a well?'

'I think I'll just go and draw, Ma. I'm feeling a bit better today . . .'

'You'll do no such thing, Milly Dawnay, you'll just help me sew some buttons on all these damned clothes . . .'

But her mother's sharp voice faded from Milly's ears as she conveniently vanished to her new secret drawing place.

She was standing, hidden, in a corner of Edmundson's back yard, peering up towards the chimney tops. There was a look of sheer, pleasurable concentration on her round face.

It was hard trying to draw a *real* chimney pot. There was so much to see: the light and the shade; the large crack on one side; the chipped edge at the top; the complete change of scene as a noisy starling suddenly landed beside it.

Ah . . . me . . .

5

She pushed the strands of long chestnut hair well away from her sharp grey eyes, and kept on. Her mouth was slightly purple round the edges from spitting on the stub of an old copy-ink pencil as she tried earnestly to draw the smoky old chimney stack perched over her own home at number six. For here, in Edmundson's back yard, was the best place to get a really good view as she stared up at the bedroom windows to the dark slate roof beyond.

She outlined the slate roof more strongly and drew clouds and clouds of thick smoke, her ten-year-old face grim with determination.

'Milly Dawnay, get out of our back yard quick, or I'll tell me Dad! You're supposed to be ill! I've a good mind to tell Mr French at school there's nowt wrong!' Hewy Edmundson was yelling at her from the back window. 'It was me and Mackie Bright as saved your life, and our mam says I've not to bother with you no more, because you're trouble with a capital T.'

Milly waved the drawing at him scornfully and pulled a face, then swiftly she ran back home, walking into her own back yard pretending to be as cool as a cucumber, but her heart beating ten to the dozen . . .

There were seven of the Dawnay family of ten squashed round the wooden kitchen table at tea-time that night. Milly's father Joe had arrived back from Manchester's Pomona Docks and was washing himself in the gloomy little scullery where the shallow brown slop-stone was.

Suddenly Milly announced: 'I'm going to be an artist when *I* grow up.' She drew the crumpled, smudged copy-ink drawing out of her green pinafore pocket in triumph. 'I'm going to draw and paint lots of pictures like that Mr Turner.'

6

'Turner? 'Oo the devil's Turner when 'ee's at 'ome?'
Her father looked alarmed. 'Unless you mean old one-eyed Tommy Turner that sells matches on Greek Street?'

'She means Turner's pictures, in art galleries, Dad. The one that did the painting of that ship in very rough seas called *The Fighting Temeraire*. Our Aunt Maddy's got one of it on their parlour wall.'

Joe Dawnay took the piece of paper Milly was pushing towards him and stared at it briefly. 'You've done the chimney right enough, lass – but what's that great lot of scribble all round it?'

'Smoke, father.'

'Smoke?' His lined, cheerful face creased into a broad smile. 'Gerraway with yer – it's bright blue skies today! You've ruined that nice chimney, so you 'ave. It just looks to me as if you was going to scribble all over it because you was fed up with it.' He brandished the scrap of flimsy paper in the air.

'Let's see it, Dad . . .' The room filled with noise as all the family pleaded to get their hands on it to give their own opinions.

'She's got ideas above her station, Mother, and she needs to be back at school,' said Effie jealously. She was helping to serve the meal, her face sweating slightly as she got some bubbling tripe and onions from a pan on the range and began to dish it out onto plates. 'She imagines she's a proper artist or summat. She spends all her time going round trying to draw silly things. Yesterday, Sid Dean saw her in Monkton Street sitting near some ashes trying to draw washing on a line –'

'Leave her alone, Effie – you talk a lot of rot yourself,' said Milly's sixteen-year-old brother Fred, sitting there with his knife and fork poised. 'It's not her fault. She's not learnt yet – proper art ain't for girls. How could women paint them really big pictures? Their muscles just isn't big enough. Take all them pictures painted on the walls of the Great hall in Manchester town Hall for a start . . .'

Everyone started to laugh: 'Listen to 'oo's talkin'. The boy 'oo knows more than the Lord Mayor . . .'

But Fred ploughed on undaunted. '. . . Painted by a *man*, they was. By *one man*, called Mr Ford Madox Brown, and Morris Moston's uncle dusts 'em with a feather duster set on a pole as long as a chimney sweep's while he stands on wooden planks set between step ladders . . .'

There was a scuffle of hands and arms and a jug nearly went flying while one of the others grabbed Milly's drawing, and by the time they'd all finished it was no more than a torn scrap of forgotten rubbish lying on the floor as everyone began to talk about something more important. Soon they were all chattering away like magpies about their own affairs.

'Stop looking so tearful, child, and get on with your food,' said her mother.

Slowly, with two small, salty tears rolling down her shamed pink cheeks, Milly picked at pieces of tender onion, amongst rubbery bits of tripe and chunks of potato in the thick, creamy sauce. Suddenly her idea of becoming an artist seemed a lost cause. It was hard enough even to find a decent pencil in their house, let alone a piece of plain drawing paper. Newspaper was the only stuff allowed. It was worth its weight in gold. It could be read; used as tablecloths or shelf coverings; saved for wrapping up parcels. Put on mattresses in case of bed-wetting; whipped out for wiping up messes of every description; produced for people to cough into when they had whooping cough or bad chests. Folded

8

up into firelighters; made into spills to light the gas; and lastly but most important ripped into neat squares and hung with a bit of string in the lavatory in the yard . . . Oh yes – that was what you called Really Useful paper. As for people who wanted other sorts like pure white drawing paper, well, that was just too bad. For no one cared a fig: not Effie or Fred or Margy or Benny or Don – or even six-year-old Betty. And as for baby Derry – he just chewed up everything in sight.

'Drawing's for idlers,' said her mother, who hardly had a moment to breathe. 'Life isn't meant for idlers, young lady.' And anyone sitting about trying to draw a picture was definitely an idler . . .

In a fit of temper and frustration, Milly looked at them all as they scraped their plates to the last trace. They were a healthy family, which was a blessing in those days, but oh how she hated them all at that moment . . . Suddenly, without giving any of them another glance, she got up from the table and was out of the house in seconds and running full pelt down the street. All signs of injury from the brick-wall episode had completely gone as she went running to the only man who understood her. Running to Mr Potter's.

Mr Archibald Potter was a retired head teacher who lived with his spinster sister, Miss Iris Potter, in quite a posh house. At least it was posh by Dawnay standards. It was smooth red brick, with attics and cellars, and had short, maroon-painted iron railings embedded in their own bit of brick wall guarding the small front garden from the flagstoned pavement beyond. This garden was just big enough to display a lump of fossilised lime-stone, some ferns, a few lilies of the valley, and a bit of pink bleeding heart.

Mr Potter had retired from Trafford Board School only a few weeks after Milly's ninth birthday. She always remembered when it was, because he had chosen her picture of a blue cornflower to pin on the display board during handicrafts week, just before he left. Hers, and Hewy Edmundson's corn poppy.

When handicrafts week was over, he had stood and watched them all remove the displays of leather work and beadwork, and embroidery and carpentry, as well as the two pictures. His long thin fingers were poised hesitantly above his grey bushy moustache, then he smiled, his monocle glinting slightly, as he said to Milly and Hewy: 'Both of you children could have good careers ahead of you. You both have great talents and don't let anyone tell you otherwise . . .'

After school that day Hewy walked out through the school gateway with Milly in a blaze of triumph. Usually he just stayed with a few of his pals. They all thought they were ten times better than girls, but after Mr Potter's words his face shone, and he talked to her as if he'd found a long-lost soulmate.

'Fancy him saying it about the both of us! We's both proper artists, we is. My dad'll be right proud of me. What'll yours say?' He took hold of Milly's hand and squeezed it tight.

Milly shook her head, suddenly overcome by shyness.

As they walked along Hewy said: ''Ave you ever kissed anyone?'

Milly eyed him proudly. ''Course I 'as. I always 'as to kiss me aunties, and Gran – and – I kisses people all the time to say hello and goodbye. It's only polite. Except some of 'em's a bit spitty and you 'as to wipe it off.'

'Would you like to try kissing me?'

10

She stared at him suspiciously. 'Whatever for?'

'Because . . .'

'Because what?'

'Ooh, nothing. Just because – that's all.'

She was just going to say no when he muttered, 'Boys has to learn to be good at kissin' to get the best girls. Let's go and do kissin' be'ind the old laundry. Just you and me . . .'

'Only if you promise not to tell. My mam says that kissin' be'ind that old laundry's different. Our Effie once got her ears boxed for doing it.'

He licked his finger and pointed it to the sky solemnly. 'I'll not tell anyone.'

They drifted along, kicking at bits of loose mortar and broken shale along the flattened muddy path amongst the grass to the old crumbling wall. They could hear the machines chugging away in the laundry, and people's voices shouting now and then, mingled with distant sounds: horses' hooves and the chirruping of birds. And they could smell the laundry smells and a slight whiff of bread from the bakery where people went for their meat and potato pies.

They stood in front of each other, then Hewy put both his arms underneath her arms and bent towards her slowly so that their noses almost bumped, and he kissed her on the lips.

'If you liked it, you 'as to kiss me now – the same. You 'as to hutch up close.'

Milly put her arms underneath his arms and hutched up close and kissed him. She felt his smooth firm cheeks and the tip of his nose, then his eyelashes brushing like butterflies.

'You're my girl, now,' he said. 'You're my girl for ever and ever.'

Milly nodded. She was his girl for ever and ever. She stared up peacefully towards the pale blue skies, and felt gentle breezes caressing her.

When Milly got home that day she was over the moon with joy and enthusiasm. Great talent ... whatever next? Should she tell Ma?

Her mother was as usual scurrying around. She was sorting out a mound of clothes for washing, next to the fire boiler in the wash house in the yard.

'Mam ...'

'Don't talk to me now. Go and do summat useful. Go and empty that po from under your bed, it stinks.'

'It's not me that uses it the most, Mam, it's our Effie.'

'Never mind giving me all that lip, child: *Do as you're told.*'

With depleted spirits she did as she was told. Somehow the po under the bed and telling her mother about her talents didn't seem to go together, and she hardly fared any better when she broached the subject again – this time with her father.

'Dad ...'

'Yes, lass? What can I do for thee?'

'Mr Potter at school says me and Hewy Edmundson has great talents ...'

'Where on earth did he get that daft idea from?' Joe Dawnay called to his wife who was in the skullery: 'Did you hear that, Clarry? Old Baldie Potter's at it again – tellin' 'em all 'ow wonderful they are and what glorious prospects they've got. If all the kids turned out like he said this world would be too full of brains to move ...' He turned to Milly. 'No, lass. Think on. Not you nor anyone else in Hatching Street is going to have this grand life he's always going on about. There's poor classes and rich classes – and niver the twain shall meet

12

– so don't you forget it. Not that it means the poor are worse than the rich, mind. We're all equal in the sight of God. It's just that Archibald Potter gets carried away because he lives in that there big house with his unmarried sister, and knows nowt about proper life.'

'But he *does* know about things, Father. He does. He had a wife and child who were drowned in a storm at sea, and he was once a soldier . . .' In vain did Milly try to explain. It fell on deaf ears.

And it was never the same at school after that, because Mr French, who took over from Mr Potter, was only interested in Internal Combustion engines, and encouraged Miss Bolsover to get the girls concentrating on knitting dark woollen knickers on thin metal needles, and making very neat samples of flannel patches with herringbone stitch round the square edges, whilst she went round the long wooden desks thumping all the backs she could stretch along to, if there was a stitch out of place . . .

Mr Potter, on the other hand, had always been a bit of an artist himself and now with time to spare in his retirement he did beadwork. He designed all sorts of patterns for any number of different purposes, from fancy purses to belts and slippers and jackets, and was so successful that with the help of his sister and a few local women working at home, a small business gradually evolved, never becoming anything more than half a hobby and a far cry from the terrible city sweat shops – for he was generous with the profits and shared them with everyone.

'Millicent Dawnay! What brings *you* here?' Archie Potter gazed down from his bony six-foot height at the small, sturdy girl standing squarely at his back door.

His sister Iris was standing behind him in his shadow. 'Invite the poor little soul in, Archie – she looks all of a fret. Bide awhile and I'll get you some ginger temperance wine, child.'

Milly sat down thankfully in their comfortable parlour with its dark green heavy velour table-cover bordered with dangling, fancy bobbles. She stared around her at the heavy quality wallpaper with its patterns of deep crimson plums entwined by diamond designs of trailing creamy honeysuckle, and the two pictures of quiet country scenes hanging above the small harmonium. There were family photographs on top of the harmonium, and the oval mirror over the fireplace reflected slight, gloomy glimmers of calm light from the window.

Milly sipped politely from the little glass of wine and nibbled at some gingerbread. Her first fury and despair had evaporated. It was hard to be dramatic with her mouth full, because of the crumbs.

'Is there anything we can do to help?' Mr Potter asked.

In fits and starts she related the fate of her drawing attempts: 'I was trying to do a really true picture of our house, see. But they never understand, or even care ... I just can't stand any of 'em, Mr Potter.'

'The Lord bless us. Never say that about your loved ones, child,' said Miss Potter, looking at her solemnly from beneath her piled up silvery hair. 'You are a very lucky girl compared to some. There are families only minutes away from this door who have never known what it is to have a comfortable bed to sleep in, or the joys of a satisfying meal. Some even have no homes at all and dread the winters. We all see them every day if we but open our eyes and minds.'

Mr Potter clicked his tongue. 'Don't labour the child with all that, Iris. Her own small problems are enough at the moment. She is a fine little artist, and she needs some help.'

He moved from his chair, went to a bureau cupboard in the corner and came back to Milly with a large cardboard box. He removed the flimsy lid, and a mass of bright colour met her eyes, much of it with a white and shining background of small beads. There were beautiful belts, set in soft creamy leather, small evening bags for ladies, and even a man's soft brimmed hat with a beaded ribbon round its crown.

'How would you like to make a few of these?' he said.

Milly stared at them. She was still in a state of amazement, for although she had seen examples of beadwork done at school when Mr Potter was there, this was much better because there were so many different designs and ideas.

'Some of the ladies round here make them in their own homes, and the money we get from selling them is shared between us, with some of it going to Mr William Booth's fund to help the starving poor.' He smiled at Milly with cheerful encouragement. 'Who knows, if you kept on with a bit of beadwork from time to time it would be an outlet that could give you your own bit of money in the Penny Savings Bank, and that's no bad thing . . .'

By the time Milly left the Potters' house about fifteen minutes later, she had already decided that she would join the band of beadworkers. 'You can come round any time,' said Miss Iris. She had shown Milly the sewing room near the kitchen. It had comfortable chairs and there was a sewing machine there, along with small tables. She noticed there were neat wicker workboxes on a long shelf, each one with a name on it: Mrs Lord, Cranly Street . . . Jennifer Cooper, Sugar Loaf Lane . . .

When she got home, she was back to her old cheerful self. Maybe it really would be true that someday soon she'd have money of her own.

'Where did your tantrums lead you to this time, then?' said her mother when she tried to slip into the house unobserved.

'Nowhere . . . I just went for a walk.' Then, seeing everyone's look of disbelief, she added: 'I was going to go round and see Babsy Renshaw, but her mam says she's always out on Tuesdays doing errands.' Then she hurried upstairs out of the way, to think again of what had happened at the Potters'.

It was going to be no use her bringing work back here to do. It would cause a real rumpus, especially the way Ma and Pa went on about so many people in the past doing dangerous, poorly paid tasks in their own living quarters to save themselves from starvation – like making matches, which involved poisonous phosphorous and caused terrible damage to their health. What she aimed to do wasn't a bit like that . . .

Even so, Mam's warning voice was in her head already: 'Good folks is sorely put upon when they're trapped an' desperate. They never knows half the take when they's doin' work for others, in their own homes.' She, Milly Dawnay wasn't as trapped and desperate as all that. Mr Potter's work was a far cry from the times of twenty years ago, long before she was born, which Mam never seemed to forget. It slowly dawned on her, too, that in her own small life she was never given time, anyway, to do 'other things' at home for more than a few spare minutes.

Yet Mr Potter's mention of her own money in the

16

Penny Bank had left its mark. She felt a mounting sense of excitement. How could she plan it so that she could go and work at Mr Potter's house – like some of the others – to do the beadwork, secretly, and regularly, away from her own inquisitive, bossy, family?

The very next day she decided to call round again and explain the situation to Mr Potter, and although he was out, Miss Iris was there. She listened sympathetically then said: 'What you must do, Milly, is to start off with a small piece of beadwork. We have some narrow canvas headbands here in the sewing room and all you'll need to do is look at some of the design books, pick out a really simple design for your first attempt, and I will show you how to trace it out ready to put on the headband.'

Miss Iris went to the bureau and produced a small, brand-new lined notebook with a shiny blue cover and handed it to Milly, along with a pencil. 'These will cost you a farthing, but you needn't pay until you've sold your very first beaded headband.' She then entered Milly's name and address on a register, writing by the side of it 'p. three', which was the page Milly's bead-work was to be recorded on. Then, turning to page three, she wrote Milly Dawnay's name in beautiful copperplate writing and the date then: '1 – Bead headband of own colour design and pattern.'

Milly's heart glowed with pride as Miss Iris then presented her with a small wicker basket with needles, thimble and scissors and some sewing canvas. Then she showed Milly the special cabinet containing numerous small square drawers, each one full of different coloured beads, and long flat drawers with sliding glass tops, where cottons and embroidery silks lay, after which she placed Milly's small wicker basket on the long shelf with the others.

Miss Milly Dawnay, Hatching Street . . .

By the time Milly was waving goodbye she was brimming with pure joy as she held her first small piece of needlework safely in tissue paper in her pocket; for as Miss Iris had pointed out, it was small enough to work on in spare moments and she could always call any time to the Potters' sewing room to do the more complicated parts.

After tea that night, Milly went to the bedroom and took out her sacred task, but within seconds her peace was disrupted.

'Milly, where are you, child? I thought you were supposed to be doing the darning, and Benny needs his shirt ironing . . .' With a sigh she put her own work away and went downstairs.

Her mother looked at her quizzically. 'Upstairs? Again?'

'She's just trying to escape doing what she knows she's supposed to do,' said Effie, who was in everyone's good books because she was walking out with a boy called Harold Flint who dressed in expensive clothes and had a father who owned a greyhound and wore gold cuff-links.

'I am not,' yelled Milly angrily. 'Why is it always me that's got at?'

'Because you're a cheeky, lazy little hussy, and there's nowt up with yer – that's why,' said Fred smugly. 'You're supposed to be seen and not heard, not heard and never seen.' He helped himself to a huge piece of plum pie and went out, as free as a lark.

During the following week when she was back at school again, Milly struggled in vain with the head-band, and by the next Monday morning she had only managed to sew two small white beads to it. She was overcome by sadness. Two beads . . . yet it was going to need hundreds. She knew that even to make the smallest of purses with beads this size it could take thousands of beads, and hours and hours of work. Whatever had induced her to be so quickly persuaded by the Potters when this was the result? She worked out that if it had taken her over a week to get these two lone beads stitched on, it would take her a year to stitch on 104 beads, which was about a quarter of one headband. At that rate she'd be fourteen and have left school before she'd even finished – and she wouldn't even have a groat in the Penny Savings Bank!

On the way back from school that day, she decided to call round and tell Mr Potter that it just wasn't working out.

'. . . You see, I never get a single second, Mr Potter. I'm nagged at to do other things all the time when I'm at home . . .' Tears began to well up in her eyes, and she blinked quickly and took out a hanky to blow her nose.

Mr Potter and Miss Iris gazed at Milly sadly as she stretched out the bare canvas headband with its two small solitary beads stitched to it. They looked like a couple of sago seeds escaping from a sago pudding.

'If only you could just manage to call here sometimes,' pleaded Miss Iris. 'You'd soon get into it all, especially if some of the other ladies were here to encourage you, and you saw your beautiful bead pattern taking shape. This very first one being completed would make you feel far more cheerful.

'Perhaps you could tell them at home, so that they could give you a bit of time off to call in here – maybe half an hour each day, on the way back from school?'

A thread of fear registered on Milly's face. 'Oh no, I

19

couldn't tell them, Miss Iris. Our mam would go mad. She has too much to do herself, see? And our Effie can't help out much because she's courting, and Mam reckons it's better for Effie to catch Harold Flint good and proper. He's got a rich father, see, and it's maybe our Effie's only chance to get up the aisle. Mother reckons that at seventeen Effie's in her prime but it's not going to last long.'

Mr Potter coughed slightly at this news and Miss Iris began to put the headband carefully into its tissue paper again. As she handed it back to Milly she said: 'Don't give up yet, child. Keep on trying. Every cloud has a silver lining.'

'What's held you up?' said her mother suspiciously when she got in. 'There's a whole pan of spuds to peel and you were supposed to be starching some collars for the lads.'

Milly pretended not to hear but when her mother persisted she said: 'If you must know, I'm a monitor now at school and I'm in charge of all the inkwells. I have to go round the classrooms checking they haven't got all blotting paper and broken pen nibs in 'em, and lots of 'em have to be emptied and washed out.'

Her mother looked down at Milly's fingers. They were pink and clean and her fingernails showed not a trace of ink. 'I thought it was Sid Wallis the caretaker as did all that, and it was always the boys who was ink monitors and they just fill up the inkwells with that long-spouted ink can? I hope you ain't telling me lies, our Milly, or it'll be the worse for you.'

'I got it a bit wrong, Ma. I am a monitor, though. I'm art monitor, and I has to count all the crayons at night and put the chalks and slates in order, so I shall always be a bit late back like I've been today. Somebody said I was going to be inkwell monitor but it turned out different.'

Clarry Dawnay scowled at her slightly then went away. She had far too many other important things to worry about without deciding how much of the tale was true, and when Milly began to get home from school every day half an hour later than usual, she assumed that Milly must have been the art monitor after all. She even went so far as to mention it to the others one day when they asked why she was always so late back.

'Our Milly's the art monitor. She has to clear everything up and count the slates, chalks and crayons.'

'You aren't half gullible, Mam,' said Effie spitefully. 'I'll bet she's no more an art monitor than Aunt Fanny. You want to watch her . . .'

Nevertheless, Milly's short, secret after-school calls at the Potters' were yielding good results and she saw her bead headband taking shape at last. There were usually two or three women coming and going from the sewing room as she sat in a small chair close to the light of the window, and they were very encouraging and showed her their own work.

'How do you like this party bag then, Milly love? Only another million bloody beads (God bless us, don't let father Potter hear me blaspheme!) then it'll be done. Anyway, chuck, I got well paid for t'other 'un – an' at least it's me own true pattern, an' it's keeping me out of mischief.' Mrs Nelson winked at her. She was a weighty woman with huge muscular arms and fat dimpled elbows, but her wrists were still thin and her fingers small and agile. 'Yours is comin' on a treat, lass. I really likes them pinks and blues. Who knows but in the Next World we might all be toffs from the proceeds. As long as we don't see Conny Roudly there – that's all I ask. Don't you let 'er ever boss you about, child. She's a right domineering old trout.'

One afternoon a few weeks later, when Milly had just left the Potters' and her beautiful beadwork was practically finished, she decided to take it home and put on the few remaining beads there, in a patch of private bliss.

She had reached the corner of Hatching Street when she heard a boy's voice calling her name. It was Hewy Edmundson.

In a sudden wave of enthusiasm she showed him the bead headband. 'D'ya remember how Mr Potter taught some of the older ones beadwork when we was only infants? Well, he runs this little workshop, see, and I'm part of it. This is my first bit of work and it's nearly finished. I even gets paid for it.'

Hewy looked hard at the band. He could see it was good.

'Did you copy it from one of them design books?'

'No fear! It's my own. I thought it up meself.'

His smooth brow wrinkled up slightly and his black curling eyelashes narrowed to a squint above his deep violet eyes. 'A bit too much pink if you ask me . . .'

'Well, I didn't ask you, did I? I'll just bet you could do no better!'

'No need to get ratchety, Milly. I'm only saying what I think. And anyway, who'd want to fiddle with all that stuff when there's machines that can stick beads on things?'

'But I get paid for it.'

'See you when you're a machine, then. Tarrar . . .'

Milly frowned to herself as she reached home. She didn't think there was too much pink in it. Hewy

22

Edmundson always said things like that because he was determined to be the best, and he got pocket money every week so he didn't need to become a bead machine. Nobody would think that he was her secret lover for ever, and they had kissed. She began to wonder whether it was the same with all secret lovers. She suddenly felt a slight pang of envy. One day he'd probably go to Cavendish Street school of art in Manchester . . .

CHAPTER TWO

The Photograph

'It isn't me, Ma. I swear it!'

Milly was shivering with inner terror and her face was like whitewash as all the family peered at the picture in the paper. It was a very poor one of a group of women displaying a whole range of goods done in beadwork, and all it said was: Women display their wares. It accompanied an article about women who worked at home, and tucked away amongst them, peering out from the front row between what appeared to be two muscular female navvies – one of them being the notorious hatchet-faced Conny Roudly – was Milly.

'You damned little liar,' said Effie in disgust. 'It's as plain as a pikestaff. Never in a month of Sundays have you been doing extra work at school – you've been going to old Potter's and getting mixed up with his sweatshop!'

Milly sat there in speechless terror. How on earth could they all have got such a terrible opinion of kind, hard-working, creative Mr Potter and his charitable beadwork?

Then all of a sudden – to her relief – her sister Margy, who was fifteen and the only person who ever seemed to come to her aid, said: 'There's no need to be so nasty just because she's in the paper. I know for a fact that the work they do at Mr Potter's is first-rate. It's for helping people to make more of themselves. It's no more a sweatshop than piffey on a rock bun. Our Effie's too sure of herself, that's the trouble. She doesn't know *everything*.'

'And neither do you, Margaretta Dawnay,' rasped Effie with a cold glare. 'Just because you work at Mrs Treddle's hairdresser's doesn't make you Queen of the May! I only wish *I* had the chance to go out to work instead of being stuck at home helping Ma.'

'That's quite enough of that, our Effie,' said Joe Dawnay sharply. 'An eldest girl's place is at 'ome doin' the 'ouse-keepin' and learning from 'er mother, like they does int' big 'ouses. Tha should be proud to do it.'

'She should, that, Pa,' said Fred with carefree smugness. 'An' tell 'er to put more sugar in the pies in future; that last one was so tart, it made me eyes water.'

Milly hung her head silently. When would she ever escape from them? It was all very well for Father to pretend they lived the same as the big houses, when he knew full well they had only three small, skimpy bedrooms with Ma and Pa and Baby Derry in one; Fred, Benny and Donny in the second-best, and her in the pokiest one overlooking the back yard, with her own rickety old bed shared by six-year-old Betty, whilst Effie and Margy slept in the other, larger one with brass knobs on it. And what was even worse, she was always being told to give thanks to the Almighty for being so well off compared to other people with only two bedrooms and even bigger families . . .

That night when Joe and Clarry Dawnay were finally

settled down for the night on their own, Clarry said relentlessly: 'It's all very well Margy trying to stick up for the little devil, but there's more in our Milly than meets the eye. She's getting into a devious and deceitful little madam, and that's not all, Joe, because you'll just never guess what I found only this morning, hidden away under a vest in the drawer...'

He grunted sleepily.

'I found she had a Penny Bank book, from school, and there's ten shillings and sixpence three farthings in it!'

Joe gave a sudden snort as the alarming news sunk in. A daughter, going on eleven, with secret money in the bank was a very worrying situation. She could have got it from anywhere. 'I'll speak to 'er termorrer.'

But Joe had one weakness: what he said he'd do and what he actually got round to doing were two entirely different things, as far as dealing with his daughters was concerned. Working at Pomona Docks was the main thing in his life. A bit of relaxation and talk in the pub, and a bit of reading of newspapers and turning his hand to sharpening the knives and making rabbit hutches and other bits of woodwork was enough to fit in after his long working hours – never mind speaking to Milly on summat he really knew nowt about, even though he always said he would see to it. And in his mind – as the master of the house and all he surveyed – when he said he'd see to it, it meant he *had* seen to it and let no one ever question it from that moment on. In fact he deliberately left all family matters linked with females to his wife. And although he could see the seriousness of Milly's ten shillings of mysterious money in the Penny Bank, he decided deep down to forget it. Though if it had been one of the lads it would have been a different kettle of fish.

But to Clarry it certainly wasn't a different matter. A secret school bankbook with all that money recorded in it, and with the name Dawnay written on the cover, needed thorough investigation. She didn't say anything about it to Milly the following morning, but she simmered with mounting fury, and her imagination soared as she peered again at the somewhat indistinct grey-and-white picture in the newspaper. Then she carefully ripped it from the page and put it in her bedroom chest of drawers, next to some hairpins and a tortoiseshell comb. Maybe it would turn out not to be their Milly after all. But on the other hand, maybe it was, for it certainly tied in with her always being late home from school. Yet if that was the case, what a little liar she was turning out to be – and after being sent regularly to church on Sundays too, and coming from a family who had always been taught to tell the whole truth and nothing but the truth, fearlessly and faithfully. For there was no getting away from the fact that this secret money dated from the very time Milly had started to become a monitor, if the monitor tale could be believed ...

Clarry slipped the bankbook under the vest again as if she knew nothing about it, and for a whole week tried to pretend everything was as it had always been. As far as the rest of the family was concerned, the newspaper picture was soon forgotten and then completely eclipsed by the news that Hewy Edmundson's father had been killed in a crane accident in the street. He had been on his way to work at the hatter's where the fur from thousands of rabbits, and some said even cats, was used for making top hats.

The whole of Hatching Street was immediately in a state of subdued shock, and there was talk of nothing else but the tragedy as the familiar sight of a funeral assembly, led by two black horses, passed along the street. Young Hewy Edmundson, with a staring white face and black suit, followed behind with his four young sisters, also in black from head to toe and holding prayer books as they hovered tearfully round their mother, who was shrouded in a heavy black veil.

'Whatever'll 'appen now wit' maister gone?' said folks, as they sent scraps of comfort to them in the way of cards and hand-stitched samplers: The Lord is Good. The Father will look after his lambs.

How would she manage with no man's wage, and no child over the age of twelve? thought Clarry Dawnay – giving thanks that nothing so terrible had struck her own family.

The frightening news of Hewy's plight made Milly more determined than ever to carry on with her beadwork, so as to escape all the talk that went on. She had seen little of Hewy as he was now off school, helping out at home with baby-minding until things were more settled, but although she seemed quite cheerful on the surface, Milly often thought about him at night as the pale, sad face she had seen at the funeral rose in front of her. She kept the grief to herself. Mass grief was a comfort to everyone, but her own family would have thought it very strange if she had grieved over-much for Hewy Edmundson's plight at her tender age.

Nevertheless her mother had not forgotten the money incident, particularly since a small new entry had appeared in Milly's hidden bankbook. On a fine day a couple of weeks later, Clarry decided on some action at last. At the close of school that day, she hovered round Pickles' corner shop, keeping her eye on all the girls who flooded out through the nearby school gates until she caught a glimpse of Milly.

Milly idled a bit at first as she talked to her pal Babsy Renshaw and they ate some sweets. Then as Mackie Bright and Arthur Fallowfield turned up and began haggling for the toffees Milly suddenly slipped away and left them, so that Clarry had to have all her wits about her to follow her. And sure enough, Milly was making straight for Mr Potter's. When she reached the Potter's house she rang the bell and the large front door opened. Milly disappeared inside.

Clarry Dawnay's heart beat with alarm. It was true after all. Her own daughter was a liar and she was going to the Potters' just as Effie had always said. So just what went on in that house, with young girls their Milly's age?

After a few minutes of agonised hesitation, Clarry stepped up to the door herself and with a trembling hand and a furious heart, rang the front doorbell.

After a few moments there was the sound of a slow tread, and Mr Potter opened the door. His shoulders were stooped these days and she saw that his face was thinner and much older, for she had rarely seen him since he retired.

'Yes? What can I do for you?' The words were kindly spoken as Archie Potter took in the small, thin, anxious-eyed woman standing on his doorstep in her ankle-length dull grey tweed coat, with the neckline of a pinny showing beneath it.

'I'm Milly Dawnay's mother. She's just gone into your house.' Clarry's eyes shone now with a gleaming challenge and her lips were set in a thin line above her clenched teeth.

'Milly Dawnay!' Mr Potter's face lit up into a smile of

happy relief. 'How good to meet you at last. Yes, she is here. Please, do come in . . .'

He led her through the lobby towards the back of the house. 'My sister Miss Iris is out at present, she will be sorry to have missed you. She could have explained everything so much better . . .

'I expect you know all about our beadwork venture in aid of the Salvation Army and all the good works it carries out to help the poor?' He smiled with genuine pleasure.

'No. I can't truthfully say I has heard of it properly, Mr Potter. But what I do know is that my young daughter has no right to be in your house at this minute.'

His face changed to dismay. 'She has never told you, after all?'

'No she has not, Mr Potter. Fetch her immediately, if you please.'

By now they were standing in the small workroom, which was entirely empty except for some scissors and a thimble on a table where a small beaded bag lay unfinished. But of Milly there was no trace.

'Where is she then, Mr Potter? Where is my girl?' Clarry's voice quivered with ill-concealed panic.

'She certainly *was* here a few minutes ago,' said Mr Potter, looking puzzled and slightly ashamed. 'I can only assume that she has left by the back door. All our bead workers just come and go as they please . . .' Then he smiled again and put out his hand to shake hands with Clarry in a farewell gesture. 'All I can say, Mrs Dawnay, is that it's been a pleasure to meet you at last and to be able to reassure my sister that you know exactly what is going on. And of course, if you don't wish Milly to call here any more, we shall quite understand.'

Speechless, and keeping her hands close to her sides, her face flaming with emotion, Clarry too left the house by the back door, and hurried back to Hatching Street.

When she got in, Effie was there ironing. 'Wherever've you been, Ma? Our Milly's just run up them stairs and banged the bedroom door like a scalded cock, and our Margy's trying to pacify her . . .'

Clarry flopped down on the horsehair sofa. 'Get us a glass of that ginger beer, quick, afore I faints.'

Effie hurried to the bit of slated floor in the scullery where the stone ginger-beer bottle was kept, and carried the beer into the living room. Then she put a newspaper on the table along with one of their four best Bohemian glasses, removed the old waxen cork from the small, heavy flagon and poured her mother the ale, with her fingers all atremble, and her young face no longer bold and bossy. 'Whatever's happened, Ma?'

Clarry hitched herself up wearily with her elbows and sipped her drink. 'Nothing's happened this time, child, but think on, our Effie – all sorts may well have happened before. Today however, I was – with the Good Lord's Help – able to nip it in the bud.'

'Mother, whatever do you mean?'

'I mean that it's just as you always said. Our Milly is never a monitor in charge of the inkwells at school; she's going round to them there Potters and is up to no earthly good . . .'

'What was she *doing*?' Effie's eyes were as round and brown as penny pieces.

Clarry hesitated. She had completely recovered now, and was enjoying her rest on the sofa. The room was as calm as an empty church, which was a rare state of affairs, and she was glad to take advantage of it. She stared vaguely towards a velvet-framed sepia

31

photograph of her own dear father and mother. 'She wasn't doing anything, Effie, because she didn't get the chance. The minute I entered that terrible house she vanished.'

Effie's face fell a mile and her natural perkiness returned. 'You mean you never even saw her in the place, Ma? What a waste of time!' Effie got hold of the ginger-beer flagon to take it back to the scullery.

'Don't take it back yet, Effie. Pour me a drop more.' Clarry could see that she was quickly losing the attention of her eldest, and favourite and – to others – domineering daughter. 'She was definitely there a few moments before I got to the back of the house –'

'And right out through the back door,' said Effie. 'Just wait till she gets downstairs, Mother, and we can have it out with her good and proper. Then, perhaps, she'll change her deceitful ways at last.'

Effie's round, healthy face assumed a look of concern for her mother's predicament. 'She leads you a real dance and no mistake. In fact she leads the whole of our family a dance with the lies she tells. She'll start to give us all a bad name. We'll be sinking as deep as those Fallowfields. One of their ancestors was mixed up in the Peterloo riots . . .' Effie's expression changed to one of thoughtful cunning. 'I should bide your time, Ma. Don't say anything to her this time. Just see if the fright of you calling has cured her. Then, if it hasn't, follow her again and try to catch her and Old Potter red-handed.'

Clarry gave a terrible gasp, and sank back on the sofa. 'You've sent me all weak at the thought of it, child. I don't think I could stand going through it all again. No . . . no . . . It would be the last straw . . .'

'Please yourself, Ma,' muttered Effie sulkily. 'But just

you remember what a little liar our Milly is. For a start she'll deny there's owt wrong in what she's doing, and second if there is summat awful going on between her and potty Potter ... If you managed to catch her in the house it would be proof positive.' Her eyes shone with sudden enthusiasm. 'He might have a hidden harem. I've just been reading *Secret Hearts* – that new paper that's giving away Princess scent free if you collect ten tokens. They had a true story identical with Mr Potter and our Milly. It was about this very old man who captured all these young girls and tried to sell them to someone like Ali Baba, but they all escaped.'

Milly had heard the person coming into Mr Potter's when she was in the back workroom and had fled when she thought she heard the voice of her own mother. Later it occurred to her that there was a very, very slight chance that it hadn't been her mam. This was because her mother – although she seemed in a very strange mood and kept wiping her brow as if she felt faint – never said anything about it and Effie too was surprisingly quiet and secretive.

So the next day, when everything seemed to be pretty well back to normal, Milly took a chance and called at the Potters' to get on with her beadwork. Everything went like clockwork, and Mr Potter even solved the mystery of the caller the day before by telling her it was her mother: 'So now you can do your beadwork with no more worries, Milly. For at least your mother knows you come here, even though she did rush away rather suddenly. Did she say anything to you when she got home?'

Milly shook her head. 'She wasn't too well. She often gets over-tired and she had to have a lie-down by all accounts. But she does have help from our Effie.'

Mr Potter nodded happily. He was glad the whole situation was open and above board. He imagined Mrs Dawnay would be glad to know that her daughter was so clever and persevering so well at the beadwork, whilst at the same time helping those in dire need and also putting a small amount of money aside in her own bank account.

By Wednesday the following week Clarry was simmering away like a cauldron as she planned once more to visit the Potters' and catch whatever was going on in the act. This time she decided she would follow Milly as before but would not go to the front door. Instead, she would slip round the back and even be so bold as to walk into the house on some pretext if the back door was open, as indeed it had been when Milly escaped from her the time before. Poor Clarry trembled at the thought of it, but the determination and fury aroused in her by Effie's horrifying insinuations had fired her resolve.

The plan worked like clockwork as she glimpsed Mr Potter once more opening the front door to her young daughter and promptly closing it. Clarry disappeared down the cobbled back entry and found to her relief that the back entry door was unlatched.

Fearfully she walked quickly through the neat, freshly washed back yard with its flat wickerwork carpet beater hanging on a nail by the back door. She looked neither left nor right, nor at any of the windows, as she pretended to knock at the door, then swiftly pressed down the metal release next to the door handle. She slipped through the door and found herself in a small inner scullery which led through to a kitchen.

Everything was as peaceful and pleasant as a children's

34

picture book as she stood in the back kitchen with its peg rug on the floor and gleaming copper kettle on the range. The large kitchen clock ticked away quietly and a cat slept on undisturbed by the hearth.

She began to waver. She had no right to have walked in here unannounced . . . She felt awkward and slightly ashamed.

Then suddenly she heard voices: Milly and Mr Potter . . . Her heart began to beat madly.

'. . . Miss Iris isn't here, Milly. So just you go and do what you always do, and I'll be along as soon as possible when I've got these dreadful old clothes off . . .'

Clarry's heart almost stopped and she began to sweat with fear. It was worse than she'd ever really imagined. With no more ado she burst out of the back kitchen towards the front hall where Milly was standing opposite Mr Potter, who was standing in some overalls holding a paint can.

But the damage was done and Clarry was so worked up that he might just as well have been standing in the nude with wings as big as the angel Gabriel. She pushed her face close to his.

'Mother! What are you doing here?' gasped Milly as Mr Potter smiled in a slightly surprised way.

'I'm here to take you back home straight away, Milly Dawnay. And you must never, never come to this house again. You've been a very naughty and deceitful child.' She turned to Mr Potter: 'And as for you, Mr Potter, you should be ashamed of yourself – trying to lead young children astray. It's an action fit for the attention of the police as far as I'm concerned. I never knew the like of it! It's totally disgraceful and my daughter's not going to be part of any of it!'

Mr Potter's face went grey. 'I fear there's been some

terrible misunderstanding, Mrs Dawnay. I had no idea you weren't aware of the whole situation –'

'I am now, Mr Potter, and what I see is greatly alarming to me and the whole of our family. What I see is my daughter – a mere ten-year-old girl – being used in some secret way in your house. And you're going to hear more of it, that's for sure!

'Come along, Milly.' She grabbed Milly's shocked, lifeless hand, and dragged her out through the back door.

When Iris Potter arrived back at the house from her afternoon bible meeting about ten minutes later, she was surprised to find her brother sitting in a chair by his desk in their best front room with a glazed expression on his elderly face and looking terribly pale.

'Archie! Whatever's happened?'

He tried to speak but the words wouldn't come properly from his lips, and when she brought him a cup of tea he was incapable of even lifting the cup towards his mouth. Hurriedly she sent for the doctor.

The following day, after the doctor had said Archibald Potter had suffered a heart attack, and must stay in bed, a letter arrived for him, which his sister decided to open.

She could hardly bear to read it, for it went on and on in a terrible tirade, accusing her brother of seducing young and innocent girls and swearing to have the law on him: '. . . For how else can a girl of my Milly's age secretly get so much money in the Penny Savings Bank?'

Slowly and sadly, Miss Iris went to the desk, opened it and sat down to reply to Mrs Dawnay:

I feel so sorry that all of us have so grossly misunderstood each other and that my poor brother has now been smitten with a heart attack, but I do beseech you not to chastise your young daughter, because she has worked so enthusiastically at this artistic craft of bead-work, and in the process has helped others less well off than herself by the funds that have been accumulated ... However, due to Mr Potter's severe indisposition, we shall no longer be carrying on with this worthwhile project. God bless you and all your family.

Iris Potter

'And good riddance! That's what I say,' said Effie when her mother showed her the letter. 'You just got there in a nick of time, Ma, before our Milly was set on the road to ruin. I only wish I had a bankbook with half as much in it as she was mounting up.'

For the whole of the next week Milly suffered the pangs of hell as everyone except her sister Margy tried to belittle her. Meanwhile her mother tried to account for Mr Potter's sudden illness by titivating her original version of her meeting with him: 'Yes ... and he was just about to take his clothes off, for some reason or other. Not that I'm saying anything about him, mind, but it only goes to show the state of their consciences ... By the way, they've suddenly stopped all their nonsense and sold out their so-called beadwork to that old battleaxe Conny Roudly from Fitzackley Street. They say she's found some rat-infested basement in Bishopton's warehouse to get it going again. But this time not with any of *our* family, thank you very much.'

Milly tried not to listen to it all, but she felt more and more miserable. Her whole body seemed to itch with nerves.

37

'What on earth's up with you, child?' said Clarry, suddenly aware at last that all was not well. 'You look quite ill.'

And sure enough she looked so unwell at school the following day that she was sent home by Miss Bolsover, and was forthwith sent straight to the doctor's surgery.

Her small world of beadwork hopes faded, and her Penny Bank was no more, except for those first ten shillings, never *ever* to be used again. Altogether, her dreams of a future of life and laughter seemed gone for ever.

CHAPTER THREE

A Sunny Day at All Saints

'Shingles? How on earth's she managed that?' said Joe Dawnay.

'I 'ope no one else gets it,' said Effie, 'even though some says it's not catching. She'd better not be around if Harold Flint calls here to say goodbye before I go off to Aunt May's farm . . .'

'. . . Anyways, she's to be off school,' said Clarry. 'Doctor Daley says it's a bad attack and the results might last quite a long time. He says only rest will cure it, along with good food.'

'I 'ope it doesn't sneak up on me an' all, when I'm away at Aunt May's,' nagged Effie. 'Some of those scabs look really runny . . .'

'And *I* hope you'll stop all that chattering an' finish getting your suitcase packed or you'll never be on that dratted holiday at all.' For quite frankly Clarry had been getting fed up with her daughter Effie since the Potter fiasco. Deep down, she now had a guilty conscience about the way she'd jumped to the worst possible conclusions – aided and abetted by Effie. And – although it was better to be safe than sorry – the whole business had proved worse than expected; what with Mr Potter now having suffered a stroke and being so much in need of specialised help that he was going into a convalescent home; while his distraught sister was moving to relations in Middleton to be nearer to him.

Milly watched Effie packing her case with morbid relief. She felt like scratching herself to bits amongst all the irritating reddened patches which were tingling painfully.

Well, at least they would all get a bit of peace from Effie at last ... Milly quite envied her going to Aunt May's farm near Southport for a trial two-week holiday as a milkmaid. If Effie fitted in she could be staying there for ever – though Milly didn't really think there'd be much hope of that, knowing how bossy and unsympathetic she was. Just imagine a cow having its udder washed and its teats squeezed and pulled by their Effie ... Milly gave a huge shudder. Her eldest sister was far from resembling the nursery-rhyme pictures of bonny looking, kindly milkmaids.

On the other hand, Milly's next sister, Margaretta, who wore small steel-rimmed glasses and always seemed overshadowed, was as kind as the gentle breezes of summer, and without her glasses Margy was the most beautiful of all, with her glimmering sheen of straight brown hair, and her sudden smiles breaking through the seriousness.

Milly began to cheer up slightly. With Effie gone, Margy in top place could make a world of difference – even though Margy would have to forsake any further schooling in order to help Mother, just as Effie had done.

During the first week, after Effie had finally settled at Sandend Farm, the Dawnays received a letter from her. It was full of moans:

★

The work here is truly awful, Ma. There's dung everywhere, and Aunt May is always getting at me. Yesterday a cow swung its filthy, muck-strewn, wet tail right across the side of my face whilst I was trying to milk it, and Aunt May went mad when the milk pail tipped up. She isn't a patch on you, Ma. How you ever managed to get a sister like her, the Lord alone knows ... She half starves me. All I ever eat is huge hunks of bread and cheese like the men and I have to share a bedroom with cousin Gertrude, who is really bossy and wets my face with a cold flannel to get me up halfway through the night to start work. And as for Uncle Toby, he's even worse. He never even speaks except to tell me to 'get yard swilled'. I know this much – I'll never, ever marry a farmer. And that's another thing, our ma – Harold Flint says he'll not come to Southport to see me in case he gets his suit spoiled.

Your saddened daughter

Effie

PS I hope our Milly isn't plaguing you with all them shingles ... and I pray to be back to help you again when this awful stay is over.

To everyone's amazement, in spite of Effie resorting to prayer, the weeks spun out until it was close on Christmas and Effie was still in Southport, complaining of chilblains, a red nose, and eating plenty of boiled onions; whilst Margy was helping Milly to get on with some more beadwork: 'Just keep pegging away at it, Milly, love – like people do with their mats and their knitting. Mother won't mind that. It was just because she was worried at you going to the Potters' house and getting so involved. It's all different now – and you'll be able to make Christmas presents.'

But for Milly it wasn't like that at all. She still baulked at the way her small personal bank account had come to an abrupt end, and the more she heard of Conny Roudly going from strength to strength in Bishopton's warehouse with the beadwork, the more she wanted to escape from school and get a job there herself, for she had passed her eleventh birthday and she knew she was now very good at the work.

One day the devil got hold of her and on the way back from school she went round by Fitzackley Street and stared at Conny Roudly's house. She gasped inwardly with amazement – what a change from all the rest in the row ... It was done up like a dog's dinner. A few years ago it had been drab like all the rest but now it had lace curtains as good as Buck House, with satin ties on them. And all the brickwork had been gone round with new, creamy looking cement, and the front door was a glossy, deep crimson with a huge, gleaming brass door-knocker. It was obvious that beadwork had done things for old Conny. With no more ado, Milly hurried along to her basement in Bishopton's warehouse.

'Well I'll be blessed! Little Milly Dawnay ...' gushed Conny with her arms folded, and her sharp eyes gleaming slightly. 'I allus thought tha might turn up agin.'

'So what can I do for thee, child? Is it work you was wanting? Come in and see the women. Three of 'em's still 'ere, including Nelly Nelson from old Potter's, and there's now fourteen more ...'

She took Milly down the dusty stone steps with their traces of rat droppings and bits of straw in corners towards a badly lit cellar room with one small, paned window of thick, grimy bottle glass. There was an oil stove in the corner, close to a small iron-barred chimney grate, and there were three large wooden tables, each fit to seat six people, where the women sewed away at their beads.

Gone was the simple, homely comfort of the Potters' domain. Gone the beautiful drawers of coloured beads and cottons, and the neat wickerwork baskets. Milly stared at it all with a sinking heart.

'The beads is in packets of a hundred. You pays for 'em yourself afore you starts. But if you can't afford it, I lets you 'ave 'em on account and you pays me one penny each time you comes 'ere to work till they're paid for. I buys the finished articles at the end, if they're suitable. But they 'as to be perfect, mind, otherwise they's destroyed. I buy nothing shoddy and nowt can be taken away. All work is ticked off and left behind in that there clothes basket with your name attached to it. Them as works the 'ardest gets the most.' She gazed beyond the top of Milly's head with a hard, superior, look on her face. 'And anyone under twenty-one had better keep what they do here completely to themselves – especially the likes of you, young Milly.'

Milly felt like turning and fleeing then and there, but the fact that she was very quick and good at the beadwork made her stay. At least she would get something out of it to start off her own savings again. But her dreams of actually leaving school to work in a place like this had faded completely.

'Thank you very much, Mrs Roudly,' she whispered.

Conny Roudly nodded with a slight smirk. 'Right you are then. I'll hold a place open for you at one of the tables. But if you're not back within the week it'll have to go to someone else on the waiting list.'

But as Milly hurried home from the warehouse, she had second thoughts. She decided to forget she had ever been there – for who would want to work in conditions like those if they could possibly help it? Surely there were better ways of making money?

Little did she realise then how circumstances can suddenly change . . .

The change came a couple of years later, when Milly was thirteen going on fourteen. Her mother had been caught, and was expecting yet another baby. And at just the same time Effie, now twenty, was expecting a baby herself – from Maurice Hayden, who worked on Aunt May's farm in Southport with her – thus finishing her chances with rich Harold Flint, who now had a solid gold watch.

And that wasn't all, because for the past month eighteen-year-old Margy had forsaken hairdressing and had moved out to work as a live-in assistant cook at a big house in Whalley Range. This meant that Milly's school days were over for ever, as she had to take Margy's place as top working drudge, the only other girl in the family at home now being her younger sister Betty, who was nine.

The work at home was even harder now, for both Benny and Donny were working. They demanded that more clothes be washed and ironed and bigger meals cooked, because they were proud wage earners with gold sovereigns in their pockets, and, oh, how Milly wished she was the same. She began to think once more of the beads, seeing them as her only escape. Eventually she decided to approach her now heavily pregnant mother on the subject.

Times were different now. Three years without the influence of Effie the young dictator always at Clarry's elbow – and with the burden of yet another child on the horizon – had made her weaker and more vulnerable.

'I'm getting right fed up with never getting any time to myself in this house, Ma. I'm nowt but a slave for Benny and Don. Why on earth can't they sew their own buttons on and starch their own shirts, *and* iron them?'

Her mother's pale face creased into a slight, tired smile: 'Talk sense, love. When did two men ever starch and iron their own shirts in a place where there's lassies? Working men don't have the time. It's not like in big houses where there are servants. Ordinary folks has to organise it all different – that's what it amounts to. Some works at home and some works at other places. The home workers does the home chores.'

'But there's *some* folks like me that wants to work at two places, Ma. Why should I work here all the time and hardly get a halfpenny piece at my age? From now on I'm going to work at Conny Roudly's every weekday afternoon and our Betty can help a bit – just like I had to – when she gets back from school. It's only fair, Ma.'

'Chance'll be a fine thing, Milly. They say that Conny Roudly never has any places and there's a long waiting list. The work they do ends up in all the poshest shops in Manchester and London and they sell for a small fortune, yet you'll be paid a pittance.'

Her mother shook her head dispiritedly, but, even so, Milly knew the words were a tacit acceptance that she could try her luck.

The next day she visited the warehouse. It had improved. The steps were clean and smelt of pine disinfectant and in the workroom the small window had been replaced with a larger, brand-new sash window,

45

and the walls were freshly whitewashed.

Yet Conny Roudly hadn't changed a scrap, standing there in her dark green twill overall, except that now she wore a thin string of pearls. She welcomed Milly with a glimmer of satisfaction. She reminded Milly not so much of an old trout, but of an elderly pike waiting in the pool for its prey . . .

'You're very lucky, love. It just so happens that Alice Shaw has had to leave, and you can have her place for old times' sake.'

By the time Milly had been working at Conny Roudly's for six months, the Dawnay household was in a complete uproar and Milly herself was nearly as thin and white-faced as her mother. Not only was she exhausted from coping with all the chores at home as well as doing her afternoon work, but there had been a family tragedy: Clarry Dawnay's baby had been still-born. Joe blamed the miscarriage on the fall his wife had three weeks before the baby was due, when she tripped over some toys of Derry's which were lying on the floor.

'You can blame them girls,' he cried in a fever of despair when he visited Clarry in hospital. 'The little varmints have never pulled their weight. Not one of 'em. And our Milly's been by far the worst – leaving everything to go off to that sweatshop every afternoon, so as to feather her own little nest. I never heard the like of it in one so young! Such selfishness is hard to beat, and as far as I'm concerned she can pack her bags and get out for ever!'

'Pass me some water to sup from that feeder, Joe love. My lips are parched.' Clarry lay there weakly as he fed her, then she said: 'We must be patient, Joe. I'll soon

46

pick up again once I'm out of here, and I'll be glad of our Milly then. She'll soon see how much she's needed at home.'

But other events were to take place that would ensure that Milly made her own mind up.

She was in an unrewarding situation at Bishopton's warehouse, for she earned far less than she done at the Potters' three years ago, and Conny Roudly had started new styles of working, to make things quicker. Mrs Roudly now had starters, middlers and finishers, along with two young 'waiters on' who saw to all the materials and did the tidying up and checking – supervised by Conny.

Milly was one of the starters and they got a farthing more for every twenty articles completed. The starters were the fastest and most accurate workers and they set the pace for the rest of the women. There were four of them: Milly Dawnay, Nelly Nelson, Lena Sefton and Moira Flit.

It was thankless work, for now they never finished any article as their own complete product but were just the start of a working chain which churned round and round all day and depended for its speed of output on the pace set by the four starters. And their own quickness was led by the quickest of their team, who was Milly Dawnay.

At first Milly had been happy to be able to work so quickly, fondly thinking in her youthful innocence that the speed and dexterity of the starters would help more goods to be produced and thus they would all get more pay. But it didn't work like that. Gradually over the next six months the tension and general inner panic about the working conditions took its toll in rows and dissension, which all boiled down to the speed at which Milly worked.

47

At first the rest of the women jibbed at her in a fairly kindly way: 'Eeh, lass. Can't tha calm down a bit? We're not part of a bloody treadmill. Most of us is a lot older for a start.'

'It's no good getting at *her*, Bessy. If we four starters slows down,' warned Nelly Nelson, 'you'll all be groaning like 'ell for want of summat to be gettin' on with – and Roudly'll be cutting our cash. We can't 'ave it all ways . . .'

Milly listened in silence and tried to go slower. But as soon as she started to go slower her concentration waned and she began to dream. She dreamt about leaving all this behind and going to the art school. Being a painter or even a sculptress, and having enough money saved up to make her own way in the world . . . Being on an equal footing with boys like handsome Hewy Edmundson and smug Arthur Fallowfield and daring Mackie Bright, and – most of all – of being able to go gadding about with her best friend, bubbly Babsy Renshaw, who only this week had just started work in the counting house of a large coal merchant where she was an errand girl.

Then, one wet, gloomy, terrible day, everything came to a head. It was a miserable Monday and Conny Roudly had been bawling her head off about the work being slow and slipshod, because the orders for bead-work belts from a shop in London had dwindled, as they could get them cheaper from abroad. 'I just don't know what's got into you all. You just aren't keeping up with the starters. 'Ow do you expect me to run 'igh standards when you acts so lazy?'

There was a stony silence. No one spoke in case they got the sack – for they knew there was a queue always waiting to step in.

And then, suddenly, young Honour Merridew – who everyone thought was beaten by her husband because of her blotchy flesh and constantly bruised looking face and arms – fell to the floor in a fit. She gave a huge warning groan, stiffened up and went purple, then began to tremble violently with her teeth clenched. Her limbs jerked in all directions and everyone thought she was going to die.

They all stood there helplessly, until Milly draped a coat over her and Nelly tried to hold her hand and someone else went to get some water.

'It's just the same as my cousin 'as,' said Bessy Fields, keeping her distance. 'You 'ave to be careful they don't swallow their tongues. She should always 'ave a spoon with 'er, with a bandage wrapped round its 'andle, to stick in 'er mouth before trouble takes over so that 'er teeth doesn't do any damage.'

'There'll be no "*always*" 'ere, from now on,' said Conny with her own mouth as hard as a trap. 'We can't put up with that again. She'll 'ave to go.'

Honour Merridew sat up at last, and peered round, then lay back on the floor again and closed her eyes. She looked like death. She was undernourished and painfully thin, but it didn't show too much because of her long clothes. She looked no more than seventeen.

Milly felt weak with the horror of it all as she encouraged Honour to have a cup of tea, which had been brewed in a large billycan, with water from the blackened kettle on the old oil stove added to a mix of tinned milk and a sprinkling of tea.

'I don't know what came over me,' said Honour as she gradually recovered. 'It's never happened before.'

The women eyed each other knowingly. They didn't believe a word of it.

49

'I can promise you it'll never 'appen again, Mrs Roudly. I'm quite sure of it, truly. I 'adn't 'ad no breakfast, see. And I've bin 'aving a bit of trouble at 'ome, with our Egbert not 'aving a job and us only just married.' Her gaze was long and pleading, but it had no effect.

'As soon as you feel well enough, you can rise from that floor and get off home, Mrs Merridew. I'll settle up what we owe each other at the end of this week.

'All this fuss has taken up valuable time, and time is money – you should know that. It's not only affected you, but it's affected everyone else. I don't want to seem 'ard-'arted, but what would 'appen if *everyone* 'ad fits every day? Where would we be then? I'm 'ere for the good of *all* my ladies, Mrs Merridew.' A spark of triumph made her jowls quiver with self-righteousness.

Slowly, Honour struggled to get up from the floor, and Milly stepped forward quickly to help her. Suddenly Milly herself was filled with a violent anger: 'And I'll be going an' all, Conny. You can settle up all my stuff at the end of the week, too – when you do 'ers.'

Conny Roudly's face fell a mile as she heard this insolent ultimatum issuing from the mouth of her youngest, quickest and best worker. 'Shut up and get on with your work, Milly Dawnay. I've never heard such tripe. What's just happened to Mrs Merridew is nowt to do with kids like you – it's me that has to see to it as the head of this establishment – so you'd better watch your p's and q's, or you really *will* be out on your ear'ole!'

She turned to the rest of them: 'Right you are then, ladies. That's enough of that. Back to your work.

'Mrs Flit, go and fetch Mrs Merridew's proper coat, and as Mrs Sefton lives close by she can see 'er safely back to where she belongs.'

50

Lena Sefton glared daggers at her: 'No fear. At that rate I'll be missing the whole afternoon's work, Conny. Why don't *you* go? You'll not be missed. We'll all manage quite well on our own . . .'

'I'll do it,' said Milly, giving Conny a proud, impudent stare. For now she had made the decision to leave she felt as free as some fairy-tale sprite with her chains of toil vanquished.

There was an ugly silence.

'Just as you like, Miss Millicent Dawnay,' muttered Conny through gritted teeth. 'But think on – there'll be no crawling back 'ere in times of need. You've burned your bloody boats good and proper now.'

When Milly finally got back home that day she was so late that the rest of them were eating.

'Whatever was up?' asked her mother fearfully, as Milly munched away at sausage and mash and young Betty scowled at her.

'Honour Merridew was taken ill and had to be taken home.' With her mouth full, she added: 'And I've left.'

'*Left?*' Everyone was dumbstruck.

'I thought you was their star worker?' said Donny, drooping over his meal like an overgrown beanstalk.

'Star shirker . . .' said Benny, looking at her through heavy-lidded eyes.

'After all the fuss you made about going there at the start – we thought it was at least for life,' grumbled Fred, wiping his plate with bread until it shone, then wiping grease from his chin with his knuckles. 'Girls is never satisfied. All girls is stupid beings.'

'If you can't talk sense, lad, don't talk at all,' said his father sharply.

Milly sat there silently, but already a plan was working out in her head. On the walk to the small, two-

51

bedroomed hovel in Laundry Close where Honour lived, she had sounded Honour out with the idea of taking a lodger: 'It wouldn't half help you, Honour, now you've got the sack. And it'd help me an' all, because I can't stand being at home any longer. Just you mark my words, Honour, I'm going to look for a proper job tomorrow – and you can come with me if you want. Then when we've both got jobs I could lodge with you and it would help you out till your Egbert gets fixed up. How's that sound?' Milly's voice rang out with enthusiasm and it was so catching that Honour agreed to meet her the following afternoon when they would both normally have been working at Bishopton's warehouse.

'Put plenty of powder on your face,' said Milly as an afterthought.

Honour smiled faintly and resolved to do as she was bid.

Later that day, whilst Milly was clearing the pots from the kitchen table, Clarry Dawnay watched her with mixed feelings. She'd resigned herself to no longer having a solid domestic helper all the time – like Effie had been, and Margy. But young Betty was a marvellous help, far more reliable than Milly had ever been, plus being a very good scholar at school.

'You'll probably quite like being back at home again, Milly,' she said tentatively. 'It's not such a bad old place for a young lady and you'll be able to take Derry out to the park, and read him stories and teach him to count.'

Milly stopped dead: 'Take our Derry for walks? Not on your life, Ma! What sort of a time's that for a person who's used to earning a wage – however small it is? You may as well know right now that I'll be out tomorrow afternoon as usual, looking for another job, and if I'm not back by tea-time, don't worry about it.'

But Clarry was already worrying. How on earth was a young girl like Milly going to get a decent job with no references and no proper skills? All she'd ever get would be skivvying, unless she knew someone who could find her something better – and there was no one round here with any influence to do that at present.

The next afternoon – with hardly any ideas of how or where to start proper job-hunting, and with her mother well out of the way on a visit to Grandmother Smith's with Derry – Milly began to get ready.

First she looked at her face in her mother's bedroom mirror and decided she would have to look older than fourteen, and disguise the scar. She couldn't prevent the usual sigh of disappointment as she regarded the livid mark which seemed set to be with her for life, slicing a path down the left side of her cheek, from all those years ago when the laundry wall had collapsed ... There was no question of only blotchy, bruised Honour needing plenty of powder on *her* face – for Milly was in the same plight.

She gazed at herself in her buttercup-coloured, ankle-length cotton sateen frock. It made her look about twelve. In a flash of summer madness and fury she grabbed some scissors and trimmed a large white net border from the flimsy, sunlit lace curtains. Then, finding her mother's rotting old straw hat with its mouse-nibbled brim, she put it on, bringing the net lace over the crown of it and draping it round her cheeks and chin like someone with a bad attack of double mumps. She tied it under her chin in a huge flourishing bow, so that it covered her scar beautifully.

Then, rougeing her lips slightly with a mixture of cochineal and cocoa butter, she powdered her face with a touch of dry starch and dabbed a trace of soot across her eyelids to give then a touch of mystery. Yes – she was looking wonderful. She could swear she looked as old as twenty-two.

When she got round to Honour's she was pleased to see that Honour too had been quite lavish with the make-up. They set off to catch a tram to All Saints, a district that featured a number of great pinnacled institutions of ornate grandeur and Doric columns in abundance. It was also a busy shopping centre complete with small, age-old taverns on most street corners, not to mention the new Grosvenor Picture Palace, which had been opened by the Lord Mayor only a couple of years previously.

'I hope we *do* find something . . .' murmured Milly, becoming ever more unsettled as they talked along the way about where the best places would be for seeking employment. Eventually they reached Grosvenor Square, where mighty All Saints church with its huge domed steeple presided over a vast churchyard paved with hundreds of flat gravestones.

Idly, they wandered near Paulden's noble department store, and Righton's the posh drapers, with its finely decorated shop front and big plate-glass window. Milly sighed to herself as she saw the Manchester School of Art in Cavendish Street close by, along with its other imposing neighbour, Chorlton Town Hall, and the busy Manchester Ear Hospital.

They found a seat and sat there amongst the greenery and neat iron railings, still pondering where, amongst all this, they should start to enquire about work.

They had hardly been there more than ten minutes, however, than they were approached by a tall man with a walrus moustache, who looked to Milly as old as twenty-five. He was wearing a high-crowned felt hat, and a shabby but very good quality suit. Behind the man were two assistants. One was a gangly youth of about eighteen with a cap thrust on the back of his head and a knitted silk white muffler round his neck. He carried a sandwich board which he laid to rest against the railings. It proclaimed: THE ADVENTURES OF A SOLDIER. CHORLTON TOWN HALL. SHOWING TONIGHT. FILMED IN MANCHESTER, BY FINER FILMS. The other assistant was much younger and was struggling in turns with both a large wooden packing case, suitable for standing on, and a huge extending wooden camera tripod.

Milly looked at him sympathetically. He was about her age and didn't seem to know whether he was on his head or his heels. Then she looked at him more closely: it was Arthur Fallowfield! She was even more surprised when along came both Hewy Edmundson and Mackie Bright, who listened carefully as the older man gave then some muttered instructions.

'Hewy!' Milly's heart began to thump. It was like someone appearing from another world. So much time had sped by since those early, almost forgotten years when his father had died. And now here he was: tall, thinner, his strong white teeth showing in a beaming smile, his eyes sparkling.

She hurried towards him, a host of memories welling up inside her, and she glowed at the thought of the love pledge they had exchanged as children, now transformed in her mind into vivid reality. Yet her words were blunt and simple and overladen with shyness: 'Fancy all you lot being here.'

His smile faded a bit. Then turning away slightly he said: 'What you got all that stuff on your face for, Milly? You can still see that scar a mile off.' Then, as he saw her look of agonised despair, he gave her a cheerful smile again to show he'd meant no harm. But the damage was done. She turned away hastily, trying to look as if she didn't care, trying to conceal the tears that momentarily stung her eyes. She returned to the bench, and when she looked up again, Hewy and Mackie had disappeared.

The man walked towards where the two girls were sitting and said in a quiet, casual voice: 'Sit there just like that and do exactly as I say, and you can be in a film show.'

They were so taken aback that they did exactly what he said, which was to sit there looking pleasant as the tripod was set up and a photograph was taken of them with what he suddenly described as a Sin Camera.

Sin Camera?

Poor Milly felt all excitement fading as she stared at Honour's heavily made-up face and thought of the soot round her own eyes, which had now loomed in her imagination to immense proportions, especially after Hewy's remark. The Sin Camera could mean only one thing. This man was one of those newfangled police in disguise who were taking pictures of ladies of easy virtue to put in a police file. She stood up hastily, hoping to make a getaway. It had caused enough trouble when she'd appeared in the newspaper photograph of the bead workers when she was working as Mr Potters', never mind *this*.

'Sit down again, Miss, er, Miss . . .'

'Miss Dawnay. Miss Millicent Penelope Dawnay. And if you don't mind, I've decided not to take part in any Sin films. My friend and I have come here to try and get proper jobs as befits respectable ladies.'

Honour nodded vigorously and stood up beside her. 'Hold it,' said the man, as the cinematograph camera began to whine and click. 'Don't go,' he implored. 'I'm not interested in sin. You are quite safe with me.'

Arthur Fallowfield suddenly realised that he recognised the face sheathed in the straw hat and the white net. 'I know them, sir. Milly Dawnay was at school with all us lads. She must think a cine camera is something to do with Bad Ways, sir.'

Milly glared at Arthur Fallowfield. He was still as smug and well dressed as ever; even, some might say, very handsome with his thinnish dimpled face and dark, floppy hair which had escaped from the soothing flatness of hair oil.

The older man sighed with obvious relief and smiled briefly. 'Excellent. Sit down again then, ladies.'

Quickly he produced a brown paper bag. It was full of fresh, glossy cherries, red and butter-coloured, hanging delicately in clusters, complete with stalks and healthy green leaves. He handed the bag to Milly.

Milly looked quickly at Honour. Was it safe to accept them? Then she looked at Arthur who was standing by. 'He's only just bought 'em from a barrer,' hissed Arthur reassuringly. 'They's what you call "props".'

Milly was flooded with a feeling of relief. 'Props' was obviously a short word for 'proper' – and proper meant safe, as far as maidens were concerned. The man, evidently seeking to reassure her further, introduced himself as Mr Bridges, and Milly responded by introducing her friend, 'Mrs Merridew'.

The formalities over, Mr Bridges asked her to place the bag of cherries on her lap and ordered Arthur to stand by with a notebook and pencil to record the scene.

A handful of passers-by began to gather and a hansom cab slowed down while its horse munched some oats. People peered from passing trams.

'Look carefully in the bag, Miss Dawnay, then draw out a really nice twig of cherries and hold them towards Mrs Merridew.

'You, Mrs Merridew, hold your left hand towards the cherries and smile – but don't begin till Arthur here gives you the sign.'

It all took far longer than Milly had thought it would, mainly because the bag of cherries fell on the floor and they were scrabbling about looking for them, with Mr Bridges still behind the camera saying 'good' and getting quite excited.

Then suddenly the episode was over and the film-makers hastily disappeared without another word, as if they'd never arrived in the first place, leaving Milly and Honour still sitting there in a daze.

'I always thought film stars got ever so much money,' said Honour mournfully. 'Do you think they've just gone to get some from the bank?'

But there was no sign of them coming back, and after about three quarters of an hour of hovering about in hope and being accosted by a man in a very tight waistcoat with a bowler hat, who asked if they could help him, but wouldn't say what with, they decided to go to Paulden's. Honour said she knew someone who worked there in haberdashery: 'She might be able to help us . . .'

They were in luck. 'I'll get in touch with Miss Frimby,' said Pauline, Honour's friend. 'They some-times need some more early-morning charwomen. Gerty Gratorix has left, as her arthritis got too bad for her to carry on, and Lotty Rogers has run off with Mr Brent, one of the floorwalkers.

'You have to work from five-thirty until seven in the

mornings, and from seven till nine at night – but at least you'll get the days to yourselves. On the other hand, they might only want to use trustworthy women with big families who need the work, rather than young girls, but I'll see what I can do. Miss Frimby's my aunt – I might be able to see her right now if you wait here whilst I tell Miss White over on the elastics and buttons where I'm going. No, on second thoughts ...' – she stared hard at them – 'you'd better come with me to our ladies' room to give your faces a good wash.'

An hour later, Milly and Honour were back on the tram again, travelling home from All Saints with jobs as charladies starting the following Monday morning. Now Milly could go ahead with her plan to go and lodge with Honour.

CHAPTER FOUR

Lodgings

Although Egbert Merridew never said anything to Milly about her lodging in their back bedroom, she knew he resented it, perhaps because he realised that his battering days were over as far as Honour was concerned, for Milly always seemed to be around at the wrong time.

As for Milly's own family, they claimed to be plain disgusted at the turn of events. Walking out of a good home at her age to live in scruffy surroundings round the corner was a terrible insult. It would have been quite different if she had been actually chucked out by her parents, for then the neighbours would have sympathised with Joe and Clarry and told them they'd done the right thing in getting rid of a thorn in the flesh and it would teach the little baggage a lesson. But the other way round meant the neighbours could look critically at a home where it was so awful to live that one of its domestic assets had left the family for worse pastures. And as for working publicly as a char, evenings and early mornings; well, it might be a virtuous task for a married woman, but some regarded it as a highly unsuitable occupation for a young unmarried girl of Milly's age – and many lascivious suggestions were aired and enjoyed behind heavy net curtains about the dangers of spending the time left in between unwisely, instead of her being chained in chastity to the constant dolly-tub.

And the time in between did indeed prove to be her undoing. It happened one morning when Honour was away cleaning at the Ear Hospital. The work at Paulden's had fired Honour into a sort of madness that she might escape from her big mistake – Egbert – by gradually building up enough funds to support herself if he should prove too violent, so she had started doing cleaning work during the daytime. Yet at the same time – in a contradictory way – she always assured Milly that Egbert would be quite all right once he had got a job to occupy himself, and that her bad turn at Conny Roudley's had had nothing to do with him as it came from *her* side. Milly didn't point out the flaw in Honour's plan: if she *did* walk out, where on earth could she go to?

Now that Honour filled her days with extra charring, she depended on Milly to do smaller tasks at her place such as bits of washing and cleaning, which so far as Milly was concerned were chicken feed compared to the drudgery in her proper home, in Hatching Street.

On the morning in question, Egbert was sitting there in his own small parlour drinking some home-brewed ale and reading an official-looking letter.

'Shift your feet, Eggy. That mat needs a shake,' said Milly cockily.

He ignored her. Then to his chagrin she began to tug at the mat with youthful zest: 'Get your clodhoppers away from it, Egbert – I want it decent for when your Honour gets back.'

'Oh aye?' He glared at her angrily without moving.

'And since when 'ave you bin the mistress of this 'ouse? You're nowt but a cheeky little upstart, Milly Dawnay, and a bad influence into the bargain. Tha'd better mind thysen or tha'll be over my knee with a good whack-ing . . .'

Milly felt herself freeze inside. His eyes had a hard gleam and there was froth on his lips from the beer. She suddenly realised now how Honour had come to look so bruised and ill. It was a state of affairs entirely unknown in her own family, for although they did a lot of shouting and yelling and threatening at each other, they never resorted to actual violence.

She turned away as if she hadn't heard him and went into the scullery, but it was a false move.

'Come back 'ere and face me, Milly Dawnay . . .' His voice was slurred and gloating.

She wondered whether to do as he said, but the hesitation was her undoing. He was already standing behind her and as she turned he grabbed her arms.

Quick as a flash, she kicked him hard in the shins. With a howl of pain, he released her and she fled from the house to the back yard, immediately composing herself, for she was acutely aware that all her move-ments would be noted by the neighbours as she walked quickly back to Hatching Street.

Her mother was sitting there alone, having a cup of tea when she arrived. 'Good gracious, Milly! To what do we owe this gift of your presence?' Then, seeing the tears beginning to trickle slowly down her daughter's face, she added: 'There, there, lass. Sit down and tell me what's up.'

Her mother's mouth set in a hard line of fury when she heard about Egbert Merridew. 'I know it never makes a blind bit of difference what I say, Milly, but you'd be better to leave Honour and her husband to sort out their own differences. I know you felt you and Honour could both help each other in the first place, but it hasn't worked out like that, has it?

'From now on you've gained a proper enemy as far as Egbert Merridew goes. And I did hear tell – though it's strictly between you and me – that he's signed up for the army.'

Milly stared at her in amazement. How could her mother, living in Hatching Street, possibly know that, when she, who had lodged with the Merridews, knew not a thing?

Her mother smiled faintly. 'You may be Honour's friend, Milly, but always remember that she's married and you're not, plus she's a lot older, even though she does look only your age. Married women never tell all their lives to young single girls – especially lodgers.' Clarry looked at her young, wayward daughter. No one ever reckoned with the cards nature and the Good Lord would deal ... 'So what's going to happen now then? I expect all your clothes will be there?' Clarry looked at her gently. 'And are you due back at that awful charring job again tonight?'

Milly nodded in total misery. 'But I can't come back here to you, Ma. I couldn't stand the boys making fun of me and Dad being awful about it. But wherever can I go?'

She began to sob.

Her mother took the teacups away then put on her coat, bracing herself for the task ahead. 'I'll come back with thee, lass, to give Egbert a bit of my mind, and you can gather your belongings at the same time. Then we'll call at Mrs Runkin's near where your friend Babsy Renshaw lives. I'm sure she'll do me a good turn and let

63

you live there for a few days till you get more settled.'

Milly flung her arms round her mother and sighed with relief. 'Oh Ma, what would I do without you?'

Her mother's face clouded over and she said nothing. There were so many families with daughters much younger than Milly who were motherless, or even orphans.

Milly had cheered up, but on the way back to Honour's she wondered whether Egbert would even open the door to them, for surely, after the way he had treated her, he would be ashamed? Maybe she would have to wait until Honour got back from work – but if she did that it would only prolong the whole sordid episode and probably cause more upheaval for Honour herself.

But her fears were unfounded as, after only a few moments, Egbert Merridew opened the door and confronted them. He looked at them stonily.

'I'm here to collect my daughter's belongings, Mr Merridew,' said Clarry harshly. 'I no longer wish her to live in your house. I'll be obliged if you'll let us in so that she can get her suitcase. It's upstairs in your back bedroom.'

'Oh aye?'

'Yes, "Oh aye", Mr Merridew. And the sooner it's done with, the better.'

His voice changed to one of cold malevolence: 'That's just what I thinks, Mrs Dawnay ... Wait there and I'll fetch it.'

They heard him thundering up the small wooden stairs, then they heard sounds of a window opening and a loud crash. He came down to them again: 'You've my permission to get the suitcase, Mrs Dawnay,' he said with a hard look on his stubbly face. 'It's in our back yard resting on top of the wash'ouse. Your Milly is a capable girl – she'll be able to reach it with the clothes prop. And if owt's missing she can see my wife whenever our Honour lands back 'ere.' And with that he slammed the door.

Clarry Dawnay hesitated. 'I think we'll leave it at that, Milly. You'll have to wait until Honour gets back. He's a very awkward customer, and we don't want to make things worse. Besides, he'll never have gathered your belongings together properly. You'll just have to find an acceptable time to call again when he's out.'

But Milly wasn't to be put off. Her temper rose to match Eggy Merridew's as she left her mother standing there outside the front door and hurried round to the back yard. She hastily grabbed the clothes prop and with a mounting rage began to get the suitcase, edging it off the roof, along with two loose slates.

She was so busy, she didn't see Egbert standing there at the back door watching her as she wrestled with the suitcase, but when the slates crashed down he left his shelter and came roaring out. 'What the 'ell are you up to – trying to wreck the bloody place?'

He might as well have been talking to thin air, as with wilful determination she was into the house through the open door he'd just left, and up the stairs to gather up all her belongings to shove into the cardboard case. Within a couple of minutes, she was downstairs and out again in the yard, leaving Egbert still standing there, dumbstruck.

Her heart filled with joy as she hurried towards her mother. 'I got it, Ma. We'll never need to come back again, an' I shan't need to trouble Honour. I'll just see her tonight at Paulden's, and explain . . .'

'You're going to have a busy day, child. The next

65

thing we must do is get round sharp to Lizzy Runkin's, and then the sooner you get shot of all that charring the better.'

Clarry Dawnay and Lizzy Runkin had been at school together and they still addressed each other by their maiden names.

'Well I'm blessed!' smiled Lizzy Runkin née Hodd. 'Clarry Smith! I was just thinking about you a few minutes ago while I was sorting out some old leaflets from one of the Pankhursts' suffragette meetings. It seems hard to believe it was as long as seven or eight years gone – when your Milly was a tot of about eight – that you got pelted with rotten tomatoes for waving a banner supporting Emmeline and Christabel during their hunger strikes . . . So, what can I do for you?'

Clarry coloured up slightly. She had never managed to live the incident down in her own house, even though she had in her own small way supported all the Pankhurst family. Richard Pankhurst was a Manchester barrister who had taken an active part in civic affairs, and his wife and three daughters had joined him in the agitation for women's votes which had begun much earlier.

Lizzy Runkin was a widow and was a member of the Independent Labour Party. She lived alone, in a larger house than the Dawnays, but was always putting people up for a few days. Often they were visitors who came to speak at meetings, or others in need of temporary help.

Without more ado Milly was installed in a large bedroom containing a brass bedstead with a bulky feather mattress, and smelling strongly of mothballs. There was a marble washstand with a wash jug decorated in purple, white and green, and a sampler on the wall with the words WOMEN'S SOCIAL AND

POLITICAL UNION embroidered in cross stitch, with a picture of Mrs Pankhurst above it.

'You can stay as long as you like, providing the room isn't needed for a greater cause,' said Lizzy, after Clarry had recounted the gist of the problem.

When Milly arrived at Paulden's that evening, she suddenly felt quite terrified when she thought of what had gone on that day while Honour was out working. It wasn't going to be as easy as she had imagined to broach the subject.

But when she eventually joined Honour with the mops and buckets she was in for a sudden shock, for Honour herself was waiting with special news for Milly. 'Shall I tell you now, before Mrs Broggins herself officially tells you?' Honour said worriedly.

'You'd better hear me out first, Honour,' said Milly in a small, unusually timid voice. 'I want to say exactly what happened at your house today when you weren't there, and why I've cleared out . . .' But as soon as Milly began to speak Honour held up her hand with a cautioning finger: 'There's no need to, Milly. I can understand only too well. I think Egbert may have been feeling a bit nervous and upset. He's going to join up, see? And there's rumours about wars abroad. He's often talked of going in the army. He needs something more to do than being at home with me – he's a very active man.'

Milly stared at her and nodded silently. She was astounded by Honour's support of her brutal husband. Why was it that she always took his side? Then Milly remembered what her mother had said about married people being left to sort things out for themselves.

'The important thing for you at this moment, Milly, is to go and see Mrs Broggins. She's upstairs working in the offices. She said you were to go and see her as soon as you got here.'

Milly made her way up to the third-floor offices of the department store where Mrs Broggins was clearing out wastepaper baskets and removing two choice cigar butts from a heavy cut-glass, ashtray. She was a heavy-boned woman of almost six foot with scrawked back hair and an ample bosom, well covered by her ankle-length overall.

She had a very soft, flat voice. 'Sit down, Miss Dawnay. I'm afraid I've got some bad news.'

Whatever was it? The atmosphere was like a funeral. 'Which place did you finish off in this morning?'

'Carpets, Mrs Broggins.' It came out pat, for she always finished there as they all had a plan of their different working areas, and woe betide them if they ever deviated from it.

Mrs Broggins nodded conclusively. 'Carpets ... In a way it was a damned good job it was carpets, Miss Dawnay, and not all the marble bits.'

Milly hardly heard her as she tried to recall how the cleaning had gone before dawn that day. Then she remembered – to be absolutely truthful, she hadn't exactly finished off in Carpets, because she'd swapped over for a bit with Alice Brent, who had some heavy furniture to move about and was suffering from a dropped womb. So Alice had come along and done some straightforward polishing of wooden floors in Carpets, whilst she'd been moving heavy furniture near Pianos ...

'Without mincing words, Miss Dawnay, your work was extremely slipshod. A large tin of polish was left with its lid open, close to expensive carpets, and not only that ...'

Milly felt like swooning. Some of the carpets cost

hundreds of pounds. A spot of grease on them could be ruination . . .

'. . . a large dollop of polish was left on the floor, causing one customer – the wife of an alderman – to slide one and a half yards and land on her back against a roll of Wilton stair carpet. Thank God she was unhurt, or we could all have been in court.'

Milly stared at her in frozen terror.

'Have you anything to say?'

Milly shook her head dumbly.

Mrs Broggins shook her head like a huge snorting horse. 'Too much polish and not enough elbow grease, Miss Dawnay. It's been the downfall of many a girl before you, and no doubt will catch many another . . .' Without waiting any further, Mrs Broggins produced a small pay packet from her pocket. I have no choice but to sack you, Miss Dawnay. 'That's your money up to this morning.'

On her way back to Lizzy Runkin's house, Milly wondered what on earth to do. How in heaven's name could she afford to live without an outside job? She imagined going back home again in disgrace and with hardly a penny in the world. How could she bear it? The small amount of money she'd been paid would hardly last towards her keep at Lizzy's until the end of this week . . .

She was moving like a reluctant snail towards a street corner near Chorlton Road, lost in her own morbid thoughts, when she bumped into a stocky figure in the fading evening light. She mumbled hastily, 'Beg your par –' Then she checked herself. After all, *he* was the one who should have apologised – barging along like that.

'Milly Dawnay, film star!'

She stopped with a gasp of sudden pleasure. 'Arthur! Trust you to be knocking everyone else over! What happened to that film then? Honour said we should have been paid for what we did.'

'It was only a casual crowd scene, Milly. You was very lucky to be in it. *And* you got those free cherries. It's more than he ever gives us.'

'Are you *all* still working for him then?'

Arthur Fallowfield's teeth gleamed white. He looked really handsome. But then he always did . . .

'Have *you* ever fancied being a film star, Arthur?'

'Not on your Nelly! We only help him out for a bit of a lark. Mr Bridges doesn't make them with film stars anyway. It's more serious stuff. We were out today photographing the Territorials at the barracks, and his next one is all about the history of trams.'

'What about me and Honour and the cherries then?'

His face was a mixture of dimples and devilment. 'It's going to be shown at Chorlton Town Hall next week, in a film called *A Sunny Day at All Saints*, but by the time it's all been gone through, you might have been cut out of it. Still, he did say he quite liked the look of you both . . . So what are you doing now then, Milly?'

'Nothing.' She felt a real fool.

'I don't mean now – this minute. I mean, since you left school?'

'I've *told* you: *nowt*! You want to get your blessed lug'oles washed out, Arthur Fallowfield.'

Arthur grinned peaceably. 'Hewy Edmundson was talking about you yesterday. If the truth be told, I think he's still sweet on you, Milly. He can't wait to see the film with you on the floor with them cherries . . .'

Milly sniffed haughtily. 'Tell him he's got a cheek. He has a new girlfriend every day of the week!' Then she said: 'When did you say it was on?'

'Next Friday night at seven o'clock, and half the proceeds goes to 'elping soldiers and sailors.'

Meeting Arthur had cheered Milly up, and when she got to Mrs Runkin's she was her old self – though with rather a guilty conscience when Lizzy made great play about her being a busy, independent young woman close on fifteen and already making her own way in the world . . .

'I know you have to be up very, very early in the morning, but you'll find a packet of Force in the kitchen cupboard and milk and sugar close by. There are also some eggs if you want to boil one. And there's plenty of bread and dripping.'

Milly nodded her head humbly. She had never actually come face to face with Mrs Runkin before that morning, even though she'd heard her name quite often in connection with women fighting for the right to vote. But it wasn't a thing that really interested her. At present, there seemed to be no connection whatsoever between elderly Mrs Runkin's life of dedicated protest and Milly Dawnay's frantic desire to find another job the very next morning.

Whilst she lay in bed that night on the huge feather mattress in the spaciousness of a large bedroom, completely unhampered by the sounds or close movements of others, she thought back to what had gone on in these past few hours, and smiled to herself about meeting Arthur, marvelling that he and Hewy and Mackie were still together – just as they'd been at school.

Her thoughts went back to Hewy again. How terrible that his father had been killed in a street accident, for it had blown his chances of ever getting to the art school

– just as her own secret hopes had vanished as the adult daily grind began to take over from her schoolday aspirations. She thought longingly of the large, church-like Grosvenor building with its arched windows and its points and pinnacles: the School of Art in Cavendish Street. It was close to Chorlton Town Hall, and Paulden's department store . . .

Then a thought suddenly struck her – perhaps the art school would need more cleaners? Just think of all the muck people like them 'ud make! All that paint splat-tered about, and all the clay they'd use to make models and things, and the dust from all the chalks and pastels . . . Her fantasy expanded as she dreamed of all the stone steps there'd be to clean, and all the marble floors to wash, and the glass display cases to polish. The place was transformed in her mind into a cleaners' Valhallla in need of constant replenishment, as bliss-laden souls flew from Cavendish Street to eternal paradise, their huge wings fluffed out with sturdy banknotes as they landed on the roofs of baronial halls tucked away amongst the tree-lined, winding country lanes of Bowdon and Alderley Edge and nested there for ever.

Next morning she was up very early – mainly to avoid Lizzie and give the impression that she had gone off to her charring job.

She stoked herself up really well and demolished almost a quarter of a packet of Force with loads of milk and sugar on it. Then, after preparing herself six slices of bread and dripping and HP sauce, she found an old paper bag and wrapped them up to eat later in the day.

She set off on foot to All Saints, aiming to save every farthing she could until she found another job. But as she neared the building a sudden fear crept into her. It was early morning and the world seemed intent on its own affairs as heavy dray horses clopped along the streets with their covered loads, and pale errand boys in flat caps sped in and out of the other traffic on their bicycles with heavy black metal carriers at the front.

Milly stood outside the art school, quaking in the cool morning air. The place wasn't opened yet but she could see that the front steps had just been cleaned and were drying off. She did not dare stand on them. She hovered, undecided, in the centre of the pavement leading to the main door.

Just as she began to turn away in mounting despair, she was brushed against by a tall, hurrying man. He stopped, fleetingly, to apologise, then as he reached the top step, he turned and stared at her, looking sharply at her brown serge ankle-length coat with its large, creamy pearl buttons and trying to recall where he had seen the face beneath the wide-rimmed velvet hat before. A face with no make-up, but with a slight scar down one cheek and the most wonderful dark, curving eyebrows beneath wavy brown hair, and eyelids drooping over grey eyes. He brushed his hand nervously across his flowing moustache. Where *had* he seen her?

Milly recognised him immediately. Her boldness returned like a ray of sunshine. 'Aren't you Mr Bridges the film man?'

The light began to dawn. 'Yes, Augustine Bridges, Finer Films. Didn't I . . . Didn't we . . .?' He suddenly smiled and came back down the steps. 'The *Sunny Day at All Saints* – I remember. You and your friend – and those cherries. It's on next week, by the way: Friday night, Chorlton Town Hall. You've both come out very well in it.' He looked quite elated. 'No need to be formal – call me Gus. And your name is?'

A few seconds ago Milly had begun to think he looked quite handsome, something of a hero, but now she felt a sudden spurt of anger.

'*My* name is Miss Millicent Penelope Dawnay. Me and my friend did you a favour, being in that film, and you went away without so much as a Thank Your Father. I was under the impression that film stars was paid . . .'

'You did get paid. I bought you those cherries.' His eyes sparkled with quiet mirth. 'It was just a fleeting snapshot. Film stars have to do far more than that.' He became serious again. 'Look, have you time to pop into the art school for a minute? I've got some tickets for the film show. They're in the modelling studio.'

What amazing luck! Milly nodded and followed him inside through galleries of stone pillars and arches, with vast curved skylights. The place was quiet and totally empty except for the two of them. The cleaners had finished their early morning work and left like unseen goblins by some other door.

Mr Bridges led her to a room set with boards and easels and dotted about with still-life compositions which included large Greek urns, Roman terracotta vases and various small palm trees in pots. 'The line-drawing room, Miss Dawnay . . .' He led her further and further – with only the sound of their two voices echoing slightly and their feet clattering over the empty floors to disturb the quiet – until they arrived at what he termed his own studio, with its huge plaster casts and plinths arrayed with moulded busts of heads and shoulders, whilst along the side-walls were panels shaped in bas-relief where the figures were modelled to stand out from their background.

She stood there looking round, soaking it all up,

whilst he went to find the film ticket. She was in a bit of a daze. What had all this to do with his film making? When he returned he had removed his coat and was wearing a long, paint-stained twill smock. His hair was a bit unruly and he looked younger than she'd first imagined, for his forehead was smooth and unlined and his hair was quite curly. Then to her complete amazement he said: 'I got here extra early to shave off my moustache. I grew it whilst I was doing all the filming. It gives an air of authority to the general public, but it's a menace to me. Especially when I'm painting. Many of the paints are very poisonous and if you're careless with your paintbrush you can get Prussian Blue on a wayward moustache and it gets spread all over the place.'

Milly frowned slightly. Was he teasing her?

'Have you time to wait whilst I shave it off before I show you the way out?'

Shave off his moustache ... Fancy doing it now – with her here! Surely no proper gentleman would have done that? She nodded to his request. She had no option. She followed him at a distance to a small sink in an alcove where there was also a kettle on a gas ring, and a chipped mirror. He produced a cut-throat razor and, after warming some water up, proceeded to soap his moustache and carefully remove it, explaining at the same time through a taut, immovable mouth with strange grunting sounds how his film making was an extra string to his bow, done mainly in his spare time.

She watched with awe as a completely different image appeared. When his moustache had been there it had drooped in bushy luxury beneath a strong, heavy nose – but now the cover was gone she saw the full curved shape of his mouth and the strong line to it that curved down slightly at the edges with a quirky sort of humour. His deep-set eyes now stood out more vividly, and his broad cheekbones. She saw his large hands, delicately dictating to the razor as he stretched his top lip this way and that.

And then, partly from boredom and partly from the want of something to say, she explained her own situation: 'I was standing outside in the hope of looking for a cleaning job here . . .'

'A cleaning job?' He put down the razor, gathered up the remnants of his moustache and threw them in a large rubbish bin. 'Why does a girl like you want a cleaning job in a place like this?'

'Because I need the money to live on.'

He sighed slightly and nodded. 'I expect you'd have to see the head. I know nothing about such things. Look, I'll take you back now and show you out again, but meanwhile I'll make some enquiries. I'll meet you again in two hours' time inside by the front door, all right?'

She nodded silently. Her hopes of anything sensible happening after this moustache episode were beginning to fade, but she knew she would turn up to meet him, unless she tried somewhere else within the two hours and found another sort of occupation.

The two hours dragged, as two hours had never dragged in her life before. She drifted round All Saints, strolling past the shops in Devonshire Street and staring impatiently into the windows of saddlers and bicycle shops; sniffing the warm luxurious smell of a bakery full of crusty cobs and wonderful fruit pies – and then hastily moving away to a seat along the railings by All Saints Church to guzzle her own packet of austere bread and dripping and HP sauce.

It was two hours to the second when she stepped back inside the art school. There was no one to meet her and her heart fell, for people seemed to regard her with curiosity as she stood there shamefacedly, feeling like some beggar from the streets.

And then he appeared. He had combed his hair and no longer wore the smock. She gazed at him with new astonishment. There was something about him ... something deep and far-seeing.

'I got in touch with the principal,' he said cheerfully. 'He reckons they could do with some general help in the pottery department. The craft workrooms down in the basement are always in need of help and the brick kiln out in the college yard needs helpers to stack it.' Then with a brusque gesture he shoved a piece of paper with what she thought was written instructions about her forthcoming duties at her, and disappeared.

She stood there and read the note. It said: 'See Miss Ponsonby at nine sharp tomorrow morning in the vase painting workshop. Good luck with your future progress ... Augustine (Gus) Bridges'. But there was another bit of paper, too. It was a white five pound note.

She decided to take a tram back to Lizzy Runkin's. As she paid for her ticket, her hand trembled slightly with shock and relief, and her heart began to beat quickly with a small pulse of hidden excitement.

CHAPTER FIVE

The Insult

The following Friday night, after her first few days working as a general dogsbody in the craft department down in the basement under the stern gaze of Miss Ponsonby – a lady who was said to wear iron stays and be ruled by a tape measure and a set of scales – Milly went to Chorlton Town Hall with Honour to see *A Sunny Day at All Saints*. It was accompanied by lantern slides about Aviation Week, which showed pictures of an airship, a Bleriot monoplane, and a Wright Biplane; plus a comic cinematograph about fishing on the canal bank.

Both the girls were cheerful, for Honour now revealed that due to Egbert joining the army she was going to live with her sister in Leeds. 'I don't suppose I shall ever be a film star again, Milly, but it turned out to be good fun, didn't it? In some ways, anyway ... And I'm glad you've got settled in at the art school.'

'I might be moving too, Honour. I might be going to live with my Grandmother Smith in Sale and be travelling to the art school from there. I'm praying it will all work out. It's Mother's idea.' Milly smiled doubtfully. She was going to miss Honour – it was always better to have someone else to share all your hopes and secrets and sorrows with. Her best friend was Babsy Renshaw, but over these past years she hardly seemed to have seen her.

Honour touched her hand gratefully. 'I wish you all the luck in the world. I'm sorry you and Eggy didn't quite get on, but it can't be helped.'

When the lights went up during the intervals, Milly's gaze scoured the place, trying to see Hewy Edmundson or Arthur Fallowfield and Mackie Bright, but the hall was so packed she could see no sign of them – and the men running the film show were complete strangers. Then suddenly she saw Gus Bridges standing there giving someone directions. She started slightly, for she hadn't seen him once since she'd begun work.

'Have you spotted someone you know, at last?' said Honour, smiling.

'Yes. Mr Bridges. The man who filmed us.' She turned her head away swiftly so that Honour wouldn't read her face. She had never told a single person of how she actually came to get the job at the art school.

'Are you sure it's him?' said Honour. 'I could swear he had a walrus moustache, that day. The man over there looks much younger.'

In the darkness as the lights went down again, Milly pretended not to hear her. She felt her face grow quite scarlet. What other girl had seen a man shave off his moustache in an art school and then had him give her a secret five pounds and get her a job?

She sat there stiffly, covered in shyness.

It was nearly the end of October, now. In the city parks a few trees stayed brilliantly yellow and orange, the last leaves clinging on in the cold, damp foggy days which now crept in. Then the leaves fell, and the darkened trunks were bare and still, bleakly waiting for the winter.

But Milly was full of the joys of spring ... She'd already been at the art school six weeks. She was still lodging with Lizzy Runkin but was due to move the very next weekend to live with her Grandmother Smith at Sale.

Grandma Smith was in her seventies and had been a widow for twenty years. She was Clarry's mother, and had a lot of money tucked away. She employed a daily housekeeper and a charwoman, and still lived in the six-bedroomed house handed down to her through her late husband's family, who had done quite well in the cotton trade. But for the past ten years the house had been divided into two flats, and Grandma Smith lived in the bottom half.

Apart from Aunty May, who lived in the farm at Southport, Milly's mother had another sister called Maddy Wilshaw, who lived in Timperley and had three very spoilt daughters, called Prudence, Charity, and Faith.

Milly's mother and Milly's two aunties were Grandma Smith's only remaining children, for although Emma Smith had borne ten children, only these three had survived, and Clarry's lot in Hatching Street were by far the poorest. Clarry herself often felt completely drained of all energy and perpetually imagined that her last day was about to arrive.

'And mind you watch your p's and q's when you get to Sale, Milly,' warned her mother. 'Your grandma doesn't suffer fools gladly and she'll expect you to be of the utmost help to her in her old age. It's almost as if the Good Lord has chosen to give you a special blessing

80

with this turning up out of the blue, and with you getting that job at the art school as well.' Clarry shook her head in wonder. 'You're set up for life, and no mistake.'

As they ate their supper the evening before Milly was due to go, the whole Dawnay family agreed how well she'd done. She was now in their good books again, with never even a sly joke at her expense from any of her brothers. Her father complimented her on getting to the art school after all, completely ignoring her humble role of general cleaner-upper. 'And think on, lass, 'ow tha used to do all them drorings when thou was but a tiny wench – an 'ow tha longed to git to that there place. And now the dream's come true.'

For a few fleeting seconds the memory of the blue cornflower rose in Milly's mind. She saw it there, clear as day, pinned up next to Hewy Edmundson's scarlet corn poppy. She gazed round the tea table. The family were still laughing at the joke of her actually being in what they called ''er spiritual 'ome', hardly aware that being a student there and being a general worker were not quite the same thing.

Yet Milly was slowly developing tact. A wry smile hovered round her lips as she listened to them all, and thought of the wet, sloppy clay she had to clear up in the pottery room. And how she often had to carry the works of art that hadn't quite made it, those monstrous disasters of creativity which had come to grief in the kilns. For there were often explosions behind the heavy brick-lined oven doors, after enthusiastic and somewhat casual students had completely ignored the solemn advice about preparing their clay until it was entirely free of air holes. The result would be not so much a romantic terracotta vase as a tortured, misshapen heap

81

of baked red brick with ugly, gaping cracks, and bits chipped off it from the flying comet offerings of other works of art within the red-hot chamber.

And as for her saviour, Mr Bridges, she had never even caught sight of him since the evening of the picture show. In a way, she was glad, for how could she have openly thanked him for the five pounds when she knew that this sort of interchange of money would never be countenanced in respectable circles? She had no idea how she could possibly pay him back at present, even though she aimed with all her heart to repay the debt somehow.

'You'll have to be up really early in the mornings at Grandma's,' warned Clarry. 'She'll expect you to scrape out the ashes in the fireplaces and set the fires ready for Mrs Frost the housekeeper to put a match to. And she'll expect you to try and get on with Sophy Trimmer, her char. That woman's been with her nigh on twenty years this coming Christmas – she'll never see seventy again. Mind you just remember how long they've all lived in this world before ever you arrived, and treat them with proper respect.'

Milly smiled politely. She was looking forward to it. Although Grandmother Smith was family, Milly felt that with the break from her own home ties she was entering, at last, the gateway to a broader, richer world – over the border into glorious Cheshire, to the tree-lined roads around School Road in Sale and along to Sale Moor where her Grandma lived and which was bordered by farms, market gardens, and small cottages. For Sale was the best of all worlds. It had good transport and a railway line and all the modern trappings of people who lived close to the local metropolis of Manchester, in a greener, purer world.

82

Gus Bridges was talking to Mrs Martinello, his model, about her pose for the life class. They were in the empty studio at the art school, and she was standing there in her kimono and slippers. Her outdoor clothes and underwear were piled up behind the nearby screen – her long cotton petticoat, her corsets and combinations, her bloomers, stockings and garters.

She was a middle-aged woman and had been an artists' model since she was a girl of fourteen. She had come from a large family – all orphaned in their early years and every single one of the twelve children having to make their own living by whatever means they could, with help from neighbours, friends and relatives, and with the dreadful threat of the Workhouse hanging over their heads.

Mrs Martinello was more commonly known as Aldina. She had straight black hair parted centrally and combed back to form a flat, shiny cap over her small oval skull, the length of her hair lying in a chignon curved into the nape of her thin neck. She had never put on much weight and was still quite a good carbon copy of the small-boned, perfectly formed specimen of her early days. Mr Bridges had decided she should try a pose lying down on the small flat cushions of the black-enamelled wooden chaise-longue, wearing the dark blue kimono, which was richly decorated with yellow chrysanthemums.

Passively she practised her pose while he carefully marked her exact position with some chalk for when the students arrived. Then, just as everything was all arranged, she said: 'I'm sorry, Mr Bridges, but this will be my last session. My husband is very ill and needs more looking after.'

Gus's heart fell. He liked older models; both men and women. Their bodies were much more interesting to draw, and there was more character to reveal. The structure of their bones showed up better, and the wrinkles and hollows of aging gave the artist more chance to concentrate on tone values and subtlety. In contrast, many of the younger models were too smooth and boringly chubby, and the younger women often became fidgety, and were unreliable in turning up. They also carped far too much about naked poses and persisted in clutching huge swathes of coloured gauze to their private parts in a most ungainly manner; complaining that the studio was cold, and muttering that they weren't paid enough.

The men, on the other hand, were quite happy to have their lower bits and pieces hardly concealed by cotton robes. One regular male model in particular complained bitterly that the use of sculptured ivy leaves on all the unclothed marble statues disguised God's supreme creation in the living world, and he always ended up in an argument with Gus about the true aesthetic shape of a male torso.

Another, older model, Mr Frank, liked to tell the story of 'a case in this very art school, where a man was carved in his moment of rampant glory. As the statue was over eight feet tall and on a pedestal, the lower half had a suitably large branch sticking out, which was used as a coat hanger, until it was broken off during some furniture removing.'

Mr Bridges himself was a bachelor, and more interested over all in his film work than in tutoring his students in painting and drawing and sculpture, but he had a very tender liking for Mrs Martinello. He had even grown his luxurious moustache in the first place so that he would appear older when she was about . . . until the day that Milly arrived. Yet never once did he consciously associate the sudden urge to become clean-shaven with his meeting such a young girl, even though he saw her as very attractive, and was extremely glad to find out how well she had settled down in the crafts' section under Miss Ponsonby's kindly, rather ancient wing.

The Autumn term passed quickly for Milly, and soon it was Christmas. She went to spend a couple of days at home, because Grandma Smith had a very old male acquaintance staying with her. Milly decided to go into town and there, quite by chance, she met her best friend Babsy Renshaw.

Babsy was exactly the same age as herself. There were only two days between their birthdays, and in the first week of January 1914 they were both due to be sixteen. Mrs Renshaw had always been a friend of Clarry Dawnay when the two girls were babies in bassinets with Virol on their dummies. But during this past couple of years since school, Milly and Babsy had rarely seen each other except for a quick catch-up on news – until this last-minute Christmas shopping after-noon in Lewis's department store in Market Street, which was as packed out as a football match.

'I'll treat you to a cup of tea and a bun, as long as we're not killed in the rush,' laughed Babsy. She was a larger-than-life girl with a mass of red curls and a round, smiling face. 'It's to cheer meself up after losing yet another job. I can't really afford to buy anyone a Christmas present – even one of these cheap picture frames with holly and mistletoe on 'em – and you know what I am for trying to do home-made things like colourful kettle holders and nightdress cases ... They always land up either knitted with the religiously holy look of dropped stitches, or ruffled up with accidental puckering – not to mention gaping seams and large tacking stitches suddenly appearing ...

'Me last job was at Mr Parrot's the bookmakers. I got the push only yesterday because a cracked inkwell leaked ink all over Mr Parrot's shift cuffs and he blamed me. He said he had a good mind to make me pay for his shirt every week out of me wages, but I said I'd as soon have the sack there and then, so he told me to leave immediately, without so much as a Christmas cracker. He's a right old beggar and no mistake ... I know for a fact he's forced to pay out three lots of seven shillings a week to three women towards their children ... and he's not even nice-looking.' Babsy stared at Milly mournfully then they both began to giggle.

'Mother was saying she heard you were all set up, working at the art school. Any chance of finding me summat?'

Milly wrinkled her brow. 'It's hard to say. I only got in myself by sheer chance, but I'll put out some feelers. The person who helped me most was one of the staff called Mr Bridges, who also makes films. I'll see what he says, though I don't suppose I'll see him till the new year.'

But the new year of 1914 found Mr Bridges missing from the art school. Later on, when the war had started, rumour had it that he was in a secret, specialised documentary film unit in the army, and was responsible for recording the events of the war. At the school, meanwhile, it was almost as if he had never even existed, Milly thought sadly. His place was taken by a tall, thin, intense-looking, dark-eyed woman called Hortensia

Longfeather, with a tongue as smooth and sharp as a viper's.

'Why are you so concerned to see him, Miss Dawnay? Have you worked here long in the crafts department? Are you sure that Mr Bridges would even know who you are? This is a very big place, you know, and Mr Bridges has many, many students . . . I'm not sure when, or if he'll ever be back. All I know is that I'm standing in for him during his enforced absence.' She gazed coldly at Milly from heavy-lidded eyes, making her feel small and inadequate.

Nevertheless, Miss Longfeather eventually decided to interview Babsy Renshaw for an art assistant's job, because she herself needed more help, and from all accounts what she needed she always got. Babsy was a more boisterous kettle of fish than Milly, who was getting more and more quiet when confronted by authority, for she realised how hard it was to keep one's job unless one was the epitome of unquestioning politeness – and no way did she wish to leave the art school.

Babsy went along to the interview clutching Milly's beautiful hand-made bead bag, which she planned to pass off as all her own work. For Milly insisted that it would help as a sort of reference: 'I'll always be there to boost you up, Babsy, and it isn't as if you're planning to *teach* beadwork. You'll only be a general drudge like me. But you just have to impress them with that little bit extra, and the bead bag might do the trick.'

'Miss Renshaw,' said Miss Longfeather to Babsy at the interview, 'what a truly delightful piece of work! I'm sure you'll fit in wonderfully well here.'

'I'm sure I shall, Miss Longfellow . . .'

'Not Long*fellow*, Miss Renshaw; Long*feather*. But not

to worry. Many far more important people than you have made the same mistake.'

Milly was glad to have Babsy working in the same place as her, but she was sad to think that Mr Bridges had vanished into thin air. It was strange the way she missed him, even though she'd never seen him much when he was there. But these emotions were soon submerged by the terrible declaration of war.

The war had come like a bolt from the blue, for although rumours of trouble to come had been simmering away, Milly never read the newspapers, and it was like a bad dream when war was actually declared on Tuesday the fourth of August following on from the August bank holiday.

It had been like any normal bank holiday, with families enjoying their annual summer day off. Milly herself had been on a trip out with Babsy to the River Bollin, and Lancashire and Cheshire had been clogged with trains, bicycles, and charabancs going to sea and countryside. But by Wednesday, all thoughts of enjoyment and days out had been eclipsed by the cataclysmic announcement.

Early on, battalions of Manchester men were medically inspected and kitted out, as the war machine gathered momentum with terrifying speed. Many men had optimistically forecast a quick finish, but the first big battle rapidly became many more battles. Fire, blood, and horror spread amongst the trenches and dug-outs of Europe, and hand-to-hand fighting became mass slaughter for both sides in the fields of France. More and more soldiers, some no more than children, joined the patriotic calls to arms. Conditions grew worse, and as the wounded were carted back home to lie in requisitioned schools and makeshift huts, and private halls and houses, many older men secretly hoped it might be over before their turn came. But it was not to be, and when they were called up, women took over their jobs in shops, in clothing and munitions factories and in public transport, whilst others worked in make-shift hospitals and war departments and as vehicle drivers for the armed forces, the Red Cross, and as civilians.

Despite all this change and upheaval, some jobs were still deemed important enough for the country's good for men to carry on with their civilian jobs. These included Milly Dawnay's two older brothers Fred and Benny, who now worked in the offices of the Manchester Ship Canal Company. But the third boy, Donny, who was eighteen, had volunteered for the army – only to be turned down because of his flat feet, so he went to work in the smoke and filth of Armstrong Whitworth's steel works, helping the munitions industry.

Those four years of war were a strange time for Milly. On the one hand there was an air of gaiety and freedom and defiant patriotic optimism as people entertained the troops and tried their best to make blighty a true heaven for returning servicemen, whilst on the other hand all sections of society stoically suffered food rationing and eventually blacked out homes, because of zeppelin raids. All this was accompanied by the fear that poison mustard gas might be used, too. Meanwhile the terrible losses of human life continued, and the concentrated savagery of the front line would lead to a generation of maimed, blinded, and badly wounded men.

The war inevitably affected the numbers of students at the art school, but even so, the school itself continued on its programmed path, for some of its buildings were going to be extended, and in 1914–15 industrial design courses were coming to the fore. It was thanks to one of these new courses, Designing For Calico Printing, that Milly, still working faithfully for Miss Ponsonby in the basement, bumped into both Hewy Edmundson and Arthur Fallowfield again.

Milly was by now eighteen, and at first neither of them recognised her. She was in a clay-spattered overall and her hair was hidden by a brown twill mobcap as she walked along the corridor carrying a mop and bucket to clear up a place where one of the students had tipped over a bucket of newly mixed glaze.

Recognising both of them instantly, she felt the blood rush to her face. Hewy was tall and more handsome than ever and Arthur was stocky with well-developed cheekbones and shrewd eyes. His childhood dimples had vanished forever into lean clefts. They were both dressed up to the eyeballs in their best suits as if they'd come to something very special.

She felt too ashamed to meet Hewy in her present state. She sensed a marked change in him, a sort of worldliness in his looks, as if he might scorn her. Involuntarily her hand went to her cheek. It was bare of make-up these days and Babsy was always telling her she was far too sensitive about it. 'It's what you *are* that counts in the end, Milly. Try and think of all the real horrors people have to suffer. Think of all the war wounds for a start. And you fuss over a small thing like that.' But Babsy spoke as a picture of unblemished beauty.

By the time they'd cottoned on, Milly had hastily turned a corner and vanished silently, but later that morning she found that Babsy had been far more open, as they took their morning break together.

'You mean to say you *dodged* them, Milly? Whatever for? I was gassing to them for ages. They've come to take these new examinations for textile designing. They're both working as clerks in Pennyfarthing's mill, which is turning out army great coats, but there's going to be art training scholarships given out to start people on these new courses, and if they get through, they aim to go and work for calico printers in the textile designing department at Pennyfarthings, and train here at the same time.'

'What? You mean *both* of them?' Milly stared at Babsy in wonder. 'I can imagine Hewy doing it, but Arthur Fallowfield was never interested in owt else but copying from comics when he was at school.'

'Well, it's all changed now,' beamed Babsy, 'an' I say good luck to 'em. I 'ope they make pots and pots of money, then we can 'ave one each. It'd be quite good in a way, because if they came here as students we'd be able to guard them as our personal property. Bags me Hewy Edmundson.'

They both laughed and as they finished off their drinks of Camp coffee, Milly said: 'Good luck to you and all, Babsy. But I'll bet you'll find him hard to get. He was always a one for the girls. My mother always says that men aren't worth the candle if you have to check their movements all the time, and as for Arthur – he's as cunning as a cartload of monkeys, and anyone's welcome to him.'

When Milly got back to Grandmother Smith's in Sale that evening, she suddenly felt pangs of sheer jealousy – about Hewy and Arthur parading round the art school done up like dog's dinners and going to take exams to get in as students. Such was her anger that after she had washed up after supper she grabbed herself a pencil and

91

on the back of a piece of shelf paper swiftly began to draw her grandmother who was dozing in the kitchen rocking chair.

She worked with feverish energy in case Grandma moved or woke up. She worked to prove to herself that she was as good as Hewy Edmundson and ten times as good as Arthur Fallowfield, even if she hadn't drawn a thing since she was ten. She was quite pleased with the result – even slightly amazed. She signed her name on the bottom proudly along with the date, and wrote: 'Portrait of my grandmother'. Then she went up to her room and hid the drawing in her suitcase, below the newspaper which covered the bottom of the mothball-scented interior.

A week after Hewy and Arthur had taken their art school scholarship examinations, Babsy met Milly at work. Babsy's face was wreathed in excited smiles. 'You'll never guess ... I actually met all three of them last night!'

'All *three* of them?'

'Yes. It was just like old times when we were kids. There was Hewy, Arthur, and Mackie Bright. And I've changed my mind, Milly – *you* can have Hewy Edmundson, and I'll have Mackie – he's turned out to be really romantic. It was almost like love at first sight after not seeing him for so long.

'On the way back to our house, he as much as asked me to marry him. I've fallen head over heels ... His kisses sent me all aquiver. I never realised how good-looking he was with that bushy hair and those deep-set sparkling eyes. He says if he ever gets his way in life he wants to spend it designing aeroplanes, and he sounded really determined.'

'But where *were* you when you first met them all?' Milly was used to Babsy's sudden enthusiasms. Babsy would probably be just the same next week if she met someone else.

'At Band Street Palais de Danse, with my sister Brenda and her young man. They turned up just after we did, and stayed with us all the evening. They weren't with anyone else . . .

'But that's not all. I've got some special news for you, my angel – Hewy Edmundson told me he's gone on you, and says I've got to get you to go out with him, and him alone, tomorrow night.'

Milly sighed and feigned a lack of interest. 'What he *says*, Babsy, and what he *means* are two different things. He might have told a hundred girls exactly the same tale. And anyway, do *I* love *him*? Just imagine if I really fell for him and he let me down to go off with some posh female he'd met . . . He's that type, Babsy.' Deep down the truth of it cut sharply. How could she bear it?

'And you're a hard-hearted person, Millicent Dawnay,' said Babsy half-jokingly. 'How can you talk about love as if it's just a fleeting fashion and not of any importance?'

Milly knew why – quite well. It was because she didn't want to get hurt. She'd been out with many a boy before, but it wasn't like being with Hewy. Most other boys wallowed in football, eating, and practical jokes. They basked in the good fortune of finding young women who were willing to wait on them hand and foot . . . and as for Art, it meant nothing to them.

What she really wanted in life was a man with the same interests as herself. She gave a slight, half hidden smile; strangely enough Hewy fitted into that category . . . but now she feared it would never work between

93

them because he always wanted to be not just the best for its own sake, but superior to everyone else. Being the winner was all he ever thought about. She'd gleaned that from Arthur Fallowfield.

She felt a stirring of shame. They were so alike really, her and Hewy, because being the winner was all she ever thought about too, if she was honest, but it was harder to do for a girl.

'I hope you're still listening, Milly. I told him you'd moved to Sale to live with your gran. He says he'll meet you outside Righton's drapery store at six pm and take you for fish and chips, and a dance.'

Milly stared at her suspiciously now. 'I just *don't* believe you, Babsy. He's kidding you on. He doesn't do things like that with his girlfriends. He might go in fish and chip shops with his pals but I know for a fact from Lotty Longshaw, who once went out with him for a bit, that chip shops are beneath his dignity. And now he's turned into a complete snob. I could tell what he's turned into when he was parading round the art school on examination day.'

Babsy shrugged her shoulders huffily. 'Please yourself then. All I've done was to convey a truthful message. Just so long as he doesn't think I never told you. Honestly, Milly, if you stay an old maid for ever it'll be entirely your own fault! It's you that's the snob. You're getting really pernickety in your old age. By the time we're twenty-one you'll be into black lace-up boots and a bonnet with a feather in it, and clutching a silver knobbed walking stick.'

The next day, before going to work, Milly mentioned to her grandmother that she might be back a bit late. 'I'm supposed to be meeting a friend, and we're going for a meal . . .'

94

'*Supposed* to be? Surely you either are or you aren't? Is it a man or a woman, love?'

'It's Babsy and one of her pals.' Milly hurried away quickly in case she got involved with any more lies. But she knew if she'd said a man was involved, her grandmother would have probed every detail from her. This way, if the whole thing was a washout and he never turned up, at least these few small white lies would make it hurt less.

It was a very wet night as she waited near the portals of Righton's without even an umbrella, feeling a complete and utter fool. She would give him five minutes and if he didn't turn up, that was *it* . . .

Suddenly a large black brolly loomed up in front of her. 'Milly, get under this quick, and we'll get to that little café on the corner of News Street. I was wondering if you'd get the message from Babsy – or even whether you'd arrive at all . . .'

'I nearly didn't. I was wondering the same about you . . .' Her face glowed with happiness as the rain soaked them. They staggered into the small café with its four little tables with black-and-white check oilcloth on them. A tramp was lolling in the corner with bleary red eyes.

'Babsy said the idea was for us to go to a chip shop, and then dancing . . .' She doubted whether any of his other girlfriends were reduced to this place as he ordered two mugs of tea and two wedges of funeral cake.

'I've had a change of plan. With it being such a terrible night, I thought we could go to my place instead? Then if it cleared up a bit we could still go out somewhere. I asked my landlady, Mrs Sprout, and she said it would be quite all right. I'm like you – I don't live at home any more. I'm in digs just off Dickenson Road. I've got some food there an' all. Some potted shrimps, tinned pears, and a bottle of ruby wine.'

Then he added hastily: 'Sorry I never said anything to you when I saw you in the art school. I didn't know whether to or not. Arthur said I should have. I'll show you some of the work I've been doing when we get back to the digs . . .'

Milly was stuck for words as she allowed herself to be guided to Dickenson Road. He was being the perfect gentleman, and she felt all her prejudices gradually leaving her, and thought only of getting to somewhere warm and dry.

The digs were quite good. He had his own front door key and even a small letter box. The bedsitting room was on the first landing. It was large, and had a small annexe for cooking and washing up.

Mrs Sprout, a stout, spreading sort of lady, was there to welcome them, but said she was going out for a couple of hours: 'So I've arranged the bell so that it rings in your room, Mr Edmundson, love — then if there's any messages or owt when I'm away, you can pass them on.' She looked at Milly with a coy smile. 'Is this your special girlfriend then? You both look well suited . . . and I'll not disturb you . . .'

'She's just a friend from school days . . .' Hewy's assertations faded on a sudden draught as Mrs Sprout hastily vanished into the street and left them to it.

Milly could see samples of his work everywhere. There were large sketch pads lying on a small green-baize card table, topped by some loose sheets of thick, high quality rag paper. And there were many designs carelessly lying about, drawn and finely painted on large, white display boards, many with bold flower patterns.

'The only one I haven't tried yet is a blue cornflower and a poppy intermingled,' he said with innocent casualness.

She was immediately suspicious. Her memory was as fresh as ever for the day their pictures had been on the wall together at school. She smiled at him in silence, and then decided it really had been an entirely innocent remark.

He began to bring a plate of bread and butter – covered by another plate to keep it fresh – out of a cupboard to put on his main table. He followed this with the potted shrimps, knives and small forks, two cups and saucers decorated with pink rosebuds, with plates to match, and finally – the ruby wine in a green bottle, and two small, rather dull-looking wine glasses.

Milly looked at the wine as he began to pour it out. It was about the cheapest stuff on the market, even she knew that. It was the sort they'd sometimes had at home at Christmas when they were very young: a beautiful bright ruby shade, and very sweet. The sort some folks drank like water.

'Here's to us,' said Hewy, raising his glass and almost finishing it at one gulp.

She nodded and took a small sip, glad that they'd at least both already had a mug of tea and some funeral cake each – for she had no intention of becoming tipsy.

When they'd finished the meal, Hewy ushered her to a small, battered-looking easy chair. He was short of chairs – there were just the two comfortable ones, and the others were old kitchen chairs.

'They go with the bedsitter. None of the furniture's mine except the folding bed, but when I get a place of my own, I'll really go to town.' He plonked down in the chair with such nervous bravado that before Milly's very eyes the whole worm-eaten relic suddenly collapsed sideways in a heap. Hewy hastily strove to free himself from the padded mess with its heritage of woodworm.

Milly stared at him in alarm, then they both began laughing. 'At least you've got *one* left! The next girl-friend you have here will just have to sit on your knee ...' The moment she'd uttered the ingenuous words she regretted it. Surely he didn't think it was a 'come hither' sign?

He looked quickly round and spotted his folding bed. 'I'll just have to get that out. It should hold us both with the pillow and a few cushions on it and at least it's got a few metal springs and no woodworm. You never know, if you sat on my knee in that other one we might both collapse with the same fate!'

She looked hastily towards the window but the rain was absolutely pelting down. She knew she was trapped. She couldn't exactly announce that she was going back to Sale straight away because one of his chairs happened to have given way.

He moved some bits of furniture and placed the metal folding bed sideways against the fawn wallpaper, with the pillows and cushions stacked on it. 'Come on, then. Come and try it out, it's even better than the chairs.'

She laughed and went and sat next to him, gradually relaxing against the cushions with her legs sticking over the edge of the bed.

He stared at their feet, for they had taken off their shoes. 'It seems silly sitting this way round with our back to the wall and our feet dangling, when we could just fit on it lengthways in true luxury ...' He got up and put the pillows at their proper end, so they could both lie there together gazing towards the window, which was still awash with torrential rain. 'We're as good here as anywhere on a night like this . . .' He turned his head to gaze at her as she lay on her back looking up at the curtain rail and suddenly feeling quite sleepy. So sleepy in fact that she hardly felt the gentle kiss on her cheek, or felt his body edging closer to hers . . .

Then his hand suddenly touched her hand and she opened her eyes.

'Milly?'

'Yes?'

'I think I'm falling in love with you . . .'

'Oh . . .' She murmured the words drowsily. 'What number am I? One thousand and two?'

'No, seriously . . . You flipping well know what I mean. It was just the same when we were at school but we were only kids then . . . Kiss me Milly. Kiss me properly.'

She turned towards him, fully awake now, her heart beating with passion and love, and found in seconds that it was her undoing as she felt the burning heat of his flesh against hers. His whole body trembled and he groaned with helplessness: 'Marry me, Milly . . . Marry me . . .'

The words broke the spell. Marry him? Surely he didn't mean it? She kissed him and tried to free herself. 'Are you *sure*? We couldn't do it this very minute. We aren't even engaged or anything . . .' She sank back. If only she could burn her boats, give herself to him wholeheartedly this very second, whatever the consequences. Tears of joy and pain flooded her eyes.

His voice had tightened with passion: 'You are the only one, Milly. You know it's true. Surely you remember our promise, our first kiss?' He pressed against her body, full length. Body against body. Every bit of them melding to each other, as he fumbled in a panic of desire with her clothing.

Suddenly, with an awful flatness, the reality of the situation struck her. Deep in her soul she knew she was waiting for the right place and the right time to show him her love. How could she submit in a place like this? It was different for men. Many of them were completely ruthless when it came to satisfying their desires. Was Hewy going to be the same? She felt a terrible misery seep through her. Would they ever be at one, in perfect harmony, knowing it was a final, lasting love?

'I'm still a virgin, Hewy. I want something better than this. It's not the right time for it to be changed. It's all too sudden. Too fleeting . . .'

The word 'virgin' brought him to his senses, as she slipped away from him and sat up, smoothing her hair and arranging her clothes properly.

He looked pale and drawn and hollow-eyed. Then, as he became more composed and they drank some wine, he said: 'Are you sure you're still a virgin, Milly?'

'What a stupid, ungentlemanly question!' She trembled slightly. 'Of course I am. Most decent girls are, unless they're engaged. But of course I mustn't ask you the same question?'

He looked away silently, then muttered: 'It's different for men. Women tempt them . . .'

Her annoyance was beginning to bubble up inside.

'I hadn't realised you might still be a virgin, Milly. At this rate, you'll soon be on the path to being a complete old maid.' He scowled at her with childish truculence.

'*You hadn't realised*?' She gasped with disgust as all her trust in him evaporated to cold fury. 'Surely you don't think I spend my time as a common tart? That's

100

the biggest insult you could ever have given me!

'So what would have happened if you'd known I *was* a virgin, then? Maybe you'd have treated me with more respect. Maybe you wouldn't have taken me to the cheapest, slummiest café in town after all. Maybe you wouldn't have tried to get me drunk on wine no better than cat's pee and try and do me in your miserable little tin-pot camp bed!' By now Milly was rampagingly mad as she struggled into her shoes and got ready to leave, with tears flooding down her cheeks. She was completely deaf to all his pleas as he followed her out of his digs and into the street.

'Milly, come back, for God's sake! I still love you and want to marry you ... Milly ...'

His voice was lost in the lashing rain.

When Mrs Sprout arrived back she remarked on how sad he looked. 'Has something happened, love? Did everything work out proper for you and your young lady?'

He nodded his head politely and tried to smile, then he said: 'But I'm afraid one of the chairs collapsed. I examined it and it was full of wormholes in the woodwork.'

'Wormholes, dear ... Are you quite sure?' Her voice became a bit harder and more cunning: 'I've never had such a thing happen before. I hope it wasn't because two people were sat on it at once. I'll need some compensation for it ...'

He hung his head in shame.

When the results of the examinations were published and Hewy Edmundson's name was there for all to see as one of the scholarship winners, Milly noticed a small star by the side of his name, and looking down to the bottom of the list she saw that the star denoted deferred scholarship.

'Would you ever have guessed that he'd've gone and joined up?' said Babsy with genuine anxiety. 'P'raps it was with Arthur never getting through. You know how close they are . . .'

Milly said nothing. She had never spoken to Hewy again after the night out.

. . . Going in the army . . . It seemed as if the call to arms was catching up with every able-bodied man on earth. Lord Kitchener's poster was everywhere:

Your country needs YOU. DON'T IMAGINE YOU ARE NOT WANTED. EVERY MAN between 19 and 38 years of age is WANTED! Ex-Soldiers up to forty-five years of age. MEN CAN ENLIST IN THE NEW ARMY FOR THE DURATION OF THE WAR. *Rate of Pay*: lowest Scale of pay seven shillings a week with food and clothing in addition.

There was even a poster in the art school and Milly knew it off by heart:

Separation allowance for wives and children of married men when parted from their families:
Wife without children 12 shillings and sixpence a week.
Wife with four children 22 shillings a week.
Motherless children three shillings a week each.
YOUR COUNTRY IS STILL CALLING.
FIGHTING MEN! FALL IN!!
Full Particulars can be obtained at any Recruiting Office or Post Office.

She went cold with sudden fear as she remembered

102

Hewy's protestations of true love. Supposing he never came back? How on earth would she bear it?

One ordinary Monday morning in 1917 Milly went to the modelling studio where a life class was in progress to collect a large box of soft-leaded pencils.

Everything was much the same as usual. The students were all standing at their easels attired in their overalls, working from a nude female model and preparing numerous quick preliminary sketches.

Miss Longfeather was there, pacing round looking at their drawings, and stopping occasionally to give words of advice. Then Milly noticed someone else – a man with his back to her wearing a smock; a man with long legs and brown hair that waved very slightly along his neck line. Instinctively she hurried towards him, her face alight with amazement and joy at his return. 'Mr Bridges! You've come back?' She was just going to say 'I thought you were dead', but checked herself in time.

He turned and stared at her. 'Milly Dawnay! How good to see you! You've hardly changed since that day at All Saints. Yes, I'm thankfully back for good, now. I was working for a government department on photography and now they've allowed me to return.' He seemed to drink her in with his gaze. 'I –'

'What was it you wanted, Miss Dawnay?' Hortensia Longfeather's voice was as quiet and icy as hoar frost at dawn. 'If it's that box of pencils, they aren't even in this direction – they're right over there in the cupboards by the door.' Her relentless gaze was like a shivering blizzard as she pointed a determined finger away from Gus Bridges.

Milly turned silently, and with deep embarrassment hurried towards the pencil cupboard, suddenly aware that she had made an enemy for life.

CHAPTER SIX

The Alder Tree

The wartime years slipped by very fast for Milly at the art school. It was a time of tension and turmoil on the one hand, and a separate, secure, daily world full of young people like themselves on the other, with Babsy and herself as energetic female labourers. It was very comfortable, compared with the awful hardships of so many, and they were thankful for it.

The working terms for the students alternated with seasonal holidays – which were periods when Milly and Babsy were still paid to come in and help with tasks which couldn't be done properly with students about, and it gave their own working lives plenty of variety. It was tons better than being tied to some poky office or draughty warehouse or factory all day.

'Just think of it ... we've been here close on *three* years!' exclaimed Babsy on a cold, foggy November morning.

Peace had arrived at last. This past month had seen a jubilant Armistice day, with Union Jacks waving in the breeze and coloured bunting decorating all the small, city streets as thousands of church bells rang glad tidings throughout the land, and people gathered everywhere in vast crowds to rejoice.

'I hope you realise we'll be twenty-one in a few months?' said Babsy. 'We'll be officially "grown-up" at last.'

They both began to sing: 'I've got the key to the door ... Never been twenty-one, before ...' and then burst out laughing. It was a milestone to freedom. Yet Milly always thought it strange that boys below this age could be called up to fight, in spite of their parents being responsible for them as minors.

The ending of hostilities encouraged a rise in student numbers again, as men began to return from the armed forces to their ordinary lives; some to find that they were without jobs. The Ministry of Labour organised special trade courses for many of the disabled in centres such as the City Hall in Manchester.

Gus Bridges was exceptionally busy now. Milly would see him wondering round the art school with his students, and noted that he was thinner than before his disappearance, and still clean-shaven, with a humorous mouth, neat teeth and expressive eyebrows below his thick dark hair.

And he was still devoted to his film making, with – to Milly's total surprise – Arthur Fallowfield as his new and permanent full-time camera man. So she observed Arthur walking in and out of the place, too, as if he *had* gained that other scholarship with Hewy Edmundson. Hewy himself had returned unscathed from the army to take up his design award, which had been held over for him, and they were often seen together. But never once, now, did he acknowledge Milly as they passed each other in the course of their work like complete strangers.

There was no doubt, either, that Hewy was the

absolute darling of the girl students, and even older ladies like Hortensia Longfeather basked in his charms as he strolled confidently through the Gothic arches of the art school planning his latest textile designs . . .

'Hasn't he got stuck up?' exclaimed Babsy. 'He just ignores you and me completely as being part of a common herd of underling servants. He never even speaks to *me*, except to issue orders. You wouldn't think we once shared the same desk together at school, or that one of his best friends is going to marry me . . .

'And as for his love life, they say he's actually courting a girl whose uncle is a sausage millionaire! Well, he can keep his sausage kingdom – give me Mackie and the municipal parks department any day!'

Babsy's half-playful words seems to ignite hidden fires smouldering deep inside Milly, which never dispersed. For a start she simply hadn't got a true and faithful boyfriend, and by the following year, even Grandma Smith was beginning to get worried about it. 'Good looks don't last for ever, Millicent. God forbid that you should become yet another old maid in these days of all our lost young men . . .'

'There's no need for you to worry, Grandma. It's my affair and I'm quite happy as I am.'

She knew it was a half-truth. At one time when she'd been eighteen or so she'd been as carefree and optimistic as any other young miss when boys went out of their way to flirt with her. But now Hewy had left his mark, for she still remembered every detail of that evening in his digs. Oh how arrogant and sure of herself she'd been, and how shocked when he'd suddenly joined the army and she'd heard no more of him. They had both hurt each other, and now it was her turn to be banished to oblivion by his stony snubs.

And her age was catching up on her already ... Over this past new year the number of young men who had jokingly asked her if they could "spoon" with her when she was eating refreshments at church hall socials, because they claimed to be short of a teaspoon on their saucer, had sadly diminished. And now, at twenty-one, far from "getting the key to the door" she felt the sudden fright of the maiden trapped in a high tower, and she began to envy long-in-the-tooth people like Hortensia Longfeather in her exalted position of professional superiority amongst all the males – including both Gus Bridges and Hewy – whilst Milly herself ploughed on as part of the general scenery.

Nowadays she sometimes gazed quite morbidly at her image in the mirror and imagined that the scar on the side of her face was getting larger and more pronounced with every day that passed – even though no one ever seemed to notice it.

'You're absolutely right, Babsy,' she said one day. 'Hewy Edmundson's nothing but a complete prig. It's sickening to see him followed around by a retinue of simpering women whilst they copy every single pencil mark he makes. I heard he was at their Victory Ball at Christmas dressed as King Canute and wearing a crown, but I notice no one ever invited *us* to it. I personally had a very quiet time this year, without a young man in sight. And as for horrible Hortensia – I'll swear she's old enough to be his great-grandmother. I saw her putting that long scraggy arm of hers round his shoulder only this morning, behind a potted palm. Gus happened to be passing, and even he was clearly annoyed.

'But I'll tell you this much, Babsy – Hewy Edmundson needn't think he's going to be king of the ash heap for ever, because I've already started art lessons myself at the Mechanics' Institute, and Mr Bresslaw the teacher there says he'll tell me exactly how I can go about trying to win a scholarship to get myself in here for a proper training.'

Babsy gaped at her, thunderstuck. '*You*? ... *You*, Milly?' she coloured up a bit 'F-forgive me, I didn't mean to be rude or hurt your feelings, and I know you were quite good at drawing at school – but honestly, in my opinion you wouldn't have a chance of getting in. Most of the scholarships go to boys, and all the girls seem to have rich parents who can afford to pay for them.'

'I'm going to try, anyway,' murmured Milly through slightly gritted teeth.

'The best of luck, then. But *I* wouldn't try it for a gold crown.'

'No ... Well, it isn't you, is it Babsy?'

'No, it jolly well isn't. Especially now I'm courting my darling Mackie Bright and he's got that job in the parks department. Give me a nice little home of my own, Milly, and some lovely children and a good husband ... That's all I pray for.'

One amazing day in Spring – amazing because it was really so ordinary and drizzling a bit and the art school was chugging away quite normally as yet another student turned out a vase with interesting drip formations of crazed glaze with the glaze all shrunk and wrinkled like an old woollen vest, while its designer proclaimed it was brilliant – Hewy Edmundson suddenly waylaid Milly in the corridor and asked her if she'd like to come out sketching with him.

'Babsy was saying she's getting married to Mackie in

a month, and will be leaving.' He stared at her hard. 'She also said you're taking drawing lessons.'

Trust Babsy to blab it all to him, of all people!

'Mmmm . . . Yes – well – I am . . . sort of. But it's my own private affair if you don't mind.'

She looked away from him but he persisted.

'She said you were studying with Mr Bresslaw. He's a very fine artist.' His deep violet eyes and his thick eyelashes had hardly changed from childhood days except they were now shadowed by the face of a man.

'Well, she'd no right to tell you, had she?'

All the time she was remembering him in his bedsitter that night so long ago now, and how he'd professed his love.

'So will you come out sketching or not?' His tone was hard-edged and slightly bullying.

'It depends where it is.' Her own voice was cool.

'Lymm – in Gus Bridges' car. Meeting outside here next Sunday morning at eight-thirty, and bring summat to eat and drink.' He had slipped into his normal tone of boyish enthusiasm.

She nodded silently, and in seconds they were both smiling at each other.

Milly had been to Lymm before, and she loved it. It had the Bridgewater canal quietly slipping through it. There was a humpbacked bridge and a very pretty church with a square tower, and the narrow, cobbled streets widened out to the place where Lymm Cross stood on its small mound of carved sandstone steps. The village stocks were close by – now past history in the book of local punishments, and more a place to photograph.

The more Milly considered Hewy's sudden invitation, the more wondrous it seemed, after all these years of silence, and what she had taken to be snobbery.

'What on earth's been happening to you today?' said her grandmother shrewdly. 'You look as if you've received the best bit of news ever.'

'It's nothing really – except I'm going out on a sketching expedition to Lymm early on Sunday morning, with some people from the art school.' She felt herself blushing beneath Grandma Smith's inquisitive gaze. 'It's an invitation from Hewy Edmondson, who used to be at school with me. I'll have to be out early.'

'And no church *again*? I never knew a girl like you for not observing the Lord's Day properly. You'll never have any hope of being the bride of a vicar.'

'There's nothing wrong with going sketching, Grandma.' Milly tried to justify her actions: 'I'm twenty-one now, and as you often say, many girls are married and having babies by twenty-one. Also it's practice for my drawing classes with Mr Bresslaw. He says I can never get too much studying done.'

Her grandmother sniffed. 'You could be dribbling along with all that fancy stuff all your life and where would you be? Nowhere! I've known others who've been just the same and it came to nowt. You'll just end up as a frustrated old maid. You need to find yourself a decent, well-employed young man who works in a legal office or is a teacher. It's no good you dallying about with the likes of Hugo Edmondson.

'. . . No need to look at me like that, Milly. I know all that family very well. They've always aimed high, and I admires 'em for it, but it works both ways, because mark my words their Hugo'll be after a better catch than you. He's there as a proper student and a grown man with good prospects in the textile designing world. He'll be after someone with a rich father.'

111

Secretly, Milly felt slashed to bits by the hard words, but she feared there was a grain of truth in them – particularly after what Babsy had once said about Hewy cavorting with the daughter of a millionaire sausage manufacturer. Yet why had he come to her so suddenly and asked her to go out sketching with them? And after all, the millionaire's daughter had only been a rumour, and she'd never once heard any more about it ...

Yet, to be honest, all rumours passed her by these days, for Babsy, her spreader of tidings, was too occupied with her own forthcoming marriage to relate them, and Milly herself had until now erased Hewy from her life as nothing but a past memory. But even so, a trace of doubt was still there. Then she chided herself. Why on earth should she imagine that Hewy Edmundson had been spending all these years never looking at another woman?

Her grandmother, sitting there blunt and unperturbed, was still returning her gaze, but Milly wasn't to be squashed like some small fly, for she knew the reason she'd managed to stay on reasonable terms with the old lady so long was that she stood up to her. 'Don't alarm yourself, Grandma. I'm not going to fade away for want of something better to do than go to Mr Bresslaw's classes for evermore, or even waste my time with Hewy. You see, Mr Bresslaw is getting me trained up to take a scholarship so as *I* can go to the art school as a student myself.'

Her grandmother sat there in her rocking chair with a slightly amused look flickering round her mouth. It was clear she didn't take Milly very seriously. 'You have to be very good at drawing, girl, and I'm not aware that you've even shown me one tiny sample of anything you've ever done. It all seems like a lot of hot air to me.'

112

Her grandmother's voice had a distinct ring of triumph to it. She always liked to come out on top in a confrontation. She nodded her head comfortably as Milly left the room and went to her bedroom.

A few moments later Milly was back. She was holding a drawing. 'Do you recognise that, then?'

Her grandmother adjusted her spectacles and peered at it carefully. 'Did Hewy Edmondson give it to you?'

'He certainly didn't! Look at it more carefully. Who does it remind you of?'

There was a sudden gasp of recognition. 'Glory be ... It's *me*! Whoever did this?'

'I did. I drew you one day when you were asleep in that chair, before I even began my drawing classes at the Mechanics' Institute. It was in my suitcase. Should I get it framed for you?'

Grandma looked at it with a strange expression on her face. 'It's very, very good, lass. You've given me quite a shock ... Now go back again, to my bedroom this time, and bring the small brown Gladstone bag from next to my dressing table.'

Milly was puzzled by her grandmother's sudden change of mood. She hurried to the large bedroom with its brass bedstead and huge black-and-pink satin eider-down, and the papered pale blue walls from where Queen Victoria still kept an eye on things, opposite the biblical text over the fireplace.

Traces of camphorated oil clung round Milly's nos-trils as she retrieved the bag from near the dressing table and brought it to her grandmother. She stood by her grandmother's side whilst the huge clasp was un-fastened.

Slowly, with a slightly trembling hand, her grand-mother drew out a small, oval-shaped photograph frame containing a picture. 'Do you know who that is?'

'Yes. It's a drawing of you when you were . . .?'

'When I was very young. When I was fourteen. It was drawn by my Stanford . . . your grandfather. There is something about the style, the way he's used the pencil . . . Take a hard look at it, Milly. It's a bit like this one you've done of me.' Grandma stared at both of the pictures in turn now with her magnifying glass, her face suddenly alight with joy.

'Yes . . . your grandfather . . . and to think I never knew till now, never suspected there was anyone else in the family who was a proper artist . . .

'It was well before your time, love. But there was one thing he often said before he died: "Wife," he said, "If I goes before thee, allus remember that if there's money left, spend it on the artist int' family." It was a sort of joke between us that I never took with any seriousness. But now it seems the time has come . . .'

Milly looked at her with sudden alarm – whatever was she trying to say?

'No need to look all afrighted, dear. You should be feeling pleased. What your grandfather meant was that if anyone else was good at art like he was, I should help them out with a little bit of money. So that's what I'm about now, lass – giving you some plain talking, to help you to get to that there art school a bit earlier than waiting to take the scholarship, which could be years and years away – if ever.

'So instead, you'll be able to sit their entrance exams and I'll see to the fees. It would have been what your grandfather would have wished . . . and you can pay me back later in your own time. You've been a good helpful lass whilst you've been under this roof.'

'But it will cost a fortune! Only very rich people can do that.'

Her grandmother looked at her drily. 'I'm not without a farthing or two tucked away, so don't you fret about that side of things. And don't feel beholden to me either for it wasn't my idea, it was your grandfather's, and it's mostly his money an' all, if the truth be known. Anyway, we'll not mention it again until you get me the art school prospectus to look at.'

On the way to the art school the following Sunday morning, Milly could think of nothing else but her grandmother's offer. She could hardly believe her luck; so much so, in fact, that she thought the best thing was to try and forget it for the time being, in case it was all pie in the sky.

She was the earliest one to arrive at the door of the art school, and waited with happy impatience.

At first when Hewy had invited her she'd thought it was going to be just the two of them until he'd mentioned Gus Bridges' car. She prayed there wouldn't be a huge crowd of other students, all with their own transport or a charabanc. She knew she'd feel awkward.

But what came about was even worse, for when Gus's small saloon arrived, who should be in the fourth seat at the back but Hortensia, and it transpired there were only going to be the four of them plus some easels and borrowed painting equipment.

The moment Hortensia saw her, Milly knew the daggers were out. 'Well, I must say, I am *slightly* surprised to find that Miss Dawnay is our fourth surprise member of the group, Gus. I had imagined that when you said it was a secret it would at least be someone like Dereta Daniels who won the diploma for botanical illustration.'

Milly shrunk further into her small corner as the car moved along the quiet city streets and into open countryside, whilst Gus, Hewy and Horty, as the men called her, kept up a triangular conversation with Hortensia breathing hard from the back seat down both their necks, and ignoring Milly completely.

'Let's go down by the canal,' said Gus when they got to Lymm. They'd already parked the car and walked round all the traditional scenic spots, which Gus pointed out would be more cluttered with other people as the day wore on, for the weather was turning out to be exceptionally bright and sunny.

Milly was happy now as they strolled along the canal bank towards a watermill. Gus led the way with Hewy, carrying some folding easels and a large stiff-backed canvas bag of paints and sketch pads, whilst Hortensia swatted at midges with her wide-brimmed straw hat and Milly lagged behind with the four small criss-cross camping stools.

The moment of truth was soon to arrive, for Milly. What on earth was she going to try and sketch? An awful nervousness rose within her. She'd been a fool ever to agree to come – knowing now that another pair of censuring female eyes would be absorbing every detail of her performance. Maybe she should have capitulated straight away and gone for a walk round Lymm on her own, leaving the canal bank entirely to its brightly painted butty boats, barges, canal dray-horses, fishermen . . . and *them*.

'We'll stop just here,' said Gus, suddenly.

He looked straight at Milly as if trying to help her. 'There are plenty of different aspects: the canal itself, that distant aqueduct, the watermill, and a village in the distance, amongst the trees.'

Milly nodded politely. What a far cry from drawing the Edmundsons' chimney pot amongst the back yards when she was ten. At least then she'd chosen her own subject. She stared round helplessly, for quite frankly it was all becoming a bit boring. The day was getting warmer and all she felt like doing was flopping down amongst the dandelions and golden buttercups, or sitting amongst purple and white clover playfully threading a daisy chain beside a sun-dappled, babbling brook – with a chance to eat her cheese sandwiches, and drink the water from her lemonade bottle.

She looked across the fields beyond a bend in the canal and saw an old farm cart near a gate, probably undisturbed since the year dot. That was the answer. She would try drawing it.

She set off immediately just in time to hear Hortensia saying in rather a loud voice: 'I think I'll wander over to that ancient farm cart. It makes a nice focal piece of draughtsmanship and has an excellent setting. I expect Miss Dawnay will want to stay close to you two for some practical hints.'

Damn! Milly quickened her step and looked grimly towards the cart. Her cotton petticoat was getting damp with sweat. Her thick lisle stockings were becoming hot and her legs were itching underneath her ever tightening elastic garters. How stupid to have put on a thick skirt. And she should never have worn her combinations. But there again – how could one ever judge spring weather properly in the north? Supposing they'd been unlucky and it had suddenly started to hailstone? Such things had been known ... Anyway, once she was well hidden behind the cart and sheltered by a hedge, maybe she'd have a wholesale removal of unwanted garments. Then she'd have a cheese sandwich and a drink of

117

water, and maybe lie in bliss and gaze at the blue sky . . . and *then* and only then, she'd start to consider drawing the farm cart.

As she drew near to it she looked back hastily to see what had happened to Hortensia, and was glad to see she had turned off in another direction. At least it meant she would not have to try and be pleasant to her and suffer all her hidden insults.

Milly walked all round the cart, taking in its position in relation to the surrounding countryside and its width and height and idiosyncrasies. It stood beside a huge alder tree whose stout branches came almost down to the ground, giving some pleasant shade. With a streak of wild abandon, Milly suddenly dragged off her long stockings and garters, then, making sure she was completely unobserved, she quickly began to unbutton her green striped calico blouse and removed it so that she could get at her combinations, which were all in one piece, and also had to be unfastened. With feverish speed she managed to slip her shoulders out of the awful coms and pull them down her legs, carrying with them her vast, elasticated, interlock knickers in one horrible, rolled up, heavy jumble. At last she felt nature's wonderful spring breezes circulating with sudden heavenly coolness in all the crannies of her body as she discarded her thick top skirt completely, leaving just her fine white lawn underslip. Then, replacing her knickers, and putting her bare feet back into her shoes, she raised her arms to the sky with thankful, childlike delight. The joyous effect was indescribable. She hung the surplus articles of clothing on a low branch of the tree and then, deciding to get down to work after all, she set out her easel a little further away, close to the cart.

She'd hardly been drawing more than ten minutes

when, to her annoyance, she saw Hortensia approaching.

'How are you going on?' Hortensia called autocratically from the distance. 'I thought I would come and tackle the cart myself. I had originally planned to stay nearer to the men but somehow they eluded me . . .

'You don't seem to be in a very good position for sketching it just there. You're standing in your own light and are far too close to it all. I would advise you to move . . .'

But her advice was already whistling in thin air as Milly suddenly turned and hurried further afield towards the canal again with her bag of painting materials and her stool, leaving only the bare easel to greet Hortensia.

Milly sat down on the grass close to the water's edge and began to eat her sandwiches, brooding on what a strange, unsettled day she was having. She knew she would have to go back to the cart eventually to retrieve her easel – and there were also her clothes hanging on the tree branch – but she planned to wait until Hortensia had gone again. Meanwhile, she began to draw a stationary barge with the horse eating grass on the canal bank.

She became so engrossed she never even saw or heard Gus Bridges until he spoke. 'I don't think you'll manage to get much more done. I hadn't realised you were so good at drawing. Do you realise we've been out here nearly four hours and we'll have to be setting off back?'

She stood up, looked at her picture critically then turned to him and smiled. 'The afternoon's turned out much better than I thought it would. This is the first time I've ever been on a proper sketching outing in my life.' Then slowly she felt her face going crimson as she realised how she was dressed.

But Gus hadn't even noticed. All he saw was her slim girlish form in a simple white cotton garment, her shapely, natural legs, and her curved arms caught with the slight pinkness of hot sun. What a wonderful model she would make . . .

When Hortensia Longfeather had finally come upon Milly's empty easel standing there in the field, she was extremely annoyed. The impudence of it all! That girl had ruined what was going to be a simple, relaxing afternoon outing between herself, Gus and Hugo, in a wonderful threesome.

Horty just couldn't think what had come over Gus Bridges that he should have told Hewy to bring someone else – a mystery person – to make up a deliberate foursome instead, with the weak excuse of saying it was to help pay the car expenses. And fancy choosing someone so gauche . . . Miss Dawnay was surely no more than an ignorant nineteen? A far distance in time from herself and Gus – and obviously never a particular friend of Hugo's, for he hadn't acknowledged her when they were within the bounds of the art school.

Hortensia settled herself down and made a conscientious, efficiently detailed drawing of the farm cart from another angle to Milly's. Some time later she looked up to see Hewy signalling to her that it was time to pack up.

Dutifully she gathered up her work, going back past the large alder tree, where a small herd of goats appeared to be chewing at some rags . . .

'Did you bring anything else with you?' said Gus to

Milly, vaguely aware now that she had been dressed differently when they first set off from Manchester.

Milly tried not to show the inner panic as she thought of her other garments hanging on the tree branch ... 'You go on ahead. I left my easel in another place.'

'I'll come with you. You may need help.'

Milly flew at him defensively: 'What on earth for? I managed quite well on my own when I set out. I'm not a small child. I'd sooner be on my own if you don't mind. I'll see you back at the car.'

Her words stung him. He nodded and went back on his own.

When Milly reached the alder tree the sun was casting shadows amongst the branches and the air was cooler. A small herd of grey goats were foraging grass in a desultory manner, half a field away. Leading towards them were scattered remnants of half-chewed clothing – bits of striped calico, still with some buttons; long, ragged strips of combinations; large, chewed up chunks of skirt; and finer traces of stockings and garters.

She stared at it all in horror. She felt like sitting down and weeping. What on earth could she do? How was she going to face the others at the car? She knew Gus hadn't seemed to notice her *déshabillé*, and maybe Hewy would have enough manners not to mention it, but a woman like Hortensia Longfeather would be sure to comment ...

As she walked slowly back to the others she began to think of her grandmother. What would Grandma say to a young woman arriving back in Sale, dressed in nothing but a loose cotton underslip, knickers and shoes, and on the Lord's Day too?

They were standing beside the car watching her

coming towards them and Hewy hastened forward to meet her. 'Where's your clothes, you daft ha'porth? You can't go back like that – you'll be set upon!'

She glared at him as all the deeper tension and worry suddenly left her. 'I didn't *mean* to be like this. Some blessed goats chewed up the whole blooming lot! Whatever shall I do?'

'God knows, Miss *Virgin*.' He added the last word bitterly, and it stabbed at her soul.

'What an awful thing to say, Hewy ... It's a sacred word.'

'You were the one who used it first, Milly – as an excuse to turn me down. I said I loved you. I asked you to marry me. What more could a man do?'

'He could show respect ...'

'Respect! 'He gave a miserable, angry snort. 'It's always the man who's to blame ... I know you better than you know yourself, Milly Dawnay. Men aren't fools.'

'And neither are women, Hewy Edmundson. But, judging by you, men are certainly more selfish and not to be trusted.'

'That's a good 'un, that is. Women's no better'n us!'

'*Some* women are ...' She gave a small, subdued sob.

They both walked to the car in heavy silence.

On the journey back everyone was very quiet, but Gus said what a good day it had been. Then he added casually. 'I'll drop you all at your own places. I'll take you back first to Victoria Park, Horty.'

'That's terribly kind of you, Gus, but wouldn't it be simpler to deposit Miss Dawnay in Sale first? We shall be driving right through it ...'

'As I said, I'll take you back first, Hortensia. Then I'll take Hewy home. And after that it'll be Miss Dawnay.'

Milly breathed with heartfelt relief. At least it would give her time to think out what to do. Maybe she would be able to slip into Grandma's unobserved, although chance would be a fine thing with that idea . . .

She could see that Hortensia was fuming at being turfed out first, and when they arrived through the gateway to the great mansions of Victoria Park, Hortensia ignored her completely and gave a weak wave towards the other two.

As soon as she'd gone, Milly heard Hewy say to Gus: 'Of course you realise she isn't decently dressed, don't you? All her stuff was eaten by goats. Trust her. We were at school together. It's just what might be expected. She's always having disasters.'

Milly was bursting with anger as she heard the old condescension creeping back into his voice. Then Gus said: 'Don't worry, I'll sort it.'

When Hewy had gone, Gus smiled consolingly and invited her to sit in the front seat. 'Quite frankly, I don't know what all the fuss is about. You look quite respectable in that outfit. Some people in other countries wear far less than that.'

Milly nodded politely. What a strange man. He obviously hadn't been brought up in Manchester if those were his views. And where on earth was he taking her? 'I hope you won't think me impertinent – but where exactly do you live, Mr Bridges?'

'Where do I live?' He began to smile. 'I'm not trying to kidnap you, if that's what you think.'

'Oh no. I know that . . .'

'You don't know that at all. You are apt to trust people far too much . . . I live in an upstairs flat in Higher Broughton and we're nearly there.' His small car turned in towards some large stone gateposts finished off on top with enormous spheres (for they were too grand to be called mere knobs). They got out of the car and as they approached the pink stuccoed Victorian house Milly could see it was divided into three flats, because three small brass plates proclaimed it, next to the large tiled portico entrance.

Gus's second-floor flat seemed bigger than her grandmother's ground-floor one, in Sale. The main room was the size of two, and what a difference in the furnishings!

The walls were whitewashed and all the furniture was plain and simple in light oak. Unframed photographs decorated some of the walls, and among them, blown up to huge proportions, Milly saw two young girls at All Saints on a summer's day, eating cherries. In a recess next to the chimney breast was a studio divan with a striped folkweave cover on it.

There were paintings, too, the best one being a portrait of a woman with shining blue-black hair as smooth and flat as a calm lake. She was lying on a chaise longue and wearing a kimono the colour of yellow water melon. Milly wondered if Gus had painted it. Then another picture caught her eye. It was a tiny framed screen print for a printed textile design of blue cornflowers interwoven in a trellis of field poppies and harvest grass.

Her own blue cornflower ... or so it seemed as the memory flooded back.

'That's one of Hewy's pieces,' said Gus.

She pretended not to hear. How she wished she could cast Hewy from her heart for ever, but still he stayed there.

'There are really four flats, but the attic doesn't actually sport a brass plate. It's rented to Hewy's pal, Art Fallowfield.'

Milly subdued the sudden urge to gasp. No wonder Arthur Fallowfield put on such airs and graces these days. She shivered slightly. She was feeling a bit hungry and rather cold now, and goose pimples had begun to appear on her arms.

'Look, we must have a meal before I take you back to Sale. You'll need a few more clothes, too. There's a linen cupboard in my bedroom and there's a good mixture of women's stuff in it. Just have a hunt through it and find something suitable, whilst I sort us out some food. As a last resort, you can always tell your grandmother you fell in the canal if she gets too inquisitive . . .'

Women's clothes in his bedroom? Milly felt herself recoiling. Unless, of course, he was honourably married . . . Whatever the case, she would be in a fix now if it wasn't for him having women's clothes in his linen press. He showed her the way to what looked like a huge double wardrobe and opened it to reveal a multitude of two-piece tweed costumes, blouses with leg o'mutton sleeves, stockings and garters by the score, and even ball gowns with bustles; while on the shelves above lay all manner of hats and shoes.

'No need to look so shocked! They're part of my humble costume department for films, even though they are painfully out of fashion. And I have an even bigger assortment of menswear in the other bedroom along with filming equipment. Suzy and Art help me to keep it all in order. Oh yes – er – well, Suzy is Mr Fallowfield's distant cousin who acts as his housekeeper and is our wardrobe mistress and secretary.'

Milly's eyes widened. Surely it wasn't that awful snivelling Suzy who never had proper hankies and used to follow him round at school?

'Would it be Susan Marsland?' she murmured.

He shook his head vigorously and said her surname was Prendlegast – and in any case her real name wasn't Suzy at all but Zeronica.

Milly looked away to stop herself from laughing. She remembered to this day the time Suzy Marsland had tried to kid her that her real name was Zeronica Prendlegast... and now here she was ... Then Gus capped it all by saying: 'By the way, Mr Fallowfield goes under the name of Art Fallows now. He finds it works better.'

She chose a deep lilac worsted barathea skirt and a rather fancy lemon silk blouse from his collection. By the time she was properly dressed, she felt that Grandma Smith would approve, even though she prayed that she would to able to get into the house and change into something else before they met. She planned the excuses she'd make: 'Sorry, Grandma, just going to get changed into summat else. I spilt paint all over my skirt and had to get it washed and dried at Miss Longfeather's ...'

Gus provided boiled eggs, bread and butter, and tea. He was anxious to get her back to Sale as soon as possible, and whisked her out and into the car as soon as she'd finished eating.

'At least you know where I live, now,' he said as they were nearing Sale, then: 'Would you ever fancy doing some modelling work?'

She stared straight ahead. 'Most certainly not. I'm quite happy with my present state, thank you. I shall always be grateful to you for getting me the job in the first place, but I've got far more important things to do with my time than sit in one position all day.

'I help my grandmother quite a lot and I'm also taking some art lessons.'

He said nothing further, but Milly herself was saying quite a lot in her own mind. A model! Surely not a *regular* one who was prepared to pose in the nude! What a complete insult. It was all right for older women who had financial problems, but fortunately she was not in that category. She felt a glow of affection towards her grandmother for what she had said about helping her financially to get into art school as a student. It was a far cry from Gus Bridges' idea of what she should do, even if it was meant kindly.

She thanked him profusely as she got out of the car, carefully carrying her picture of the barge on the canal, with the horse munching grass on the canal bank. She felt quite proud of it as she stood and waved him goodbye.

Walking along the garden path to the back door, she realised she would have to give a reason why she hadn't actually got her own clothes with her. Oh well, it could just be that kind Miss Longfeather had urged her to leave them behind to be properly pressed and collected later, from Victoria Park. The address itself would be enough to soothe things. For one thing Grandma revelled in was a description of a suitably salubrious location.

Cautiously Milly opened the door and crept in quietly. The grandfather clock ticked with remorseless solemnity – it was almost nine-thirty. She could see a light shining from under the closed sitting-room door but she slipped past hastily to her own room and quickly divested herself of the borrowed clothes, hastily slipping on a grey cotton frock with a feeling of relief. After she had combed her hair and made herself look totally calm and respectable, she picked up the painting again and went to the living room. At least her grandmother would know her granddaughter had something to show for the day out and that Milly was indeed a chip off the old block where art was concerned.

'I'm home!' Milly's voice range out cheerfully in the sleepy silence.

Her grandma was sitting peacefully in an easy chair looking at a newspaper. She hadn't even heard Milly come in the room, and when Milly stepped forward to kiss her, she still made no movement. Milly stooped over her briefly and then recoiled, for the cheek was stone cold . . .

Grandmother Smith was as stiff and dead as a doornail.

CHAPTER SEVEN

The Studio

What a shock her grandmother's death was. It took Milly some time to get over it as all the family turmoil began.

There was an immediate flurry among the relatives as everyone squabbled about the funeral arrangements, and Clarry Dawnay's posh sister, Maddy Wilshaw from Timperley, took over with her three daughters; even going so far as to banish Milly from the flat immediately.

'Your place is at home with your poor mother now, darlin'. Just like my three dear girls are going to be staying right here with me for the time being, in Sale and in this house. For when all's said and done, Milly love, it's not as if you was being chucked out into the cold, cold snow at your ripe age, is it? You're a mature maiden lady now, and you'll just have to look round for summat else if you can't get on with all your own lot.'

Her face folded into an expression of bland and determined leadership: 'Quite truthfully, it's just not your place to be here any more, petal, now poor Mother's gone. My own three little treasures will stay with me, and we'll hold the fort until the funeral's over.'

Milly stared at them with mounting anger. She was extremely nettled to be called a maiden lady at twenty-one – especially since her three gargantuan and over-cosseted cousins were all in their mid-thirties – but the jab also served as a reminder that one day she would be galloping along to middle age with absolutely nothing to show for it. Babsy's words came flooding back about wanting nothing better than a home, a husband, and some children. Indeed, Babsy and Mackie had already found themselves a small house in Levenshulme and Babsy's waistline was expanding steadily, with their firstborn on its way . . .

'But Aunt, what about dear Uncle Beltane, all on his own?'

'Don't you fret about him, Millicent. It's not your place to pry into our affairs.'

Grandma Smith's will specified that the house should be sold – complete with the sitting tenant upstairs – and the money divided between her three daughters. This led to even more interminable chuntering, which was finally resolved by Maddy's husband Beltane triumph-antly acquiring the whole place himself with a loan which the Wilshaws partially recouped when they received Maddy's third share of the will. They then deposited their own three, willing, unmarried daughters – Prudence, Charity and Faith (who all had very good clerical jobs in the offices of company directors) – in the ground-floor flat, keeping on the services of Grandma Smith's ancient, almost immobile housekeeper, and the charlady.

As for Milly, with her wonderful promise of financial help completely evaporated, she received nothing except for a very old box of oil paints, brushes and a palette, wrapped in half a linen curtain with a note inside saying they had once belonged to her grandfather.

'I never knew your father had anything like that, Clarry?' said Joe Dawnay to his wife.

'Neither did I, Joe. But our Milly's lucky to have got anything at all. None of the other grandchildren received so much as a groat.'

It was the end of Hatching Street as far as the Dawnays were concerned, and they moved to a modern three-bedroomed semi-detached house near Longford Park in Stretford. The three eldest boys were now in digs and courting, and the only two children still at home were Betty, now seventeen, and Derry, nearly eleven.

Milly felt both glad and sad: glad that Mother and Father had at least received some recompense from the will to bring comfort to their later years, but sad that Grandmother Smith had died so suddenly, carrying with her many of Milly's hopes and dreams. Now she was worse off than ever.

She hastily found cheap lodgings near Denmark Road in Manchester, and banished all ideas of ever becoming a student. These days it was enough to cope with keeping herself in the same steady job.

But there was far, far worse to come. Hardly had Clarry and Joe Dawnay and their daughter Betty and young son Derry settled down happily into their modern home and new life in Stretford than they were victims of a scourge of Spanish Influenza which was sweeping the whole country. Within a few days of each other Clarry and Joe both died in hospital.

Once again, like some terrible nightmare, Milly was embroiled in more sadness, heartache, and loneliness.

Her younger brother and sister were too upset even to stay in the new house near Longford Park, now. Thankfully they were offered a long holiday with Aunt May at Southport, leaving the house empty until further arrangements were made.

About two months later, just as the Dawnay sons and daughters were beginning to get sorted out, Milly's sister Effie, along with her son Paul and her husband (who had changed from farm work to being a motor mechanic), decided to come and live in their late parents' new house in Stretford, to give support to Betty and Derry. This meant that any small hope Milly might have had of herself joining her younger brother and sister in the family house was finished for ever, and so she stayed on in her terrible digs.

One pleasant summery day Milly received a message from Gus at work asking her to meet him in Paulden's for a midday dinner.

As they sat there, eating roast beef and Yorkshire pudding, Milly felt a sudden overwhelming sense of normal life returning again after the deadening effects of her family grief. How restful and reassuring it was amongst the pleasant everyday warmth and bustle of the place with its muffled clatter of silver-plated soup tureens; how intoxicating those lingering odours of mouth-watering roast potatoes and rich gravy. She felt enveloped in the refined homeliness of the place, with its stiff white damask dinner napkins and curly clothes-stands heavy with overcoats and bowler hats, and the small violin quartet strumming away in the background.

Milly had hardly seen Gus Bridges or Hewy to speak to since the day at Lymm, but Gus knew about all her misfortunes and the fact that she'd moved back into Manchester.

'How's it going, then? What are the digs like?'

She pulled a face. 'To be truthful, they're absolutely dreadful. It's a very noisy place, and the man in the room on the same landing as me is a heavy drinker. I can hear him vomiting and thumping about when he comes in at night. But I mustn't grumble, because the place is very cheap, and that's what matters most at present.' She tried to brighten up and smile.

He stared at her thoughtfully. 'Strangely enough, I have a proposition for you, and it's to do with living accommodation, though I'm in two minds as to whether you'll turn down the idea immediately. It's to do with my place . . .'

He saw a beam of interest flicker and then fade from her face. No way was she interested in getting tied up with him when what she was really looking for was a good, entirely independent place of her own.

'. . . Well, not actually my place, but the second flat on the ground floor, which is empty and has just changed hands. The new owner, Algernon Hawkesly, is in the same line of life as me and wants to keep the place as a studio with a live-in caretaker, but he's just gone abroad for twelve months, to do some painting. He'll be employing other staff for heavy work so it doesn't matter if it's a man or a woman who's actually there, just so long as they are resident. There's a very comfortable bedroom and sitting room, and a large kitchen and bathroom. The main room looks out onto the back gardens . . .

'No need to keep shaking your head. You'd be well paid, that's the main thing. It would probably work out better than working as a general skivvy at the art school, if you wanted to do more art work yourself.'

Milly felt herself going into a bit of a daze. What an amazing bolt from the blue! For, truth to tell, she hadn't imagined she'd be paid at all. She'd been thinking to herself that never would she be able to afford to live in such a luxurious place as that on her small weekly wage.

'Think about it, anyway,' he said as they finished their meal. Then he changed the subject: 'Done any more drawing and painting since our outing to Lymm?'

She shook her head ruefully. 'Everything's been too much at sixes and sevens, but my grandmother left me some old oil paints belonging to my late grandfather and they're still in good condition; almost brand new. I was going to ask you sometime about how to start off with them. I've never touched oil paints in all my life.'

'If you took up this offer, I could teach you easily. Tell you what, why not give it a try? You could just live there for a few weeks rent free, and keep on with your job at the same time. You wouldn't be any worse off than you are now.'

She laughed. 'I could *never* be that, believe me!'

That afternoon she tried to puzzle out what to do. Was there a catch in it? It seemed too good for words. Supposing it wasn't as perfect as it seemed and she had to go hunting for somewhere else yet again? She knew she wouldn't be able to stand that.

The very next Sunday Gus collected her early from her squalid living quarters and transported her to the tall chess-piece chimney pots and pink stucco of Sundower House in Higher Broughton.

On this second visit the place looked larger and the sprawling building more complicated as Milly tried to take in every detail – for she had to be sure it would be all right if she did decide to move in.

'There are two flats on the ground floor,' said Gus, 'and yours is the biggest.' He said it casually as if it was a foregone conclusion she would accept.

There was a brass plate engraved TWO on the flat's own white, panelled, carved vestibule door. The door was inset with stained glass panes of richly coloured fruits and flowers, and was at the back of the house, close to the conservatory. In fact it was difficult to tell that the door was at the back, since the house itself was a mass of interesting doors and windows looking onto the gardens. Mundane things such as coal supplies were allocated to a place at the side, partitioned by its own driveway, high brick walls and many outbuildings.

The hallway of the flat was decorated with encaustic tiles of a beautiful geometric design: coloured clays in dove grey, slate blue and sage green. The simple kitchen had brown lino on the floor and contained an old black iron fire range, a deal table and four stout kitchen chairs, along with a large kitchen dresser.

To Milly it seemed like a palace as she looked through the window, close to one of the sinks, and out towards a trellis of small rambling roses.

The bathroom had a free-standing bath with large claw feet and brass taps. The wash basin stood in the corner with marble surrounds and a well-used, rather stained mahogany cupboard beneath it. The basin was patterned with flowers.

'And this is the bedroom . . .' said Gus, as they moved on.

Milly drank it in: the homely room with its low ceiling and wooden planked floor. The neat, unobtrusive flat-woven carpet. The restful design of the flock wallpaper in delicate greens and lemon. The two sash windows to greet her, with their cushioned window seats, the paintwork faded white, and shaded by pale lined sateen curtains with frilled peplums. And a copper coal scuttle by the fireplace.

In the corner stood a roomy rosewood wardrobe with a full-length mirror. And what a bed! It was heavily carved with a double bedstead, next to an inlaid mahogany chest of drawers.

An ebony-bordered screen decorated with dark flowers and leaves enclosed the marble-topped wash-stand with its gleaming green bowl and jug.

Milly walked across to a small armchair. It was perfect. She brushed her hand across the oval table with an oil lamp on it, and gently stroked a tapestry stool.

'The bed has no mattress, as you can see.' said Gus, 'but Algy Hawkesly says he'll provide a new one.'

And, finally, with almost reluctance in his steps, Gus led her to the largest room of all – the living room, with its huge French windows.

Milly frowned slightly. She'd been looking forward to this part, but it was remarkably bare, apart from its rouge marble fireplace and ornate, heavy-looking black clock on the mantelpiece, for there was nothing else in the vast space other than a number of battered-looking, non-descript chairs and a heavily finger-marked glass-fronted bookcase housing ancient-looking encyclopaedias.

She noticed a strange oval-shaped sign on the far wall, drawn in black ink, rather like the rough draft of some future idea, in a puzzling combination of letters.

'This is where we all meet,' explained Gus in a quick, low voice.

'Meet?' Milly stared at him. 'How do you mean, *meet*? Meet who?'

He didn't seem to hear her at first. 'I'll just show you the sitting room,' he muttered hastily. 'It's ideal for one. It's very comfortably furnished.'

He was right. It was cosy with a plain fireplace and a hob for a kettle. It was painted in pink and there was a five-sided table complete with three dining chairs, as well as a chest of drawers and two plush velvet easy chairs. A mirror reflected light from the garden.

Milly stood there silently. She felt most unsettled now about the whole idea. As soon as he'd mentioned the word meeting it had been like a bucket of icy cold water.

'So what do you think?' He was looking quite anxious.

'Well ...' she gulped with sudden nervousness. 'Of course, it's absolutely wonderful. The size of it's as big as three houses put together, if it were in Hatching Street ... The bedroom alone is as big as some ordinary town flat. This "small" sitting room is the size of my bedsitter in Denmark Road!' She hesitated. 'But ... what was it you said ... about "*meetings*"?'

'Let's go back upstairs and I'll explain.'

Whilst Milly sat in Gus's whitewashed studio room, reminded once again of her own past existence by the photograph of herself and Honour eating cherries at All Saints, and catching sight of Hewy's textile design of blue cornflowers and poppies, so small yet so vivid, she suddenly realised that her future fate lay here – in this house – whatever the outcome. For with the death of both her grandmother and her parents it was the only

137

place that could still give shape to her life in her present, unsettled state. But even so . . . what had he meant by 'the meeting'?

'The truth is,' admitted Gus as he poured her out some port and offered her a cream cracker and some rather stale-looking dried up cheese fit only for a mouse trap, 'we've formed a small group of painters, sculptors, designers and film-makers. We call ourselves the Post-War Visualists, and all our work will bear the initials PWV within an oval shape as a sign of new life and ideas. And your living room downstairs is the place we plan to have the meetings.'

He looked at her with serious intensity, and she could do nothing but nod her head solemnly, for now she had committed herself to accepting his offer of the flat she had no other option, and at least there was the cosy little sitting room. It was all quite exciting really . . .

'Our president is Algy Hawkesly, who's away for the year and who now owns this house –'

Milly's eyes widened. 'Owns this whole huge house? I thought it was only the one flat downstairs?'

Gus shook his head. 'He bought it lock, stock and barrel, and we're very pleased. He's the heir to Portal Benson's, one of the manufacturers of clothing for His Majesty's Forces. He was in the war himself.'

After a second small glass of port Milly let it be known that she was quite happy to take up the offer of the flat.

'You'll never regret it. It'll be just like home for you,' said Gus with a sudden gush of brotherly love and delighted enthusiasm. 'You already know most of us – there's me, there's Hewy –'

'Hewy?' She gave a nervous start of surprise.

He nodded his head and his smile became a bit

bleaker. 'He's a member, but he's a bit involved with Minny Dee, one of the students. She's linked with Falethorpes Pork Sausages and she's a bad influence – she's just a social butterfly. He doesn't join in nearly enough. All good art needs plenty of hard work and you have to keep at it, as he well knows.'

Milly tried to look sympathetic, aware only that Hewy had not changed one jot. Her fears about his dilly-dallying and those rumours of the sausage millions were true. But what could she expect? Why was she such an utter fool to care so much? It was her own fault. Did she enjoy all this inner turmoil and torment? Men always sought after pastures new, but oh how she longed for him. Longed in vain to be back at his humble, seedy lodgings on that rainy night so long ago. Longed to have told him how much she cared and how much she wanted to be his wife.

'Then there's Art Fallowfield, of course. His girl-friend Zeronica sometimes models for us, and there's Stewart Kilkraddy – I don't think you've met him – he's a sculptor ... and a couple of my pals from the films. Not a large group, but just right. Oh – and Hortensia, of course. That goes without saying ...' He looked at Milly awkwardly.

'Hortensia Longfeather?'

'Exactly so. She's terribly keen, and with her coming here to live in flat number one it's –'

'– Live *here*? But she lives somewhere else, doesn't she?' Milly went scarlet.

'Not now. She's due to move in here in less than a week. Quite one happy family, so to speak.' He hastily poured himself another drink. 'The fact is, Milly, she's well in with old Algy, and Algy rules the roost as it were ...' Gus suddenly looked miserable. 'It's not quite how

139

I had envisaged the group at first, but I'm sure we'll all merge together ... especially with a girl like you being in it. You'll keep us all on the rails ...' His voice had a slightly blurred edge to it.

'*Me*? Where on earth did you get that strange idea? Supposing I change my mind after all?'

But she knew she wouldn't, in spite of Horty. For what other real option was there? She could see even more clearly that if she went back to her noisy beer-swilling digs near Denmark Road she would be almost like an exile – with not even Babsy these days to cheer her up at work. She would just be a small, drifting, single speck outside the real core of this art world she now knew so well ... No, she would just have to grin and bear it, hoping that Her Royal Highness Horty Longfeather would keep a safe distance in flat number one. Maybe Hortensia would be a different sort of person in the privacy of her own personal surroundings, for people often showed two faces to the world. Perhaps, after all, they would be like ordinary neighbours in any other moderately normal place where the only link was an occasional mention of the weather.

Then a horrible thought struck her. 'Does Hortensia know she will be living next door to me?'

Gus gave a sickly smile. 'She doesn't, actually. It might be better if we didn't mention it for the time being and just let her get settled in for a week or two whilst your flat's empty. Then you could edge yourself in one day just as if you'd been there all along, and by then you'll have all the rest of us there to soothe troubled waters if there should be a sudden storm. Er, you see, Milly, it's a bit complicated, and as I said, she is very closely linked to Algy. I can't really go into the whys and wherefores right now, but ...'

Milly began to see red. She had never realised how much Mr Augustine Bridges was within the tentacles of grasping Hortensia Longfeather. 'I'm afraid you'll have to think that one out again, Gus.' She said icily.

'Beg your pardon? I don't quite get you.'

'You really *do* want me to come here, don't you, Gus? You're just not *saying* it, or anything? I seem to remember you even mentioned my stopping working at the art school altogether as the payment being made for me to be an acting caretaker here would be as much as – if not more than – my art school wages, plus free lodgings?'

'Yes, of course. So?'

'So I'm moving *in* right now, Gus. You can take my note to Cavendish Street in the morning saying I'm indisposed and not available for any further work.'

'Isn't that rather sudden? Whatever will poor Miss Ponsonby do without you in the basement? And especially with Babsy gone, too.'

'They'll soon find someone else. They'll have queues miles long for jobs like that in these hard times.' Her temper cooled down. 'I'll always be grateful to you for getting me the job in the first place, Gus, but you are the one who suggested the change! They were your very words today.'

'But not as quickly as this, surely?'

The expression on Milly's face hardened. No way was she going to be the one hanging around whilst Lady Hortensia tripped lightly onto the scene, leaving herself to be the approaching thorn in the flesh . . .

'So if you'll take me back to my digs, I'll get out of them right now. I'll have just enough cash left to last out until I start to get paid by Mr Hawkesley. Will that be in about a week?'

Gus gulped and nodded his head. 'No need to worry there, Milly – I'll guarantee to pay you. Perhaps you're right about not going in again. It might have been a bit awkward if you'd had to keep it a secret from Horty all the time. This way round might be easier, even if it is a shock for her straight away.'

'Shock for *her*? What about *me*?'

'She's rather formal, that's all. She likes to keep within very strict social bounds as far as art is concerned. She doesn't even like mixing with first-year students in the social sense. I know it sounds terribly snobbish, but there you are ... Although I do feel you both got on very well on our outing to Lymm.'

With amazing mildness, Gus did exactly as he was told and within a couple of hours Milly was back again, with her belongings, at Sundower House in Higher Broughton.

'The only thing is, you have no proper mattress on the bed,' he said, smiling, as they sat in his place eating balm cakes. 'You can stay here if you want, until it's fixed up, and I'll use a camp bed.'

She stared at his studio divan with its folkweave cover, and a sigh rose within her, a sigh of weariness and longing. When, oh when would she really be in her Own Place?

'It wouldn't work, Gus. People might think we – I mean – there's Arthur Fallowfield up in that attic for a start, with Zeronica. They'd be sure to think we were being exactly like them, and it wouldn't be true.'

'Got it!' He smiled at her triumphantly. 'There's a divan in flat one, and seeing that Horty's not due in it for a few days you can settle in there. I'll get the key and show you. It's not as well padded out as your place, but I've got lots of spare sheets and blankets. She'll be bringing some furniture of her own when she arrives.'

That night, when Milly eventually went to bed in flat one, she didn't give Hortensia Longfeather another thought as she sunk almost unconscious into the soft pillows.

When she awoke the sun was streaming through all the windows. It was practically dinner-time! Gus would already be at work.

She sat up hastily. There was a shadow by the door, a figure standing there silently . . .

It was Hortensia.

CHAPTER EIGHT

The Paper

'*You?*'

Hortensia Longfeather just could not believe her eyes as she saw Milly Dawnay staring up at her, bleary-eyed.

Early that very morning, during the morning break at art school, she'd heard from Miss Ponsonby that Miss Dawnay had suddenly left.

'You could have knocked me down with your little finger,' quivered Miss Ponsonby. 'I was very, very sad, I can tell you. And it mean's I'll be extremely short staffed. She was like one of our very own bricks in the wall of my pottery shed, she'd been there so long. But what a trick to play . . .'

Miss Ponsonby stared at Hortensia with subdued rage. 'What on earth could she have been thinking of? Unskilled young women of her type could never hope to find a more pleasant and suitable way of life than remaining here in this civilised atmosphere.' A genuine tear welled in the corner of one of Miss Ponsonby's pale, elderly eyes. 'She even claimed to be interested in Fine Art herself . . . so why leave?'

Hortensia nodded this way and that. She neither

knew nor cared. If it hadn't been for the shortage of labouring staff affecting everybody, in every department, she would secretly have muttered 'good riddance' – for after her memorable day out to Lymm with Millicent shoved upon her, she felt there was more to that madam than met the eye ... She was very pushy with men, for a start, especially Gus Bridges – and even Hugo Edmundson seemed to be at her beck and call. Hortensia knew that if she herself had not been a married women of long standing and above such things, she could have been quite alarmed by Miss Dawnay's seductive ways.

But why was she here now – in Higher Broughton, in this very room, in someone else's flat ... *her* flat on *her* divan, at midday?

Horty's eyes glinted. Surely there hadn't been some sort of drunken orgy in her absence? She had led Gus to believe she wouldn't be moving in for at least another week or so, and it was quite by chance that she'd come today with her tape measure to check up measurements for fresh curtains.

Drunken orgies ... She thought of her husband, Algy Hawkesly. That was one of the real reasons she'd been so glad to see him clear off to paint abroad for a year. He could be such a boozer if given the least excuse ...

If he had been a poorer man she might well have left him years ago – especially as they had no children – but his own redeeming feature was his inherited wealth, which she tried to keep secret as much as possible, along with the fact of their marriage, for married women were pretty well barred from teaching jobs in most places. And the secret had been made even harder to keep with this sudden madness of his in buying this huge house and planning to run it as a sort of rest haven for some of his pals – the main one being Augustine Bridges, for they had been students together.

The ultimate insult, however, was that he had assumed she would leave her own well-paid job as an art teacher and act as a housekeeper-cum-caretaker in this rambling place. Yes, actually *give up* her own work to act as an unpaid nanny for a lot of happy-go-lucky males in another of her husband's artistic schemes. In this latest one he planned to form a new nucleus of post-war art, bringing together various influences and ideas: abstracts like the various versions of White on White; other subjects, such as animals in boggy ground with moons and rainbows behind them; and preliminary paintings for larger works of heaven and hell no smaller than twenty feet by twelve.

But she was too angry to ponder the merits of her husband's artistic scheme. It was the housekeeper scheme that concerned her. What total and utter cheek! – only outdone by the fact that he'd sold their home in Victoria Park over her head so that she had had no choice but to come here to this small flat for the time being in order to continue with her own art school job.

Her gaze was still on Milly, as she simmered inside.

Hastily and with muttered apologies Milly scrambled to her feet and stood there in her shrunken, dowdy, cotton pyjamas. 'I had no idea you would be . . .' Milly's voice tailed off weakly. 'There was no mattress in my own flat . . .'

Hortensia froze. Her pale face was like a noble marble statue with live, dark, burning eyes that pierced Milly with steely rapiers. '*Your flat*? Since when has anywhere here been *your* flat?'

'Since today,' Milly was almost beginning to doubt it herself. Was it all a dream or had she really and truly made that permanent arrangement with Gus Bridges? And had she really left her longstanding job which she'd managed to survive in and appreciate up till now? Had her own dreams of studying at the art school vanished? And would she ever make her own way well enough to consider herself on an equal footing with Hewy?

Hortensia stood like a field marshal waiting for Milly to beat a retreat as, without another word, Milly shuffled back to flat number two, dragging sheets, blankets and pillows with her whilst Hortensia turned and began measuring windows with her tape measure.

Milly closed her own front door with profound relief. Well, at least Horty knew part of the truth now, so the best thing to do would be to keep out of her way as much as possible . . .

That afternoon, when Milly was properly back in focus again and Hortensia had vanished, she began to explore the house more thoroughly. There was no one else about and the place basked in sunny, placid peace. The doors of all the flats were closed but Milly couldn't resist the temptation of climbing high up to the attics to see where Arthur Fallowfield lived with his girlfriend. As she stood there gazing with curiosity at the small, ordinary wooden door with the name Art Fallows painted on it in a scrawling, confident signature, she heard footsteps behind her. Before she could turn round, a hand was placed on her shoulder.

'Milly Dawnay! Gus told me about you coming here. Who'd have guessed it?' He had grown a bright ginger beard and wore an old dark blue smock. 'Come in anyway and have a look round – Zeron's out getting a bit of shopping done. I'm working on some railway holiday posters at present . . .

'So what's all this about you being the resident

caretaker and becoming a member of our new group? Are you still doing those lessons at the Mechanics' Institute with Lewis Bresslaw?' He began to look for a couple of mugs for a drink of tea, and to move some painting materials from the table.

'I haven't actually given up, but I haven't been to any classes for ages – everything's been in such a turmoil.' She was grateful for his words, which decided her not to let Mr Bresslaw's painstaking tutelage vanish for ever.

In fact, Arthur's enthusiasm for her to get moving with her art again was so strong that the very next evening she turned up at the Institute once more to ask Mr Bresslaw if she could continue.

'I expect I'm getting too old now to go in for one of the scholarships, but all the same I'd still like to come to your classes . . .'

'Too old? What's got into you, girl? No one's too old in the art world if they're prepared to work.' He peered at her quizzically over the tops of his rimless glasses. He had a shining bald pate and curly grey hair round his ears. 'I'll enter you for the 1920 one, and even if you fail, you can always have another go if you're still keen. How old are you at present?'

'Nearly twenty-two.' She felt as ancient as the hills.

'Forty years younger than me then. You've still got plenty of time.'

What a darling man he was!

Milly was so swept along by Mr Bresslaw's cheerful influence, and his flexible methods of deferring payments by running his own small 'never, never' club for the more hard-up students and paying their fees himself in the name of posterity until the payment was caught up on, that she began to work with fanatical zeal both at evening classes and at her flat. So much so that she was entirely unaware that Hortensia had finally moved into flat number one, or that Gus was busy making arrangements for her full initiation into all her forthcoming working duties.

During this first month everything had been complete paradise. She was left entirely free to please herself, and the first payment for her name-only position as resident housekeeper was made at the end of the month, as promised. But soon the honeymoon was to be over . . .

It began the moment Gus announced that they would be having a general meeting of the Post-War Visualists in her large living room the following Sunday and that it would last all day.

Post-War Visualists. What a complicated title. A far cry indeed from blue cornflowers and red field poppies. Was she going to be entirely out of her depth?

'I reckon everyone will turn up – even old Algernon,' said Gus enthusiastically. 'He's supposed to be calling back, briefly, to make sure things are going all right, and to buy a batch of coloured inks at a cheap little place in Hanging Ditch. You'd think he'd get his stuff in Switzerland now, because that's his main bedding-down area, but not him . . . His heart is always here and always will be.'

Gus began to look thoughtful. 'He's got some strange quirks. He's neurotic about the quality of his water-colour paper, and insists on getting it in Manchester, where he's always got it. He's one of those impatient blighters who does all sorts of strange things with it, with the sudden patience of Job. Mucks about with his work for hours and hours to get it just right, almost at random. Trial and error for evermore. The paper has to be as tough as God himself – a miracle of flexibility and forgiveness. Sometimes he puts as many as thirty different coloured ink washes on it.'

Milly smiled. Mr Hawkesly sounded fairly normal. She'd been at the art school quite long enough to realise the propensities of artists for strange working techniques. Maybe their dreadful title of Post-War Visualists was more alarming than what was about to take place, once they all got together. Perhaps Algy Hawkesly would be a really good artistic influence, just like darling Mr Bresslaw. There was nothing like encouragement from a far-seeing eye.

'All *you'll* need to do will be to see to refreshments, and perhaps take a few notes throughout the proceedings in case we can't come up with someone willing to be the secretary. One of our members from Salford – a photographer – had planned to do it, but he has left due to pressure of other work.'

Milly had virtually ignored the living room since she'd been there, and now as she went and stood in the centre of it she realised how neglected it was. There was no sign of any other hands at work in the general cleaning and rough work. She hadn't seen a whisper of a charlady since the minute she'd arrived, in spite of Gus's previous grandiose assertions that Hawkesly would be employing other staff for heavy work.

With mounting reluctance she picked up the inevitable cleaning materials: scrubbing brush, mop bucket, Jeyes Fluid, feather dusters, stiff hand-brush, an ordinary sweeping brush and shovel . . . the list was endless. Once more she became a beast of burden, laden with dusters and a carpet sweeper, as she started to remove cobwebs and mouse droppings. All the time she worked she comforted herself with the thought that Hewy might turn up. She imagined him greeting her with his old familiar smile as if nothing had ever gone wrong between them. She dreamed, idly, of finding them both a quiet spot in the flat where they could work together as twin souls – with never a bad word between them.

She cleared all the heavy books from the glass-fronted bookcase, and polished and washed every bit of glass, including all the windows, with water and ammonia. She pounded masses of dust out of the battered old chairs and dusted all the walls. She removed mildew from the window frames and polished all the brass trimmings she could see, until the place looked a far better sight than previously.

'No need to kill yourself, Milly,' said Gus casually, as he popped down from his own flat on the Saturday to see how things were going. 'The place was pretty well all right before you started. It only needed the chairs putting straight.'

She stared at him to see if it was a joke, but he was entirely serious.

'All we need now is a fair amount of food, and a few drinks. I'll get Zeronica to fetch some meat pies and some loaves and a few sardines to make sandwiches. Arthur will see to the drink situation. All you'll need to do is to sit back and relax.'

She bit her lip to control her amazement at his utter ignorance. The true proportions of the work entailed were evidently a closed book to him, from the way he gazed at her with absent-minded innocence.

'How many people will there be altogether, Gus?'

'Well, there's you and me for a start. And Hortensia, of course, and Algy. Then there'll be Arthur and Zeron, and Hewy and maybe Minny Dee . . .'

Hewy. So he might be turning up after all? Milly felt a sudden flood of happy relief. She'd been right to hope. These days he was often no more than a distant stranger – it was ages since she'd even spoken to him . . .

Then a rush of sadness and guilt took over. Was she merely holding onto a strange, juvenile fantasy? Carrying a torch for old infant rivalries? Perhaps what she felt was just an immature love, not suitable for consummation.

'And there'll be Stewart Kilkraddy the sculptor with his girlfriend Rosanna Porteus, as well as Micky Craddock, Osbert Formby, and Percy Shell from Finer Films . . . So how many's that?'

Milly hardly heard him.

'Oh, and Ralph the boiler man. I was talking to him only this morning. He might come. He paints miniatures. I reckon it could be about fourteen or fifteen if everyone turns up.'

On the Friday evening before the Sunday of the meeting, Milly was surprised by a caller – a man in a military-type raincoat, tall and sunburnt, with a lean face and grey, restless eyes. His slightly bleached brown hair was as short as a convict's, and he was carrying a canvas portmanteau.

As soon as she opened the door he stepped inside without any invitation. 'Tell Hortensia I'm here if you please.' His tone was so autocratic that Milly felt like curtsying immediately. She was standing there in an apron and cotton dustcap – she had been finishing some extra cleaning before this special weekend.

'I'm afraid she –'

'Don't argue, young woman. Do as I say. She's expecting me. I was supposed to have been here tomorrow, but I've managed it earlier.'

152

'Miss Longfeather doesn't live in this flat, *sir*!' Milly glared full force.

'She does, you know!'

'I'm sorry, sir, but she does not! Flat number one is where *she* lives.' A sparkling, indignant anger lit Milly's face. What absolute arrogance!

'Look, girl, get me your mistress and don't damned well *argue*!'

'I *am* the mistress.' She stared at him coldly. 'I'm Millicent Dawnay, the caretaker for Mr Hawkesly, who owns this house.'

'What are you talking about? *I'm* Hawkesly!' He scowled at her for a few seconds, then his face broke into a wide, engaging smile revealing sharp-even teeth. 'So *you're* Milly, eh? The girl Gus told me about. The little angel I'm paying ...' He began to look embarrassed. 'I do apologise. I hadn't realised my wife was going to move to the other flat."

'Your *wife*?' Gradually the truth seeped through, though how Hortensia could be his wife at all was very strange, particularly considering how different in style they were.

He gazed about the place. 'I was aware she didn't want to take on the housekeeper job, but I thought she'd still keep this flat because of all the space ... I presume you know her?'

Milly nodded reluctantly. 'I see little of her, though, or the others. They're out working.'

'Got anything to drink?' He followed her to the small sitting room, promptly seating himself as if he'd lived in the room all his life.

'I can make you some Camp coffee or tea. Or there's some sarsaparilla ...? We'll have some proper drinks for the meeting, though.'

He stood up again. 'Tell you what – you put the old kettle on, and I'll go and rattle the other front door to see if my beloved is there. Then we'll both come back to you here for the tea – right?' He lowered his eyelids with what seemed to her to be a slightly flirtatious gesture. Then, remembering he was an artist, she decided it must be an entirely innocent mannerism caused by constantly making visual measurements of scenes he was drawing . . .

She smiled back at him, and out of some streak of sympathy immediately lowered her own eyelids too. 'I'll put the kettle on the fire right now, Mr Hawkesly.'

Hardly had she done it, than he was back again. 'Not in, I'm afraid – and neither was Gus when I called at his place earlier. I hope I'm not disturbing whatever you were doing, Miss Dawnay,' he said with sudden solicitude. 'You looked as if you were quite busy?'

She took off her cap and hung it on the hook behind the door, then removed her apron too as she shook her hair to loosen it to its normal curliness. 'I have been quite busy. It was my last cleaning session before Sunday. Tomorrow I shall be arranging the food. I'm going to the meeting, myself, to take notes for Gus, so there's been lots of preparation.'

'And you are getting your salary, from Gus?' He looked at her gravely.

'Yes. Oh yes . . . It's all sorted out.'

'Do you know them all?'

'I know Gus, and Mr Fallowfield, and Mr Fallowfield's friend Miss Prendleghast. I'm also acquainted with Hugo Edmundson . . .' She coloured up slightly. 'And of course Miss Longfeather. But not the others.'

'You don't know Kilkraddy the sculptor then?'

'Only by sight.'

'That's all you need to know of him, I warn you. And

never believe a word he tells you – including outlandish tales about me.'

She looked shocked. 'Of course not!'

What a motley crew they were when Sunday morning arrived – as sure enough they all turned up – even tubby little Ralph, the boiler man.

Some of them stood up, smoking cigarettes, others half lounged in their chairs and the rest lay on the floor. The exception was Mr Kilkraddy, the hungry-looking sculptor, who sat cross-legged in front of the table where Gus and Algy Hawkesly were presiding, draped in a long, white, flowing overall and looking like a Buddha, with a plump, docile brown-and-white spaniel on a long leather lead beside him.

Milly sat to the side of the group in one of her own small easy chairs from the sitting room, with a notebook on her knee to record the proceedings. She wasn't going to get any time to herself.

Hewy and Minny Dee were sitting close by. Minny Dee was dressed to kill, in lime green and silver-grey. Her skirt was as small as a postage stamp, and her long, shapely legs were encased in salmon-pink silk stockings, slim and provocative. Hewy smiled at Milly. Immediately, with an almost reflex action, Minny Dee's hand clasped Hewy's and she gave him a huge, glamorous smile, ending with a steady gaze towards Milly.

Milly ignored it and bent her head towards the notebook. She felt she was in a field full of female hand grenades, with Horty giving her the cold shoulder, and Stewart Kilkraddy's girlfriend, Rosanna Porteus, whom she'd never seen before, eyeing her in quick covert glances. So she was glad of the open, ordinary friendliness of Arthur and Zeronica, perched unobtrusively in the background, and the homeliness of Ralph Tonks, who explained that his wife would have liked to have been there but she had to cook Sunday dinner for ten, even though she was more interested in flower painting.

'So what are your ideas for a programme of work?' asked Gus an hour or so later when everyone had taken a fair amount of liquid refreshment and all the sardine sandwiches had vanished. 'We mustn't forget that one of our most important acquisitions will be a regular and reliable model, and if that isn't forthcoming we shall all have to take turns ourselves.'

There was a mumbling period as everyone looked at everyone else and names floated through the air. 'What about Esmeralda Nogson and her long neck ...? Why don't we give old Charlie Cook another go and tell him to keep his stomach covered more? His chin is his main asset ... Has anybody thought of asking Tortoise Trevors – his legs are out of this world ...?'

Then Algy said casually: 'Is there anyone here who'd like to do it on a regular basis for proper payment ... Maybe one of the women?'

'Count me out straight away!' exclaimed Hortensia with alacrity.

'Me, too,' purred Minny Dee with innocent charm as she pulled a solid gold, ornately mirrored powder compact from her small pochette and began to powder her pert little nose. 'I'm still mastering the art of managing to draw a circle freehand ...' She looked round at everyone and flapped her false eyelashes with magnetic savoire-faire.

Milly busied herself writing down all the suggestions, glad that she couldn't be dragged into the actual problem herself. Then Zeronica, after a few whispered words to Arthur, offered herself for the job. She needed every bit of extra cash she could find to help make ends meet, in order to give herself a small amount of financial independence. At the moment she spent what little spare time she had modelling for "Art Fallows" calendars and posters – and it was always done gratis.

The day went by smoothly as various plans were made. Opinions were aired about what the group actually stood for in terms of post-war art, with its ramifications of sculpture and film photography.

'Realism. That's what we need,' cried Gus excitedly. 'Realism. Realism in all its forms ... None of this airy-fairy stuff with maidens festooned in silks and satins, seated on fanciful swings in apple orchards with ropes of ribboned flowers. Those days are gone!'

The meat pies were all demolished and then it was the turn of the bread, cheese and pickles, accompanied by mass swillings of ale, whisky, brandy and port. By the afternoon everyone's mood had changed to complete torpor, and the room was filled with the sound of heavy breathing, and in some cases downright snoring – especially by Ralph, who normally had forty winks on a Sunday afternoon but was now sleeping off lethal effects not so easily reached by his usual roast beef and Yorkshire pudding.

Hortensia had chosen to return with the excuse that she had some students' studies to see to, and Hewy and Minny were wandering around in the glass conservatory. Milly wondered whether to join them – just to see how Hewy would react. The thing about Minny Dee was that she was quite nice, really. You could never actually hate her. You could understand men falling for her. Milly sighed gloomily. She was up against a formidable opponent.

Then, to Milly's horror, Stewart Kilkraddy, Rosanna

Porteus and Algy Hawkesly, accompanied by two of the photographers, and all with sketching pads, suddenly drifted into the bathroom and slammed the door loudly. Then she heard the sound of running bath water.

'They don't want to be disturbed,' warned Gus.

What in heaven's name was happening? Milly felt weak at the knees as all the terrible tales throughout history involving various bathing scandals, from Rome onwards, flooded through her mind, for it was positively indecent for a group of half-sozzled men and a woman to be in a place like that – even though there was the redeeming feature in this case that the WC was entirely separate.

Then she heard great gales of laughter and Algy's drunken voice roaring for more and more water with instructions to swish it about far more. 'We should have all brought our bathing costumes,' he blared. 'I advise Miss Porteus to remove that dress immediately. She's already drenched to the skin. I can see the ribs of her stays . . .'

Unable to bear it a moment longer, her heart bursting with moral indignation, Milly went to the heavy bathroom door and turned the huge brass door knob with all her force. It wouldn't move, but a sudden silence ensued from within.

'Warra ya want?' Hawkesly's slurred voice had a dangerous tone. 'Shift away from that door knob, damn you!'

Milly hesitated. She was trembling. After all, he'd seemed quite civilised when she'd first met him, in spite of his commandeering ways. Then resolutely she gripped the door knob again, pushed the door hard and walked in.

There was water everywhere, and standing in the

bath with his trousers off and his woollen long johns rolled up to his substantial and hairy knees, which were streaked and mottled in green, yellow, pink, and purple, was Algy, surrounded by sheets of floating watercolour paper, some of it scrawled with coloured ink.

He glared defiantly at Milly. 'Well – warrisitt ...?' Come to see the damage?' He was waving a large, purple, ink-stained loofah at her. It was utterly ruined for washing with, and the bath itself had a myriad of vivid stains which she knew would take hours to remove. She stared at the rest of them. They were mildly spattered with sprays of coloured ink, but poor Rosanna Porteus was soaked to the skin and her rather pretty cotton dress had absorbed a plethora of extra colour, as she stared with silent anguish towards Milly.

Meanwhile the two photographers were well employed, sketching and scribbling copious notes while they tried to ignore the general chaos, and Stewart Kilkraddy the sculptor was measuring the bath and babbling on about 'Venus emerging ... in marble and twelve feet tall'.

Summoning all her courage, Milly marched over to Algy. 'It's time to get out of the bath, Mr Hawkesly. There's going to be a lot of cleaning up to do, and it's getting quite late.'

'Time to get out?' He looked at her petulantly. 'But it's *my* bath! I own it. I own the whole of this house and if I want to stand in my own bath it's not me that needs to get out, it's you lot, ya buggers ... It's all you lot.' He suddenly turned on them all, waving his arms dangerously. 'Gerrout, the whole lot of ya! D'ya hear?'

Everyone filed slowly from the bathroom, leaving Algy to get out of the water, remove all the dripping, sopping sheets of paper and pull the plug out.

'The work's not finished yet,' he bawled. 'Warrabout all this paper? Warrabout the research on its quality? Warrabout its colour reaction to the inks? Warrabout its weight when wet? Warrabout how it's going to dry out and how long it'll take?' Then he gave a huge groan and slipped to the floor ... by which time everyone had hastily assembled in the living room to try and decide what to do with him.

'I'll go and fetch his wife,' said Milly, pale and trembling.

Hortensia was a long time opening the door. 'Yes ...? What is it?'

'It's Mr Hawkesly. He's in a bit of a state. He was doing some research in the bathroom about different qualities of paper, and ink absorption, and it seems to have got a bit out of hand. Gus would like you to come and sort it out.'

Hortensia sighed slightly. 'I expect he's drunk ... It's one of his weaknesses. That's really why he's supposed to be away for a year abroad. He's in a special non-alcoholic pension in Switzerland, run by friends, where he can do his painting. He should never have called back.' With her usual dignified mien, Hortensia returned to them all and persuaded Algy to go back to their own flat, assuring everyone that he had a very quick recovery rate.

The next morning, when the whole nightmarish episode had been dispersed and both Horty and Gus had gone off to work for another Monday morning, Milly stood there surveying the mound of clearing up she had been left. Please God, there would never again be another meeting quite like this. It was going to take her all day to get the bathroom back to normal, and the bath

160

would always have a faint shading of rainbows.

She turned towards her bucket and scrubbing brush. Was she destined to be one of the eternal charwomen of life? Then, just as she was feeling at her very lowest – the doorbell rang.

Don't say it was Hawkesly again – she just didn't feel she could bear to see him, ever, and now her heart quite bled for Horty having to cope with him. Little do we know of what other human beings put up with in secret.

When she opened the door she was surprised to see Hewy standing there. He looked bright and normal in the morning sunshine, his face shining and clean-shaven, his neat striped grey suit immaculate. The perfect answer to any millionairess.

'Hewy! Back again already after the terrible debacle? What's happened? Don't say Minny left her powder compact in the conservatory?'

He laughed and shook his head. 'She's not that careless, Milly. I just called to see how you'd gone on with old Algy. If Minny Dee hadn't been there, I'd ...'

'Yes?' She waited eagerly. 'You'd ...?'

'Oh never mind. What a performance it was ... He's noted as being a bit of a tearaway, always has been. I met him and Horty when I was on the way here. She was just going to see him off at the railway station. He looked as right as a trivet. She was the one who looked under the weather! Apparently she was getting him sent back to his "cure" straight away.

'Meanwhile I'm going to call in on Arthur while I'm here, about some textile designs.'

There was a short silence then he said hastily: 'D'you fancy coming out with me for a snack later? Arty was saying last night you've started your own classes again with Bresslaw ...?'

'Yes. But if you lot have meetings like yesterday's in this flat very often, I can see it all falling by the wayside again.'

He was genuinely concerned. 'Don't say that ... Get your hat and coat. Let's get away from it all, right now. I can always see Arthur any time. Where shall we go?'

They chose a small ivy-strewn private hotel, open to non-residents, which overlooked the race course and was renowned for its good food. What a change from the day he'd taken her to the awful little café on News Street with its black-and-white check oilcloth on the table in that war-time world that had now vanished. She fell silent with the memory of it all, and what had happened in his digs ...

When the meal was over and they were alone at the hotel entrance, he said: 'I wish we could do this every day, Milly ...' He suddenly pulled her towards him and hugged her gently in his arms – right there, just as they were standing, as if there was only the two of them in the whole universe. Then he kissed her with relentless passion. She felt her whole face throbbing, her eyes fluttering, her mouth accepting, her breasts tingling. But all she did was to remain perfectly silent. Afterwards, she resolutely kept the conversation on trivial, light-hearted things.

She waved him goodbye as they parted without showing a flicker of the deep emotion she felt inside. When would this core of fear deep inside her break and dissipate? This terror of being let down if she trusted him too much? It was no use suffering a broken heart, pining for Hewy, when it was too late. He was a man of the world now, not just 'the boy next door', and she was an independent woman. Yet she was still bound by their shared childhood memories. She would only have herself to blame, whatever she decided . . .

Yet later that day, in the sudden loneliness of her new life of seeming luxury in her own flat and amongst friends with the artistic background she had always sought, she hastily blinked back the tears. Was there after all no real, simple, settled happiness to be found as one grew older and more alone, with past memories still so clear?

Then, like a shaft of sudden sunshine, a vision of Mr Bresslaw's kind face and round bald head with the grey side curls rose before her, as she heard his quiet voice: 'Too old, girl? . . . Nearly twenty-two . . . Forty years younger than me . . . still got plenty of time . . .'

She suddenly realised she had a lot to be thankful for.

And it was brought home to her even more a short while later when to her grief and shock she found that Mr Bresslaw himself had died peacefully in his sleep and her lessons with him were ended.

CHAPTER NINE

The Baby

Hewy Edmundson had been given an ultimatum by his long-standing girlfriend Minny Dee.

'When are we going to get *properly* married, Hewy?'

Hewy twisted about uneasily. It was a factor he refused to face. There was always a niggling feeling of needing to escape the actual deed . . .

He'd met this rich, nineteen-year-old heiress – who was the niece and protégée of the sausage millionaire Herb Sansome – when she was a fairly worldly fifteen-year-old. They'd met quite by chance at a garden party in aid of soldiers during the war when Minny was in charge of the pony rides.

These days she wore a small silver eternity ring given to her Hewy, even though they had no proper engagement contract. Her guardian, Uncle Sansome, realised that unsuitable Hewy Edmundson was her constant beau, but listed Hewy as a non-starter in the wedding-bell stakes. Herb Sansome took his duties towards his niece seriously, feeling bound to make sure that she married into the top bracket before she was twenty-one. Never for one second did he realise the true nature of Hewy's relationship with Minny as she tumbled in and out of bed with him in secret and discussed the finer points of birth control, constantly mentioning Marie Stopes, who was the new leading light on such secret affairs. All this was going on while Uncle introduced her to likely lords of the manor and Hooray Henrys at hunt balls and charity events; and she appeared regularly in the pages of the *Tatler* and *Cheshire Life*, a picture of captivating and unblemished innocence in a cloud of silk organza and diamonds ... ready and waiting for official plunder.

All this was in complete contrast to Milly, whose own love life had been regulated in a more austere fashion right from the start, and birth control meant not Doing It at all ...

A week had passed since her casual outing with Hewy, when she saw him again. He tapped at her sitting room door, a mass of smiles and carrying a huge canvas, which was firmly wrapped up.

'I was wondering if I could leave it in our meeting room, Milly? It's for the next Spring Exhibition, but it needs a few small finishing touches. I know it'll be safe with you. I won't show it to you ... I'm a bit super-stitious about it, but I reckon it's the best one I've ever done.

'D'you fancy coming out again for a meal? I sold three textile designs for a pretty good price yesterday, so I'm in the money. Shall we try another place this time? What about the George and Dragon?'

And so Milly and Hewy began to see each other regularly, easy, friendly outings which nonetheless began to strike deep into her soul – even though it never showed. She appreciated Hewy's company all the more since the loss of Lewis Bresslaw's teaching skills and all the encouragement which had gone with them, along with the fact that she and Hewy had shared so much in the past.

'You should try putting something in the Spring Exhibition yourself, Milly,' he told her one day. 'It's completely open to all, and your work is well up to standard. It would be worth framing one of your water-colours of the garden at Sundower House and trying out. It's got great freedom and individuality. It reminds me of the French Impressionists.'

Milly smiled with pleasure.

She knew she was living a sheltered life these days, away from the hardships of the real world with its perpetual confrontations between government, miners and other low-paid workers in trade unions as they struggled for better conditions, their families hovering on the borders of severe malnutrition and even starvation. And then there were the troubles in Ireland, featured in every newspaper. Oh yes, these things could hardly be ignored ... They lay there like the black side of the moon.

Yet here in Higher Broughton, in this huge, rambling house set in a garden that showed the seasons of nature rather than those of heavy northern industry, it was another world threading like a bright ribbon between all the grime and misery, as she strove to improve her artistic skills and be a credit to Lewis Bresslaw.

One day, when she was showing some of her work to 'Art Fallows' in the top flat, Arthur said, 'Have you ever thought of painting *proper* pictures?'

'Proper ones? What on earth do you mean? They *are* proper ones! What a thing to say ...' Milly's face fell a mile, and she stared at him reproachfully. 'Hewy's even suggested I send one in to the Spring Exhibition.'

'He would,' said Arthur bluntly. 'He's just buttering

you up because he wants a good, reliable place to store all his big canvases. He can't keep them all at the art school in case someone spills a can of turpentine on them or they get gnawed by rats or painted on by someone else. His large stuff is completely different from his small textile pieces and not many people like them. I find them a bit gruesome myself – if the one I happened to see by accident is anything to go by.' Arthur looked at her quizzically. 'Shall I describe it?'

She shook her head hastily. 'No thank you. I never see them. He's very superstitious about that sort of thing.'

'And no wonder!' The light from the window caught a glint of gold from Arthur's ever growing, bushy ginger beard. 'But never mind him – he's quite capable of shifting for himself. What about you, and proper, *saleable* pictures? Hewy's got a bit of a cheek telling you those wishy-washy watercolours will make it to the front ranks of exhibitions. You've got as much chance as a cat in hell. What you need is to get out of your shell and strike out with something really good in oils. And there's no need to glare, Milly. I'm telling you for your own good. It's no good being one of those closet artists who never makes a bean. I know that sort of thing all too well, after moving into the commercial world. You need to make a bit of a splash – something not too outlandish but that will catch the public's eye nonetheless. Summat for their living rooms if it was taken up by a firm and printed. Maybe a picture with a horse on it . . .'

'A horse?' Milly looked amazed. 'I've never tried to draw a horse in my life, Arthur. I just wouldn't know where to start . . .' Her voice trailed away. It wasn't quite true – she had once tried . . .

'Well, now's the perfect time then, isn't it? There's enough of them in the streets. You can't say you've never seen one.' His challenging eyes met hers.

A horse ... As Milly went back to her own room she pondered on what Arthur had said. Was he right? Should she *really* get going with oil paints and canvas and paint horses? She was suddenly reminded of the day at Lymm and the barge horse there, by the canal. She began to hunt through all her stuff amongst piles of folders, watercolour blocks and canvases to find her painting. Eventually, with a gasp of relief, she glimpsed the smallest corner of it, immediately recognising the thick, ivory-coloured rag-paper she'd used on that special day.

The painting was deep down, entirely buried by other, larger works. It was small and simple, yet when she drew it out, the colours were as bright as the day it was painted. She peered at it with narrowed eyes, an excited awareness dawning of its potential for enlarging to an oil painting, using the memories of that day: the large alder tree; clothes drying on a branch close to the moored, brightly painted barge and the noble, heavy dray horse, which rested from its labours beside the grassy towpath; with maybe a child playing nearby with a small dog – for she could draw human beings and animals like dogs quite well.

Without any more ado, she put on her outdoor clothes and collected a small sketch book and three pencils: hard, soft and medium. She planned to set off to study horses in more depth. Grosvenor Square, All Saints, would be a good stopping place because of all the grey, polished granite drinking troughs for horses there, and the seats close by. The easiest option was to ask Gus Bridges if he would give her a lift to All Saints. She knew he was in, since she could hear him moving about in his flat, on his midday break from the art school.

'Yes, of course I'll give you a lift, Milly. Are you going shopping?' Gus looked at her with brotherly affection. These days he was pinned firmly by the talons of Hortensia, and had been ever since Algy had gone back to the continent.

Gus spent an abnormal amount of time in Horty's flat at the moment, but, so far as Milly was concerned, it was having quite a good effect, for Hortensia had mellowed. She often smiled at Milly quite freely. She had become slightly plumper in the face and her dark hair was shortened and shaped to a younger style.

Milly didn't tell Gus about the horses. There was a sort of respectful barrier between them at present.

'I'll drop you off outside Paulden's then?'

She nodded happily.

When he'd gone she walked to the seats near a double set of horse troughs. It was a mild day. It had rained earlier and washed the streets, but now the sun shone brightly on the cobbled setts as she sat there making numerous quick sketches and small studies of horses.

The time just flew by, and it was almost four o'clock before she stopped for good, proud of all the information the careful studying had given her. She was just collecting her things together when, out of the blue, a female voice hailed her cheerfully. It was Minny Dee.

Her appearance was an undeniable show-stopper. She was always wonderfully dressed in expensive fabrics of daringly gaudy colours, and today it was peacock blue with a small hat to match, with one small fluffy feather curled round lightly above her smooth fair hair and arched eyebrows. 'You must be a stickler for punishment, Milly. You'd never catch me sitting in such a public place drawing them – even if I do adore the darling creatures.

'One day you must come round to nunky's place when he's away and I'll show you round his stables. You'd be able to sketch his thoroughbreds. He might even buy the result! Especially if you managed to do something good of his favourite, Northenden Hero.

'I'll ask Hewy to bring you sometime.' She said it with casual confidence. 'I'm away to meet Hewy this very minute. We're off for a spin this afternoon.'

When she'd gone, Milly packed up her things and went to catch a tram back to her flat. As she sat on the top deck she wondered if Minny Dee knew anything of her own regular outings with Hewy. Probably not, for there was nothing much to them except a bond of friendship and a common interest in art. Her heart welled with profound disappointment. Was it the usual pattern for all men to be dallying with two women at the same time? Then her common sense took over. There was a lot of difference between dallying and Doing the Deed. She might even dally with more than one person herself in the future – who could tell?

Just as she was putting the key into her front door, she was met by Gus Bridges coming out of Hortensia's place. Looking rather guilty, he hastily assured her that Horty had wanted him to sort out some special work.

'How did the shopping go? Get anything good?'

She smiled. 'I met Minny Dee.'

'She'd be shopping too, no doubt. Getting ready for her wedding to Hewy. Quite frankly, I think he's a fool to be marrying her in his final year at art school with all his exams pending. They're really man and wife already in some senses ...' Gus murmured the words absent-mindedly, almost to himself, and Milly felt herself stiffening with shocked surprise.

'Getting married? Will it be soon?'

170

'In two weeks at the Registry Office. Her uncle's fuming, but he's allowing it. He's always tried to pretend Hewy didn't exist, but he's finally accepted it. Hewy softened him up – drew an exceptionally fine portrait of the old boy's horse Northenden Hero. A master stroke by Hewy, that. It's probably that huge thing he's got resting over here for the Spring Exhibition.'

Milly felt herself going scarlet. Minny Dee had been stringing her along with all that twaddle about nunky and the horse. What hypocrisy! Especially when Hewy had already trodden the same path.

'You look quite miserable all of a sudden, Milly. Have I said something wrong?' His face brightened. 'Anyway, there is one good piece of news. You're going to be invited to enter for one of this year's admission bursaries to the art school, based on the glowing reference sent in by Lewis Bresslaw just before he died about the high standards of your work. You should be receiving an official letter any day now.'

She looked at him gratefully. 'Will you stop for a cup of tea or anything?'

He shook his head. 'I'd like to, but I have to rush back again. Hortensia will be wondering what's happened. Oh, and by the way, I met Art Fallows a few minutes ago, looking for you. I told him you'd gone shopping.'

When Gus had gone, and she'd made some sardines on toast and a drink, and looked once more at all the work she'd done that day, Milly climbed the stairs to Arthur's small attic studio.

The door was ajar. The place was bathed in silence, with a lingering aroma of Lancashire hotpot.

He was painting a picture of Zeronica. She was in a tomato-red satin dress, her head lifted back in a seductive gesture, her long fingers and painted finger-nails caressing a cigarette in a long, gleaming cigarette holder, while a toy black cat lay across her knees.

'A Craven A cigarettes advert,' explained Arthur, not looking up from his work. 'Nice to see you, Milly. Hast thou thought owt else about Donkey Walloping and such? The horsy scene?'

Zeronica put down her arm and slowly stretched her limbs as she abandoned the pose and stood up. 'You came just as the right time, Milly. I'd almost changed to stone. Which reminds me ... We've got a favour to ask you about the next meeting of the Visualists. I shan't be able to model for them this next time because I have to visit my sick sister down in Croydon and give her a hand with all her children when she gets out of hospital. 'I'll probably be away about two weeks.'

Arthur's face became troubled. 'Do you think you could stand in for her as the model, Milly?' He pushed his work to one side. 'I was talking to Gus and some of the others, and we'd all be extremely grateful ... You'd be fully clothed, of course.'

'I should jolly well hope so, Arthur!' Milly's face broke into a smile. She had never for one second envisaged anything else; especially for a complete novice.

All the same, the reality of posing as a model was the last thing she had ever considered, except perhaps sitting there in an armchair asleep and unaware that she was being drawn. And although she had joked in an accepting way, her brain was already trying to find an escape hatch, especially as she knew only too well what a fiasco the first weekend of the Visualists had proved to be.

Then Arthur smiled at her, his face glowing with

unspoken thanks. 'What a relief if you could just help us out this once, Milly.'

'I do so need the work, Milly.' Zeronica was smiling too. 'I can't afford to turn down even one sitting. I know Arthur is having a bit of luck at the moment, but we live from day to day, almost hour to hour if the truth be known, and what with my sister's illness – all of that is going to be added expense, even the cost of travelling down there . . . You'd be helping me to keep the links of my chain of work.'

'And I'll help you all I can to ensure you submit a really good picture to the Spring Exhibition, Milly, so that it'll be exhibited and sold at some enormous price. How's that?' joked Arthur.

They all smiled at each other and Milly felt a sudden warm glow of comfort from their friendship, and from Arthur being so earnest about helping her to get her work into the Spring Exhibition. It was the least she could do now, to agree to this simple request. After all, it wasn't as if she was going to have to go to some strange art class or a draughty village hall to shiver in the buff.

The weekend meeting of the Post-War Visualists brought in a fuller contingent than ever, including two young girls of no more than fifteen who were introduced by Stewart Kilkraddy, the sculptor.

The only person not there this time was the mainstay of the whole outfit, Algernon Hawkesly, who was still comfortably bedded out in Europe, and exhibiting his intricate ink-work in Paris.

Milly had breathed with relief when she heard he wasn't coming, and wondered if his latest bathtub would be a feast of rainbow hues, and if it would ever be cleaned or, instead, become an artistic gem in its own right. She had slogged and slaved away getting ready for the weekend, with the added gloom of being the model thrust upon her, which she tried not to show, as everyone else seemed extremely enthusiastic, particularly Gus and Hortensia.

She had dressed carefully for the weekend in a long, grey, ankle-length cotton frock chosen from Gus's film-work wardrobe upstairs. It had a very big starched white collar, giving it an old-fashioned, Quaker appearance. She had decided that if she looked like a simple Quaker girl it would not be as easy for them to ask her to undress and become something else ... with the added factor that many artists liked grey and white in their pictures. It was the perfect garb for sitting there on a wooden chair near a window where she could gaze out at he garden at the same time.

After everyone had arrived, there was a formal welcome and general introductions from Gus Bridges. A short message of apology and encouragement was conveyed from the absent Hawkesly, while Hortensia helped Milly to offer refreshments before the real work began.

Milly waited to see if the question of a model would arise but was thankful to find it didn't as most people stayed and talked in groups and displayed their work for discussion, whilst a few others wandered about outside in the thankfully dry weather with their equipment. Others had brought their own small collections of still life to study, such as fruit or onions with a suitable container and a bit of drapery. A new, rather morbid woman with penetrating eyes and dramatic gestures had produced a bunch of dead flowers and a cracked vase which she said signified the end of the world, and would be her finest work.

'As long as the world doesn't finish too soon, Pauline,' observed Arthur Fallowfield cheerfully.

At first there was no sign of Hewy or Minny, but they arrived later on in the morning, with Minny looking her usual glamorous self; although Hewy, in Milly's eyes, appeared to be quiet and withdrawn.

It wasn't until the afternoon that anyone brought up the subject of The Model. It happened just after Kilkraddy's old brown-and-white spaniel had cocked its leg up against a table and left a small, seeping pool on the carpet; whereupon Stewart, believing that the best form of defence was to attack, hastily revived the question of a model. 'As ye can all see, I've two bonny ones wi' me, but it's their weekend off. My Rosanna' sent 'em to keep me on the straight an' narrow whilst she looks after our bairn.' His cadaverous dark face peered around expectantly. He had a Scottish name and a bit of a Scottish accent, but he had never stirred farther north than Leeds in all his life, from his home in Harpurhey.

'Zeronica is unavailable this time,' said Gus, 'but Miss Dawnay is willing to help out if required.'

Everyone gazed lazily at Milly in their afternoon haze of liquid goodwill.

'She looks very well dressed,' said Ralph the boiler man rather pointedly.

There was a few seconds of tactful silence, then, out of the brandy fumes, a new, strident young voice arose. 'I only came here for the model – which one is it?' A stocky, strong-featured student with frizzy blond hair and eyes as sharp and brown as an eel stood up and looked all around the room as Milly put up her hand to reveal herself formally.

He stared at her hard, then said disgustedly: 'Surely

we aren't supposed to deal with all that clothing? I only came for The Life.'

'Well, Tommy White, you'd better go and find The Life somewhere else,' said an angry male voice. It was Hewy's.

Immediately everyone began to shout at once. 'Come off it, Edmundson, the lad's quite right. We didn't come here to do junior art school exercises in costume drawing. We expect a bit more than that from a model, or this whole exercise is a bloody waste of time . . .'

'Where's Gus Bridges . . .? Get him to put it to the vote . . .'

'But what about the lady? Supposing the lady doesn't want to do it? I know my wife wouldn't.'

'Then you shouldn't have one, should you, ya turnip.'

'What's she afraid of? Has she got a wooden leg or summat?'

'My wife wouldn't, either . . .'

'Your wife 'ud never be asked, Barny.'

'I knows this much – my girlfriend Mabel wouldn't touch it with a bargepole . . .'

'What's all the damned fuss about? We never have this trouble in professional circles. Aldina Martinello worked at the art school for nearly half a century, in the nude, with never a squeak . . .'

Milly felt her knees turning to jelly. It almost seemed better to go and strip and lie naked in front of the whole nattering gang rather than suffer all this eternal bickering. Whatever would poor Zeronica have thought? It would never have happened if she'd been here. Milly felt she was letting Zeronica down, but she knew with absolute certainty that the act of displaying her own naked, vulnerable body to all these prying investigative

176

eyes – no matter how noble and dispassionate the reason – was not for her.

'To see or not to see – that is the question,' guffawed an aged buffoon with a pointed beard sitting in the corner.

With passive reluctance, Gus put the whole topic to the vote on a show of hands, and there was a clear majority for the nude model.

There were three abstainers, Gus, Hewy and Arthur. Over twenty people voted in favour, including the two, nubile young models Kilkraddy had brought along. But the other females, including Hortensia and Minny Dee, voted against, for deep in their minds was the knowledge that Millicent Dawnay might well be quite a competitive danger if seen in the raw.

'It is now up to Miss Dawnay as to whether she accepted the verdict,' said Gus. 'She is quite willing to act as a clothed model. Nothing was ever officially stipulated about the state of undress; and in any case, by the time our next meeting comes round, Zeronica will be here.'

Milly hung her head slightly. 'I prefer to stay clothed.' she said in a low, apologetic voice as if she was a worm who had committed the greatest sin on earth.

'Well, *I* am going home!' said the frizzy-haired student imperiously. 'We may as well stay and draw Kilkraddy's dog, for all the good it'll do with her in that grey and white shroud.'

'There's nay wrong with humble doggies, laddy,' growled Kilkraddy. 'And I'm quite willing to offer his services, even though he is apt to scratch himself. Landseer never sniffed at dogs.'

'Even if they sniffed at him,' chortled old pointy beard.

'And if you're so damned clever at complaining about people not wanting to be in the nude,' said Arthur with sudden anger, 'why the hell don't you be the perishing model yourself and get stripped – or don't *you* like undressing either?'

Tommy stared back at Arthur then, with a huge mock sigh, as if he was dealing with a lot of dunderheads, he said: 'All right then. If that's what you want. No one can accuse of me being a hypocrite – except the ladies might not like it . . .'

'I'll find you some swimming trunks,' said Gus hastily.

By tea-time, a peaceful calm had descended as most of the group were absorbed in dealing with the graphic problems of Tommy White's young, well-padded challenging body, with even Milly talking part. He even agreed to pose again the following day so that people could finish off their work properly.

'Or there's the choice of the Quaker Girl,' said Gus.

So Sunday found Milly sitting there on a wooden chair, gazing towards the window. Most of them seemed more polite this time, she thought. But no sooner had she settled comfortably into the pose than she heard some muttered words close by. It was like an angry wasp buzzing round her ear: 'Miss Prissy, the grey disaster, sitting there like a lump of plaster, Titian would turn in his grave . . .'

Did she *have* to put up with such rudeness? Her cheeks burned with anger and she stood up. 'Excuse me. I have to go.'

Gus stared in amazement, and the guilty student came up to her. 'I hope you don't take any of my protests personally, Miss Dawnay. I often say things when I work. One has to make a stand in life . . . Tarrar.' He hurried away.

Looking neither to right nor left, Milly marched out of the room. All the weekend she'd slaved away. She'd been like Patience on a monument. And all she got were cheap insults because she chose not to expose herself to all and sundry.

'Milly, come back! Take no notice. You always get the awkward ones. Surely you know that?' Gus was trying to catch up with her, but she hurried from the house in a rage, the long grey frock flapping round her slim legs, and the stiff white collar showing a slight rain of paint. She strode along lanes, streets, and byways in an angry trance, walking for miles, until she came to a bridge over the canal. By then she had finally cooled down. She was glad she'd left them all to stew. She smiled to herself defiantly, a steely satisfaction filling her heart as she stared across to the huge railway viaducts in the distance. It was a far cry from her painting day at Lymm with Hewy and Gus, but even in the city, canal banks had a lot to offer the artist with their sudden changes of scene as they wove their way across the land. She thought about Arthur nagging her to get a proper oil painting done. Well, at least she'd been hard at work studying horses recently. Maybe it was now time for her to go back to the canal at Lymm and get a fresh impression of the whole scene for her final triumph.

The cobbled road where she was standing was completely deserted as she gazed down at the water. She followed its progress from beneath the darkness of the bridge to where the view ahead freshened out to trees and thick, green grass. The towpath became wider and more interesting once it had left the old brick warehouses and towering chimney stacks behind.

Suddenly something caught her eye. It was an oval shape, the size of a small pillow, floating half-submerged in the distant water . . .

She froze with sudden fright. Oh Lord above! Surely not? She rushed from the bridge and down to the towpath. The bundle was drifting almost in the centre of the canal, yards ahead of her. She could see the loose arm of a small, pale yellow knitted coat and something bright pink. As she got closer, she glimpsed about a quarter of submerged head in a pink bonnet floating face downwards. She looked around helplessly. There wasn't a soul about. She knew she was a poor swimmer, but she tore off her long frock in feverish seconds and plunged into the cold, secretive water. Whatever the state of the small child, it had to be rescued.

Milly just about knew how to keep her nose above water. She prayed to God with all her might that she might reach the baby. Her eyes closed as dark torrents gathered her up, and she prayed once more, that she would not drown. Her only skill was a sideways dog-paddle. It carried her valiantly towards her goal, but as she drew nearer the body always moved in the water so that it was difficult to get a hold.

She began to get tired, and panic bubbled up inside her. The canal was much broader across than she'd imagined when standing on the towpath. Water was blinding her eyes and her nose was choked as she gasped and struggled, and tried to grasp the lengths of clothing which almost lapped her clutching fingers. She must rescue it . . . she *must*. Either that or they'd both sink down together.

Her hands were beginning to go numb when suddenly, like a miracle, the floating mass buffeted against her in a slight eddy of movement and in the distance she was aware of a voice calling her name and the noise of powerful, splashing strokes in the water which drew ever nearer. Then she heard a gasping, spluttering male voice: 'Do exactly as I say, Milly, and I'll get you back to the side.'

'The child . . . The child . . .'

She felt herself being forcefully propelled through the water. She was vaguely aware of being dragged out onto the towpath, lying on her stomach and retching up all the filth of the canal.

'Can you manage to stagger to the car?' said Gus a bit later.

She nodded weakly than glanced towards the water. It was all calm again. The bundle was still floating there. She tried to speak.

'It was a baby doll, Milly. All dressed in children's clothes. The clothes helped it to float. It could have fooled anyone. It fooled me at first.'

On the way back, as the car chugged steadily along, he said: 'For one awful second I thought you were trying to do away with yourself until I saw the small body floating there. I thought it was a child – just like you did.'

The pair of them were in a terrible state. Gus was soaking wet and white with the strain of it all, and Milly was shivering uncontrollably.

'When you walked out on us, Milly,' said Gus when she was safely home, wrapped in a warm blanket and watching him make them both a hot drink, 'I realised you were totally fed up. Something made me follow you in the car from here to try and . . .' He shrugged his shoulders wearily. 'I don't quite know why, but there you are. I just followed you at a distance, then I lost you, close to the canal bridge. Anyway, let's try and forget it. You'll be fine after a good night's sleep.'

In bed that night, Milly lay there feeling deeply

depressed. What a fool she had made of herself. What an idiot to put her life at risk for an old toy doll wrapped in a bundle of clothes. Whatever must Gus have *really* thought of her? And supposing she *had* been trying to commit suicide – just imagine all the trouble there would have been, and how the whole of the art group might have been involved in some awful police investigation because of the way she had suddenly walked out on them during the modelling session. And as for rescuing the baby ... She turned in the bed and curled up in a ball, sobbing her heart out. The baby ... The baby that never was ... Oh how she longed for a baby of her very own, in a proper, peaceful, ordinary marriage. A child of love. Was it ever, ever to be? If only she and Hewy ... If only ...

She blinked tearfully into the damp pillow slip. Why was he so determined to desert her? She thought of his past accusations of prudery and wept again. Such deep-held convictions didn't seem to matter when it came to Minny Dee ... The course of true love never did run smooth ...

The following day, Gus greeted her with a cheerful smile, and all he said was: 'It was some day, yesterday, Milly. Yes. It was certainly Some Day ...' His forehead wrinkled into a thoughtful frown.

It was never mentioned again, but later in the week Milly took hold of her sorrows and brooding, and walked back to the spot where it had all taken place. Was she being stupid to harp on it? She hardly dared to look over at the canal when she reached the canal bridge again, but, opening her eyes wide, she forced herself to scan the water. There was a barge moving slowly along, pulled by a horse from the towpath. It was a quiet, sunny day and there wasn't a sign of the bundle still floating there. She stared at the scene, then, with a quiet, sad smile, she made her way back home.

'You seem to be keeping very quiet all of a sudden,' said Arthur jokingly to Milly, one day towards the end of the week. 'Anyone'd think you'd been going through a bad time since you walked out of that weekend art set-up. You really stirred it up, didn't you? I doubt if they'll have any more of 'em.' He had invited her to share a can of soup with him, and news of Zeronica. 'How's your own work going on? The oil painting for the Spring Exhibition?'

'I haven't actually started it yet, Arthur. I've got it all planned out, but –'

'But me no buts, Milly; you'll need to get a move on. You've got to allow at least three months for the oil paint to dry out properly.'

Milly could see how right he was as she worked with more and more concentration on her layout for the oil painting, and showed him her preliminary sketches and compositions, until by the end of the two weeks whilst Zeronica was away she was like putty in his hands; for Arthur seemed determined that her picture of 'Horses by an Alder Tree' should be one of the pictures to be selected.

'Just imagine, Milly, if yours got through, and that mysteriously secret canvas of Hewy's got rejected . . .'

'What an *awful* thing to say, Arthur! I'd never want that!'

'You must have changed a bit since your young days then . . .'

Milly blushed to the roots of her hair. 'I was only a child then. Art is above such things.'

'You can bet your life it isn't,' said Arthur craftily.

'Well it is for me, anyway, Arthur. All I want to do is to produce the most satisfying and pleasing picture possible – and all my own work.'

'With my constant advice, Millicent. Don't forget that. No one ever got very far without a bit of expert advice. I mean, take these sketches lying here, based on your own barge picture from Lymm – it's clearly no use having just *one* horse for your larger oil painting; you'll need two. If I were you I'd keep the original one in the background shade of the tree, then I'd find a good picture by George Stubbs and carefully copy one of his horses to put in your field.'

Milly was horrified. 'I couldn't do that! It wouldn't be *me.*'

Arthur scowled at her irritably. 'What do you mean, *you*? Of course it'll be you if it's in your picture. It's almost like saying Art Fallows isn't me, because my proper name's Arthur Fallowfield.' He knew there was no real logical link, but he was getting more and more irritable over the whole affair. Trust a woman to niggle her way into some sort of false predicament, by dragging in unimportant aspects. He began to wish Zeronica was home again, quite forgetting that she too was a woman. He was getting completely fed up with devoting so much time to Milly's trivial picture, even though he knew it was all for his own gratification in seeing it make it to the walls inside the Mosely Street Art Gallery, which he himself had not yet accomplished. Oh how he wished he'd never got involved!

'Look, Milly. Stop being so damned negative. If there's one set of things I know about, as a commercial artist, it's colour, composition and dramatic effect. And as for not wanting to copy a Stubbs horse – how in heaven's name do you think he became so good? It was because he taught himself from an early age from others who'd copied from the old masters, plus his own anatomy drawings of dead horses, which have been studied by famous artists throughout the world.' He glared at her with triumph. 'If you ask me, Milly Dawnay, you're getting a bit above yourself, not wanting to have one of *his* horses in your picture.'

Meekly, Milly finally agreed to his suggestions as he altered the whole of her original composition and even found her what he considered to be the best Stubbs horse to put in the picture.

'Believe me, Milly, it'll be a winner.'

But it no longer mattered to her. All the joy of the work had vanished, and although she worked diligently and neatly transposed the whole altered picture to canvas with careful precision all her own spontaneity had been blotted out.

Six weeks later, when the picture was finished and Arthur and Zeronica were gazing at it with awe and approval, Arthur stroked his beard with joy and said: 'It's absolutely first-rate, Milly. A real stunner. The gloss on that horse's coat is absolutely terrific. The planes of light and shade on its body – pure Stubbs. He would be proud of you, just like we are.'

'What about the barge then, Arthur?' It was the only bit he hadn't tried to alter.

'Quite good, for someone like you. The whole canvas is admirable and worthy of any professional artist. It'll get you in, Milly. You mark my words.'

She was beginning to hate Arthur these days; beginning to notice his superficial, gushing turns of phrase. And as for the actual picture – she felt like thrusting it into the nearest bonfire.

'Leave it with me and I'll get it suitably framed for

you,' he said now, glad that at last it was all going to be over and that he had some more commissions for mustard advertisements.

'Do what the devil you like with it, Arthur. Quite candidly, I'm just fed up with the whole lot. I shall certainly never, *ever* enter for the Spring Exhibition again.'

'Of course you will, Milly darling,' said Zeronica soothingly. 'You've just got tired out with all the work of it at the moment. Just like I was when I got back from my sister's. But there is one important little thing to remember, dear – you haven't signed it.'

'I have!' said Milly indignantly. 'It's down there amongst the buttercups.'

They both peered at the picture then Arthur looked at her sharply. 'Is it a joke?'

'It is not a joke, Arthur. I can't take *all* the praise for George Stubbs' efforts.'

Zeronica peered at the buttercups again into a rather dark little patch, then stared at her in alarm. 'Georgina Stubbs! Milly, are you *sure* that you want this to be your signature?'

'I can't think of anything better,' said Milly between tightened lips.

'You sound really mad. I hope you aren't trying to blame Arthur or anything. He was only trying to help you.'

Milly softened. 'I know. I'm sorry. It's just as you say; I've got over-tired.'

'– And you couldn't have done it at all without your own original studies in the first place to base it on, it's just that Arthur wanted you to have a real taste of success.'

Milly nodded humbly. She knew she was making a bit

of a fool of herself. Then, thanking them quietly, she left the wretched picture with them and hurried downstairs to her own flat.

Nevertheless, when she finally filled in her application form, she wrote: Georgina Stubbs, c/o Milly Dawnay.

Early the following year, Milly was stunned to receive a communication addressed to Miss Georgina Stubbs congratulating her on her painting being accepted for hanging in the 1921 Spring Exhibition. And on the very same day, Hewy came round to tell her that his own offering had also got in.

Hewy was aware she'd sent in a picture based on the Lymm outing, but he didn't know the half of it – or even that it wasn't in her proper name, for he had been far too busy with his own catastrophic marriage to Minny Dee.

And Milly had never known what *his* actual picture was like, because she'd been far too busy getting herself ready for her new role of what was termed a 'mature' full-time student at the art school, where she had won an admission bursary, much to Gus Bridges' delight. Hortensia had confined *her* delight to guarded congratulations.

And as for Zeronica and Arthur, it was a question of sending them a postcard to let them know the news about the picture, for they were away at Zeronica's sister's whilst Arthur was being interviewed for some work to do with posters for the London Underground. Milly blessed her lucky stars they were not in Manchester – for her relationship with Arthur had never been quite the same after she had signed her name Georgina Stubbs.

Previews of Spring Exhibitions were quite lavish affairs, attended by the Lord Mayor and Manchester dignitaries as well as the artists, many art critics and members of the press, along with others – including Gus and Horty and countless known and unknown faces from the smart sets, all sipping their drinks and looking at their catalogues.

'Would you care to come with me, Milly?' said Hewy. 'My own relatives won't be going until later.'

She nodded. She hadn't even mentioned it to any of hers.

She would have liked to have asked him if Minny would be there, but thought better of it. She hadn't seen Minny once since Hewy had married, and he never mentioned her. It was all very strange.

Milly put on her best black chiffon dress, threaded with silver and gold, with flowing, transparent sleeves. It was second-hand, found by chance in a white elephant sale, and once she had washed it carefully in warm soapsuds it had come to life like some film star's garb. It went perfectly with her small crystal earrings and velvet cloak. Decked out in her finery, she waited to meet Hewy.

He gave an inward gasp when he saw her standing at the door of the flat.

'You look wonderful, Milly.'

'You too, Hewy. I hope we enjoy it all. I feel quite nervous.'

'No need to – Gus and Horty will be there, for a start. It'll all be very civilised. Not a bit like *our* artistic gatherings in Sundower House!'

When they entered the galleries their names were ticked off by a smiling woman in navy blue silk. They signed the visitors' book and accepted a glass of wine and a programme each. It was a large show, and Milly was soon lost in the magic of it all as she and Hewy drifted away on different paths.

After a while, with a sudden shock, she came face to face with her own painting. She was suddenly embarrassed and was glad she was alone. She could hardly believe she had actually painted it and that it was hanging so prestigiously in this mellow light amongst such ornate surroundings; hardly credit that it appeared so accomplished and professional.

She gazed at the catalogue: 'Horses by an Alder Tree ... Georgina Stubbs'. She blushed at the number of guineas Arthur had told her to put for its price.

She wandered on amidst polite voices and knowledgeable opinions bursting from waves of subdued chatter, against a scented background of chinking wine glasses.

Then another, quite familiar-looking oil painting caught her attention: 'Barges on the Bridgewater Canal'. She looked at the name and could hardly believe her eyes: Georgina Stubbs! Surely it was some terrible joke? Then, as she moved on again, she came across two more paintings, both with canal background, and both by Georgina Stubbs. She felt like fainting.

She was in such a trembling state that she hardly noticed the small, irate crowd who had gathered in front of a large painting in the next gallery. It was in a very modern style: an abstract geometrical pattern shaded in overlapping colours. It was called Portrait of Minny. Someone had just thrown a tomato at it, and been escorted from the gallery by two hefty-looking attendants, whilst other people stood about, arguing.

'No wonder it had summat chucked at it,' said a gruff voice, followed by a high-pitched shriek: 'Minny must be devastated by a picture like that, poor dahling . . .'

'It's an insult to humanity . . .'

'They say her husband did it . . .'

'He won't be *that* for long at this rate . . .'

'Fancy wasting a martyr on it . . .'

'There's never a dull moment when you come to these things.'

'There certainly isn't!' bawled another angry female voice. 'Especially if – like me – you've found a blatant forgery of your own pictures hanging on these very walls!

'I want to state here and now that number 78 in this year's catalogue – "Horses by an Alder Tree" – has nothing whatsoever to do with me, even though it's signed with my name. The horse in it is a shameful copy of one of my famous namesake's horses, and the price this impostor is asking for such rubbish is *outrageous*. I shall be bringing up this whole matter of forgery with the Arts Management Committee.'

Already Milly could see that the true Georgina was being surrounded by interested newspaper reporters with their notepads open and their pencils poised. The woman was large and elderly with flashing indignant eyes and a deep fringe of black hair. She wore an oatmeal-coloured hessian tunic and scarlet-beaded moccasins, and her false teeth were a bit loose.

Milly was almost sinking to the floor with dread, when she felt a firm, steady grip on her elbow. It was Hewy.

'Have you seen what happened to my Work of Art?' he said with calm bitterness.

She nodded sadly. 'Have you heard what's happened to mine? That voluble dame over there says I'm an impostor and my picture's a forgery . . . I never in heaven's name thought there'd actually be a painter here called Georgina Stubbs. I only called myself that in a fit of pique because of Arthur interfering so much with my work and making me so mad.'

They both stared at each other miserably, then Hewy said: 'Come on, let's beat it.'

Like prisoners on the run, they fled outside into the misty Manchester air.

CHAPTER TEN

Naples Lodge

Milly lay wide-eyed in bed, in her flat. The night was dragging by. The moon cast sudden shadows then brightness in a wind-wracked sky, as she thought about Hewy and wondered what to do.

It had been nearly three am when she finally arrived back. He'd taken her to his home at Bramhall, assuring her they would be alone, as Minny had vanished to France on sudden impulse to visit Algy Hawkesly at some small place in Côte d'Or. Hawkesly had extended an open invitation to all members of the Post-War Visualists to visit him at any time – an invitation which had brought an expression of cynical disbelief to Hortensia's face, for she knew all too well how unreliable her errant husband was. It was a rare opportunity, not to be taken up by many, for such journeys were completely out of the bounds of ordinary Manchester life, especially that of penniless artists.

Milly had refused when Hewy first suggested going home with him, after fleeing the Spring Exhibition, but eventually she agreed to keep him company. They could have come back to her place in Higher Broughton, but it would have meant meeting all the rest of them in a sort of post-mortem. She knew both Hewy and herself would have been enveloped in sympathy, and she wouldn't have been able to stand it, especially from Arthur and Zeronica.

It was still early evening when they reached the beautiful Victorian villa set foursquare in its own neatly designed gardens. Hewy led her along an avenue of beech trees, then through the wrought-iron gate to an Italian-style front door flanked by small marble columns.

'No need to look so apprehensive, Milly. We'll be entirely alone.' His face had set to a hard mask. 'Min saw to it that all the staff were dismissed before she set off for France.'

Milly went cold with shock. What a terrible thing to do. Only a real hate could have produced such enmity . . .

They went inside to the small drawing room. It had delicate electric wall-lights with pink glass shades shaped like hyacinth bells; and two narrow silver vases with swirling leafy patterns decorating a light oak bureau. It was all very modern.

They sat together on a velvet sofa, and gradually the whole story of Hewy's awful mistake came out.

'She's still just a girl, Milly. She has no intention of settling down. I thought it would be different once we were properly spliced, but she's a complete liability and spends her money like water. It's an awful situation, really, because I'm the one with no reliable income until I leave art school. She's the one who's made the running. I admit she's twisted me round her little finger and it's been a complete disaster . . .'

Milly sat there silently, her brain in a whirl – and caution nagging away in the background. Hewy seemed to want to have his cake and eat it. What a paradise he was in, living here in the countryside of Bramhall, so close to the rambling hall dating back over 700 years, with its patterned facade of black timber criss-crossing over white plaster, and its panoramic setting of lordly trees and ornamental lakes. What a contrast to the smoke-blackened viaducts of Stockport and places like Hatching Street, where her own and Hewy's childhood roots lay. How lucky he was to be living in this bijou mansion, married to a beautiful young woman with pots and pots of money. Surely it was every man's dream?

She glanced at his handsome face. She knew quite well the magnetism that lay there. What traps men and women laid for themselves ... She felt his shoulder leaning more and more towards her, and she tried to sit entirely upright. Smelt the faint scent from his clothes of cigar smoke and brilliantine, knew that she longed to nestle closer and console him but dared not – for both their sakes.

'It was the painting of her that finally did it. She sat for me, but she thought it was going to be an orthodox portrait and there was a hell of a row when she demanded to see it. She said I was completely insane! What a statement, coming from a woman who's rushed off to visit an elderly madman like Hawkesly. I just can't make head or tail of her and never will ...'

He suddenly moved away from Milly and stood up. 'Enough of me. I'll find us something to eat and drink, while you tell me how things are going with you. It seems strange to think you'll just be starting at the art school when I'm leaving. You've done marvellously well, Milly. But then, you always were good. I was quite jealous of you when I was a boy.'

'And I was jealous of you ...'

194

They both smiled.

After their meal he began to show her photographs of himself and Min. Clearly, he was still obsessed by his young wife and still in love with her. Milly saw page after page of society life: hunt balls, champagne, horses, aeroplanes, racing cars and well-dressed, high-spirited, smiling people. What worlds away it was from most people's plodding daily toil.

'The trouble is,' said Hewy, as if reading her thoughts, 'Min expects our life to be like surface froth the whole time, and it can't go on. We shall destroy each other.'

He looked at Milly calmly and for some perverse reason a streak of anger rose within her. Why was he telling her all this? What on earth did he expect her to do about it? She began to fidget and wanted to get back to her flat, almost as if a warning light was shining.

'I really think I'll have to go, Hewy. I do hope things will work out better than you say. After all, you haven't been married very long, and although I'm not married myself, I'm sure things will take a turn for the better. Maybe a dose of Algernon Hawkesly will make her see some sense.'

Her anger died as quickly as it had risen, and she decided she wouldn't leave, not just yet ... Hewy put more logs on the fire and they sat in its warm glow, staring at flickering shadows in peaceful silence and becoming drowsier and drowsier.

By now they were completely worn out by all the problems of that day, and it was to Milly's amazement that she woke some time later to find herself lying in Hewy's arms. He was fast asleep.

She lay there wonderingly, not wanting to disturb him. It seemed so right for them to be together at this moment – just as if it had always been this way and always would. But as she looked at the softly ticking clock and realised they were halfway through the night and saw again her rich surroundings in another woman's home, she knew she was deluding herself.

Hewy woke with a sudden start and stood up. 'I went out like a light.'

'So did I, but I'll have to get back, Hewy.'

'Couldn't you wait till morning?' He yawned and stretched and gazed at her pleadingly. 'Stay in one of the spare bedrooms. You'll come to no harm. We could set off early, after breakfast.'

She shook her head. She dared not . . .

'We should never have fallen asleep. I should have returned, hours ago.'

Reluctantly, he agreed to take her back. As they got into the car he said: 'Is it always going to be like this, Milly? All we ever seem to do is avoid each other in the end.'

She didn't reply – how could she? And how could he, a newly married man, say such a thing?

When they finally reached her flat, they crept in quietly.

He looked tired and white-faced. She offered to make him a drink but he refused. There was a dry ring to his voice: 'I'll go back and sleep all this off with a bottle of Bell's. It seems to be the fate of most men . . .'

He hesitated, then kissed her on the cheek and went.

What a relief to be alone at last, to try and get things sorted out in her mind, but above all to sleep in peace and wake to a better day, led by the blustery shadows now crossing that silvery moon . . .

Then, like the guttering of a candle, she was lost to oblivion.

Brilliant sunshine met her the next day, piercing the slight openings in the curtains as she awoke to great clatterings at the door. It was the window cleaner, demanding payment for cleaning all the windows of Sundower House.

Hastily, she got up, put on her blue quilted satin dressing grown, and faced him. He was being completely obstreperous. 'You may not be aware of it, lady, but I've cleaned every single pane of glass in this establishment for the last two bloody months without ever a penny piece being paid.

'Oh yes, it's very convenient, isn't it, for Mr Hawkesly to be abroad at an unknown address and everyone else to be elsewhere whenever I call? But this time I've just 'ad it up to 'ere, so don't blame me if the windows all goes to rack and ruin and lands up wi' bricks hurled through 'em – cos I just shan't be around, lady, and that's a fact. I'm not a man to be trifled with. I've got an honest working life to keep up, as well as a wife and nine kids.' He glared at her. 'Not like *some* . . .'

Hastily Milly went to the small metal cash-box in the bureau and drew out the required money. She stood there firmly whilst he wrote out a receipt in copy-ink pencil, wetting its point with a stream of spit as he went along, to a flourishing Received With Thanks, H.T.W. Pilson, on a torn piece of lined paper from a battered red exercise book dragged from his jacket pocket.

Milly frowned to herself. She was finding that there were more and more demands to her personally for payment, but when she'd mentioned it to Gus Bridges once, he'd merely told her not to worry – just to hand them Hawkeslys' main address in Switzerland, and tell them he'd be back soon.

'There's nothing anyone can do about it, Milly. Even Hortensia says the same. She's completely washed her hands of him, when it comes to paying all his personal bills and debts. But don't worry . . . it'll all work out in the end. He is a very wealthy man. It's like a bottomless gold mine, really, made by the last generation. It's just a question of catching him at the right moment and pinning him down.'

Milly peered gloomily into the small black tin cash-box. The money this time was actually her own. She knew she couldn't have faced the hassle of dealing with the window cleaner and his veiled threats if she hadn't paid. But if it happened again, she saw herself getting into proper debt – for like everyone else, she had no real guarantee of ever being paid back by Hawkesly. Her mind began to fill with terrible thoughts: supposing Hawkesly was so besotted with Minny Edmundson née Dee that they became the biggest spenders in all the world and left Sundower House and its inmates to stew for ever, surrounded by his creditors?

The more she thought of it, the more terrified she became, for hadn't she taken on the flat on the understanding that she was a live-in housekeeper? And she had to admit that until now she had been having a fairly comfortable time of it compared to normal people, in these days of uncertainty.

Yet yesterday's episode at the Spring Exhibition had set a different tone to her whole life. It had caused an awkwardness with Arthur and Zeronica, which was complicated by Hewy's row with Minny, and Minny's chase after Algy Hawkesly . . . And on top of it all, she was due to be a student herself at the art school, with Hortensia and Gus Bridges still working there, whilst their clandestine affair was being carried out right next door to her. What a fiasco . . .

The thought of it all overwhelmed Milly so much that all she wanted was immediate escape. Oh for the simplicity of a normal, humble, single life in some small, manageable lodgings of her own – though not like that last awful place, which had made her move so thankfully to the life she was in at present.

But was a single life *really* what she wanted? Sometimes these days, on the occasions when she heard from her old friend Babsy Bright, who was now a thoroughly laden down mother with numerous young children, she felt a deep pang of envy and thought that perhaps she was missing out on something – yet at other times she breathed with relief that she had never been trapped into such a path so early. For there was nothing so bad as being a penniless mother, without any freedom of choice or true independence, and half one's youthful energy already evaporated. And yet . . . Babsy looked exceedingly well on it and all her brood were thriving. Perhaps it was just the luck of the draw . . .

The straw that broke the camel's back came some weeks later. Hortensia appeared at Milly's front door. 'I need to speak to you urgently and in complete secrecy, Milly. I hate asking people for help, but you're the only one I can turn to. Please say right now if you want me to go. I shall quite understand.' Horty's face was a picture of dark-eyed misery.

'Come in, for goodness' sake. I'll do all I can to help.'

Milly put the kettle on, and as they sat there some minutes later, sipping tea, yet another tale of woe began to emerge.

'I never realised it would happen so late in life. You've probably realised I'm not quite looking myself. I'm starting to go through the change. It's a terrible time, Milly, so full of ups and downs. One minute you see a period, the next you don't.'

Milly nodded.

I'm worried about my job at the art school, too. I don't want to have to leave to make way for someone younger, and what with Algy always being so unpredictable, I try to be as independent as possible. The truth is, Milly, I'm very ill at the moment . . . very ill indeed. My nerves are in shreds and I don't know which way to turn. I'm quite sick with fear. I doubt if I shall even keep this cup of tea down without starting to vomit.' Tears of panic and frustration began to run slowly down Hortensia's cheeks.

It was a great shock for Milly to see the worldly, autocratic Hortensia looking so helpless and vulnerable. Normally she was as cool and self-contained as a clam.

'I don't want to admit it even to myself, Milly, but I saw my doctor a week ago and he seems to think I may be pregnant. I just can't believe it after all these years . . .'

Milly shivered slightly. She thought of Algy hitting the high time abroad with Minny Edmundson, then she cheered a bit. Maybe this news about his wife would bring him back home and sober him up enough to pay all his bills instead. Maybe her fears about him were unfounded.

She smiled comfortingly, but in truth her mind was too full of her own problems to be burdened with someone else's. For she was already trying to work out how she could move away from it all. Even so, she suppressed her own preoccupations, and tried to look pleased.

'What a nice surprise, if it's true. You and Algy will

have to make lots of new plans. It could be really exciting. I quite envy you . . .'

'Algy! What on earth do you mean? How could it possibly be Algy's child when he's never here?'

'Y-you don't mean it's . . .?' The light suddenly dawned on Milly and she saw the whole picture. No wonder Gus Bridges had been to Horty's flat so often. She knew that Hortensia had always had her eye on him from the flashes of jealousy she'd shown whenever Gus paid any attention to Milly.

Hortensia stared at her askance. 'Not *him* . . .! Surely you haven't been thinking Gus and I . . .?' Her voice faded and the cool, disdainful look returned. 'You obviously don't know much about *his* history . . .'

'His *history*?' Milly looked puzzled.

'His time in the last war when he was in the film unit, and came back early to the art school. He was ill during the war with a germ which left him completely sterile. It was a tragedy, really, because he had got married just before he became ill, and his wife left him because she wanted to be with a man who could have children. The strange thing is, she refuses to go through with a divorce. I suppose it's her way of getting back at him by making it impossible for him to put the whole miserable business behind him.'

Milly was so staggered she hardly heard the next few words.

'No . . . if this is going to turn out to be a pregnancy, the father will definitely be Art Fallows.' Hortensia's mouth was now set in a grim line.

'Art Fallows . . .?' Milly gaped. 'There must be some mistake! You don't mean Zeronica's Art Fallows – Arthur Fallowfield – surely? I honestly just can't believe –' She bit her lip. She was saying too much. It only

201

showed how little she knew of what anyone else was up to in this place, and the sooner she left, the better.

'I couldn't quite believe it either, at first, but he's the only person I've cohabited with in recent years since Algy and I went our own ways, even though I'm still Mrs Hawkesly by right.

'My affair with Arthur started some years ago, in a casual way, before Zeronica went to live with him. Then we slept together again when Zeronica was away – almost an old-times-sake sort of affair, which I felt would be quite safe due to the change. I thought I was safe by now, at my age . . .'

She gave a slight smile. 'You look really stunned, Milly. It's all part of human nature . . .'

Milly tried to compose herself. She still couldn't believe that Arthur would have been such a complete two-timer and so unfaithful to hard-working, patient Zeronica. How little some people – including herself – knew of each other's secret ways . . . But there again, Arthur always had been a bit of a deceiver, and he'd been quite ruthless over her own picture in the Spring Exhibition.

She tried to blot Horty's words from her mind, for after all, it wasn't her business. And what would happen once Zeronica found out that Horty was pregnant with Arthur's child? She turned away as a rueful smile crept to her lips. How different from her own cautious ways – she couldn't even bring herself to stay with Hewy for part of the night, quite honourably, in a bedroom in his wife's house whilst the woman was absent.

'Of course I pray I'm wrong. I'm not *absolutely* certain, but if it *is* true, I shall have the child and make the best of it. I wouldn't want to have it adopted or anything. And that was why I wanted to ask your help, Milly.'

Milly felt a rising panic: whatever next?

'I wanted to ask you to help me out, and when the baby's born, to be its nanny whilst I'm working – for I'm pretty sure I'm right. I shall be seeing this doctor friend again, in complete confidence, later today. That's why I needed to see you so desperately. The bare truth is, I have no one to turn to – not even relatives.'

Milly felt dizzy. What a thing to ask of her! 'I can't just promise all that this very second, Hortensia. You said yourself you weren't *quite* sure. It could be that you're ill and tired from all the trouble you've had with Algy and just need to rest more. And I couldn't possibly be your nursemaid because I'll be starting at the art school myself as a student . . .'

Milly's voice faded as she considered her own predicament. She was due to start at the art school, yet she had no proper income to keep going if she suddenly left Sundower House. How would she be able to pay for digs anywhere else, and where would her day-to-day cost of living come from once she had left this place?

The following day she was feeling worse than ever about it all and hardly dared to face Hortensia, even going so far as to wait until Hortensia was out of the house before she ventured from behind the locked doors of her own flat, in case Hortensia should catch her yet again to embroil her in some future domestic plan based on Hortensia's own survival. Milly realised that although Hortensia now treated her on equal terms and even used her to confide in, deep down, Miss Millicent Dawnay was a small, expendable ship in the night as far as the good ship Hortensia was concerned.

Then, to her alarm, her front doorbell began to ring. It rang and rang . . .

She hesitated . . . Then, bracing herself for the worst, she went to unfasten the door and greet the next lot of fate. Hewy was standing there.

'Whatever's up, Milly? You look as if you're peering out of a cave!' He was as cheerful as the bright day itself. 'I just had to let you know . . .' His deep, violet eyes sparkled with joy. 'I've landed myself a top designing job at MCPA. They print original designs for fabrics all over the world. And that's not all – they want me to act as a sort of mentor for other artists of talent and to encourage them to submit their work for consideration. Can I come in?' He gazed at her with enthusiastic expectancy.

She nodded and stood aside for him. 'I can't quite take it all in. What wonderful news . . . I'm truly glad for you. I'm sure Min'll be delighted too. In fact, everybody will. Has she come back from Europe yet?'

His face clouded slightly. 'Never mind *her*, it's *you* I've come to see. Don't you understand? It's you I can help to get a foothold in the commercial world. It'll be a step towards the hard earning of regular cash for your talents – and the sooner you can do that, the better. You could well decide to leave this place for good now you're going to work as a full-time student.'

A thread of cold shot through her. Was he a mind-reader? How could he possibly have guessed she was wanting to escape from this impossible trap?

'Stop looking so alarmed, woman. Whatever's got into you?' His tone turned milder and more affectionate: 'I'm saying all this, Milly, so you can be thinking about some artwork ideas over the next few months.' He looked at her solemnly and said softly, 'Always remember The Blue Cornflower . . .'

Her face lightened into a smile. 'What little demons we were . . .'

Maybe this meeting with Hewy would change the whole pattern of the dilemma she was in.

'... It's just that it's a bit of a shock. I wasn't even expecting to see you – and, as far as the other idea about my submitting work to the Calico Company goes, well ... it would be almost a dream come true, but I've hardly done any, compared to you. And what with living here free, and being paid to look after this place, I can't see things getting any better. It's far more complicated here than I ever imagined ...'

He looked at her knowingly. 'You can say that again. The worst thing you can do is to live in an artistic colony in a place like this run by an absent and unreliable landlord. Anyone could tell you that.' Then he added: 'Which reminds me: I shall ask Arthur, too, if he'd like to put any designs forward. He's a dead cert for commercial work ...

'What's the matter? Have you suddenly gone off Arthur, or what? You looked quite ill when I mentioned his name. What's he been up to?'

She shook her head in embarrassed silence. Far be it from her to talk about Arthur, after what Hortensia had revealed ...

'I think I might look around for another place to stay, Hewy, in due course. You were quite right to broach it. My job here – trivial as it might seem to some – just wouldn't tie in with my art school studies. But the chance of being able to afford somewhere else seems pretty hopeless ...'

'Come and live with me for a bit, then.'

At first she thought she hadn't heard him properly.

'I said – why not come and live with me for a bit until you finally get settled, Milly? Come and be *my* house-keeper ...' He was smiling at her cheekily.

'Hewy! How could you? It's a serious matter!'

'I am serious, Milly. Deadly serious. I received a letter from Min today. She says she's not coming back. She's met some rich playboy – a pal of Hawkesly's ...' His face went as gloomy as sin but he tried to gloss it over, adding with childish bravado: 'So why shouldn't you come and be housekeeper, seeing as she sacked all the servants when she went?' He took her hand impulsively and held it in an urgent grip.

'Please come back with me, Milly. I *need* you ... You're the only person who really understands me. I'll treat you absolutely honourably. You won't be living like a loose woman or anything. You'll be the straightforward housekeeper of Naples Lodge. You'll have your own small flat and be able to employ your own choice of useful maid and daily cook, until the mistress arrives back home – if and when that ever comes to pass ...'

At first she could hardly take in the offer. It seemed so absolutely ludicrous and unbelievable: her, Milly Dawnay, going to be the housekeeper to wealthy-through-marriage Hewy Edmundson, her childhood rival. In a way it went against the grain, for whatever anybody thought, a housekeeper was a paid servant and lower in status than the master of the house, and no way did she consider herself inferior to Hewy.

She stared at him and saw the pleading look still there. It was quite genuine and she realised that at present Hewy and she were equals. But would it always be so, if she became his employee, paid from his and his wife's income?

'I don't think it would work, Hewy. Especially with you starting in your new, highly paid post with MCPA and me going to art school. I'd hardly be doing much to warrant being employed as a housekeeper.'

'Leave me to decide that, Miss Dawnay. But please ... oh please, Milly, give it a try. It's you who'll be saving my whole career. I need someone like you to be there to boost my morale. We'll be a good support for each other. A man with an erring wife is in a poor way – whatever his financial circumstances.'

'So is a woman with an erring husband,' said Milly bitterly as she remembered about Art Fallows and Hortensia and the plight of innocent Zeronica.

When he'd gone she sat there silently for ages, then with a sudden spurt of forced determination she decided to take the bull by the horns and accept his offer. "Never look back" thudded her brain ... "Take this chance and make the most of it."

Two days later, still in the same frame of mind, she hastily packed a suitcase – enough for an interim stay, and to show him that she was seriously accepting his offer. Then she set off to Bramhall, her heart in a surge of flowing excitement, yet not daring to consider now what the future might hold.

The walk was long and tedious from the bus to the long avenue of beeches which led to the small marble columns of the entrance to Naples Lodge.

She could see smoke curling from its chimneys in the peace of early summer as blackbirds and thrushes moved fearlessly in thickets of damp green undergrowth, their noise quite slight compared to the revolving rattle of a lawn mower in the background, and the trotting of large point-to-point chestnut horses, ridden by expensively clad, buxom girls. She smelt the rowan blossom and saw a burbling, rushing brooklet by a meadow ... What a place to live! Yes, she had definitely made the right decision.

With a deep breath, her face flushed with fresh air

and effort, she hurried to the front door – glad to be able to dump the heavy suitcase at last. She pressing the bell and relaxed, fancying she saw Hewy's outline beyond some ornamental stained glass.

But as the door opened, she realised she must have been wrong – for the person who opened it, wore exquisite pale grey kid shoes with sparkling diamanté clips; and the eyes that stared at her were those of Mina . . . Minny . . . Min. The eyes of a girl with as many sides to her mercurial nature as she had pet names, and the official lady of this particular manor . . .

Without waiting another second, Milly turned with her suitcase and, with her face flaming like a furnace, dragged it back towards the bus-stop.

She could hardly see as she stumbled along with torrents of tears flooding her eyes. What an idiotic fool she'd been! What foolishness to succumb to such a rash plan; to take the plunge, only to find no water there, but the mistress of the house barring her way instead . . .

Milly Dawnay had never felt so humiliated in all her life as she cursed herself over and over again for putting her full trust in Hewy. All she longed for now was to get back to her own flat and to try and forget the whole miserable episode. She stood there, waiting, alone, and seemingly for ever in a heavy shower of rain, with never a bus in sight, and a car hooter blaring in her ear.

She looked up and glared at Hewy's car drawing up beside her then turned away swiftly.

'What on earth's going on, Milly?'

She tried to ignore him as rivulets of rain ran down her nose, but he got out of the car and came towards her. He took hold of her suitcase and walked back with it to his car: 'I'm taking you back again.'

'Back where, Hewy?' She glared at him bitterly.

'You just don't understand, Milly.'

'I understand all right . . . My eyes don't deceive me when your wife Minetta Edmundson opens the door of your house . . .'

'I didn't have a chance to let you know,' he said plaintively. 'She only arrived last night. She came to tell me it's all finished.' He looked at her beseechingly. 'She want a divorce. She's going to marry a French Count. She was waiting for a taxi when you knocked at the door, and now – she's gone for ever.' He gave a low, helpless groan, then, grasping her arm, he tried to guide her to the car but she pulled herself free. 'Take your hands off me, Hewy Edmundson! I'm not your personal prisoner. Never, in a month of Sundays, will I ever visit your place again. Take me back to my own flat – right now!'

Meekly he complied with her wishes, and for some time they drove along in a brooding silence, the future hanging like a black cloud between them. Then Hewy said: 'I'll never manage on my own, Milly. All I want is you, and it always has been you . . . deep down. Please come back.'

She gave him a stony stare. Her heart was as heavy as lead. She had no idea what to do now, except for knowing that never in her life would she set foot in Naples Lodge again. God strike her down if she told a lie . . .

'Let me come and live with you then?'

'Live with *me* . . . What a suggestion! You said yourself that Sundower House was a bad place to be and the sooner I was away from it the better. And as for us living together in my flat, it would be a pure insult. I've no intention of being described as a rich man's tart, Hewy – for mark my words, that's how it would turn out in the end.

'Oh yes . . .' Her voice was tired and quiet now. 'I know I came to you to accept your offer of a post as housekeeper, but for *you*, a married man, to come here would be quite different.'

They had just neared the corner of the main road crossing which led to Sundower House, when, to Milly's horror, Hewy swerved nervously to avoid an erratic rag-and-bone cart which was careering towards them on the wrong side of the road. The cart vanished in seconds down a small side lane, but the damage was done as Hewy smashed full-tilt into a hawthorn hedge to avoid barging against a parked van.

The car ripped through the hedge and lay there, tipped on its side, with the engine roaring itself to a standstill and the air heavy with petrol fumes.

Hewy struggled to clamber out and drag Milly with him. They were both half-numb with shock, and Milly prayed to God that Hewy was all right. With painfully slow progress and expecting the car to blow up at any minute, they managed to get clear of it into a large pony paddock, where Milly closed her eyes and knew no more . . .

The next thing she heard was the voice of a police constable.

'The best thing you can do, sir, is for you and your lady to get back home as soon as possible once you've been checked over at the hospital. You'll most likely be able to order a taxi from there to take you back to Bramhall, and your own doctor can visit you at home.'

Back to Bramhall? Was she hearing aright? Milly closed her eyes again as she heard the ambulance drawing up on the roadway.

210

CHAPTER ELEVEN

Chrystalised Syrup

'How's the patient today then, Miss Dawnay?' said Dr
Martingale cheerfully as he strode towards Hewy's
bedroom at Naples Lodge.

It was three days since the accident and Hewy's face
was a swollen contusion of mauve, purple and yellow
with angry red abrasions everywhere – whilst Milly
herself was nursing bruised legs and a badly sprained
wrist.

'I can see a marked improvement in both of you this
morning. Another seven days should do the trick. You
were both very lucky to escape with such minor
injuries.'

Milly smiled at him gratefully. He'd been wonderfully
helpful. It was soothing to have such a wise, fatherly sort
of man take control. He'd even sent in a District Nurse,
besides finding them a charlady and a daily cook, with
the ease of a magician: 'I've been here so long. I know
the needs of everyone so well ...' He murmured the
words humbly.

News of the crash had soon travelled. They'd already
had visits from Hortensia, Gus Bridges, and Zeronica.

You'll not want to come back to your own flat again

after all this luxury, Milly,' joked Gus.

'Hewy won't want to part with you!' laughed Zeronica. 'I expect Mina will be jolly glad he's got you here to act as his nursemaid whilst she's away . . .'

Milly smiled silently. And to think how she'd sworn almost on the Holy Bible never to grace this place again! Life played some awful tricks.

But after Milly had been there another fortnight, Dr Martingale came round with yet more helpful tidings.

'You know you said you were looking out for lodgings convenient for the art school, Miss Dawnay? I was wondering whether you'd be interested in living close to the Ear, Nose and Throat Hospital, at All Saints? My young nephew has a surgery there and Miss Allershaw, the widow who's looked after it since the year dot, has retired to go and keep house for her invalid brother in Huddersfield.

'It's rent-free in return for keeping charge of the keys and seeing the place is kept up to scratch by the cleaners. You would also need to make sure the mail was properly delivered, and be there to answer phone messages at weekends. It might be ideal for a mature art student like yourself. I only mentioned it, just in case . . . There's no obligation . . .'

Milly gulped with sudden joy. She felt like flinging her arms round his neck but instead she said calmly: 'It sounds ideal, Dr Martingale. I'm extremely thankful.'

But when she mentioned it in passing to Hewy, her joy was quickly dampened by his reaction.

'Move *there*? *You*, a single woman, all on your own . . . Looking after some drab doctor's surgery, full of every ailment under the sun, in the middle of the smokiest parts of the city? It's madness!'

'It isn't madness. It's a wonderful offer. Hundreds of

212

people would jump at the chance to have a home to live in *free* at a doctor's surgery.'

'Then let *them* do it. You don't need it. You can stay here with me, *free*. You know we get on.'

She shook her head slowly. 'It wouldn't work, Hewy. It's different at present because of the accident. I just can't forget that this is still Min's home, until you're officially divorced.'

Angry colour spread across his face. 'Mina, Mina, Mina. When will you get it into your head that she's already left me for good? Actual divorces often take half a lifetime to organise.'

Milly set her lips tight. Even if Min had gone, Hewy had never breathed a word about a divorce until she'd mentioned it just now, in spite of the talk about Mina getting attached to a French Count.

French Count! How often had she heard that one? Continental Counts were as plentiful as buttercups if Milly went by the tales she'd heard of people bumping into them when they were on Cook's Tours ... She glanced at Hewy warily. He certainly wasn't quite better yet. She didn't actually want to dash away and leave him in the lurch. They both needed a bit more recuperation ...

They were floating along in a pleasant limbo. They both gradually recovered, and Hewy started to get back to some of his artwork. All their friends visited them and they both continued to get on exceedingly well. But it was an artificial situation. They were living in perfect comfort, and to be quite candid she was enjoying her existence as a peaceful spinster. It was so much more simple and uncomplicated than being embroiled in the passions of men – for never once had there been any suggestion of her and Hewy being anything but a

213

couple of childhood friends brought together in a temporary way.

About a week later, things began to change . . .

It was a pleasant August afternoon, and they were outside in the back garden at Naples Lodge. The air was filled with the busy hum of bees visiting the honeysuckle, and Milly was enjoying the sight of a red squirrel jumping across the branches of the larch trees.

She noticed a small, scarlet two-seater tourer drawing up outside the house with idle curiosity which quickened to real interest when a tall, pleasant, fair-haired man sprang out and came striding into the garden.

'Am I in the right place for finding Miss Dawnay?'

She put down the shallow woven fruit basket in which she had been gathering plums and hurried forward to meet him, her long linen apron gleaming white in the sunshine.

'I was just passing . . .' He smiled towards Hewy, who had come to see who it was, then held his hand out to him in greeting. 'I'm Dr Michael Dodds – Dr Martingale's nephew. I believe he mentioned me?' He looked at them both in the manner of a large, friendly puppy. 'It's about someone taking over the small house where my surgery is and being at hand. As you know, the caretaker, Mrs Allershaw, is due to leave next week, and Dr Martingale said Miss Dawnay might be interested?' He looked at Milly and raised a bushy blond eyebrow quizzically, but as she smiled back at him she was aware of the tenseness in Hewy's manner as he stood there stiff and expressionless. They had not discussed the idea of her looking after the doctor's surgery again after his initial angry outburst.

She began to stammer slightly: 'Y-yes . . . I – well, yes, I've been looking forward to hearing from you. I told

D-dr Martingale I would be only too glad to accept.' She avoided Hewy's cold, hard glare and looked towards Michael Dodds. What an amazingly cheerful, uncomplicated, and straightforward person this man seemed to be. It was like a breeze of cool mountain air from a land of waterfalls after the claustrophic, temperamental life she had been landed with at Sundower House, with all its attendant worries.

Michael Dodds turned towards Hewy. 'I expect you'll both be glad she's found somewhere. It's a friendly place. It should work out quite well. A nice cheerful solution for you both, after that accident. You'll be able to catch up on your own separate lives again.'

Hewy didn't even nod back in reply, but Dodds didn't appear to notice as he shook Milly by the hand. 'Look forward to seeing you next Sunday afternoon, then, Miss Dawnay. Just to show you all the whys and wherefores of the place, ready for Monday morning. I think we'll all fit in very well.' In a couple of minutes he was back in his car, waving at them, then, with a roar from the engine, the small car shot off down the beech-lined drive.

Milly's face shone with joy. 'So that's that, then. What a marvellous stroke of luck...'

'But not for me,' muttered Hewy darkly. 'And don't you be too sure that it'll all be June roses in a place like that. For a start you'll find you'll never be able to get out of the place because of having to hang on for messages for the doctor ... And what happens if the cleaners never come in? You could find yourself doing all the charring. So where does that leave all your beloved artwork? You'll be back to square one. Believe me, Milly, you're as innocent as a newborn babe –'

'Innocent? At *my* time of life? I know more about the

215

ramifications of ordinary life than you'll ever know, even though we did grow up together!'

He sniffed and turned away. 'Don't say I didn't warn you. And don't expect to come running back here for a bit of comfortable living . . .'

She could hardly believe her ears. What snobby superiority! 'I certainly shan't! You've already started to treat me as your servant . . .' She hurried away with angry tears in her eyes, and as the days sped by she almost counted the hours until Sunday when she was to visit the house and surgery. It would be a completely new era. She would be truly independent, just as she'd always wanted; and, best of all, she'd be starting out as a real art student, at last.

Moving in to Michael Dodds' surgery proved quite a painless affair, for once Hewy saw she'd made up her mind, and that Michael Dodds and Dr Martingale were helping her all they could, he became quite detached and found that his artwork was at a crucial point where he had to devote himself to it completely, except to help her to get her few personal belongings safely transferred from Sundower House.

Number twelve George Terrace was a typical doctor's surgery. It was a two-floored, smoke-darkened, red brick house with a cellar basement guarded by black iron railings. The steps leading to the front door with its etched glass panels were brightly donkey stoned with a light cream sand block both mornings and late afternoons, and the brass nameplate was polished at the same time to make sure it was perfectly free of fingermarks from people pressing the bell.

There were two names on the brass plate. The first name, Dr Archibald, had clearly been there the longest and had been polished the most, but old Dr Archibald was now semi-retired and only appeared at the surgery in good weather, coming in a horse and carriage from his home in Bowdon to see one or two personal friends. He was a man with strong opinions and an exceedingly loud voice, who spread mild terror throughout the neighbourhood and bludgeoned the general public with carbolic soap, Jeyes Fluid and brandy in every sentence. He said scubbing floors was exceedingly good exercise for pregnant women as it was a natural position that stretched the peritoneum, and he advised all men with problems to sit in rocking chairs and smoke their pipes with a pint mug of tea by their side, laced with brandy, and a copy of the pink 'un to read.

Little did Milly know, when she first settled down so happily in her own, large upstairs flat, that old Dr Archibald was going to impinge drastically on her own life . . .

The flat itself had very little furniture, but Michael had assured her she could furnish it just as she pleased. 'By all means use part of it as a working studio if you wish. It's entirely yours to do what you want with.' His cheerful, enthusiastic face beamed at her with humorous pleasure, and she felt an overwhelming sense of safety and peace at being in surroundings entirely suited to her at last.

At first the whole situation seemed to be heaven, and although Gus Bridges and Hortensia stressed their disappointment at her leaving them, and said it was hard to find a replacement, she managed to stay on an even keel at the art school itself, keeping her distance from them as much as possible and gladly taking on the role of a student who hardly ever spoke to the teaching staff except for moments of genuine instruction.

In her first term there, it was as if even her sojourn with Hewy was a distant memory, for she never enquired about him, or even had sight or sound of him. He had obviously wiped his hands of her completely and she began to feel glad of it.

One thing did strike her, though: Hortensia was getting fatter and fatter, and had taken to wearing very long, shapeless flowery robes and leaving her dark hair all loose and flowing like a portrait of one of the Pre-Raphaelite models of Dante Gabriel Rossetti. Even some of the students remarked on the transformation, saying how bonny and changed she was.

'It's middle-aged spread,' explained one girl to Milly. 'My mother once looked a bit like that, before she got really old. You often put on weight . . .'

Milly nodded, wondering privately how Hortensia was managing her pregnancy, and whether poor Zeronica had any idea what the true situation was . . . And whether Horty had ever declared the state of affairs to "Art Fallows".

One day, when she was walking through the Textile Gallery to one of her classes, she suddenly bumped into Zeronica carrying a small canvas holdall.

'Zeronica? What a surprise – I haven't seen you for months.'

Zeronica laughed. 'We're both so completely immersed in work these days. A good state to be in if you ask me . . . Gus has asked me to help him out with a bit of modelling. Their main woman has retired to live in luxury with a man who's painting a mural for a town hall and wants her by his side day and night. So how's life at the doctor's surgery?'

'Oh, fine . . .' Milly's expression clouded just a fraction. 'It's really been absolutely marvellous, but sometimes, I must admit, it is a bit lonely being entirely on my own. Especially at the weekends. But there again, it means I concentrate on my artwork more and more, so I've no right to utter even a small squeak of complaint. I expect no human beings are ever quite satisfied, even with paradise ...' She hesitated and gave Zeronica a quick glance. 'How's Arthur doing?'

'Very well indeed at the moment. Hewy's got him loads of designing work to do, and I'm so busy myself that it's rather like two people going past each other on a railway station and just waving.'

Zeronica changed the subject: 'By the way, have you heard about Horty?'

Milly gave a faint start, and looked at her cautiously. 'No ... Well, at least not since two days ago when someone said she's been put on yet another special board of examiners. She seems to be blooming beneath all those robes ...' Milly looked away hastily, hoping Zeronica would change the subject.

'She's got a large cyst. She went into hospital only this morning. The specialist said there was nothing to worry about, but she will be away from the art school for about two months, which includes convalescence time. And Algernon is coming back to Sundower House, to be at hand. Aren't they a funny couple? I thought he'd vanished for good!

'She was telling me in confidence one day how sorry she was never to have managed to have any children, and a few months ago she actually imagined she was pregnant! But apparently, on rare occasions, women can imagine themselves into false pregnancies so much that it begins to look like a real one – especially when they begin to put on weight and swell up a bit ... But enough of all that. How would it be if Arthur and I called to see you one weekend, seeing as how you can't get out too easily?' Zeronica beamed at her cheerfully.

'Yes – do. Anytime. Come this weekend if you like. How about for a meal on Sunday night?'

They both nodded their heads and Milly felt a wave of relief that Hortensia's dilemma had evaporated, though not quite in the way anyone would have imagined.

She was quite excited when Sunday arrived. It was the first time she had ever had visitors since being at the surgery. She bought two bottles of Spanish wine and spent almost all day preparing roast duck and orange salad followed by rice pudding, all to be set out on a battered-looking mahogany table covered by a linen cloth with a crocheted border. She hoped there'd be enough to eat, but knew she had plenty of bread and a bit of funeral cake in reserve, as well as a few apples and pears.

As the hands on the clock moved round to seven she fidgeted about nervously, trying in vain to sit there serenely in her new green velvet dress with a satin bow on it. Then she sprang like a panther as she heard a faint tinkle from the front doorbell downstairs.

She rushed down the stairs almost two at a time and flung the door wide open to greet Zeronica and Arthur. Then she blinked in slight disbelief. Someone else was with them.

'We dragged him along with us, Milly. He didn't need much persuading . . .'

It was Hewy.

The meal was a great success. Not a scrap of food was left.

It was as if Milly was meeting Hewy for the first time, for no mention was made of any personal gossip as they all talked easily and busily about the art world for hours and hours – which fled by in seconds until Zeronica said they must go.

Then, to Milly's surprise, Hewy said, just as they were leaving, 'And the next time, you must all come round to my place. How about next Sunday?' He turned to Milly, but didn't quite meet her eyes. 'It'll give you a full week to inform Mike Dodds you're having a Sunday night away from his cage at last.' There was a slightly sarcastic twist to his mouth. His tone was firm.

She hesitated. It always annoyed her when he started to say what she should and should not do, but Zeronica was already smiling with full approval. 'He's quite right, Milly. You've got to assert yourself occasionally as far as time off is concerned, or they'll take it for granted you don't need any. Then if you complained later they'd say it was your own fault for not letting them know. It always turns out like that.'

Milly nodded. As if she didn't know...

'I'll be seeing you at art school anyway, Milly, so I can see to it you *do* come ...' Zeronica waved cheerfully as they all disappeared and Milly smilingly closed the front door again. Yes, it had been a good evening. She must forget the past and go with Zeronica and Arthur to Hewy's, just as if she'd never been there before. Things were completely different now. Her whole lifestyle had changed. She was completely independent, and savouring every second of it. She actually enjoyed being a spinster.

'Dr Dodds, could I have a quick word with you please?'

'Of course you can.' His face broadened to a welcoming smile as he put away his stethoscope. The very last patient had left his Monday night surgery.

'I just wanted to ask if it would be all right for me to be out next Sunday evening? Some friends have planned supper. It wouldn't be a very late affair . . .'

'No problem at all. I was only thinking the other day that you never seem to get out much. As long as I always have due warning of when you'll be away so that I can leave a message in the waiting room for patients to contact me at my home address in case of emergency, it's fine . . .'

'How's your work going at the art school? Are you finding the two sides of your life fit together all right? Everyone seems delighted to see you in the house. Is the flat comfortable?'

She nodded and smiled at all his questions. 'Everything's perfect.'

He looked at her a trifle shyly and said: 'I'm quite keen on art myself, if the truth be known – have a dabble at country scenes now and again. More as a hobby, really. I don't get a lot of free time for such activities.'

She politely expressed interest, then turned to go upstairs to her flat. He called after her: 'D'you fancy coming out for a spin sometime and showing me how to paint something decent?'

She burst out laughing. 'I couldn't presume to do that. I'm still a beginner myself. In fact, every picture and design seems to be a new beginning. But, yes . . . I should be delighted to come out sometime.'

When she got upstairs she felt entirely contented. Her whole life had reached a point of homely, untrammelled equilibrium – topped off by Michael Dodds' suggestion.

Somehow, when she went round to Hewy's the following Sunday, the thought that Michael had actually asked her to go out with him made her feel calmer and more reassured as Hewy welcomed the three of them inside.

'What a luxurious place . . .' murmured Zeronica. 'I think I'd have stayed here for ever if I'd been in your shoes, Milly.'

Hewy was on his best behaviour, the perfect host. He was wearing a dark grey lounge suit, which must have cost oodles, and his flowing violet and green satin tie accentuated his deep, perceptive eyes. Milly kept a cool, friendly distance, trying hard not to be suddenly swept away by him.

'You should all feel very honoured. I cooked the whole meal myself. I wasn't going to be outdone by *you*, Milly Dawnay . . .' A streak of humour lit his thin, handsome face as they settled down to tatie pot, mutton rissoles and red cabbage followed by bread and butter pudding and washed down with regular draughts from a fancy claret jug containing iced claret, brandy, sugar and mint, which was so potent that Milly asked for ginger beer, instead.

Everything swam along happily until Zeronica said in a slightly slurred, rather sly tone: 'Mina's a fool to leave such a good cook all on his own . . .' She lowered her eyelids in artless drowsiness, a cigarette dangling from her small, slim fingers, then said tactlessly: 'Fancy leaving all this comfort and mollycoddling for some ancient pseudo Count . . . Algernon Hawkesly reckons she's been taken in completely . . .'

There was a terrible silence.

Milly could have hit Zeronica for even mentioning any of it as she saw Hewy bristling up and Arthur helping himself too liberally to more drink.

'Never mind all that,' said Milly hastily, 'what about Hewy showing us those design sketches he's sold?' She looked towards him with a pressing urgency. 'The ones you promised, Hewy. The ones you said were going to be in the Royal Insurance Banqueting Hall . . .'

When he'd gone to fetch them Milly stared at Zeronica reprovingly. She'd never realised before how quickly Zeronica changed after too many drinks. And as for Arthur, he was lolling there like a goggle-eyed scarecrow with his tie all askew and a vacant smile hidden somewhere in his overgrown ginger beard. Yet they had been perfectly all right last Sunday at her place . . . Was it the slightly chilling smell of hospital disinfectant permeating the surgery that had kept them all in order? Or maybe her two humble bottles of wine had been less lethal than today's main brew. Unless of course she was being over-sensitive about the whole situation . . .

Hewy returned with the sketches and they all assured him how good they were. Milly noticed how swiftly he removed them out of harm's way as Zeronica gathered up steam again: 'If there's anything I can't stand, it's women who drift from one rich man to another and men who are unfaithful . . .'

Arthur made a rude snoring sound, but Milly could see Hewy getting quite agitated and her heart bled for him, for she had hoped they'd have a pleasant, happy evening. He turned to her, then said with quiet sadness, 'Have another drink, Milly. It's going to be one of those nights of just drowning our sorrows.'

She didn't really want one, but almost to try and reassure him, she let him fill her glass with some ordinary claret. Gradually they all became more and more careless in their conversation, and her own eyelids began to feel like lead.

In fact, she could hear herself talking away without

even knowing what she was saying. Vaguely, she realised that all of them were completely drunk. She could still hear Zeronica rambling on about Algy Hawkesly and Hortensia again.

'Not a shingle person at the art school 'cept old Gussy even knows she's a married woman. She's Mish Longfeather to all of them and always will be . . .'

'An' whatsh wrong wiv that then, Ronny?' burbled Arthur. 'Thatsh jusht 'ow it should be.'

'It'sh jusht that it'sh shuch a funny set-up, love,' said Zeronica, stroking his beard. 'She was longing for a baby . . . Jush like me . . .' Zeronica began to whimper slightly. 'Longing for one, Arthur, and that rat of a hushband left her to it and she was forshed into that shordid affair with Gus . . .'

Hewy sat there with his eyes closed, splayed out in a large pink and grey plush armchair, but Milly, though completely k-lyed, was following the conversation.

'Affair with Gus . . . Zeronica? . . . Exchuse me, but she never ever had a proper affair with Jussh. Jush Bridges is a married man – jush like she's a married woman . . . But he never tells anyone . . . Shurely you knew that? Jus Bridges ishn't the type for affairs . . .'

Milly tried to stand up. 'An' – if you want the *real* trooooof, it was your *Arfur* she was carrying on with . . . Yesh, no need to look so gawpy . . . Your darling Arthur . . .' Milly flopped back to the velvet settee, and heard a shrill scream leave Zeronica's lips.

'What a bloody lie! Take those words back – *immediately*!'

Even in her bleariness Milly realised she had dropped an unforgivable clanger. She looked across at Arthur. He was dead to the world. But not for long . . . Zeronica staggered across to him and clutched at his shoulder,

prodding and poking at him with drunken determination. 'Get up, Arthur, we're going!'

He tried to open his eyes. 'Going? Where?'

'Going home. Back to our own flat. And *never*
mention Milly Dawnay's name to me again – *ever.*'

Everyone seemed to sober up suddenly, and in a few
minutes all four of them were standing in a group in the
centre of the room, looking puzzled and indignant.

'All I know is that Milly Dawnay inshulted me,'
drilled Zeronica relentlessly.' An' it'll never happen
again because I'll never be speaking to her again . . .'

'What did she say?' A sudden streak of alarm shot
across Arthur's face. He drew out a large hanky to blow
his nose to hide his confusion.

'Never you mind what she said, Arthur. We'll be
discussing that as soon as we get back –'

Milly tried to put her hand on Zeronica's arm. 'I'm
terribly sorry, Zeronica. I must have been out of my
mind. It was all the drink. It went to my head. I never
meant to upset either of you . . .'

'Well, you have done, haven't you – and it's too late
to apologise. And to think how Arthur helped you to get
that picture in the Spring Exhibition! He almost painted
the damned thing for you himself. It's taken me until
now to find out what a scheming little liar you are. What
a fool I was to regard you as a true friend!'

Milly felt ill with shame.

'Come off it, Ronica. Milly's apologised and if we
hadn't been so sozzled it would never have happened.'
Hewy's voice was harsh. 'It was all my fault entirely –
dishing out that claret cup.' He began to scowl angrily.'
I agree with you, Ron – get yourself and Arthur back
home again as soon as you like. I'll order you a taxi.'

When they'd gone, Hewy said to Milly: 'What in

heaven's name was all that hullabaloo about? Anyone would think you were the most deceitful creature who'd ever walked this earth . . .'

Milly said nothing. She was totally miserable. It was no use adding fuel to the fire. Her face was shadowed with gloom as she helped him to tidy up and wash the pots, even though he said the maid would do it in the morning.

'I must get back, too, Hewy. I think we all need a good rest.'

Suddenly he put his arm round her.

She was so taken by surprise she fell against him for comfort, wishing only for this awful evening to be over. They both collapsed together on the velvet sofa.

'Forget it . . .' murmured Hewy, placing his hands gently against her cheeks and kissing her slowly.

She felt all defence fading . . .

Then, rolling softly to the floor and the silky warmth of the thick carpet, in the glow of embers and whitened ash from the log fire, Hewy pulled her down beside him and embraced her passionately. They lay in perfect peace and quiet amongst the flickering shadows.

Half an hour later, they were in Hewy's bed together, like naked twins in some dream world.

She had no regrets . . .

Early next day, after a brief breakfast of coffee and toast, Hewy took her back to the surgery. She breathed with heartfelt relief that she had got there before Mrs Trixy the daily cleaner arrived to do the front doorstep and polish the brass plate . . .

'Shall I call in and see you tonight?' said Hewy as they were parting.

She nodded.

'It might be a bit late if I'm held up anywhere, but I'll call in just the same.' He kissed her lingeringly. 'We should have done this years ago, Milly . . .'

As she went upstairs to her flat, she agreed with him. Yes, it might have been . . . *could* have been, years ago, if she hadn't been so stubborn and cautious. But who could dictate to the vagaries of life, anyway? Perhaps if the affair had started sooner it might have ended sooner. Perhaps this would only be a small flame of a thing . . . All she knew was, she was glad it had happened.

All that day whilst she was at the art school, she thought of the previous night and how it had turned into a small disaster as far as the evening itself was concerned. Especially when she caught a glimpse of Zeronica outside one of the studios and saw Zeronica freeze, cut her dead and go in the opposite direction.

In fact, the effect of the day and what had gone before was so wearing that she decided to ring Hewy up at Calico Designs and tell him not to call round, as she wanted an early night. 'Maybe later in the week, Hewy. I just need to take stock of things a bit. I've a fair lot of work to get through myself, and being cold-shouldered by Zeronica hasn't made me feel any better . . .'

Reluctantly he agreed.

That night she was in bed and fast asleep by nine o'clock . . .

The following evening too, she went to bed early but was awakened at about eleven by sounds from downstairs coming from the small dispensary next to Michael Dodds' consulting room.

Hastily she put on her dressing gown and slippers and, arming herself with a walking stick once left behind by old Dr Archibald, she set off fearfully to find out what was going on. She went downstairs, opening a landing window on the way down in order to be able to call loudly for help if the need should arise, feeling thankful that this part of the neighbourhood was well populated and well policed.

As she opened the dispensary door she heard a sudden scuffle and the smash of glass as a youth hurled himself into the street. There was immediate pandemonium as shadowy groups of people gathered on the street, and soon after the police arrived along with Dr Dodds.

An hour or so later, to Milly's startled surprise, along came old Dr Archibald.

'I'm here to look after *you*, Miss Dawnay! I own this place, and I intend to stay until morning to see things are tidied up properly.'

His long white whiskers quivered with menacing fervour. He was a tall, well-built man, not to be trifled with in spite of his age. His next move was to make himself a mug of tea laced with brandy and to settle down with it in a rickety old rocking chair in the bleak downstairs kitchen.

'And after this, lassie, I shall retire to that spare bedroom next to yours and we'll all hopefully continue with some well-earned snooze . . .'

The next day, Milly noticed that Dr Archibald showed no signs of moving back to Bowdon. He had made himself thoroughly at home, talking to the police and gossiping to people who live locally. 'Yes, Mrs Hinks,' Milly heard him say to one old lady who called round, 'I'm staying on just this second extra night to make sure Miss Dawnay is completely safe.'

He even had Dr Dodds jumping about like a cat on hot bricks: 'And see you're here really early in the morning, Dodsy. I want you here no later than six am, with my horse and carriage and old Crumbles, me driver, outside here at seven, ready to take me back home – got it?'

Michael Dodds nodded respectfully. It was more than his life was worth not to follow every command to the very letter.

'I think, just to be on the safe side, in case the old boy suffers apoplexy, I'll make sure of things by staying over myself and bedding down on the camp bed in my rooms. It'll be far easier. He can be a bit of a devil if things don't run according to his personal plans.'

Michael Dodds seemed so hypnotised by Dr Archibald that even Milly began to get slightly nervous and was up well before six in her dressing gown and nightdress, setting the breakfast table for him. He was up with the lark, singing his own rendering of "She was Only a Bird in a Gilded Cage", followed by "Boiled Beef and Carrots" as he washed himself, then, finally – fully dressed – he settled down to porridge, issuing exact instructions about his boiled egg the while.

He'd just got to the words 'two minutes and sixty-one seconds' when he noticed something was missing from the breakfast table: his Lyles Golden Syrup . . .

'Where's the syrup? I always have syrup on me porridge. Always have done. You can't beat the stuff. There should be a tin somewhere about. It lasts for years. Always kept some around . . .'

Syrup . . . Milly had never seen a sign of any – even though there was honey and sugar on the table.

She hurried downstairs to Dr Dodds, who was still lying there in his camp bed. 'Have we any syrup anywhere?'

He stretched himself, yawned and looked up at her

pleasantly. 'Syrup...?' He was wearing pink and maroon striped pyjamas. 'Don't look so harassed, Milly.' He stared rather lazily at her pale blue flowered cotton nighty, then he glanced at the alarm clock across on his desk. 'Good God, is that the time? Must have forgotten to set the damned thing! Is the old buffer up yet?' He got up hastily, almost knocking her over in his haste. 'What was all that about syrup?'

'For his breakfast. He swears there's a green tin of Lyles Golden Syrup somewhere.'

Michael Dodds glanced at the glass cupboards containing leather-bound medical tomes and moth-eaten monthly journals, then his gaze softened. Bare-footed, he lunged over to the cabinet and from the very top shelf, in what appeared to be a dark, unnoticed gap, he produced a small tin of syrup. 'It must have been there for years. I seem to remember he kept it for if he ever had his breakfast here ...' A slightly coy smile swept Michael's face. 'Mrs Allershaw occasionally entertained him ...'

Milly grasped the tin like a mesmerised relay runner ready to dash upstairs again, but the sight of Michael's twinkling eyes was too much for her, and she burst into helpless giggles.

Ever since Hewy had slept with Milly he'd been constantly restless. All the time his mind kept taunting him. Supposing it was a one-off situation? Supposing she said it had all been a terrible mistake?

He was only too well aware that he was still a married man, and that Naples Lodge was based mainly on the riches of his younger, erstwhile wife.

All the time he had this hauntingly mad desire to visit Milly Dawnay and see if she was still as loving when in her own territory at Dodds' surgery as she'd been in his. Yet, since she had put him off about their Monday arrangement, he hadn't heard a word from her . . .

But at the same time he didn't want to push himself. For a start, he was very busy with his own work, and he realised that she too was heavily committed with both the art school and the surgery. Inwardly he cursed the smooth, smiling Mike Dodds. A place like that was no proper home for a dedicated art student. One thing he'd remembered, though, was how Milly had mentioned she would be free of classes this Thursday morning because Mr Grantley in the textile department was away.

Hewy paced about his bedroom. It was hardly six am – he'd slept badly. He longed to see her . . . Then why didn't he get round there really early before anyone arrived and suggest they both spend the morning together? They could even go round his own studio at Calico Designs in the large MCPA Building . . . After all, he'd said he would act as her mentor and pass on her designs – just as he was already doing for Art Fallows.

No sooner had he justified his somewhat convoluted plans – which were basically to test out his further love life with Milly – than he was washed, dressed and ready for off. He reckoned she would be up by about half past six, for she had told him she was always an early riser and liked to get everything entirely shipshape before she set off for art school each day.

He parked his car in a side street and walked to the front door of the surgery. He could see a few lights on, so he knew he'd been right about her being up. Then, on second thoughts, so as not to attract the attention of nosy neighbours, he decided to go round to the back entry and through the yard to the back door.

232

The door was already open and he was quite surprised to see lights coming from under another door;
the one leading into the consulting room.

'Milly ...?' He walked into the consulting room
quickly to reassure her it was only him. Then stopped
dead. His mind was racing.

All he was aware of was a dishevelled camp bed with
half the blankets on the floor and Milly sitting there in
her nightdress next to Dodds in his pink striped
pyjamas, and they were laughing ...

They both stood up in flabbergasted surprise to face
him.

'Hewy ... What on earth –?'

He ignored her completely and, walking coolly
towards Michael Dodds, he tried to grab him by the
throat.

CHAPTER TWELVE

The Mother

Hewy lay semi-conscious on the floor with blood streaming from his bruised nose, whilst Michael Dodds grumbled to himself: 'The bloody fool! Surely he didn't expect me to stand there like a little lamb ready to be throttled.' He looked at Milly pleadingly. 'I wouldn't mind, but he's made a hell of a mess of this bit of carpet. We'll need to remove it before the patients start to arrive.'

Milly was already kneeling by Hewy's side with a white enamelled, blue-rimmed basin, her fingers trembling as she used cotton wool to swab his face.

'You'd better dab his nose with this astringent, too, whilst I go and see how old Archy's going on upstairs. If his man Crumbles had turned up with that posh rag and bone cart on time he'd have been on his way back to Bowdon by now and the whole scene might have been different.'

But before Dr Dodds could say another word, loud shuffling steps were heard as a foghorn voice bellowed to know what was happening, and Dr Archibald appeared. 'What in heaven's name are you all doing? Tell him to get up from that floor immediately.' He peered at Hewy disparagingly. 'Raise yourself, lad. No good lying there like a sack of spuds. Get moving, boy!'

Hewy struggled hastily to his feet in a daze. He felt an absolute idiot. He started to apologise.

Dr Archibald glared at them all, then looked accusingly at Mike and Milly. 'Why are you two still in your night attire? And who *is* this fool with the bloody nose? Did he try to break in?'

Dr Dodds and Milly both began to speak at once.

'It was you and that wretched syrup for your porridge, sir. Milly came down here to ask me to help her find it . . .'

'And then my friend Hewy arrived,' said Milly in a low, ashamed voice. 'I expect he was going to ask me about going somewhere . . .' She could think of no other reason for him to be there so early. Hewy was startled that she'd guessed almost correctly.

'That's right,' he said hoarsely. 'I knew she always got up early to get the surgery ready and I wanted to see her before I went to my own work.'

'So meanwhile you decided to attack Dr Dodds for being with your ladylove and he hit you back – right?'

There was a certain wise satisfaction in Archibald's voice, but he wasn't in the least amused, and as soon as his carriage arrived he got in it silently, then chuntered to himself all the way home. 'Bloody disgustin' – what the hell do they think they're playin' at these days? Patients deserve better treatment than havin' all that rubbish goin' on before the place opens. It just won't do. In my day they'd have had a proper fight on the common at a selected time and got it over with. It's an insult to normal people, having all that argy-bargy. It's worse than *Peg's Paper*! There'll have to be a new arrangement. There was never a scrap of this sort of

235

puppy trouble when old Marge Allershaw was there . . .'

As soon as he got back to Bowdon he was on the phone to the surgery. 'All squared up yet, Dodds?'

Michael Dodds was just in the middle of sounding someone's chest and hearing a long tale about bronnical tubes: 'Everything's fine, Dr Archibald.'

'It isn't fine at all, Michael. That Miss Dawnay will have to go. We can't have a repeat of that sort of thing. I'll expect to see her bags packed by the end of this week, and meanwhile I'll look round for a mature woman to take her place. Old Ruby Hinks from round the corner'll fit the bill. She'd have known where that damned golden syrup tin was straight away!'

Mike Dodds was fuming. 'Sorry, sir, I'll have to ring off. I'm just checking someone's chest. Goodbye, sir.' He had no intention of getting rid of Milly. In fact, the sight of Edmundson lying vanquished on the surgery floor had sparked a sudden animal pride in his heart. He dreamed of all the delightful painting sessions he and Milly could manage together. What she needed was someone to care for her and protect her from people like Edmundson . . .

As for Milly herself, she felt completely humiliated. The atmosphere was icy when she'd shown Hewy out of the front door and told him never to call on her again at such a stupid time in the morning. They made no further arrangements to meet again.

Michael Dodds completely ignored Dr Archibald's instructions that Milly be replaced by Mrs Hinks. Their friendship blossomed and he spent more and more of what spare time he had practising painting bowls of oranges and bananas and discussing the results with her. In fact, his cheerful, handsome, reassuring presence had such an effect that Milly gradually began to bloom ... It was almost like capturing the romantic dreams of her teens as they laughed together and read each other's thoughts as if they had been born to it. In a strange sort of way, Milly almost blessed Hewy for causing all the trouble that had finally brought this wonderful new man to comfort her and take over her life completely.

A couple of months after the surgery trouble, just as term had finished at the art school and another Christmas was on the doorstep, Michael Dodds went down on one knee in Milly's flat and asked her to marry him. It was an impulse; a tentative query; almost a joke – for he had a bottle of iodine in one hand, which he hastily put in his pocket. 'I mean it, Milly. I've always known I wanted to marry you – ever since I saw you that day gathering plums in the garden.' He frowned ever so slightly. Edmundson's garden ...

Milly was bowled over with pride and love. What more could she ask for than this handsome, caring, faithful man actually proposing marriage to her at her time of life? She knew that any woman over the age of twenty-five was considered to be no spring chicken; and one's chances of finding a decent husband were often on the road to decline after the twenty-five watershed ...

All the same, she remained slightly cautious. It was only a very short time since she'd got to know him, and she knew nothing whatsoever of his social background or his relations – any more than he knew about hers, for all their meetings were confined to the surgery or odd outings around Manchester.

'I'll need time to think about it, Michael. It's a wonderful honour ...'

237

His face fell. He was completely downcast. 'You mean, you don't really want it too? It's not "an honour", I'm not presenting you with a badge, Milly. I *love* you. Don't just try to be kind to me. I couldn't stand it.'

She nodded. 'I do love you, Michael. It's just that I mustn't be rushed.'

As she lay in bed that night she tried to justify her actions. Of course, she must accept. It *was* an honour, and she *did* love him.

What could be more wonderful than being married to a handsome young doctor who loved her and was so easy to get on with, a man so reasonable and level-headed and calm? A man with a settled, well-paid future. A person cherished by the local community. The wife of a doctor ... and maybe a happy family of her own at last, just like her friend Babsy Bright. A happy ending, where she could settle down for ever in a nest of comfort.

And all the time these thoughts circled in her mind another vision intruded persistently: Hewy lying on the floor of the surgery...

Mrs Dodds was busy organising a small dinner party at Oakside for her friends the Spenders.

The Doddses lived near Manchester in the village of Flixton, in a large Victorian mansion. Oakside stood near some small private tennis courts on Irlam Road, just before you got to Goldsworthy Road.

Flixton was rather a pretty little place, ruled by a country squire and blessed with lots of corn fields. The main features of the village were a blacksmith's forge on Flixton Road, a square-towered church near the Jubilee tree, and a link with Irlam via the rowing-boat ferry across the Manchester ship canal at the bottom of Irlam

Road. The ferry was often at the heart of local news when bold men with too much drink inside them toppled out of the boat into the murky waters, usually at Christmas time. Time and again they would challenge each other to swimming matches, only to end up sinking like stones.

Mrs Dodds was very proud of Michael, her one and only son. There were no other doctors in the family, apart from Uncle Martingale. Mr Dodds was a mechanical engineer.

Their two daughters had married well, one to a bank manager and the other to a Chief Constable, but Doctor Michael Dodds was still – rather worryingly – an unattached bachelor at the ripe old age of thirty-three. Although Dorothea Dodds knew he was kept well occupied with his work as a General Practitioner, she also knew she would never feel entirely happy until he was successfully married to a suitable young bride with an impeccable family tree.

Mrs Dodds was a busy, beady little woman with eyes as sharp as a robin redbreast, and when Michael came home from his small, bachelor service flat at Platt Fields one weekend she spotted the change in his demeanour straight away. His fair hair was curling slightly, as if he'd forgotten to get it cut, and he seemed particularly absent-minded and dreamy.

'Mother, where do you think would be a good place to buy a small, inexpensive house?'

'You can't talk about *inexpensive* houses, dear. Those so-called cheap new ones are jerry-built, and hardly bigger than a butler's pantry. They certainly aren't worthy of a doctor in your position. And anyway, I thought you were quite happy living at Platt Fields, amongst other professional men. You're on your own level there with all those professors and lawyers.'

'I need to settle in a place of my own –'

'I know you do, dear, and with a nice wife, if you ask me. You couldn't do better than Felicity Budge. She's only twenty-two and . . .'

He turned away and left the room in exasperated anger. The only person he wanted to marry at this moment – or at any moment ever – was Millicent Dawnay . . .'

Milly was rereading an extremely rude, bombastic communication, written in the crabbed handwriting of Dr Archibald:

Dear Miss Dawnay,

I hope you are aware that I commanded Dr Dodds to dismiss you instantly after the incident that took place at our surgery. Unfortunately, he chose to ignore my instructions and made an impassioned plea for you to stay on. I therefore conceded, with the proviso that your friend Mr H. Edmundson never visit our surgery again under any pretext whatsoever.

I feel I have to stress this position even though a few months have passed, for quite frankly I am still not happy with this state of affairs.

I am,
Yours faithfully,
Hyram C. Archibald, FRCP, Lond.

Milly put the letter down slowly next to the designing work she was doing, and looked around her flat. She was settled in and comfortable. She had all her artwork well organised and there was plenty of space to store her working materials. She could hardly hope for a better situation – for a woman of low income and uncertain prospects. She thought of Hewy and a cold glow of sudden hatred welled up. Hatred because she kept remembering him so often. Why did he always seem to wreck her life? Why did she take any notice of him? What a fool she'd been to succumb to him on the night of the meal with Zeronica and Arthur! What a fiasco the whole episode had been – with both Zeronica and Arthur treating her now as if she no longer existed.

She looked back at the letter. At first she was going to crumple it up and put it in the wastepaper basket, but then she thought better of it and slowly took up her fountain pen and began to write.

Dear Dr Archibald,

You may depend on it that the incident concerning Mr Edmundson will never have the slightest chance of happening again. He behaved disgracefully, and our friendship is now at an end. Please convey my sincere thanks to Dr Dodds for being so understanding on my behalf.

I am,
Yours faithfully,
Miss Millicent Dawnay

Christmas that year turned out to be a quiet affair for Milly, apart from visiting her friends Babsy and Mackie Bright. Babsy was expecting yet another baby, but she seemed to accept it cheerfully enough. 'I'm lucky, really, Milly. I have them easily, and fortunately we both love children. Of course it's made a terrific difference with Mackie having a secure occupation. He's had a pay rise

241

this Christmas, and he's being promoted in the new year. I wouldn't change any of it.'

She and Milly were always happy in each other's company. In some ways they looked quite alike. Their hair was now shingled into boyish haircuts, and Milly's had a slightly unruly short dark fringe.

After Christmas, as 1923 drew to a close, Michael Dodds invited Milly to Flixton to meet his parents on New Year's Day.

It was an unexpected invitation and quite welcome, for this year, for the first time in Milly's life, New Year's Eve itself was due to be a lonely affair. She would be spending it on her own and she was not sure whether local people in the streets around would welcome her into their first-footings, for she was a newcomer, isolated in her flat, and not one of the established community. And no doubt the whole neighbourhood would already be well informed about the fracas between Michael and Hewy, thanks to Mrs Trixy the daily cleaner, and Dr Archibald's gossipy old pal Mrs Hinks. It would all have been a different matter if Mrs Allershaw had still been in charge . . .

And so it was no surprise when she found herself sitting alone on New Year's Eve, reading a book, aware of all the noise and revelry outside as she waited for midnight and the sounds of church bells, train whistles and ships' hooters, with people all visiting each other to welcome in the New Year.

She tried to focus her mind towards the following day, the first of the new year, when she would be visiting Flixton. She wondered nervously what she should wear to meet his family. Her best frock, a pale green crepe de Chine, had hardly been worn. It was very short-skirted with a pointy, scalloped hem and bootlace-thin silk shoulder straps. It was her favourite, but would it do to wear in an unknown situation? Many older people didn't approve of such skimpiness – in their eyes, the sight of bare arms and an excess of silk stocking was linked to irresponsible, party-going flappers. Maybe she should be more covered up especially if she was going to some cold, draughty old house. The trouble was, she didn't really know what to expect. Michael hadn't said much about it all after his initial invitation.

In the end she chose a longer, Prussian blue, velvet dress with long sleeves and a square neck set off by a gold locket. The locket contained a tiny photograph of her mother's and father's faces, as a good luck talisman.

Milly had grown far away from family life these days, apart from Babsy's brood, preferring to forget the sadness of her own background and how both her parents had died in the Spanish Influenza epidemic. That tragedy had resulted in the Dawnay family strands drifting further and further away from each other.

As the church clocks struck twelve and the new year arrived, she wondered hopefully if Michael might call on her with a small lump of coal and other symbolic gifts, but nothing happened.

And then, just as she was about to get ready for bed at last, she heard someone ringing the front doorbell downstairs.

She hurried down, feeling a surge of joy and excitement. She had not been forgotten after all . . .

She opened the door, smiling, then her face changed.

'Happy New Year, Milly.' Hewy was standing there in the semi-darkness. She saw the brightness of his eyes in sudden patches of light, and the paleness of his face. He was carrying a bottle and a small parcel. He put a hand in his pocket and drew out a small piece of coal. 'A Happy New Year!'

She stared at him in amazement. This dark-haired, so-called bringer of good luck was the last person on earth she would have expected to grace this doorstep after what had happened.

'Aren't you going to invite me in?'

The small lump of coal now lay in her own hand. She faltered and hesitated, then, with a fatalistic show of determination, she said: 'I'm sorry, Hewy, it's not to be.' She closed the door sharply. Then, with a moan of anguish, she rushed back upstairs and wept her heart out.

Michael Dodds had arranged to take Milly over to Flixton immediately after his morning surgery on New Year's Day, for inevitably there were always a few emergencies after the night's festivities. He was free after that for a full two days, as there was always a "locum tenens" rota of other doctors working during Christmas, New Year and other holiday periods.

'Last patient seen off the premises exactly on the dot,' he joked as they went out to his car at eleven o'clock.

Milly felt relieved that New Year's Day was turning out so well. Her spirits lifted further still as thin, wintry sunshine smiled on them during the journey, despite the cold, north-westerly winds that swept the skies. She had never been to Flixton before, since it was slightly off the beaten track from the main Altrincham to Manchester route.

'Here we are at last ...' They turned into the driveway of Oakside and his small car crunched its way over the granite chippings toward the house. To Milly's mind, the place seemed large and gloomy and in complete contrast to the man sitting beside her with his fair complexion and cheerful, energetic nature.

A small housemaid of no more than fourteen opened the door to them. Her little white cap was slightly lopsided and she looked very flushed.

'Good morning, Sal. This is Miss Dawnay.' He helped Milly off with her coat then took off his own heavy navy-blue crombie overcoat, woollen scarf and leather gloves and piled the whole load into Sal's small thin arms. 'Are they all here?'

Her face peered over the top of the pile of coats. 'Not yet, sir, and might never be. Mr and Mrs Lonsdale may not be coming as Mr Lonsdale has a touch of bronchitis, and the bank window was broken during the night. And Mr and Mrs Cooper have had an urgent call to visit Mr Cooper's mother in Rochdale. Mr Dodds is away for a walk to the Church Inn, and Mrs Dodds is in the dining room poking the fire.'

'Is that you, Michael?' His mother suddenly appeared, and Milly's initial impression was of a neat woman with thick brown hair set in careful waves. She walked quickly towards them and shook hands with Milly. 'How lovely to see you . . . Michael has mentioned you quite often. Not the best of days, but I suppose we mustn't grumble. It could always have been worse. We've been having a bit of trouble with the back boiler, but as the Good Lord would say: These things are sent to try us . . .' She gave Milly a quick show of teeth.

'We seem to be the only ones here at the moment, then? That's a bit of a relief,' Michael commented as she led them into the drawing room, where a grand piano stood on the thick, warm-looking Turkish carpet.

Milly and Michael established themselves on the flowered, cretonne-covered sofa and then his mother

245

said casually: 'Felicity is here too, but she's just upstairs in the bathroom, gargling.' Maria Dodds turned to Milly and smiled. 'Miss Budge is a friend of ours, and she has a beautiful voice, but you know how it is these days, Miss Dawnay . . . Miss Budge was cut out to be an opera singer, but at present she does clerical work for her father, who's a local business man. She's an only child and her mother is one of my best friends. Felicity has chosen to stay with us for a few days whilst her parents are visiting other relations.'

Milly blinked slightly at this torrent of information. Miss Budge must surely be an infant prodigy, but how old was she? She looked at Michael for guidance. He stood up and paced about in front of the marble fireplace. Instead of being his normal friendly self, he had turned into a glowering red-faced bull.

'Staying *here*, Mother? At this time? Aren't you taking on a bit too much?'

'It's delightful to have her here,' smiled his mother. 'And after dinner she's going to sing for us all. I've invited the Sheerbournes over to listen.'

'Well, you can count Milly and me out,' he growled. 'We'll be going for a walk this afternoon as soon as dinner is finished.'

'Oh, don't say that, dear. How impolite!' She turned to Milly hastily. 'He's very rude to be deciding things without even asking you, my dear. I'm sure *you'd* like to stay and listen, wouldn't you, Miss Dawnay?'

Milly nodded enthusiastically. She was curious to see this wonderful female, and she didn't really fancy a proper walk because her shoes were too flimsy.

'That's settled then,' chirped Mrs Dodds thankfully.

The moment Felicity Budge walked into the room Milly felt a spasm of envy. It was clear that Felicity was

246

only just into her twenties, whilst Milly was on her way out of them. She stared at the long golden hair piled high on Felicity's head, and noticed her small diamond earrings. She was a petite creature with an impressive cleavage that was shown to advantage by her emerald-green silk dress, which clung to her like delicate, shimmering seaweed. Milly began to wish she had worn something more modern after all.

You'll have to forgive me,' whispered Felicity in hardly audible tones, 'but I'm saving my voice till after dinner.' She turned towards Michael and fixed him with a dazzling gaze that would have been suitable for The Annunciation.

Dinner was a no-nonsense affair: stuffed roast pork and apple sauce with cabbage and mashed potatoes, followed by treacle roly-poly and white sauce.

Felicity picked at the meal delicately and removed a large piece of crackling full of roasted bristles to the side of her plate. Seated next to her, Mr Dodds – who'd arrived back from the Church Inn bulging with fresh air and bonhomie – beamed at everyone, ate every scrap of dinner and never said a word except when a piece of Felicity's diaphanous skirt was trapped on his chair. He retrieved it hastily from underneath his buttock, apologising profusely, and then related a tactless tale about a lady losing the whole of her skirt in a lift in Kendal's.

'Thank goodness my Maurice is such a marvellous piano accompanist,' remarked Maria Dodds once the meal was finished and cleared away and they'd retired to the drawing room again.

Felicity reached for her music from a flat brown leather case with metal rodded handles.

'What is our treat to be today, dear?' trilled Mrs Dodds.

It turned out to be 'All through the night there's a tiny brown bird singing/Singing in the night of the Darkness and the Dew/Singing in the Ni-i-i-ght of the darkness and the dewwwww/Tra-la-la-laaaar ... ar ... My lonely heart is winging ...'

She sang and she sang.

"Come into the garden, Maude/For the black bat night has flown ..." And "Your tiny hand is frozen/Let me *warm it into loife*!" Her piercing and far from timid, slightly off-key voice swept along like a river torrent, filling the drawing room, and eventually subsiding to polite and enthusiastic applause laced by a couple of 'bravos' from her happy pianist as he bowed both humbly and numbly from the tapestry piano stool. The performance over, Mrs Dodds helped the maid to dish out afternoon tea from a wooden tea trolley.

When Michael returned Milly to her flat that evening, she wondered whether they would make any further arrangements to meet during this time off. But to her disappointment, he made no such suggestion.

'Seeing *her* there was a bit unexpected, Milly. Quite honestly, I had no idea she would be staying. It's completely wrecked all my own plans, because I was going to suggest to Mother that you stayed over with us. But you know what mothers are, once they've planned things *their* way ...' He smiled with boyish ruefulness and she almost felt like hitting him. It had been a revelation to see him in his own background instead of in his role as a doctor, with all the respect that entailed.

He rambled on, quite unaware of the wrath he was causing. 'Actually, Felicity's quite a nice girl, really. She's growing into quite a beauty and I think her singing has improved tremendously. Did you notice how blue her eyes are? Almost the colour of corn-flowers ...'

'Cornflowers!' Milly tried to stifle a snort. No one need tell *her* what colour true cornflower-blue was, and Felicity Budge's eyes were nowhere near that colour.

'She's quite appealing with all that enthusiasm for her music, isn't she? I'd never even noticed it until today ...'

Milly nodded and smiled.

'Well, we mustn't stay here for ever. See you in another two days then, my darling, when we're all back to normal here at the surgery.'

He turned to leave the flat, but then he caught sight of the small piece of coal sitting on the mantelpiece, and a small unopened parcel next to it. 'Did you have a New Year's visitor then?'

She was taken aback for a few seconds. 'A visitor?'

'The first-footings. The New Year. You know – tall dark stranger ...' He was staring at her with a look of cynical disbelief on his normally merry face, then he glanced at the small lump of coal again.

She felt herself going scarlet. 'No – I didn't take part in any of the local things ...' She knew this part was true, but he knew it wasn't the full tale.

'You're lying, Milly. You're trying to cover something up.' She could see his temper rising, just as it had on the morning he had dealt with Hewy. 'I can't stand liars, Milly – especially in a woman like you.'

She began to stammer something defensive, not knowing what to say, but as she regained her composure her own temper shot up. What infernal cheek to expect her to reveal her every movement to him! Was this the man she had thought so tolerant and easy-going? She began to see him in a different light. Why hadn't she

249

seen that all the jealousy so apparent in Hewy's nature was just as strong in Michael's?

He said no more about the coal, but within seconds his whole attitude had changed.

He looked at her cautiously then muttered casually, 'Why don't you come back to my place sometime, Milly? Come back to my bachelor mansions and I'll cook us supper.'

There was something strangely suggestive in the way he said it. Why had he never invited her there before? Did it imply that he thought she was freer with her favours than he'd first imagined when he'd taken her to his parents' home, and that he hoped this might now be proved in his own pad? And all because he suspected she'd received an unknown visitor during the New Year, yet had chosen to lie about it?

'Thank you, Michael, but I'm feeling very tired now. It was lovely coming to Flixton with you . . .'

He hesitated, then suddenly pulled her close to him, sweeping her almost off her feet, and kissed her hard and full, bruising her lips against her teeth in a sudden fury of passion. 'I love you, Milly. And I forgive you everything, even if you're the biggest trollop on God's earth.' His mouth sought hers again in a fever of pressing haste, and, with overpowering strength, he pushed her down to the sofa, murmuring endearments all the while, but at the same time manipulating her body like someone in a wrestling match. She struggled to free herself. His insulting suppositions about her moral behaviour stabbed at her heart like an ice-cold dagger. What a fool she'd been to dupe herself into a false idea of romantic love with a man like this!

She finally wriggled free of him, forcing him to release her by giving him some stubborn, unladylike jabs with her elbows. She was sure he wasn't actually a rapist, but she knew now that he was a man entirely given to having his own way – by the rules of the rugby field, she told herself indignantly.

He lay there unmoving on the sofa as she got up, feeling slightly dizzy with shock and anger. She decided to leave him to it. She grabbed her outdoor coat, her keys and her handbag, then hurried downstairs without a backward glance, slamming the front door and rushing out into the street. Her mind raced: where on earth could she go now? The only haven open to her was her friend Babsy's place. Yes, she decided, she'd go and plead a place on Babsy's old couch in the kitchen until morning.

Babsy was almost ready for bed and Mackie was already there, for he worked long hours and had to be up early.

'Milly Dawnay! What on earth . . .?'

'I can't say much now, Babsy, and it's nothing to worry about, but could you put me up on the couch till morning? I'll explain then. It's just that I needed to be away from the surgery till tomorrow, and you were the only person I could think of for help . . .'

'Of course you can. There must be some good reason why you can't stay there, and I'll not nag you. You can sleep in the parlour. I'll just bank up the fire a bit more, and I'll fetch a blanket and some coats to keep you warm. Would you like a drink? The water in the kettle's hot.'

Milly shook her head and settled down on the couch. 'I'll stay put till you've got Mackie off to work, Babsy.' She kissed her friend gratefully, and Babsy squeezed her hand to comfort her.

The next morning, Milly returned to her own flat at the surgery. Finding that the locum Dr Frances was already busy, she sat down and opened the letter she'd found addressed to her.

Dearest Milly,

Why the devil did you rush away? I shall ring you tomorrow to see if you are back again. I was a fool to treat you so badly and to doubt you. I must also apologise for my brutish lovemaking. Please forgive me – I was beside myself with jealousy and suspicion in case you ever left me, for I love you more than ever.

I was upset, too, about the way Mother had parked Felicity at our house. Mother is so strong-willed, yet she means well, and I don't like to hurt her feelings if I can help it . . .

I sensed immediately that I'd said the wrong thing when I invited you to my flat, but believe me it was meant sincerely, though of course I realise it was tactless and blundering of me to do so.

Please let us start again, my darling, and do all the things we'd always planned, like going out sketching, and catching up on those walks in Derbyshire, and visits to the Hallé orchestral concerts . . .

Yours for ever,
Michael

Milly read and reread the letter, pondering over its contents. She felt guiltier and guiltier. How could she have thought those awful things about him being jealous and insensitive when, as he had pointed out, it was all due to complete misunderstanding?

She thought back to the time she'd first glimpsed him, when he'd come striding past the honeysuckle along the path at Naples Lodge, and she'd looked up from gathering plums ... What brightness and hope he'd brought into her life when he took her on as housekeeper, and how he had pleaded with Dr Archibald to allow her to stay after the fiasco with Hewy on that disastrous morning ...

She frowned to herself. The sudden reversal of her love for him had happened since she visited his house and met his mother and that other girl. And yet ... reluctantly, she forced herself to acknowledge something else: Hewy's visit ... Yes, Hewy's New Year's Eve visit had been the real cause. If Hewy had never come round, that whole episode of Michael Dodds forcing himself upon her with such relentlessness would never have happened.

Later in the day there was a phone call for her. 'Milly?' His voice sounded anxious. 'Did you find my letter?'

'Yes.'

'I'm sorry about it all. I was a fool ...'

'I was a fool too, Michael. I can see that now. I went to stay with my friend Babsy for the night, to get over it all.'

'Oh good. I was worried about you. By the way, Felicity's gone home. She said she had a sore throat and preferred to rest in her own place until it was over. Do you fancy coming out for the day with me tomorrow and then back here for tea?'

Milly hesitated.

'You needn't worry, Milly. There'll only be the two of us. Ma and Pa have gone to visit one of my sisters.'

'Yes. I'd love to.' Milly smiled with pleasure. It was working out right at last.

The following day Milly decided to wear a tweed skirt and jumper for her day out. As she fastened the buttons, she was aware of an unusual tightness around her breasts, and her stomach felt swollen. It was something, yet nothing ... She went to the small calendar on the sideboard and checked the date. Her heart sank. It was ages since she'd had a period. It might be due to all sorts of things – even a touch of anaemia – for *surely* that one time with Hewy could not have done it?

She went to her bed and lay down for a few minutes, feeling quite faint. Then, getting up again, she got ready to see Michael.

CHAPTER THIRTEEN

A State of Fate

I want to be happy,
But I can't be happy
Till I've made you happy too . . .

Milly could hear the music coming through on her
cat's whisker crystal set. It was from a musical comedy
called *No, No, Nanette.*

She felt anything but happy, for now she was convinced she was pregnant, but she didn't dare mention it
to anyone. And, even worse, she couldn't go to a doctor
anywhere near All Saints in case it leaked through to
Michael Dodds.

She was in a terrible state, utterly forlorn and
depressed. She felt sick at the sight of food, was
perpetually running to the lavatory, and was convinced
she would die completely if Michael turned on her and
she was chucked out of her flat. She just didn't think she
could possibly stand it.

And as for Michael Dodds himself – he was on top of
the world now that he had squared himself with Milly
again. Concerts in Manchester and small painting
sessions with Milly in his bachelor apartment had
begun, which gradually ate into Milly's studying time

for her work at the art school. It did not occur to Michael that Milly's own work might be suffering as a result, but he could not fail gradually to become aware that something was troubling her.

One day he decided to voice his concern, as tactfully as possible: 'What's wrong, Milly? You seem to be all on edge. You hardly let me kiss you these days.'

She half-smiled and thought about fobbing him off, but underneath she was wondering whether to confess the real reason and get everything cleared up and into the open; for although it was impossible for the child to be Michael's there was no reason for her to say *whose* child it was.

'. . . I – I don't think I'm altogether well at present.'

He was puzzled. 'Not well? How do you mean?'

'It's just that I have certain worries on my mind. Perhaps we should stop seeing each other for a while. It's not that I'm *ill* or anything. I'm quite capable of looking after the surgery routine, but there are other, private things . . .'

'Look, why don't you go and have a word with Dr Martingale? Then it will be entirely private. Although he's my uncle, I can assure you that you wouldn't get more understanding care from anyone. He'll have you right in a jiffy.' Michael beamed at her confidently.

She didn't like to turn the idea down too obviously. She nodded and smiled. 'I've probably been making too much of it, but all the same, I think I'll just have a couple of weeks of pure spinsterhood. I do have quite a lot of artwork to get through, apart from anything else.'

'That could be precisely the cause,' he said firmly. 'Overwork is at the root of most ailments . . .' He looked at her thoughtfully. 'Would you like me to find someone else to do a stand-in whilst you go away for a couple of weeks and have a really good break from everything? I'm sure it could be managed quite easily.'

She nodded hastily, hardly daring to say another word in case she broke down and told him the true situation. Maybe she *should* get away for a couple of weeks so that she had a clearer view of what to do. But where would she go?

'Don't worry too much. I'll get it all fixed up for you to be off for two weeks starting next Monday. How's that?'

'It's ever so good of you, Michael. I feel awful about it.'

'No need to. We all go through these bad patches.'

When she was on her own the next day, she went over and over the situation in her mind, trying to work out what to do and where to go for the two weeks. And then, just as she was almost giving up hope of ever finding a suitable solution, Gus Bridges approached her at the art school on an entirely different matter.

'Milly, I was wondering if you could possibly do me a favour?'

'Why, yes. Of course.' It wasn't often that Gus asked anything of her. She suddenly noticed how strained he looked.

'It's a bit complicated, is there a chance you could come back to Sundower House to discuss it this dinner-time? It's to do with helping out a bit at the college. I know it's a lot to expect when you have all your other work, but we're in a desperate situation . . .'

Milly gulped. What on earth could it be?

'I'll pick you up at the entrance then, at the end of classes.'

He was silent on the journey to Higher Broughton, and Milly was silent too, brooding mournfully on her own problems. There wasn't a hope of this two-week 'holiday' solving her true dilemma. Over the last few weeks, she had noticed more and more signs of changes within her body – the problem was not going to go away. And now, on top of all that, there was this good turn. She was mad to have agreed so easily. Yet how could she have turned down a plea from Gus of all people?

As they went into Sundower House she was miserably aware of changes there – and none of them for the better. The place was in a state of terrible neglect, even though Gus's own flat looked much the same as always.

He put the kettle on and made some hot Bovril. Then he buttered two barm cakes and put cheese in them, spiced up with some HP sauce.

'Don't just stand there like an orphan, Milly. Find yourself a pew.' He gestured to an old armchair with a sagging seat. 'The fact is that this week has turned out to be the final act of a long and complicated saga. What it all boils down to is this. Hawkesly has finally sold all this lot to someone else. We actually thought he'd already done it a while ago, but there was a last-minute hitch, and some of us said it was sold, whilst other denied it. What a cock-up! Anyway, it's really true now. But the main point – with you in mind, Milly – is that three days ago he was back here to collect Hortensia, and he's taken her back with him to Europe for good.

'It's all been so sudden that we haven't been able to line up a proper replacement for Hortensia at the art school, and we won't find one for some time. I'd even thought of getting Arthur to hold the fort as a temporary stand-in, but – as if the Hortensia news isn't bad enough – he and Zeron have shot off to London. Zeronica reckons she can get more modelling work there, including work for magazines.

'I'm staying on here, of course, but the rest of this place is going to be let to students. The person who owns it now is a bit of a philanthropist and supporter of the arts, and the flats will be let out fairly cheaply to anyone in full-time education.'

His eyes crinkled in a kind-hearted smile. 'But none of that luxury caretaker stuff now, Milly. He's getting a man and his wife who live in a street nearby to do all that, and there'll be no more exotic meetings of those Post War Visualists. Those days seem like a dream world now. So ... What do you think? Will you be able to help me out whilst we find a replacement for Horty?'

'It's all so sudden, Gus. I don't quite know what to say ... I –'

'You don't need to make up your mind this very second.'

'As a matter of fact, I'm supposed to be taking two weeks off from my surgery job – for a sort of rest – and I was wondering where to go ...'

Gus's face lit up with pleasure. 'Come here, then. There's loads of space until they get this student idea working properly. Or you could stay in Art and Zeron's place – there's still the bed left there. Free digs for your two weeks! Also, it'd give me the chance to work out a proper timetable with you so that you can fit in the teaching with your own studies.'

By the time the midday break was over, Gus had arranged to take her back to the surgery to collect all the belongings she'd need for her two weeks away. Never would she have dreamed she'd be back at Sundower House again, and staying in Arthur and Zeronica's flat.

'You'll get payment of course, Milly, and this two weeks'll be a good trial period, because you can judge how it ties in with all your other commitments when you're back at the surgery again in a fortnight.'

She smiled enthusiastically, completely forgetting for a few minutes her real problem as it ticked away like an invisible time-bomb . . .

On the first night, curling up in bed in the attic flat with the name "ART FALLOWS" still on the door, and relishing the peace and quiet, she felt she had come home at last.

Gus was like a real protector, taking her backwards and forwards to the art school and always on hand to help her. He was an angel in disguise, she realised, this large, rather bumbling, slightly absent-minded man, beginning now to show his age and always so patient with her, yet asking nothing in return.

'Gus . . .'

'Yes?' He was looking at a film script. He had continued with his film making when he wasn't at the college, for though it was an arduous and complicated business, it was an integral part of his life.

'I need to see a doctor. It's nothing *very* serious, but I don't want to worry Michael Dodds with it. I'd prefer to keep it private. Do you know of anyone I could go to?'

'Not the slightest idea, Milly, love. Never ask me for any really serious advice in case it all turns out wrong. All I can suggest is for you to go and see the doctor you visited when you were a child. If he's still there he might well remember you – some of these old 'uns have memories like elephants.'

'Dr Daley . . .' Suddenly Milly remembered him from all those years back, and involuntarily her hand touched the almost invisible scar on her face, received when she'd fallen from the wall in the old laundry works.

The following evening she decided to see if Dr Daley's surgery was still there. To her relief, it was. She took her place in the waiting-room queue, thinking how uncanny it was that it all seemed the same as it had always been, even though her own life had changed so much.

Her heart beat nervously as she waited to see him. He had always seemed old to her when she was a child, and quite severe, so what must he be like now after at least fifteen years?

A sharp mechanical bell sounded for the next patient and as she walked into his room she was assailed by the familiar smells of aniseed and ipecacuanha with a whiff here and there of disinfectant. Just the same as it had always been. And so was he, in his fawn suit with his rimless glasses and his dark, slightly yellowing face and high cheekbones. 'Miss Dawnay?'

She was quite taken aback until she remembered that she had of course given her name to the receptionist when she had come in.

He was looking at a card with her particulars on it. 'Ah yes ... Hatching Street. But no longer there. So what can I do for you?'

'I was wondering if I was ...' The word pregnant trembled on her lips, almost choking her, then the whole sad tale began to flood out in torrents.

He listened attentively, then said briskly, 'Right, let's examine you.'

Obediently, she lay on the horsehair examination table behind the screen with a white sheet beneath her; and his nurse stood beside her whilst he palpated her abdomen and asked her questions, and arranged for a sample of urine.

'Yes, Miss Dawnay, you are quite right.' He looked at

her solemnly. 'Do you still live at home?'

'No. My parents died. I live alone . . .'

'Do you have any friends close by?'

'I do have one friend in the flat downstairs . . .' She didn't dare reveal it was a man.

'You'll need to come and see me every month, and we'll see about getting you fixed up with a midwife, or maybe a cottage hospital, with it being your first. But there's plenty of time yet.' He hesitated, then bending his head to write something on her card, he said casually, 'any idea who the father is?'

She felt herself going crimson. It seemed such an insult – as if she had just walked the streets, waywardly submitting to any passing man. But what could she expect when she was single and pregnant? She was what her own parents would have regarded as "a fallen woman".

'Do you or don't you know who the father is, Milly?'

His voice was kinder this time.

'I do know, but I'd rather not say . . .'

He did not pursue the matter any further.

On the way back to Sundower House she was filled with a mixture of fatalistic gloom and utter disbelief that she really was pregnant after that one night with Hewy. Maybe Dr Daley was wrong after all . . . she thought of the Hortensia episode, when Horty had been convinced she was with child, only to find it was not so. Might it, by some miracle, turn out to be the same with herself – Miss Millicent Dawnay, this swiftly aging spinster? For that was how she was beginning to see herself, at the relatively young age of twenty-seven. Perhaps all the rumblings and movement within her were due to wind . . . Maybe she'd been eating all the wrong things, and coupled with nervous worries . . . Her brain was beginning to go round in circles.

Then her imagination came to a cold, realistic halt. She knew she was trying to delude herself, to escape the unforeseen consequences of what had taken place on that one evening at Hewy's.

Her visit to Dr Daley's had revealed a confusing mixture of feelings she tried hard to deny: a trace of excitement, and even hidden pleasure, overlaid by anxiety for the future from knowing she was entirely on her own without anyone there to comfort her, let alone the father of her child-to-be . . .

Then reason came to her aid. It was no good beginning to feel sorry for herself when she hadn't even told Hewy what was happening. At least he should be informed. Her heart sank. Easier said than done. How on earth was she going to break the news?

The months flew by. With machine-like precision her baby grew inside her and she suffered all the passing phases of feeling faint, and morning sickness. Yet each time she saw Dr Daley he pronounced her to be as fit as a fiddle.

'You're a lucky woman, Milly . . .'

And all the time she said nothing to anyone, least of all Michael Dodds, for she had returned from the attic flat at Sundower House after her two weeks away from the surgery as if her life was completely the same.

'I managed to get Felicity to help me out,' said Michael Dodds happily. 'Naturally, I missed *you*, Milly, but I must say Felicity did absolute wonders considering she'd never faced a similar situation before. She didn't stay in the flat, of course, except to practise her singing a bit in quiet moments. I collected her each day from her own home and took her back again, and we managed to have all extra messages to the surgery seen to by Mrs Spinks. Felicity's father was extremely happy to lend her to me for that small break. She's a wonderful girl . . .'

He beamed at Milly, then added quickly: 'But not as wonderful as you, of course. You seem to be absolutely blooming after your two weeks off.' He held her hand gently and gazed into her face, but she jokingly moved away.

'I'm afraid it's going to be just platonic friendship at the moment, Michael. I have a terrific amount of final work to get through at art school. I hope you'll understand.'

She could see he was puzzled by her rebuff, but she had to try and stave him off until she was properly sorted out. She knew the baby didn't show. Her body was firm, and with it being the first her muscles were all trim and in good shape so that any extra expansion round her waist looked to be nothing but a bit of extra weight. There were no prominent bulges yet . . .

No, her main concern was not whether or not to tell Michael, but the task she had yet to carry out, of seeing Hewy and revealing the truth to him . . .

One morning her self-imposed duty finally met her full in the face in Gus's studio at the art school. They were both taken aback. There was complete silence.

She took a deep breath. 'Hewy . . .?'

'Yes?'

'There's something important I've been wanting to say for ages. Would it . . . Would it, er . . .' She took another breath then gabbled quickly: 'If I could come round and see you, Hewy? It's something very important, something we need a bit of privacy for . . .'

Gus had walked into the studio. He looked at them both and smiled. 'I expect you'll be able to get her loads of work once she's finished her course, Hewy?' There might even be a job going for her here, too – replacing Hortensia.'

Hewy gave a thin smile and one eyebrow quirked slightly. 'Congratulations. Yes, I daresay I could find you some work, Milly, but our paths in life seem to have changed.' His voice was cool.

Gus frowned slightly. 'Not changed all that much, surely? I thought you were going to get together sometime on textile designing?'

Hewy turned away, but when he walked out of the room Milly went after him. She knew that if she didn't collar him now to get the situation sorted out, she would never have the courage again.

'Hewy, please wait. I do really mean that I need to speak to you in private. Please don't ignore me . . .'

'You were the last person to do the ignoring, Milly. Remember New Year?' His voice was low and accusing. 'It was the final turn down. A man can only take so much . . .'

'Please, *please*, Hewy. I just need to talk. It won't take long.'

He melted slightly. 'Naturally, we could go back to my place, but knowing how much you resent being present in another woman's property . . .'

She ignored the jibe. 'Yes, I'll come back with you.'

They hardly uttered a word to each other on the way to Naples Lodge.

The place was beginning to look a bit neglected. There was some loose stonework next to the gate and the grass needed cutting. The small summer house had a cracked window and the paint was peeling, but inside the elegance still surmounted the untidiness.

The velvet sofa was still there. She sat down, and

amazingly he sat down beside her. 'Come on, then. What's it all about? Why all the sudden drama? Why the determined urge to talk?'

He stood up restlessly and walked away, then came back carrying a tray with two drinks. She could see it was whisky.

'Not for me, thanks, Hewy. I'd better say what I want to say right now and get it done with.'

Everything was so quiet now that she could hear birds chirruping outside, beyond the sunblinds. "The fact is, Hewy ... The plain truth is ... Well, perhaps you've noticed it ...'

'No?'

'I'm pregnant, Hewy.' She stood up and placed her hands one on each side of her stomach. 'It's our baby, Hewy.'

He took a long, cool swig at the whisky. 'Say that again, Milly.'

'I'm not saying it again. I came here to tell you and that's what I've done. I thought it was right for you to know. It's just six months now. I've been lucky that it hasn't shown much yet, but soon it'll begin to show properly.'

She saw his eyes gleaming with a thin sort of anger as he touched his mouth nervously with his fingers. Then he said slowly: 'You may well be pregnant, Milly, but it's a bit much to turn to me for help.' A sudden scorn filled his face. 'It's taken you a long time to find a father if it's been there for six months. Was I your last resort?'

They were both standing now, facing each other. With one almighty swipe she caught him across the cheek with her clenched fist, her whitened knuckles hitting him hard.

He grabbed both her wrists in a grip of iron. 'You

can't fight your way out of this one, Milly. What about Dodds?'

'Michael has nothing to do with it. We've never ever –'

He shook his head cynically. 'Don't try and make a fool of me. I just can't stand it any more. You'd better go.'

Milly went, her head held high, her heart thumping with angry shock. She felt a lurching movement inside. She walked almost blindly with hard, dry eyes towards the bus stop, miles away. If that was how Hewy Edmundson wanted it, so he should have it. If he wanted his child – girl or boy – born a bastard, on his head be it. She had tried to do her best. She had informed him. But he refused to believe it. How could there be any proper love between them if he would not believe her words, even though he could not deny that they had spent that night together?

When she finally got back to her flat at the surgery she was violently sick and began to have griping pains in the stomach. Then, just as she was looking for her smelling salts, she swooned to the floor and knew no more until she found Michael Dodds standing over her as she lay in bed.

She wondered what on earth had happened, but before she could ask him, he said quietly: 'You were groaning away about being pregnant, Milly. And I have a feeling you could well be.'

She looked at him with true sadness. 'You're right, Michael. It's no good trying to hide it any longer. It's Hewy Edmundson's child. That's why I've been so offhand with you. I knew it wasn't fair to you to be too encouraging, because of all this ... I'm glad you know about it at last.'

She sank back against the small pillow and closed her eyes. 'I won't be able to go on with this job. Maybe Felicity would like it ... I can't thank you enough for employing me in the first place. It might have worked out so well, except for this, if ...'

If ... There were so many ifs in life. What would happen now? Well, it needn't be Michael's concern. At least he knew the truth now. 'I'm six months gone, Michael. I've been attending my own doctor.'

He summoned up a smile. 'Well, that's a good point about the doctor, anyway, and I expect Edmundson will help you out ...'

'I'm sure he will.' She turned her face away from him and faced the wall.

Hewy sat alone in the drawing room at Naples Lodge in a state of near despair. He groaned aloud as he thought of his awful meeting with Milly that morning. Whatever had induced him to be so harsh? He knew Milly wasn't a liar, and he remembered every moment of the night they'd spent together. All the same, how could there be any proper proof that the forthcoming child was really his when she was so bound up with that smug idiot, Dodds?

She had sent him away so wilfully at New Year. It had been the most depressing moment of his life. He'd hoped to start afresh but she'd snubbed him. And now came this final straw over the pregnancy – the double hurt.

Any man in the same circumstances would have acted the way he'd done. What a fate it would be to be cuckolded, left to look after some cuckoo not his own ... it was different if you agreed to have another man's child under your roof, but to be deliberately used, and lied to ... Who wanted that? He began to feel better as he justified his actions to comfort himself.

The very next day, out of the blue, Hewy received a telegram from his wife Mina.

HEWY – ARRIVING HOME FRIDAY. FOR GOOD. YOUR WIFE MINNY DEE.

Why did she always use her maiden name? Hewy thought irritably.

'Any reply, sir?' The telegraph boy stood there beside his red bicycle in his navy blue and red uniform, waiting.

Hewy shook his head. 'No reply.'

So what had happened to her Count? Hewy shrugged his shoulders. The only way to deal with Mina was to let her arrive under her own steam and hear the whole tale when she was back at home.

He even began to feel pleased at the thought of seeing her again. He forgot about Milly entirely as he looked at the broken stonework by the gate. He'd better get it mended straight away, *and* the grass cut ... He ran a hand through his thick, unruly hair – *that* needed cutting too ...

He became more and more high-spirited. It was sheer good luck, this telegram arriving. Especially now he was so busy with his work. The place had been needing a woman's touch for some time and she'd be sure to re-employ the servants as soon as she got back. He went to the small rosewood table near the grand piano and stared at the photo of her. It was surrounded by a broad silver frame embossed with cherubs. What a young beauty the girl was! A combination of frivolity and strong will; a power based on always being rich. He had taken her so much for granted until she went, treating

269

her as an overgrown, spoilt child, yet he had always felt slightly inferior to her. But now, on his own – oh, how he longed for her again.

On Friday he was extremely busy and hardly in the house, but he knew she would have her own keys. In fact, he was keeping away from the place because he wasn't quite sure what would happen when they met.

When they did finally meet it was in the evening. He opened the front door and walked into the drawing room, then stopped short momentarily.

She didn't stand up. She was sitting there solidly, smiling at him incorrigibly – the same old Minny Dee. 'Hewy . . . my dearest darling!'

He walked across and bent over to kiss her. She was wearing glasses with bright blue frames. He'd never seen her in any glasses before, except sunglasses.

He had never seen her fully pregnant either. She was huge!

He did a few swift calculations, reviewed the dates when he had seen her. Could the child possibly be his?

CHAPTER FOURTEEN

Just a Statue

Milly saw the announcement quite by chance in a copy of the *Manchester Guardian*.

She was in the attic flat at Sundower House, where she was now permanently installed, folding up an old newspaper into long strips then tying the strips into small circular shapes to light the fire with. Suddenly, she froze.

EDMUNDSON: a son, Karl, for Hewy and Mina.

She stared at it with amazement. The date of the paper was only a few days after she had told Hewy she was expecting his child. She frowned slightly, remembering how his cruel words had forced her to strike him. Maybe he had behaved like that because he'd already known Minny Dee would be back as a full-term mother, due to have this other man's baby? Yet it hadn't seemed a bit like that . . . And to think how he'd treated her over his *true* forthcoming offspring when this one – so publicly celebrated – was clearly not his!

Her own baby was apparent to all, now, and many people had asked her if she was expecting twins. Only two months to go . . .

Throughout the last, traumatic month, her only real friend and faithful help had been Gus Bridges. He was the man whose shirt she'd drenched with tears, and who'd tried to calm and comfort her when she had poured out her terrible woes. And he was the one who had provided her with a sanctuary, steering her firmly back to Sundower House.

'There's nothing to be done at present, Milly, but at least the child will know who its true father is, eventually. All we can do is wait and see if Hewy will become more reasonable. The most important thing at the moment is to look after yourself, for the baby's sake.'

He restrained himself from saying anything to Hewy, for he knew it was an entirely private affair and nothing to do with him. He'd suffered his own share of marital disharmony and chose to steer clear of any entanglement in other people's problems as much as possible. As for himself, he still hoped that eventually he would obtain a divorce from his wife of long ago.

It was obvious that he regarded Milly's state of fecundity as a precious gift from God, made all the more poignant by his own inability to produce children due to his past illness. He looked after Milly with concern and delight, insisting on sketching her many times and saying that a pregnant woman had a certain majesty, never manifested at any other time. Milly indulged him with amusement, but she didn't believe a word of it and longed only for the day when her proper figure would be released from all the extra bulk.

Gus even wanted to lay his head against Milly's belly to listen to the baby's heartbeat. He smiled with triumph at the small pulsing, living sound of new unknown life, and felt the movements of the baby's limbs, small knobbles that gently poked about beneath Milly's domed abdomen.

She felt completely at ease with him by now, the more

so since they had gradually come to share all their secrets with one another including the sorry story of his marriage and the reason for its failure.

One day during the art school holidays he asked her: 'Is there any chance I could make a sculpture of you, Milly?'

'A sculpture? In *this* state? Whoever would want a sculpture like that?'

'I would.'

'Not a nude one, surely?'

He looked slightly embarrassed. 'Well, yes, but you could remain covered most of the time and I've already done a lot of sketches. I would take care you didn't have to pose for a long time or stand for too long, and I know you've never done much modelling before . . .'

'*Much* modelling?' She could see the funny side of it, for the only time she'd ever tried modelling was that memorable occasion when she'd done Zeronica a favour and sat on that chair, fully clothed, at the meeting of the Post-War Visualists. And afterwards she had vowed never, never to do it again!

'I shall abide by what you say, Milly. Just say no if you'll find it too distasteful.'

'You know I wouldn't find it distasteful, Gus.' She knew how different his request was from the crude demand that had been made of her services on that day long ago. 'In some ways it would be quite an adventure. It's not often that women have sculptures done of them when they're in this state. And as you say, it's a proud period in a woman's life in many respects, and a natural one. Though I expect many people might be quite horrified by the idea.' She smiled. 'And anyway, how on earth would you make a sculpture in two months? How big would it be?'

'It wouldn't be too large. I'd make a plaster cast, and then see if it could be finished in bronze.'

She was startled. 'Bronze? It would cost an absolute fortune!'

He looked amused. 'Never mind the cost, Milly. The point is, would you agree to it?'

She nodded silently. He kissed her affectionately and went back to his own flat.

The last two months flashed past like wildfire. She had stopped helping out at the art school but had continued with her own studies, and Gus had sold some of her textile designs for her. She had no proper income of her own now, so she blessed him secretly more and more, and gladly modelled for him.

The sculpture started off as a series of small, rough clay shapes. The best of these was then fashioned into a larger, carefully worked clay sculpture which Gus planned to finalise in plaster of Paris, with a view to casting it in bronze sometime in the future, when he could afford it.

Milly was startled by the swiftness and passion of his work. It was as if she was watching the emergence of a new, better woman, yet a woman of clay; something being created which was herself yet not herself; an independent being. She stood there, composed and entirely silent, looking forward to the time when the clay would be transformed into a white snow maiden, ready for some time in an unknown future when it could become a bronze woman for all the world to see.

Gus worked away, standing back from time to time and murmuring, 'Not long now ... Soon ...'

Soon ... until he covered it all with a piece of sheeting.

'So what do you think of it Milly?'

The white plaster of Paris sculpture was on a revolving plinth in the workroom of his flat, facing the world outside the windows with triumphant perfection. It stood exactly two feet eight inches from head to toe and was finished the night before Milly's labour pains began.

She stared at it in wonder. 'I think it's marvellous. It's a wonderful portrayal of pregnancy. All the best parts, all the optimistic future . . .'

He hesitated. 'It isn't quite perfect – but what creation ever is? But it's a true memory of this time, Milly. And it's the first sculpture I've done in years, what with all my films and other artwork. I'm very proud of it. And just you see – when it's cast in bronze it will be a masterpiece. The beauty of plaster of Paris is that provided it doesn't get chipped or scratched it can be kept for any length of time for the final metal casting.' His eyes shone with enthusiasm, and he looked at her so earnestly that tears came to her eyes.

How could she ever manage without him? She felt so safe. She knew he was so utterly reliable.

But later that night, as she lay alone in her double bed in the attic flat and felt the first period-like pains of something brewing, she knew that not even Gus could make this part any easier.

She looked across at the chest of drawers. It was full of nappies passed on to her by Babsy, and knitted baby clothes, many of which had been given to her by friends at the art school. There was a second-hand white enamelled baby bath on a low wooden stand in the corner, and against the far wall lay a small wooden trundle cot, already made up with cotton sheets and baby blankets.

For a few hours she lay there, wondering if this was the start of her child arriving and whether it would come very quickly. Perhaps she should get in touch with the midwife? Then, as nothing further happened, she dozed off to sleep, only to be awoken again by a much stronger griping pain, in her loins. She climbed out of bed and walked around the room, rubbing her back gently. She wondered whether to warn Gus. But nothing more happened, and once more she got back into bed and fell asleep.

When Mrs Benson the midwife called round the next morning Milly had felt no further rumbles and was entirely all right.

'False alarm. The first rehearsal ...' Moll Benson smiled. 'You have to watch out, mind, because some people never get a false alarm. False alarms can often be about a month before it's due, but in this case you *are* due, so I'll keep popping in during the day to see if you've had any more hints.'

The day went on. Gus called in to see her. He had to go out, but not for long.

'I shall be quite all right, Gus. I haven't had a single pain lately, and Mrs Benson will be calling again.'

'Are you quite, quite sure, Milly?'

'Absolutely sure, Gus. You go. I prefer to be on my own.'

Everything went quite normally until the afternoon, when gradually the pains began to come more regularly: dull, cramping aches, which took their time to go. Each time Milly gasped and wincingly counted the seconds to their waning, sighing with relief as they faded once more, then grabbing at the short bliss of normality before yet another wave came belting to the shore.

'Plenty of time to go yet,' said Moll Benson when she arrived.

Plenty of time to go? How long was she going to have to stand it all? Even though Mrs Benson had decided to stay with her, Milly felt so alone and helpless; so defenceless. She tried to look on the bright side. But all she wanted to do now was to get the agony over as soon as possible without having to have chloroform.

Gradually, as the contractions became more frequent, she got into a pattern of bracing herself then trying to relax into them. But she was in labour a long time and by the time the baby was born twelve hours later she was worn out and sweating with exhaustion. Never, never again would she go through all that. She had been a lone fighter in the battle only women had to face, with not even the comfort of a caring husband and relatives to share the eventual joy of the birth.

Well, it was, God be praised, born at last and bawling its head off. She lay there gasping, groaning, half laughing and half crying with relief at the final proof that nine months of waiting was over, and had been more than worthwhile. Her harrowing memories of only a few hours past were already dimming in the new and thankful present. She could glimpse the baby's shining blue umbilical cord gleaming and still trailing from its belly button towards the placenta, and its small body covered in creamy vernix as if someone had smeared it with cream cheese.

'A beautiful girl,' smiled the midwife. 'What will you call her?'

'Clarinda,' said Milly firmly. 'After my mother.'

The baby was wrapped up and given to Milly to hold. Gus, who had been pacing up and down in his workroom as anxiously as any expectant father, came in to see her. Pleasure and release from the burden of it all were written all over his face, and they smiled joyfully at each other.

277

On Milly's medical notes were the words:

MILLICENT DAWNAY,
spinster.
Religion: C of E
Baby: female, CLARINDA DAWNAY, 7lb 4oz, b.
23.07.25.

'I'll put notice of it in the *Manchester Evening News*,'
said Gus proudly.

'No, don't do that!' The joy of the birth was shrouded
in a sudden gloom. How could she openly announce in
the paper the birth of an illegitimate child, unclaimed by
its true father?

But then, as she looked at Clarinda sleeping peacefully; saw the tuft of black hair on her crown and the
little, screwed-up face with its strong features; felt the
thankfulness of the whole miracle of this small, live
human being; a sense of loyal defiance rose within her.
Why should she shrink away from the announcement
because she was a single mother?

'Yes, Gus, on second thoughts it would be a very
good idea. Put it in as many papers as you want.' She
smiled at him gratefully. What more amazing happening than this could she hope to proclaim and celebrate?

By the time Clarinda was six months old, Milly was
firmly settled in the attic flat and Babsy had become her
baby-minder whilst she went back to work at the art
school.

'Let's face it, Milly,' said Babsy, 'the money for
looking after her will come in handy now Mackie and
me have moved to a larger house, and I love children. I
promise that if I find it too much I'll let you know.'

One day a couple of weeks after Milly had gone back to work, Gus came into her flat looking very tense. There was an unusual undercurrent of excitement about him. Without any preambles, he burst out: 'Guess what, Milly? Pauline, my wife, has agreed – after all these years – to a divorce at last! So all that remains is for me to ask you to marry me.'

She gazed at him in wonder. Over the years the story of his wife had become like a faded legend in her mind, never to be changed. Her own relationship with him had been a purely platonic affair, in spite of people who said there could be no such thing between a man and a woman. Yet how much had he given of himself in kindness, love and faithfulness? How could she possibly refuse this noble, unassuming man?

'Yes, Gus. I'll marry you.' She stepped towards him and they fell into each other's arms.

That night, as they lay together for the first time in the same bed, they planned to marry quietly at a registry office when the divorce was finally settled.

And in spite of the fact that she was still not married in the official sense, Milly felt as if a lingering cloud had lifted at last from the horizon as they settled down together as secret man and wife.

It was a beautiful day in 1926 and Milly was in the kitchen making a birthday cake for Clarinda's first birthday, whilst Clarinda was having a sleep in her cot. Milly put the cake in the oven and went to look at her daughter. Her hair curled softly around her dimpled, bonny face and thick curling eyelashes shaded her sleeping eyes. She was the absolute image of Hewy Edmundson . . .

Milly had finished her studies at art school and had

279

already been offered a proper teaching post there, beginning in the Autumn term, which she had accepted. Her life was progressing easily and pleasantly, in spite of the general climate of strife and hardship resulting from the economic depression. She was even continuing to sell her textile designs. There was just one slight snag, which hopefully was to be ironed out at any moment: Gus's divorce had not yet materialised, despite his wife's final agreement to proceed.

When he came home that evening, his face was alight with pleasure. 'You'll never guess what happened today, Milly! I met someone who I worked with during the war. Now he works in documentary films, and he wants me to go and direct for him. He's been away from this country, but now he's back, he's started up some studios in a large country house just outside Knutsford.'

Gus looked serious again. 'It'll mean I'll be away quite a lot during the art school vacations, but one good point is that I'll have a bit of spare cash to get the statue cast in bronze.'

She sensed he'd added the bit about the bronze just to cheer her up, for surely the real truth was that once more she was going to be fending for herself, with no close companionship except that of her baby daughter. She struggled to put a brave face on it.

'Well, Gus, at least I've plenty to keep me occupied when you're away, especially with Babsy still able to look after Clarinda whilst I'm at college.'

She knew it would be harder, though. For one thing, there wouldn't be as many comfortable motor-car rides for herself and her child. From now on it would be pram trolleys, trams, buses, trains and Shanks's Pony. But most of all, she would miss Gus himself, always so comforting and reliable.

Gus was amazingly prompt in fulfilling his promise about the statue, and after his first three-week stint away, he came back and announced he was having it cast in bronze at last. 'I wasn't just saying it to console you, Milly, I really meant it.'

He was so full of enthusiasm every time he came back from a stint of his film directing that one day it slowly and painfully dawned on her that in spite of his loyalty to her and his never-ending love and kindness, the thing dearest to his heart was his film making.

She brooded on it for hours whilst he was away, knowing he would never admit it. But, there again, was it fair for her to be here, waiting to be his wife and expecting him to support Hewy Edmundson's child?

One day towards the end of the year, Milly walked into the large studio room at Sundower House to find a surprise awaiting her on the small oval table. There, by the casement window where she had spent all those hours of modelling for it, was the bronze glory of pure, simple, pregnant motherhood.

'And all ready for display in the new Frederick Ingles Studios in Mosely Street, Milly.' Gus stepped forward, smiling. 'But not for sale. I don't think I could ever really part with it.'

They put their arms round each other's shoulders and silently appraised it as a work of art.

The Frederick Ingles Studios had only just opened and were regarded as being extremely modern and forward-looking. The pieces they showed were a far cry from fig leaves over private parts . . .

Frederick Ingles was not what you'd call parochial. He was a stocky man with a short grey beard. A man with no frills and a bit of a sense of humour, not to mention a bit of cash to spare, to nourish his own tastes. He embraced all forms of art, both local and worldwide, at a time when L.S. Lowry was exhibiting his Manchester work abroad and when Pablo Picasso, Paul Klee and Joan Miro were the talking point at arty parties.

Gus was pleased to have his bronze accepted for exhibition at the Ingles Studios. He knew it was good. The statue followed a classical style, rather more in the path of Rodin than of Jacob Epstein. But although pregnant women were fairly common sculptural symbols in world terms, there weren't many of them popping about in Manchester.

About two weeks before the opening night preview of the exhibition, Gus realised he wouldn't be able to go. 'There's some crucial filming work on hand, Milly. Will you be able to manage on your own? Perhaps Mrs Maybury could come and sit in with Clarinda whilst you were out – she's always very helpful. I think at least one of us should be there.'

Milly nodded. 'I might try asking Babsy if she'll come. She never has a night out.'

But Babsy turned the offer down. 'It just wouldn't be worth it, Milly. By the time I'd got all the children to bed and seen to Mackie's supper, I'd be exhausted. And then I'd have to hire a taxi or something. No, I can't see it working. But I'll come round with the children sometime when the statue's back at home, and you can tell me what went on.'

Just after Gus had left to do his filming, a letter arrived addressed to Gus Bridges and bearing the name Ingles in a blue crest on the envelope. Since Gus had instructed Milly to take charge of all the mail whilst he was away, she opened it.

Dear Mr Bridges

Due to some misunderstanding, I note you have put "Not For Sale" on your bronze study of The Pregnant Woman. I must ask you as a matter of urgency to state how much the price is before the opening viewing. Perhaps I did not make it clear that the exhibition is only for work that is for sale.

Yours faithfully,
Freddy Ingles

Milly stared at the letter again and again. She knew it was impossible to get in touch with Gus except by telegram, and she felt that an urgent telegram was not quite warranted. There was no doubt that neither of them wanted to have the statue sold. But at the same time, Gus was very keen to have it exhibited . . .

Hastily she took up her pen and replied.

Dear Mr Ingles,

I am writing on behalf of Mr Bridges, who unfortunately is away at present. He is sorry he misunderstood the terms of exhibiting The Pregnant Woman, and asks that a price of 700 guineas be placed on it.

Yours sincerely,
Millicent Dawnay (For Mr Augustine Bridges)

Milly sealed the letter and posted it with a flourish of satisfaction. The high price she had put on the statue was a sure way of ensuring that it would *not* be sold, knowing what Manchester people were like . . .

When she got home again she wrote and told Gus,

and a couple of days later he replied saying he agreed with her.

Milly went to the private showing at the gallery alone, and with some trepidation. She was very thin now, slimmer than she'd ever been in all her life, and a far cry from The Pregnant Woman. And, to distance herself from it even further amongst all the bubbling, well-dressed crowd, she was wearing a plain, severely cut, charcoal-grey two-piece costume.

The very first person she saw when she entered the gallery with its deep damson curtains and its carefully arranged lighting effects for the exhibition preview, was Minny Dee . . .

Milly froze in her tracks.

Who could have failed to miss this vision in front of her? Mrs Hewy Edmundson stood poised in a silver lamé dress with a small piece of mink thrown across one shoulder, and wearing a close-fitting, sequined, silver-beaded cap on her shapely head.

Milly began to turn away. She felt like leaving immediately, but the place was so crowded that she took heart again and decided that in her own unobtrusive clothes she would be unnoticed. She began to peer at her catalogue with undue concentration, whilst edging nearer and nearer to where she thought the bronze statue was.

'Milly! What on earth are you doing here?'

Suddenly, right in the squash of it all, there was Hewy with the long stem of a champagne glass balanced in his fingers. His eyes were sparkling, his face smooth and happy. It was as if life's troubles had passed him by completely and there had never been any history between them.

She met his gaze with a mixture of anger and defiance.

'Why on earth shouldn't I be here?'

He faltered slightly. 'Sorry ... It was badly put ... How are you, anyway? You look stunning. Someone somewhere said you were back at Sundower?'

She nodded and smiled briefly. 'I'm here to see a bronze of Gus's.'

'Gus, sculpture? That is not usually his line, is it? To tell you the truth, I haven't bothered with the sculptures much. I was looking at the etchings ... Mina's here somewhere – have you seen her?'

'I think so.'

'You must come round and visit us sometime.'

'Yes ...'

There was an uneasy silence. They exchanged bright, insincere smiles, then Hewy drifted away.

Milly looked down at her catalogue again and found the etchings – "23: Child in a Cornflower Field, Hugo Edmundson". Her mouth set hard.

'Excuse me. Are you Miss Dawnay?' A tall man in an untidy suit was standing next to her with a pleasant look on his face. 'It's taken me quite a long time to find you in all this scrum. I gather you know something about the bronze sculpture by Mr Bridges? It's certainly a striking piece of work.' He gave her a disarming smile. 'Someone said Dr Raphael Del Shaugnessy of the obstetrics department at Saints is interested in buying it for the hospital.'

Milly stared at him. Who was this man? And how on earth had he managed to track her down in all this crowd when she had been sure no one would know her? Was it some sort of joke?

'It's quite a price, isn't it?' said the man cheerfully. 'You've hit lucky in a way. I expect Mr Bridges will be quite chuffed when he hears about it. I hope he isn't ill or anything?'

'No, not at all. He's away doing film work.'

'Busy man, eh? Very versatile.'

She nodded her head.

Then the man said casually: 'Someone said the model for it was you. Is that true?' His face was completely bland.

She frowned. 'Who on earth said that? And what does it matter anyway? It's the sculpture that counts.'

'Yes, yes, of course. I quite agree with you, Miss Dawnay. It's a marvellous piece of work and it's causing quite a stir. I wouldn't mind buying it myself if I had any money and wasn't married.'

'What exactly is *that* supposed to mean, Mr – er . . .'

'Charterson.' He swiftly produced a card from his pocket. 'Miles Charterson, Editor, *Blazonby Bugle*.'

When he'd melted away again into the chattering crowds, she found the sculpture. It was on a plinth in a corner, and not very well placed, for it needed to have space all around it for it to be seen at its best. But even so, she felt a glow of pride as she looked at it.

So, had the man been right in what he said about someone wanting to buy it? She half hoped it was untrue, yet if it was going to a hospital it would really be quite an honour . . .

As Milly returned home she was torn both ways about what might happen to the statue. But in the end she knew it would rest on what Gus himself decided.

Six months later, when Gus was still travelling backwards and forwards from his film making, and the sculpture was resting quietly back at Sundower with never another cheep about anybody wanting to buy it, he finally received notice of his divorce being complete. He began to make arrangements for his marriage to Milly at the registry office.

Milly was relieved at the news. Her life had settled into a regular pattern and she was busy herself with her artwork, and bringing up Clarinda, who was changing from a baby to a lively two-year-old in what seemed like seconds.

She had asked Babsy and Mackie to stand for them at the ceremony, and everything was going along smoothly until the day when Gus came home and said they would have to change the date: 'Not for long or anything, but if we could just make it at least two weeks later so as to get some film work done. It's absolutely crucial for the weather effects. We're in this dry, sunny spell which is set fair for some time. It would be madness to ignore it, Milly.'

She sighed inwardly. She knew he was right, but it was so upsetting to have arrangements perpetually changed. It would mean telling all their friends it was off and putting all of Babsy's family out of kilter.

'It's only for a week or two, Babsy . . .'

Babsy gasped with ill-concealed annoyance. 'Really, Milly! He absolutely takes the biscuit for not wanting to get properly spliced. It's excuses all the way!'

'It's not quite like that, Babsy. Filming is terribly capricious. The moment has to be taken advantage of, so to speak. It isn't Gus's fault . . . I just have to be patient. I feel awful about it from your point of view, but . . .'

Babsy smiled and gave a huge mock groan. 'Go on, then. We'll wait for the next date . . .'

The next date was fixed and this time there were no hitches at all.

Milly arranged everything perfectly. Clothes, food, everything.

Gus accepted it all in his usual manner, without a hint of resistance. He bought the wedding ring and ordered all the flowers. They set off in the car together, with Clarinda travelling with Babsy and her family.

Then, just as they got to the steps of the registry office, Milly felt a terrible faintness enveloping her.

'It's no good, Gus . . . I can't go on with it.'

White as a ghost, she swayed dangerously and clung heavily to his arm.

He supported her as they went inside to the waiting room where the others were and she sat down, trembling. 'I'm sorry, Gus, it wouldn't work,' she muttered. She shook her head from side to side then rested it against his chest. 'It'll all have to be cancelled.' She closed her eyes.

Everyone stood about uncertainly, then Gus said: 'She's ill. It's finished. Sorry and all that . . . I'll have to notify the registrar.'

Babsy and Mackie took Clarinda home with them and Milly went home with Gus, who put her to bed.

After a couple of hours' sleep Milly woke up. She felt completely all right. In fact, she felt better than she had done for ages. She was suddenly aware of a freedom she'd never even sensed before.

When Gus came creeping in with a cup of tea, she said: 'It was inevitable, Gus. Neither of us really wanted it. You were being kind to me . . .'

'I wasn't, Milly, I swear it.' His face reflected his despair. 'All I want is for you to be happy . . .'

She stared back at him and tears began to roll down her face. 'But how *can* we be happy when I know that Clarinda is Hewy's child and he won't even acknowledge it, and *you* are having to bring up Hewy's child and act as her father? It just wouldn't be right, Gus. I

288

couldn't bear it ... I would be doing you an injustice. No, I've got to get it cleared up properly with Hewy, for the sake of all of us, including Clarinda ...'

'Don't leave me, Milly, that's all I ask.'

'Of course I won't leave you. It's just that I see now that I can't marry you. At least, not until Hewy admits he is Clarinda's father, and who knows how long that will take?'

A couple of days later, Hewy Edmundson was idly reading a gossip item in the *Evening News* by 'Grape Vine'.

'We see that Saint Raffles is causing another rumpus in the region of female expectancy by pressing his need for a bronze statue of female fruitfulness to be acquired from hospital funds to grace the main entrance of the Obstetrics Department. This has caused many Bearing Down spasms. Most of the noble committee felt it was an affront to the dignity of womanhood and all agreed that they could not countenance their wives or daughters being faced by such vulgarity. This sentiment was echoed by many pregnant women themselves – one saying that a woman attired in a flowing night dress might have been more acceptable and refined.'

Hewy put down the paper and went out into the garden to play with his son.

CHAPTER FIFTEEN

Confrontation

Minny Dee was getting ready to go out. The only other people in the house were Nanny (forty-year-old Miss Travers, who looked after Karl), and Hewy, who was in his private studio working in splendid isolation.

Minny Dee was exceedingly restless these days. She was bored with the art world; bored with nannies; and bored with Bramhall.

She was getting reading to go out dancing. Her frock was slightly too short for parochial do's, and through its creamy silken fringes her plump, dimpled knees clad in pale-pink silk stockings beamed out invitingly. Over the frock she wore a satin, highly embroidered stiff-shouldered jacket with purple silk revers. Her hair was shingled almost to an Eton crop, and her emerald and silver cigarette holder lay ready on the dressing table as she carefully painted her nails pearly green.

She wasn't going to a posh affair. A posh affair was an occasion when you went along with your husband in his bow tie and tails, and were announced by flunkeys at the top of winding stairs leading to sumptuous ballrooms where orchestras soothed the air and women in mothballed fishnet gloves fanned themselves.

No, this was a local hop full of Charleston fanatics at the Palais de Danse, and she was being met at the bottom of the drive in twenty minutes by Ramsay Browne, the window cleaner's seventeen-year-old son, and the son's girlfriend, hefty Shirley Pringle, who wore a long string of Woolworth's pearls, a band round her head and a coney fur coat.

'They'll keep you safe, Mrs Edmundson,' said the window cleaner, winking, when he heard how Hewy was otherwise occupied and how Mina pined for a good night out. 'They're good affairs at that pallay, and you'll 'ave a reet good neet.' He looked at her solemnly. 'I 'ope you isn't completely k-lied and knock-kneed after a night on the tiles with that there Charleston. They do say it's good exercise, mind, with all them joints flapping and clacking, an' all them beads a-swinging and a-throttling. It cures as many as it injures . . .'

The Palais was packed, and within five minutes Ramsay and Shirley had vanished for good. Mina was swept into the cavorting crowds by a clothes prop of a man in a large bow tie called Shorty, who said he owned a bread shop, and asked her to marry him at the end of the first dance. By the end of the final cooling-down 'Who's Taking You Home Tonight' waltz, Mina was clutched in his arms like a melting sardine, quite unaware that Milly Dawnay was also at the Palais on a night out with her friend Babsy.

Milly and Babsy looked askance at the crumpled vision before them.

'Fancy Minny Dee being here with *him*!' gasped Babsy. 'He almost lives here. He was doing the self-same thing the last time we came. Whatever's happened to Hewy?'

Milly shook her head vaguely. She wasn't particularly

interested at the moment. Her heart wasn't really in the Palais and she was looking forward to getting back home. Yet she always came with Babsy because she knew how much Babsy enjoyed getting away from the family for a while. Mackie was completely clueless as to where they actually went – probably because Babsy always took her knitting bag with her, containing her dance shoes, and a piece of wool hanging out of it ostentatiously.

When Milly got back to Sundower House that night, she was quite absent-minded when Gus spoke to her. She had begun to think about Minny Dee again. Whatever had induced her to go to a place like that – Mina, the queen of luxury?

Babs was quite right to ask what had happened to Hewy. Her heart almost missed a beat. Surely he and Mina hadn't split up? What a disaster if they had, especially with the complications of Hewy's one and only true child – her own darling little girl, Clarinda – and his assumed child by Mina.

It was two weeks later that she received more than the answer she'd bargained for when she came face to face with Hewy outside the city art gallery in Mosely Street. That day, the wind and gales were so strong that people's umbrellas were getting blown inside out. She was standing there trying to put hers right and fold the spokes back into position, when her green velvet beret blew off, almost into the tracks of a heavy dray horse, except that some man swiftly caught it . . .

It was him.

'Hewy!' She gasped his name with sudden, natural relief, then immediately felt ashamed that she had responded to him in that way when she always claimed to herself to feel so bitter, and even to hate him.

'Milly?' His dark hair strayed across his forehead in rain-drenched curls. His face gradually changed to a wide smile. 'What a day! Let's get in here and shelter.'

They went up the steps into the gallery and stood just inside the door beyond the pillars and portico. Their voices were lowered to a whisper because everything echoed so much in the vast space of the entrance hall.

Milly took a deep breath. A unique blend of Mansion polish, pine disinfectant and mature paint varnish assailed her nostrils.

He stared at her quite tenderly. 'How's the artwork? By the way, I was sorry to see that bit in the paper about Gus's pregnant woman bronze and that bunch of Philistines on the hospital board . . . Where is it now, then?'

'In pride of place at Sundower House, in the living room. I never wanted it to go in the first place. We put a high price on it to stop that very thing happening . . .'

He hardly seemed to hear her. 'I'm starving. Let's go to Paulden's and have some hotpot. My Ford's parked round the corner.'

'I shouldn't really. I've got to get back to work on my designs, then I have to collect Clarinda from Babsy's. Gus is off again tomorrow . . . He's away a terrible lot on his filming these days.'

When they were settled in the warm luxury of Paulden's restaurant, with its thick carpets and gleaming white starched tablecloths and silver-plated dishes, and the delicious smells of dinner wafting everywhere, Hewy spoke above the background sounds of violins and piano: 'I expect your daughter will be about the same age as my son Karl. . .' He looked sad. 'I only wish Mina was a bit more of a mother at times . . .'

'Gus has been a marvellous father to Clarinda,

especially considering she's another man's child.' Milly stared at him hard. 'I expect you're in the same boat too, in a way, Hewy ...' She blurted out the words before realising properly what she was saying.

He stiffened, and his face reddened angrily. 'Me, in the same boat ... How can I be?'

The hotpot had arrived. Their plates were placed in front of them and the waitress was putting a double tureen of potatoes and peas between them, but they ignored it all in a sudden, secret challenge.

'Go on then, Milly Dawnay, what *exactly* are you getting at?'

'Nothing,' she muttered in a low voice, 'except that Karl has a different father, just as Clarinda has a different father ...'

He looked as if he was about to strike her, then collected himself just in time. Taking a large tablespoon, he put two huge boiled potatoes on his plate and helped himself to hotpot. Then, stabbing the potato viciously, he said coolly: 'Where on earth did you get that daft idea?'

'Because Minny Dee was supposed to have left you, Hewy. Then back she comes, pregnant ...'

He glared at her scornfully, with his mouth full. 'And do you really mean to say that on that flimsy amount of evidence you've concluded that Karl *isn't* my child?' He gulped down the last bit of food and then spoke in a harsh, swift stream of words: 'The stark truth is, Milly, that Karl was conceived during her earlier visit to see me at Naples Lodge, if you must know. When she finally came back for good, it was precisely because I *knew* it was my child that I wanted her back, for the sake of *my* son.'

There was silence as they both picked very slowly at

their food, while the musicians continued playing pieces from *The Student Prince*.

Then Milly spoke up: 'But not your *daughter*, eh, Hewy? Not my Clarinda ... One of these days, maybe, you'll come round to the truth. But by then it'll be too late. Clarinda may have started hidden in that bronze statue, but every day she grows more and more like you for all the world to see, so that you'll never be able to deny it!'

She got up hastily from the table and grabbed her coat, then hurried from the dining room with his voice still ringing in her ears. Oh what a terrible, terrible mess it all was ... She began to wish she'd never met him again. How was it that there was always trouble in the end between them?

That day she hardly worked at all. The trauma of her meeting with Hewy had revived memories – memories of the small scraps of good time, of the moments of true love so quickly lost like wisps of magic.

As she prepared Clarinda for bed that night, combing her bonny curling dark hair and bathing her, she longed and longed for a normal happy family life like Babsy had, even though she knew it could never be quite like that because their lifestyles were so different and her artwork was so deeply embedded in her being. But now, at this moment, she was so lonely, what with Gus absent so often – though that was partly her own fault, the way she had turned him down at the last minute. How could she really grumble when in the end she was always the one who ran away from a permanent commitment? Was she going to end up as the eternal escaping bride?

That night she sobbed silently as Gus slept heavily beside her, until finally she began to slumber, drifting slowly away from the welter of sadness and confusion.

★

Zeronica was homesick for Manchester.

She and Arthur had done well in London. They were part of a circle of artists in the Euston Road, but all the same, she longed to get back to the North Country, and she was forever singing: 'On the oak and the ash and the bonny ivy tree, they-ey flour-rish at home in the North coun-treee . . .' as if her life depended on it, and in spite of the same trees flourishing elsewhere . . .

'Arthur . . . why don't we chance going back?'

Arthur shook his head doubtfully. 'It's a terrible time to move. We must thank our lucky stars we've got any work at all these days. 'For they'd already experienced the effects of the general strike and all its repercussions at first-hand. 'Going back there'll be like going back into the lion's den, Ronny.'

Zeronica shook her head mournfully and longed for the Sundower House era again, little realising how completely it had changed from the old days, for she had never kept in touch with anyone.

Then, like a bolt out of the blue, they received a postcard from Gus Bridges saying he was coming up to London and could he call on them?

Zeronica was full of exuberant excitement as she cleaned up the flat and dashed off to a delicatessen to prepare a welcoming meal fit for heroes.

'Gus! How wonderful to see you! You don't look a bit different, Arthur's just gone round the corner to get some fruit; he won't be long . . .'

They sat there talking about old times and new times, then Gus spoke more and more about the film work that was absorbing him. It was strange, but for some reason he never mentioned Milly or young Clarinda once. It was as if he had entirely forgotten them as the hours flew by . . .

'Although a lot of the small-scale film makers have been forced out since the coming of the talkies, some of us have managed to cling on by our bootstraps.' Gus smiled thankfully. 'Which includes Finer Films, with all those memories of old Art and Hew and Mackie helping out . . .'

Zeronica began to look anxiously at the clock. 'Wherever can Art be? I know how he's a bit of a devil for getting embroiled with his pals, but he was only going to get a few apples and oranges and some grapes – and he swore he'd be no more than ten minutes.' Her face had gone quite pale. 'It's just not like him . . .'

'Hello there . . . Anybody in?' It was a loud, unknown male voice bellowing from outside the door of the flat. 'Is this Art Fallows' place?'

Zeronica was trembling so much that Gus went forward to the door.

Her worst fears were realised.

'Afraid there's bin a bit of an accident. Mr Fallows has bin knocked down by a motor car on the corner of the square an' he's bin taken to hospital.'

Gus and Zeronica sat gloomily in the ward waiting room, waiting to see the sister.

'He's down in theatre at the moment having an emergency operation to try and save his arm,' she told them when she eventually appeared.

Two weeks later, Arthur Fallowfield was still in hospital and Gus had come back home with the news that although the hospital had saved his arm, he would not be able to use it for fine work. It was his right arm, and the hand he had used all his life to do his commercial work.

The blow for both him and Zeronica was tremendous.

'Whatever will they do then, Gus?' said Milly. 'However will they manage to make a proper living if he can't use his hand again?'

Gus looked at her cautiously. 'They'd been thinking of coming back here, and this has probably made Zeronica keener than ever. But of course the situations's so different now. Their old attic flat is occupied by other people . . . There could be one solution, though. They could help me with the film work, and come and stay with us in this apartment whilst they find accommodation of their own. We'd have loads of space if we cleared some of the junk to one side . . .'

Milly felt her heart fall. Her relationship with Zeronica had never been the same after the row they'd once had about Arthur and Hortensia. And as for Arthur himself, she knew from experience that he had a very domineering streak after the fiasco of her picture in that Spring Exhibition . . .

'What on earth's the matter, Milly? You look quite put out!'

'It's just that I wonder if it would be a wise plan for them to stay here in the same flat as us.'

He frowned. 'It's not like you to be so uncharitable, and you know how fed up you get being on your own if I'm away. It could work out very well, besides being handy for my film work. It would make a heck of a difference to have them here, on the spot: two people who've already got experience of the whole set-up . . .'

Quickly, she agreed; glad he was so keen and settled about it for his own sake, but actually dreading it for hers.

Alas, her worst fears were well founded. When Zeronica and Arthur decided to return a month or so later, their greetings to her were like ice. And when she and Zeronica were alone in the flat it was only the cheerful prattle of Clarinda that kept things remotely normal, as Zeronica tried to pretend that Milly didn't even exist. As for Arthur, he spoke to Gus about film work, but wouldn't address a word to Milly.

Milly began to get desperate. Surely she wasn't going to have to move yet again? She didn't feel she could bear it. But what could be worse than getting this awful cold shoulder all the time – which Gus seemed to be completely unaware of?

One day things came to a head. It was when Zeronica was out and Arthur was looking at some film-set notes Gus had left him to read. He was smoking a cigarette with his left hand and could just about manage to keep the paper under control with his right one, whilst Clarinda ran about the room, and Milly did some of her own work in the bedroom.

'Milly, are you there?' Arthur called out irritably. 'Can't you do something with this child? She's getting on my nerves . . .'

Milly pretended not to hear. After all, the bedroom door was wide open and Clarinda was quite free to come and see her whilst she was working. In fact, she knew that if she could hear Clarinda scampering happily about it was a far better sign than if things went very quiet, because that would mean Clarinda was up to something, and Milly would have to stop her own work to investigate.

'Milly! Did you *hear* me?' Arthur's voice was as harsh as a hacksaw. 'How the hell can anyone concentrate on anything with her charging about the place?'

By this time, Clarinda, knowing how bad-tempered Uncle Arthur was getting, had retired to a quiet corner next to Milly and was looking at a crayoning book of nursery rhymes. Arthur thumped out of the room nonetheless, muttering wild threats, and quite unaware that in his fury he had left his burning cigarette close to the film-set notes ...

Suddenly Milly smelt smoke. She dashed into the room and within seconds had managed to put out the flames by smothering them with soil from a pot of geraniums and a metal tea tray.

Both Milly and little Clarinda stood there in state of shock, staring at the burn marks on the large armchair.

'Let that be a warning to you never to smoke when you're grown up, or ever, *ever* play with matches,' said Milly to Clarinda in a shaky voice. 'It was an accident.'

'And Uncle Arthur did it, didn't he, Mummy?'

'Yes, he did, but it was an accident.'

Milly tried to soothe her small daughter. When they had both calmed down a bit, they put on their coats and went out for a walk to get away from the whole episode, and to feed some ducks on the nearby pond.

Milly could see clearly now that it was hopeless staying on at Sundower House any longer. As if echoing her thoughts, Clarinda said tearfully: 'Mummy, can we go away?'

'Yes, dear, we can. But we'll have to make some arrangements first. Uncle Arthur and Aunty Zeronica are a bit upset at the moment because of Uncle Arthur hurting his arm. They're looking for a house of their own, but it takes a long time. We're going to try to find one as well'.

That night Clarinda woke up screaming from a nightmare, and Milly began to feel desperate to move out. She needed to buy her own house, but she was as poor as a church mouse ... Well, she decided, it would have to be a case of grasping at anything – however awful – as quickly as she could so as to make a clean break from Sundower House.

The very next morning she rang the art school and said she wouldn't be able to go in to do her teaching that day. Then, leaving Clarinda with Babsy, she set off house-hunting.

Within two hours she had come across the derelict cottage that Babsy had mentioned only that morning: 'My great aunt Jonson's been living close to it for years. It's just off Lapwing Lane in West Didsbury, but it's in such a terrible broken-down state, no one seems to want it. It's called Mrs Clocker's Cottage, and when she died six months ago it was left to rot . . .'

When Milly saw it her spirits sank like lead. Even she hadn't envisaged such a wreck!

It had a chewed-looking thatched roof and was built with timber framing, with a red brick chimney that looked as if it had been added on as an afterthought. The bottom half resembled a stable and had wooden casements which, from their silvery, coarse-grained, warped appearance, had received a good battering from the elements over the years. In one of the spider-ridden broken windowpanes was a filthy bit of paper: 'FOR SALE. Fur there perticulars, see Mrs Sims at number 6.'

Milly stood staring at the tumbledown exterior for some time, then she peered through one of the windows. There seemed to be only one room downstairs, with an old slopstone in it; and she supposed there was only one room upstairs, from the one tiny window.

She walked slowly along the dank-smelling alley next to the cottage and found the garden: a few broken paving stones in some rough grass that was overgrown with dandelions, and a large elderberry bush. All three garden walls were composed of bits of other houses. There were two bent zinc buckets lying about with holes in them; and an old, empty coal sack, grimy with black dust, that lay covered in dead leaves.

Then, just as Milly was turning away, the sun came out from behind the scurrying clouds and shone full at the rear windows like a golden beam of hope. She turned back again and stared. Maybe, with a bit of imagination, maybe with some goodwill, and a very, very cheap price, she could transform it? For in some ways it was in a good situation. It wasn't isolated, and the larger houses on either side sheltered it.

Feeling slightly more hopeful now, she set off to find Mrs Sims, hoping against hope that she would be in.

'The people as owns it, love,' said Mrs Sims, who was already standing at her garden gate, peering towards Milly with her brawny arms folded, 'is some cousins of the old lady 'oo once lived 'ere. They 'as a telephone and lives at 'uddersfield. They've writ me out bits of paper with their name and address on 'em and the telephone number. Would you like one, love? Would you really?'

Milly nodded enthusiastically, then followed Mrs Sims up her donkey-stoned steps into the lobby then through to the kitchen, which still had newspaper on the red quarry-tiled floor because Mrs Sims had only just finished washing it.

Mrs Sims looked behind a small brown wooden clock and drew out a sheaf of papers. 'There y'are, love. Take two of 'em in case of emergency. An' I 'ope you gets it, dear. We need a few young ones to 'elp us old 'uns … Tarrar then.'

It took Milly two weeks to get it all settled. She arranged to rent the house for six months with a view to buying it at the end of that time, and she was allowed to paint it and decorate it and do anything else she thought necessary without altering the actual structure of the building.

It was a real relief to her, for it meant she had somewhere to go to mull over her options before reaching a final decision on whether to try and find the money to buy it. It would be a valuable stepping stone.

She didn't tell anyone about her plan, not even Babsy, for she wanted to break the news to Gus first, and the only way she could bear to do that was as quickly as possible on the very day she intended to move into the cottage.

She waited until all three of them – Gus, Zeronica and Arthur – were out, then she left the pale blue envelope on Gus's large deal table with a bowl of fruit sitting on the corner of it. She had given him her new address and said she would call back later for the remainder of her few possessions.

Then, taking her suitcase and a rucksack for herself and Clarinda, she left Sundower House, just as she had once before, but this time, with her small daughter by her side, she knew for certain it would be permanent.

CHAPTER SIXTEEN

Lone Souls

The Hon. Belvedere Constantine (a twenty-one-year-old, weighty Adonis, known to his pals as Belly Button) had spent the last two years of his life rollicking around in a minefield of pending paternity suits, while frantic women chased after him.

He'd spent much of this time drifting happily about Europe, away from rainy Manchester fogs, enjoying himself as the heir to a lordly family fortune. But now, in 1928, with the comfort of having Glover, Bliss and Cress, the family lawyers, to fight off all claims against him, he'd returned to the fold on the borders of Cheshire, and was helping his sisters with the estate. The only trouble was, it was early spring and the blood was surging in his veins again . . .

He decided to look up an old friend, and the next sunny day found him cantering happily along the leafy lanes of Bramhall, hunting idly for the country seat of dear old Minny Dee – or if people wanted to be really fussy, Philomena Edmundson, wife of Hugo.

'Where in heaven's name *is* her bloody place? Here am I, sat on this confounded, grass-munching cuddie and gazing out towards jolly old Bram'all Hall, with ne'er a Naples flippin' Lodge in sight ...'

Then suddenly he saw it.

He dismounted, tethered his horse, Teacake, to a tree and strolled up to the front door.

Mina opened it. She nearly swooned with amazement. 'Be-Bee! Don't say you've come all the way from France on horseback?'

'Course not, you silly old sausage. My God, Mina, do my eyes deceive me? Or are those *bags* under your limpid orbs?'

Mina looked at him reprovingly. 'I'm *older*, darling. Worn out looking after *your* piece of night-time mischief. He's nearly four, now.'

'They all say that, my beloved.' His eyes flickered a trifle coldly.

'And I'm the one who says it and *means* it, Belvedere. Anyway, whatever induced you to come back to boring old Bramhall?'

'You, my darling ... apart from Mater and the girls ...'

They smiled at each other shrewdly. Their general prattle concealed what they really were: a pair of hardened socialites who could do battle with anyone if they cared to stir themselves.

'Come with me into the orchard then, my prince, and look at your son for yourself: hair the colour of carrots, eyes like blue forget-me-nots, and as sturdy as a beer keg. He's even got your ears ...'

They both looked at Karl as he came towards Mina.

'This is a relation of yours, Karl. His name's Be-Bee.'

Karl looked up at the huge mountain before him, then Belvedere picked him up and sat him on his shoulders.

A bit later, when Karl was playing in his sandpit

outside and Mina and Be-Bee were sitting in the drawing room, Be-Bee said: 'Mmm, there is a *slight* likeness, but you've no real proof. And anyway, I'm too young to settle down yet.'

He got to his feet restlessly and then both went outside again through the French windows and sauntered round the vegetable patch, which was showing a bit of spring cabbage.

'Anyway, Mina, you always swore you were never cut out to be a wifey, and just look at you now – loving every minute of it.'

'I am *not* loving every minute of it, Be-Bee, and to be quite candid, Hewy was not placed on earth to look after *your* son. He only does it because he thinks the child's his.'

By the end of the afternoon, and a couple of small brandies later, Belvedere was in a forlorn state and ready to leave. He zig-zagged across the grass to his horse and made off for home. He had learnt there were some hard and ruthless women in the world and that Mina was definitely their leader.

She had threatened him resolutely: 'I'm just thoroughly sick of it here, Belvedere, and what you need is someone like me to look after you properly and keep you on the straight and narrow. Hewy is far too wrapped up in his art world. He has tunnel vision as far as any other part of life is concerned.'

Belvedere had looked at her plaintively, crumbling away like Cheshire cheese. 'B-but Mina . . . I'm so much younger than you . . . Damn it all, I'm only a mere stripling of twenty-one. You can hardly expect a young sproggit of my tender years to take on someone like you? You'll be an old hag in a few years . . .'

'Don't talk such piffling nonsense, Belvedere. Just go

back to Beltermain and tell your mother flat that Minny Dee is going to get a divorce and *you* are going to take her on, complete with the child your loved one already has. You've no need to tell them Karl was yours in the first place. And don't think I'm just teasing, Be-Bee – I mean every word of it, and my lawyers Glover, Bliss and Cress will always see to it that I win.'

Belvedere winced painfully. 'Not – *them*, surely?'

'Yes, *them*! So think hard about it and let me know by next week.'

She hadn't even bothered to wave him off.

When Hewy arrived back from the studio, Mina told him: 'I had a visitor today. Someone I knew when I was abroad . . .'

Hewy raised his eyebrows in mild surprise. 'Man or woman?'

'A man, actually. Anyway, let's have a meal first . . .'

Afterwards, when Karl was in bed and Nanny was out of the way, Mina said: 'You know that man I mentioned? He's Karl's father.'

Hewy froze. '*What?* Say that again?'

'He's Karl's father. His name's Be-Bee Constantine. I know all his sisters. He's a bit younger than me. He was out there when I was.'

The blood that had drained away from Hewy's face came back in full force and he gaped at her in fury. 'What the hell's got into you? Are you mad? He's *our* child! You damned well know it. It can even be dated to the very night you came back to Naples Lodge to tell me about your French Count.'

She half smiled at him. 'It can't, you know. Hewy dear, surely you don't think a girl like me would be so stupid as to give you free rein when you know full well

307

I've always supported Marie Stopes, right since you met me?'

He went pale as death again and brushed his hand across his forehead.

'The only thing with Be-Bee,' said Mina thoughtfully, 'was that we slipped up and drank too much. He caught me unawares ... But I'm a bit older and wiser now.

'I know it must be a terrible shock for you, Hewy. I do really. It was a terrible shock for me, too, when he turned up out of the blue this aftey ... But it was right in a way that it should happen, because it's all ironed out properly now, and everyone knows what's what.'

'Except our child ...' said Hewy bitterly.

'Not *our* child any more, Hewy dear. You've just got to face it ... *His* child.

'So ... I want a divorce as soon as possible. My lawyers will soon get it all settled, and I shall arrange for me and the child to go and live with Be-Bee on his estate. He needs very firm handling.'

That night, Hewy and Mina slept in separate bedrooms, and it stayed like that until two months later when she finally left him.

'You can keep the lodge, Hewy. I don't want to haggle over it.'

Fury entered his heart again as he thought of the small darling boy he had nurtured and been so proud of being torn from him like some cheap toy, and going to a playboy father who had never even cared for him or bothered to find out about him in the first few years of his life ...

'I don't want any of it, Mina,' he said in a choked voice. 'Keep the bloody lot. I never want to see Naples Lodge again.'

He strode from the room with tears in his eyes and sobbed secretly in the garden.

Milly was sitting talking to Gus in Mrs Clocker's Cottage. In the six months she'd been there she'd worked like a demon every moment of her free time to get it sorted out from the complete wreck it had been.

The people round about had been very good. Their hearts had gone out to her as a woman on her own with a small child, and they could see that improvements to the place were a blessing for the houses next to it – rather than it remaining a crumbling wreck.

'It's turned into a real little gem in no time,' said Mrs Sims as she and her friend stood gossiping to Milly at the shop one day. 'I must say, I never dreamed that even the thatch could be repaired. I was really chuffed when old Bob Mountford offered to do it. I'd have thought he wouldn't even have been able to get up a ladder at his age . . .'

'Come off it, Myrtle,' said Amy Sopworth. 'He's not as old as that. He's only ten years older than Fred, and Fred's only thirty-seven. He was a steeplejack an' all before he took to running the 'ardware, an' if a steeplejack can't do it, nobody can. That's chicken feed to him, that is, specially as 'is dad was a thatcher.'

Yes, life in Lapwing Lane was going very well, thank you . . .

Milly was staring at the bronze statue on the table, which Gus had brought with him: 'I want you to have it.'

'Oh Gus . . . are you sure?' She was quite overcome.

At first when he'd unwrapped it she'd wondered for a few seconds whether it was the final goodbye to all their past. Perhaps he aimed to forget her so completely that he wanted no memories of her whatsoever? For she had caused him such pain, while he had done so much for her, with such love and kindness . . .

But it wasn't like that after all, and after the first shock of her sudden flight from Sundower House, Gus had calmly accepted the situation.

'I'd sooner you took it, Milly. It'll be much safer with you and better looked after. I know I'll always be able to see it whenever I visit you, and my own plans are in a bit of turmoil at present. I'm concentrating completely on film work now – with Arthur and Zeronica – and I'm clearing out of Sundower to lodge with a distant relation who lives in Brooklands, near Framingham Road, where all those modern houses are. I'm putting every bit of spare cash into the films. It's my whole life now, Milly.

'Art and Zeron are taking over my flat – and by the way, Zeronica's expecting . . . so howzatt?' He beamed at her with a sudden smile. 'Also, as if that isn't enough good news, I've found an old warehouse to rent with a view to buying it, and we're going to start making our films there. It's in Rusholme, just near Dickenson Road . . .'

After they had finished exchanging all their news, they both sat and looked at the statue for a while in awed silence. What an age it seemed now from the days when she had posed for him in her pregnancy . . . And how marvellous it was still to have those memories wrapped up here in this bronze . . .

'Anyway, I mustn't stay any longer, Milly. Duty calls . . .' He stood up and kissed her lightly on the cheek, and just as he did so there was a knock on the front door.

They both walked towards the door and Milly opened it, her face happy and animated from Gus's visit, but the man who'd knocked had turned round and was disappearing down the lane.

'Someone trying to sell something,' said Milly sadly. 'Half the population seems to be doing it . . .'

When Gus had gone she put on her old clothes and began to do some painting and decorating, making the most of her free time whilst Clarinda was in West Didsbury at dancing class. It was Saturday, and Milly always enjoyed Saturdays. Then she tidied herself up again, prepared dinner, then set off to collect Clarinda.

Just as she was approaching Miss Swanson's Dancing Academy, she fancied she saw Hewy in the distance – or at least, the back of him. She smiled to herself and dismissed it. There were a million men who looked slightly like Hewy.

CHAPTER SEVENTEEN

Summer

It had taken Hewy until 1929 to get settled down properly after Mina had gone off with Belvedere, taking Karl with her.

He had found himself a pleasant upstairs flat to rent in a large Victorian house in Sale. 'The Limes' stood on Alexandra Road, in a salubrious area dotted with old cottages and market gardens. The elderly sisters who lived there, Francine and Faith Mulberry, had decided to take in one paying guest.

In some respects the traumatic episode of Hewy's break with Minny Dee had turned out to be quite civilised in the end, and for the sake of the boy whom he had fondly regarded as his true and only son, Hewy went to visit Mina occasionally to see five-year-old Karl. But it was always at the same place – her aunt's in Studley Road, Hale – and Hewy was now known as 'Daddy Hewy', as distinct from Karl's true father.

'"Daddy Hewy" looked after you whilst your father Be-Bee was away,' explained Mina to her child, 'and he's very fond of you.'

Hewy chose to ignore all references to Mina's new country house and estate. He buried himself in his artwork and worked harder than ever, ironically becoming extremely wealthy in the process. Yet he continued to live in his simple but pleasant bachelor apartment, and he still drove the two-seater Belsize convertible with the dickey seat that he'd bought in 1923 for £280.

He realised that in many respects he was now one of the luckier ones, for unemployment was getting worse and worse and the hardship suffered by people all around him was painful to accept. Like many others, Hewy found a release from gloom in getting out into the country, and so he joined a Sale rambling club and spent most of his weekends in the Peak District in Derbyshire, around Hayfield and Glossop, and on the far reaches of Kinder Scout.

He'd also, quite by chance, renewed his friendship with Gus, for they'd run into each other one Sunday morning in the Brooklands Hotel. It was a cosy, rather sophisticated place and almost a halfway house for each of them to stroll to – so that it became a regular Sunday morning rendezvous for them both. Gus kept him up to date with the film world and the doings of Arthur and Zeronica and their child Angelina, and Hewy kept Gus supplied with details of the textile designing world.

Not once did either of them ever mention Milly, even though Hewy was convinced that Gus was Milly's unofficial lover. He still remembered going to the small cottage on Lapwing Lane when his anguish over Mina and Karl was at its height, to try and make things up with Milly and seek some grain of solace. Yet when he had got there on that awful day and the front door was opened, Gus had been standing behind her . . .

Hewy, covered in self-conscious shame, had turned away like lightning, vowing never to return.

*

Milly had found Clarinda a very nice little private kindergarten to go to. It tied in well with her own work and although it was some distance away, it had such a good reputation that parents took their children there from far afield.

Milly was lucky enough to have found a friend, Blanche, who took her own child Melissa there by car: 'I'll take them on three days then, Milly and you can take them on the other two days.'

On one of the days when it was Milly's turn to collect the two children from Barroway House, she stood watching over them as they slithered about on the floor near the coat hooks, struggling to put their outdoor shoes on and to put their house-shoes in their slipper bags, in the usual mêlée of nannies and mothers. Then, gradually, she became aware of another woman . . .

They looked at each other in surprise.

Minny Dee was struggling with Karl to get his shoe buttoned as he tried to chase after his friend, Thomas.

Milly was the first to speak. 'Mina!' Her mind flooded with sudden embarrassment, for she had tried to wipe both Mina and Hewy out of her mind completely ever since Hewy had been so cold-blooded about Clarinda. In fact, after that point she had broken off relations so entirely that she had never even been involved in any more artwork with Hewy, and they swam in entirely different artistic pools. She didn't even know that he and Minny Dee had finally parted . . .

Milly looked towards Karl. He bore not the slightest resemblance to either Hewy or Mina. He was red-haired and very chubby, with a turned-up nose.

She saw Mina staring hard at Clarinda, then Mina said slowly: 'Your daughter reminds me of someone, very much . . . Strangely enough, it's a man I was once married too ...' She looked at Milly now with cold, viperous eyes.

Milly tried to ignore her tone. She replied in a small, low voice: 'Forgive me, Mina, I didn't realise you and Hewy had left each other. I've been too busy with my own problems ...' When Mina didn't respond, she carried on bravely: 'There were lots of changes last year and the time seems to have flown. Did you know that Gus has left the art school and gone to live in Brooklands? He's got a proper film studio now near Dickenson Road.' She mentioned it only as something to say, for she knew that she and Mina had nothing in common except for bits of the past and the children.

Mina shrugged, then grabbed Karl firmly, tidied him up and took him by the hand. 'We're sure to meet again,' she said crisply, before whisking him out of the room.

On the way back to West Didsbury with Clarinda and Melissa, Milly couldn't stop thinking about the news of Hewy. What on earth could he be doing now, without even his son to look after? Was he all on his own at Naples Lodge, or had he found another female companion?

Every time that Milly caught glimpses of Mina again at the kindergarten after the first shock meeting, she was nagged more and more about what had happened to Hewy. And in the meantime, back at home in Mrs Clocker's Cottage, Clarinda, who was an inquisitive four-year-old, plied Milly with perpetual questions of her own: 'Mummy, why haven't I got a daddy? Karl at kindergarten has two daddies. He has his proper daddy, Be-Bee, and he has Daddy Hewy. And I haven't even got one!' Her round, eager face – so like her father's – looked up at Milly reproachfully.

Milly chose her words carefully: 'There are lots of children without daddies, darling. Everybody has to have both a mummy and a daddy to start with – just like you have. But some people never manage to see their daddies much if the daddies live somewhere else.'

'Does my daddy live somewhere else?'

'Yes, dear.' Hurriedly Milly changed the subject. 'Go and get me those socks that need washing from your bedroom, there's a good girl.'

When Clarinda came back with the socks she said persistently: 'I wish I had a Daddy Hewy, like Karl . . .'

'You *have* got a Daddy Hewy,' said Milly consolingly.

'Can he come and see us?'

'Perhaps he will, one day. But never mind all that.'

Milly breathed with heartfelt relief as someone knocked at the door. 'Here's Mary, come to play with you, Clarinda . . . Come in, Mary,' She called out enthusiastically, then almost flung her arms round the child as the whole episode of daddies came to a swift end.

But it hadn't come to quite such a swift end in Milly's own mind, and a chance meeting with Gus whilst she was shopping in Fallowfield the following day ensured that she would not be able to forget it.

'Come and see the studios, Milly. Arthur and Zeronica are both there . . .'

She tried to think of an excuse. The minute he'd mentioned Arthur and Zeronica she'd felt uneasy, but he already had his arm entwined in hers and was walking her towards Dickenson Road. 'They'll be really pleased to see you. Zeronica's always asking how you're going, and I'm sure she'd love you to see their infant. He's called Gus, and I'm one of his godparents. She brings him with her when she comes to work.'

Milly walked into the huge barn-like warehouse with its high rafters to find Zeronica sitting there in the corner on a wicker trunk, with her son on her knee, and Arthur standing nearby, talking to her. They both greeted Milly like long-lost friends.

It was as if none of them had ever had a cross word in all their lives, and Milly realised that all that part of the past was forgotten, as baby Gus smiled up at her.

'By the way,' said Gus casually, after he and Milly had said goodbye to Arthur and Zeronica, and he was walking with Milly a few yards down the road, 'I've been meaning to tell you ... I've met up with Hewy again. He doesn't live far from me. We sometimes have a drink at the Brooklands Hotel.' He fished out his fountain pen and one of his own cards with FINER FILMS written on it. He wrote Hewy's address on the back and handed it to Milly. Then, without another word, he gave her a small wave, turned and walked quickly away.

All the way back home on the bus, Milly kept looking at Hewy's address on the card.

Should she, or shouldn't she? Was it inviting yet more trouble and complications to her life if she set out to trace him? Was it worth the terrible hurt of raking up the ashes of the past and the sadness they'd caused each other? And could she bear to hear him cruelly deny that Clarinda was indeed his child again, and then forgive him?

Her spirits sank to rock bottom. No, it was too much to ask of any woman, to suffer such heartache and indignity yet again ...

She began to wish that Gus hadn't given her the address. For a few fleeting seconds it had seemed like an answer to her prayers; but now, sitting on this bus to West Didsbury, looking out at the cold, grey world, it all seemed different.

When she got in she made herself a cup of tea.

A whole load of artwork was piling up, yet somehow, in these past few weeks, she hadn't been able to concentrate on anything.

It was her turn to collect the children today. She always went in her own car, although she hardly used it for much else, since she tended to find it more relaxing to travel on buses, trams or trains, they were so frequent.

She looked the car over. Should she go in it now – to Sale? Should she just have one quick glimpse of Alexandra Road to see where he was living? At least it would be some consolation, and it would settle her mind to know exactly where he was . . .

She drank her tea quickly. Suddenly her whole mood changed to one of optimism and cheerfulness. Yes, it was right, she thought confidently, that she should chase him up, for the sake of their own little daughter. After all, he wasn't an ogre or anything. It wasn't as if he was someone she hardly knew.

But then she hesitated. Did she really know him properly any longer?

Finally, stopping herself brooding once and for all, she got into her car and drove to Sale.

She reached Alexandra Road quite quickly. Steeling herself, she climbed the large stone steps leading up to the front door of The Limes and rang the bell.

A maid opened the door. 'Who was it you were wanting?'

'Mr Edmundson. Mr Hewy Edmundson. He lives in a flat . . . I have his address here.'

The young girl's face lit up with recognition. 'Oh yes, Mr *Edmundson*. He's sort of . . . private, really. The Mulberry's don't usually rent out bits of the house. Yes,

318

I know him all right, but he's no longer here, madam. He cleared out yesterday. Went without rhyme or reason, he did. The only thing could be said was, he never left the ladies without paying. He was a real gentleman. It was all in an envelope in their dining room, and he said thank you.'

'I don't suppose you've any *idea* where he might have gone?'

'Nobody knows, ma'am – nor ever will, from what I suspects . . .' The girl smiled apologetically and tried to close the front door on Milly as gently as possible.

Milly turned away dispiritedly. What now?

Then an awful thought struck her. *Don't say he's reached the end of his tether – don't say . . .* She began to imagine the worst . . .

Not the canal, surely? Or a railway bridge? Please God, he hadn't got as fed up as all that?

After she'd collected Melissa and Clarinda later that afternoon, and the children were laughing and chattering amongst themselves, she felt as if an awful void had come into her life.

It was no use. She just *had* to find him!

When Hewy had first arrived to stay with the Mulberry's, it had seemed like a gentle haven opening up for him at last. The two ladies were kind and thoughtful. They went out of their way – but not too much – to make sure he had every comfort.

Hewy sat with his head cupped against his hands, trying to trace back when the rot had set in. It wasn't hard to track down . . .

And when they found he'd forsaken them, even the Mulberry ladies themselves began to realise that they were partly to blame in the way they'd looked after their perfect paying guest. For the truth was that they had, in the end, fallen into the trap of mothering him just that bit too much after all.

'We should never have introduced him to Pansy,' said Francine mournfully. 'I sensed it was a dire mistake the moment we'd done it. It was your fault, really, Faith – you should never have told her it was a man we were letting our rooms to.'

'It was *not* my fault, Francine. You shouldn't even have breathed to her that he was young and fancy free. Or that he needed someone to care for him; or that he was quite well off and wore good-class shoes and had a good job ... Pansy has always had an eye to the main chance, even if she's never quite managed to make it work for her.'

The two sisters stood glaring at each other irritably in their lovely drawing room with its floral Aubusson carpet and the hand-crocheted antimacassars on all the chairs. Both of them were thin and rather handsome, and both wore long, dark dresses. They still dwelt on sad memories of the Great War and all the loved ones who'd never survived it – including Pansy's mother, their only other sister.

Pansy Fusser was now thirty years old, and lived with a friend in a small house round the corner. They did not like the friend much. She had a passion for canaries and budgerigars, which were allowed to fly all over the house in rather an unhygienic way. The sisters were always hoping that one day Pansy would meet the man of her dreams and move out, for she too was becoming extremely tiresome.

The day Hewy first met Pansy Fusser he was feeling happier than he'd felt in months, and he was at his glowing, manly best when the Mulberrys introduced them to each other. She seemed to him, on that sunny, breezy day, to be a fresh, open-faced woman with lots of charm – for she had a good set of smiling teeth and spoke lots of common sense.

He thought about her quite a lot after that first meeting and wondered whether he could call it a day as far as thoughts of other women were concerned. Maybe he should settle down to simple and straightforward domesticity with a person like Pansy? Clearly the glamour of Minny Dee had done nothing for him, nor the childhood friendship of Milly Dawnay . . .

Perhaps the secret of a stable life with a woman was not to expect too much, and to settle down with a nice, plain no-nonsense woman who would share his bed, darn his socks, guard him like a lion and give him Force out of a cardboard Sunny Jim cereal box every morning.

At first everything went swimmingly. He and Pansy launched out on a few rambles with knapsacks on their backs and dubbin on their boots, which clearly disturbed Pansy's friend Elayne, who twittered in the background about being left to look after the birds all the time.

Then one evening it all came apart. He was sitting with Pansy at her place, with only the glow of the fire to light the room, when Elayne's green cockatoo escaped from its cage. Hewy was just sliding his arm round Pansy's shoulder to see how romantic she was – for he had begun to sense a domineering streak creeping in, especially when they were striding along on rough grass.

'Trust that bird to escape at a moment like this,' said Pansy.

'Can't we just forget it?' murmured Hewy, nuzzling a bit closer.

'Certainly not! It gnaws all the picture rails, clutches at the cushions and pecks every perishing piece of loose material in sight! And I can't stand its continual squawking and screeching either. Trust Elayne to be out . . .' She got up restlessly. 'I suppose we'll just have to try and catch it.'

Hewy began to get annoyed but he tried not to show it. He had no intention of chasing round the house trying to catch a rampaging cockatoo, and right now the bird appeared to be fairly quiet behind a curtain, so he had no intention of disturbing it. 'Let's go out for a while.'

He tried to put his arm round her but she shrugged him away.

'I can't possibly go out until we've got that bird back in its cage, Hewy, and it's up to you to do it.'

'And *I* think we should go out and leave the damned thing where it is, Pansy. If it belongs to Elayne she can jolly well put it back when she gets in.'

'Don't say you're *scared* to deal with it?' She looked at him like a brisk and rather frigid headmistress.

'Not scared exactly, but frightened that if we disturb it chasing it round the place we'll just cause more havoc.'

She gave a huge snort. '*Men!*'

'What would you have done if you'd been on your own then, Pansy?'

'I should probably have read a book and waited until Elayne got back.'

The cockatoo episode wasn't exactly the end of the affair, but as their outings and meetings continued, Hewy found that his dreams of connubial pleasantness and his willingness to come to a somewhat stodgy compromise in his love life were thwarted by Pansy's overridingly rigid and military nature, which grew more and more obvious. She became an over-bearing and constant companion, domineering every free minute with her clamours for him to mend leaky hot-water cisterns and chop wood.

And as for any love life – he found that one brisk peck per meeting was all that was allowed, and was also the only reward for chopping twenty sticks for the fire, or setting at least six mouse traps.

Was it any wonder then that one day he felt the time had come simply to vanish? He packed up and left.

'You're the cream in my cof-feeee,
You're the milk in my tea . . .'

The music was streaming out from someone's open window into the sunshine as Milly sorted out some flower designs at home.

She had stopped worrying about Hewy. There was something about gorgeous, carefree summer weather that banned all misery, and obviously nothing tragic had happened to him, or it would have been in the Manchester newspapers.

It was now the summer holidays for schools and kindergarten, and she was relieved. She'd decided to find Clarinda a school closer to home next term. Milly knew deep down it was mostly because of always having Mina there in the background with Karl and his 'two daddy' theme, but it was also because Clarinda had made so many more friends locally.

The morning's post plopped through the letter box. Among the dreary business letters was an invitation from Gus, asking her if she'd fancy an alfresco meal at the Brooklands Hotel in the gardens. 'Might as well do it now whilst the weather's so good. I've invited Babsy and Mackie Bright too, and it'll be like a reunion from those early All Saints days. It's to celebrate a new and very good film contract. Turn up any time round midday next Saturday. All the best, Gus.'

Milly smiled with delight. How wonderful always to have Gus there in the background . . .

The day was true to the sunshine forecast as she and Clarinda set forth, but Milly felt pleasantly cool in her shady straw hat and sleeveless jade silk frock.

She had never been to the Brooklands Hotel before. It was a nice, countrified-looking place, partially covered with white stucco, and the gardens were idyllic, with white wooden tables shaded by parasols set on the smooth green lawns.

Everybody looked happy and well because the spell of sun had brought colour to their faces and limbs. Clarinda joined the other children, who were romping about happily, most of them in bright cotton sun-bonnets with broad frills across the napes of their necks.

All the adults were sipping iced orangeade through straws from heavy crystal glasses, and Milly accepted a glass as she sat down. Gus was ambling about among his guests with smiling good nature. When he reached Milly he said casually: 'Oh, by the way, I saw Hewy yesterday. He's been away in Holland on a business trip. He's bought himself a small house in Northenden, and he said he might join us.'

The sun seemed to go cold as Milly looked at Gus disbelievingly. How typical that Hewy's name should crop up again, just when she'd finally wiped him from her life and was perfectly at peace at last and completely settled with her daughter!

She began to look around like a prisoner hunting for

an escape. Maybe she should leave right now. What a miserable end to this glorious day if he actually turned up and completely ignored both her and his daughter ... 'Oh, by the way, Gus. I meant to tell you, we won't be able to stay for the actual meal. I only came just to see everyone briefly, but we'll have to leave almost immediately. It's a shame, but ...'

'But what, Milly Dawnay?'

She turned round. He was standing there looking at her, smiling all over his face. Standing there, caught by the sun in an open-neck shirt and grey flannels. Standing there holding the hand of his daughter.

'Look what Daddy Hewy's given me, Mummy. He picked it from the flower border. He's naughty, really, isn't he? You should never pick flowers from other people's borders, should you, Mummy?' Clarinda was smiling up at her father as he quickly swept her up in his arms and kissed her.

She was waving a blue cornflower about.

Milly looked at Hewy. Her knees felt like jelly. She was trembling like a leaf. He put Clarinda down.

'How will it be if I pick up Mummy instead?' he said. With a sudden surge of relief and joy, Milly felt his body against hers, as he swept her half way into the air and kissed her too, then gave a mock groan: 'What a ton weight!'.

'Daddy, can I get another cornflower to give to Mummy?'

'No,' he laughed. 'This time it'll be a bit different. This time it'll be the picture of a poppy, *and* a cornflower together ... but you'll both have to come home with me first.'

Milly stood there now smiling at them. Her eyes were blurred with tears. She put her hand to shade her forehead pretending it was the bright sunlight.

'A cornflower, *and* a poppy?' Clarinda looked from one to the other.

'Yes, my sweet – a cornflower and a poppy. For ever, and ever, and *ever*,' said Milly quietly.

<u>DASIA</u>

Joan Eadith

Manchester, 1926. Sixteen years old, strong willed and with a cloud of red-gold hair, Dasia Greenbow lives with her parents and older sisters in their large, dilapidated house. Working begrudgingly but resignedly in her family's pawn shop, she one day accidentally opens a letter addressed to her father – and discovers to her horror that her family is not all it seems. In a desperate bid for independence she runs away to her Aunt Dolly's boarding house, and finds work as a maid.

But when a handsome young medical student, Hal Wrioth, asks for Dasia's hand in marriage, her fortunes seem to take a turn for the better – especially when she then gets a job on the Gloves counter of Baulden's department store.

But in the depths of the Depression, no one's job or future is secure, and although she can always turn to her irrepressible Aunt Dolly, Dasia must contend with hardship, pregnancy and the ever-present threat of the bailiffs. Still there are youth and determination on her side, and Dasia is determined some day to claim the mysterious legacy that is promised to her . . .

Other best selling Warner titles available by mail:

☐ Dasia	Joan Eadith	£4.99
☐ Ivy Violet	Joan Eadith	£4.99
☐ Hospital Girls	Joan Eadith	£4.99
☐ Cygnet of Melmere	Joan Eadith	£5.99
☐ Skinny Lizzie	Elizabeth Waite	£4.99
☐ Cockney Waif	Elizabeth Waite	£5.99
☐ Cockney Family	Elizabeth Waite	£5.99

The prices shown above are correct at time of going to press, however the publishers reserve the right to increase prices on covers from those previously advertised, without further notice.

WARNER BOOKS

WARNER BOOKS

Cash Sales Department, P.O. Box 11, Falmouth, Cornwall, TR10 9EN
Tel: +44 (0) 1326 372400, Fax: +44 (0) 1326 374888
Email: books@barni.avel.co.uk.

POST AND PACKING:
Payments can be made as follows: cheque, postal order (payable to Warner Books) or by credit cards. Do not send cash or currency.

All U.K. Orders   **FREE OF CHARGE**
E.E.C. & Overseas   25% of order value

Name (Block Letters) _____

Address _____

_____

Post/zip code: _____

☐ Please keep me in touch with future Warner publications

☐ I enclose my remittance £_____

☐ I wish to pay by Visa/Access/Mastercard/Eurocard

Card Expiry Date

☐☐☐☐☐☐☐☐☐☐☐☐☐☐☐☐☐☐☐   _____